"Caleb, help me." It was the barest whisper and he almost failed to hear it. He held her closer, careful of her injuries, as he struggled to give her the warmth of his body.

"I'm here, Wren, I'm here."

Throughout the long, endless night, Wren cried out for Caleb and he would answer, his mouth pressed against her ear. His strong, sinewy arms held her. From time to time he kissed her cheek in tenderness.

And through the night, as her chills began to abate and her sleep became lighter, her words became clearer. As Wren told him what she had suffered before coming aboard his ship, he wrapped his arms protectively around the girl who slept so trustingly in his arms . . .

CAPTIVE SPLENDORS

CAPTIVE SPLENDORS

FERN MICHAELS

BALLANTINE BOOKS • NEW YORK

Prologue

Soft sounds emanated from the center of the large four-poster bed which dominated the geranium-silk-draped room. Impatiently tossing back the bedcovers and exposing their naked bodies to the chill air which even the fire in the grate could not dispel, Caleb van der Rhys rolled over onto his back and brought her with him. In the fire's glow Celeste read his features, seeing there his unadulterated lust and thrilling to the gleam of dominance in his night-dark eyes.

Grasping her hips firmly, he lowered her body onto his, watching the display of emotions cross her face. Her fingers tore into the furring of soft hair on his chest and stroked the tight cords of muscles banded across his ribs. His hair was tousled and dark against the pillow and his eyes bore through her, seeming to command her senses, greedily enjoying the pleasure he was giving her. His strong, lean thighs accepted the burden of her weight; his hands caressed her breasts, then strayed to where their bodies merged, becoming one.

From below, the throb of music could be heard, and the familiar clinking of taproom glasses blended with laughter. As her passions mounted, Celeste lost

1

her awareness of the sounds in Madame du Toit's bordello. The man beneath her was all-consuming.

She felt his eyes burning into her, watching for the approach of her ecstasy. Low moans of desire escaped from deep in her throat, her pulses raced, and a thin sheen of moisture veiled her skin. Suddenly she felt herself tumble backward against the mattress; he followed her movement, burying himself deep within her. And still his eyes watched her, triumphant now, realizing the power he held over her senses, fulfilling her passions while he slaked his own.

In the two years Captain van der Rhys could be counted among Celeste's clientele, she had always found herself looking forward to his next visit. Lusty and powerful, he was a magnificent lover, showing many sides to his expertise. Even now, as she watched him dress, she realized the power he exuded, the heady, masculine strength and potent domination he held over women.

Demanding, forceful, yet with a boyish charm which most women found irresistible, Caleb sat on the edge of the bed and pulled on his soft knee-high boots.

"If you like," she whispered, her voice a soft, contented purr, "I could meet you outside Madame du Toit's."

He smiled, seeming to weigh her words. "Meet me where, my sweet? My ship is my home. Ships' captains don't usually keep apartments in port."

"Marseilles is a very big port," she pouted. "You come here often. I could keep the apartment for you, see to things . . ."

He threw back his head and laughed, the sound filling the room. "Could you, now? Celeste, don't ruin the evening. I've told you before, I have no need for an apartment and less need for a woman to keep it for me. Isn't it enough that the time I do spend in France I spend here with you?" To soften her disappointment, he leaned over and buried his face in her breasts.

2

"No! It is not enough! Once again I will be the laughingstock among the other girls. I am the only woman you seek out here at Madame du Toit's, and yet you care so little for me that you do not keep me for yourself." Her lower lip jutted out in a display of pique, and her finely arched brows came together over the bridge of her upturned nose. "I think perhaps you have other women."

"Certainly I have other women!" he answered good-naturedly. "Just as you have other men!"

"But that is my business!" she retorted, throwing back the covers and kneeling beside him, wrapping her scented arms around his neck in gentle persuasion. "How would I live otherwise? I am sick of Madame du Toit's. Why is it you never bring me out to your ship? I could stay with you, be there whenever you wanted me, instead of only for a few hours at night."

Her petulance was beginning to grate on him. He reached for his waistcoat and pulled it on with a fury. "I've told you I never bring women out to my ship."

"Yes, yes, something about it being a sacred shrine where your father and stepmother realized their love for one another. Bah! I never thought you could be accused of being sentimental!"

Once again Caleb regretted ever having told Celeste about the history of his ship, the *Sea Siren*. He owed his foolishness to the liquor he had consumed and perhaps to a barely admitted loneliness. Instantly he knew he would never again return to Madame du Toit's. Celeste had begun to bore him with her strident demands and pleas.

As if realizing she had pressed too far, Celeste became immediately contrite. She drew herself against him, her lips near his ear, whispering that she would never plague him about his ship again.

His hands found her wealth of golden hair and pulled it viciously until she was once again lying back on the pillows. His mouth came crashing down upon

3

hers, his breath hot and wine-scented. Her pulses throbbed rhythmically, her fingers tore at his clothing, her hips arched in offering. His lips trailed a familiar path from her mouth to her breasts; his hands possessed her, igniting fires she had thought were quenched.

A slow, sly smile tugged at the corner of her mouth and her long, slanted eyes gleamed with conquest. He forgave her; he always would. In time she would manipulate him, make him see he couldn't live without her. She wanted him, needed him; in all her experience she had never known another man like him. His touch could fire her passions, his lips could conquer her desires. A slow curl of heat warmed her like a summer sun, and she knew she wanted him, again, and again . . .

When she had reached a dizzying height, Caleb tossed her away from him, leaving her hanging over an empty abyss. "That's right, Celeste, you'll never plague me again."

His boots were almost soundless on the carpet as he strode to the door and banged it shut behind him.

Chapter One

Tyler Payne Sinclair strode down the wide gallery which winged out over the main staircase and entrance hall of his London town house. As he glanced at the impressive row of family portraits lining the wall, he again realized how difficult it was for him to comprehend that, since his father's death, he had inherited the title of Baron and taken his father's place in Parliament. All the dire threats put forth by his parents to disinherit him if he should ever marry his distant cousin, Camilla Langdon, had not come to fruition. When Camilla's jackanapes father had finally met his end at the hand of Sirena van der Rhys, the elder Sinclairs had experienced a change of heart. Or so they had told themselves and Tyler, explaining that Camilla, once free of Stephan Langdon's evil influence, had been found to be a girl of exquisite taste and a loving nature. It had never been spoken aloud that they would sooner have cut off their arms than alienate themselves from their only son.

Tyler's dark eyes became thoughtful as a squeal of girlish laughter rang in his ears. He would sorely miss Wren when she left with Sirena and Regan, who were expected in London within a fortnight. Now that Camilla had at last come into her own with approaching motherhood and little else filled her thoughts, he would be lost without Wren's exuberance for life and her flattering dependency on him.

How alike the beautiful Sirena and Wren were, yet how unalike. He supposed he should resign himself to the fact that he would always worry about her in the manner of an older brother. He could never seem to gain the detachment toward her that even the role of a substitute stepfather would designate during these years in which Wren had come under his care. He sighed heavily. It was time for Wren to return to the Spice Islands with Sirena and Regan and find her place in life, whatever that might be. Just as long as it didn't include that dandy, Malcolm Weatherly.

God! How was he to explain that fop to Sirena? He shuddered as he pictured how those emerald eyes would spew fire when she was told that her little Wren was bent on marrying that rapscallion as soon as he could properly ask for her hand. A grudging smile split Tyler's handsome face. If Malcolm Weatherly managed to escape Sirena's fury, he would find he still had Regan to deal with. Tyler imagined he himself should be chagrined to consider that Regan might be able to gain control of a situation where he had not, but he soothed his spirit with the thought that Regan had not lived under Wren's charm and winning ways for these past three yeears.

Tyler had found it impossible to deny Wren anything, and Camilla had found herself in the same predicament, especially where it concerned Mr. Weatherly's courtly attentions. In fact, Camilla's fondness for Wren was surprising on all accounts. Tyler smiled again as he thought of his pretty blond wife. Camilla had come a long, long way from that pretty, empty-headed young girl he had known and loved in spite of her selfish, self-serving behavior. She had grown into a loving, tender woman, and Wren, as well

6

as he, was grateful for her cloak of maternal regard. The only area where Camilla was disapproving of Wren lay in the young girl's friendship with the Puritan, Sara Stoneham. But even in that Camilla was being protective and defensive of her little family. The Puritans were speaking out dangerously against the King's control of the Church of England, and there were even rumblings of civil war.

As a member of Parliament, Tyler knew Camilla's fears were not unfounded, but he refused to allow his own concern to color his feelings toward Wren's young friend. Sara Stoneham was a lovely girl from a notable family, one he had known for years. If her religious preference was different from his, it mattered little to Tyler. Besides, how could he, in all conscience, have turned Sara out into the street when she had come here, at Wren's invitation, to await the arrival of her parents in London?

Tyler quickened his step toward the elaborately carved door of Wren's apartment to bid the girls good night. He had lifted his hand to knock when the sound of their voices penetrated the thick panel.

"Wren! In the name of all that's holy, I didn't think you were ever coming back! What could you have been thinking of? Sneaking off with Malcolm and staying out so late! What if the Baron or the Baroness popped in to say good night? What would I have told them?"

Wren spun around the room, her blue and mauve striped silk skirt ballooning away from her slim legs like a brightly colored parasol. She hugged her arms close to herself, an expression of rapture softening her features. "Ooh, Sara, don't spoil this for me. You're always so disapproving every time I'm with Malcolm. Not tonight. Please?" Wren's eyes glowed softly in the light of the lamp, her thick lashes casting feathery shadows on her smooth cheeks.

Sara noticed the huskiness in Wren's voice and that

7

her hair was disarrayed and wispy tendrils curled toward her ivory brow. There was no mistaking that look of voluptuous satisfaction which pouted her kissbruised lips, nor the languid, sensuous expression in her eyes. Sara was familiar with these outward signs of lovemaking. She had seen them branded on her own features after slipping out of school for a spring night's rendezvous. And, like Wren, but unknown to her, she, too, had spent breathless hours in Malcolm Weatherly's arms. She knew how the touch of Malcolm's hands on her flesh could transport her to worlds never before imagined . . . how his lips could plead and then tease until she was half mad with wanting him, with wanting to give herself to him. Then, suddenly, it had ended. The secret notes had stopped arriving; when she had slipped out of the dormitory at night, hoping to meet him, she had waited until the chill, damp, early-morning air had penetrated her clothing, causing her to shudder from the cold and from the deeper, more painful quiver of love lost.

After several weeks of pining for Malcolm and experiencing rapidly dropping grades, Sara had heard it rumored that Wren van der Rhys was keeping trysts with a handsome stranger. Her suspicions aroused, Sara had managed to befriend Wren and learned that indeed it was Malcolm Weatherly who tempted the innocent, young Wren to brave the dark and perilous rose trellis for a few moments in his arms. It was torture being here with Wren and knowing she was Malcolm's new love, but Sara was beyond helping herself. In some undefinable way, being close to Wren was like being near Malcolm.

"You don't like Malcolm, do you, Sara?" Wren said quietly, touching her friend's sleeve. "I know you've gone along with my little deceptions, but underneath you disapprove, don't you?"

Sara turned so that Wren couldn't see her face. She wanted to lash out, to scratch Wren's beautiful face, to force her to face the truth. Poor silly little Wren. Couldn't she see that Malcolm was more interested in her family's wealth than he was in her? Sara wished she had the courage to tell Wren that Malcolm had loved *her*, Sara, until he had discovered that the Stonehams had lost favor with the Crown over some loose remarks about the King's failure to call together a session of Parliament. Times were uneasy for Puritans, to say the least. A swift seizure of properties, and the Stonehams were on the verge of bankruptcy. But to reveal this to Wren would mean a certain end to their relationship and to her vicarious closeness to Malcolm. Sara's only satisfaction lay in the fact that Malcolm didn't love Wren. It was just a scheming, self-serving game he was playing. Sara knew she should hate Malcolm Weatherly, and she'd even experienced twinges of guilt because she was keeping the truth from Wren, but she couldn't hate him. She loved Malcolm Weatherly more than she had ever loved another person in her entire life. I must love him, she told herself; otherwise what kind of person am I, to have allowed him to do the things he has done to me?

A sly smile tugged at the corners of Sara's generous mouth when she remembered the nights alone in Malcolm's arms, the things she had done, the things she had permitted Malcolm to do to her. No one in the world knew what they had shared, and Malcolm certainly wouldn't tell.

"Sara, answer me," Wren persisted. "Why don't you like Malcolm?"

"Wren, it's not that I don't like him. It's just that . . . how will you explain Malcolm to your . . . to Sirena and Regan?"

"Why can't you ever bring yourself to refer to Sirena and Regan as my parents? They are, you know. They're the only parents I've ever had, and they consider me their very own daughter," Wren announced defiantly, her amber eyes lighting from within.

"Not in the true sense of the word, Wren," Sara said falteringly. She recognized that light in Wren's eyes, and it only meant an ensuing argument for the unfortunate person who dared to cross swords with her. Sara swallowed and pressed onward. "One of these days you're going to realize that Sirena doesn't belong on a pedestal and that she's a human being like the rest of us mortals. And you must stop thinking about the infamous sea witch—you're always talking about her and making her your idol. For shame, Wren! Here you are, contemplating marriage with old Mally, and it's time to leave such fantasies behind. Now that you've finished school and are ready to meet society, you must put all that nonsense behind you. Do you understand what I'm saying?"

Sara faced Wren and saw that her ploy had been successful. Once again she had put doubts in Wren's mind about the relationship between herself and her parents. She was quick to see that the seeds she had sown weeks ago as to Wren's rightful use of the van der Rhys name had taken root and had begun to flower. Besides, this well-worn path of conversation was a perfect distraction for Wren's too-personal questions concerning Sara's opinion of Malcolm.

Outside the door, Tyler massaged his temples. He hadn't meant to eavesdrop, but hearing that Wren had slipped out of the house for a clandestine meeting with Weatherly had stunned him. He hadn't realized things had progressed so far. Now he found himself anticipating Wren's answer. Sara was correct. Wren had been living in a make-believe world, and her fantasies were the prime reason she had fallen prey to Malcolm Weatherly's charm. The stories about the Sea Siren, infamous piratess, told to Wren when she was a child, were meant to be just that. Stories. Fairy tales for a child to dream about, not a basis on which Wren should build her life.

10

"Sara Stoneham! There is a person, a real person, who was the Sea Siren! I really don't care if you believe me or not, but you're wrong—she doesn't occupy all my thoughts, and I know you think I'm trying to pattern my life after her, but I'm not! There could never be another Sea Siren." A wistful note crept into Wren's voice. "The Siren was the most beautiful creature who ever rode the seas. Long, flowing hair, eyes the color of emeralds and skin like spun honey. She was a master of fencing, and there wasn't a man who could best her. I could never hope to compete with her, either in looks or in actions. My eyes are the wrong color and my skin is too pale. And I'm too short, much too short. And try as I might, I'll never equal her skill with the rapier."

"See? Listen to yourself! Do you hear you compare yourself to that sea witch in such an unfavorable light?" Sara grasped Wren's wrist and dragged her over to the pier glass. "Look at yourself! Look!" Reluctantly, Wren lifted her eyes to the glass. "Now, tell me that what you see there is not more beautiful than any fantasy about a female pirate! Tell me that just the sight of you doesn't turn all men's eyes. I've been to the Royal Exchange with you, Wren. I've seen the effect you have on the masculine sex. Didn't Rolland Chalmers send you love notes that nearly singed the fingertips? What did he say to you? That your hair was a cloud of dark night and your eyes were golden embers and your skin—"

"Stop it, Sara!" Wren wrenched herself away. "I never said I was ugly!" she protested.

"True. But you compare yourself to this sea witch and it eats at you. Admit it, Wren. Why can't you put these thoughts behind you? Take a word of advice from an old friend. You'd better concentrate on the problem at hand. Prepare yourself for what your guardians are going to do when they find out about Malcolm. Somehow I can't see the van der Rhyses giving your their blessings over old Mally, not after what you told me about them."

"They'd better give it, otherwise I'll run away," Wren declared recklessly.

It was time to intervene, Tyler decided. Privacy be damned. He knocked and opened the door at the same time. "It's late, young ladies, and you need your beauty sleep. Or so my wife has been telling me all these years." He looked from one girl to the other. Sara was tall and slender, like a yellow tea rose, he told himself. And Wren was like a tapered candle flame. Right now her eyes were like banked fires, ready to flare into flame if the conversation were allowed to continue. The girl had an ungovernable temper where it concerned Sirena and the Sea Siren.

Sara laughed, tossed her white-gold curls and quickly embraced Wren. "Baron Sinclair is right, Wren. We get along so well and we're best friends. Let's not spoil it now. Besides," she added coquettishly, "Baron Sinclair has been so kind in allowing me to spend these few days with you before my parents arrive, I must insist that I am on his side."

"I didn't realize we were taking sides," Wren snapped as she wriggled out of Sara's embrace. "Tyler is right, though. We do need our beauty sleep—at least I do. Malcom is taking me to the country tomorrow and I want to look my best. Don't frown so, Tyler," she said as she threw her arms about him. "Sirena will love Malcolm just as I do, and believe me when I tell you she won't hold it against you that I've been permitted to see him. She's going to love him, you'll see."

"Somehow, little one, I can't share your optimism."

"You're behaving like the new father you soon will be," Wren teased, yet there was a ring of steel in her voice that could set Tyler's teeth rattling. He knew in his gut that Sirena would take one look at the modish Malcolm Weatherly and rip out her rapier and cut him

12

to pieces. Also, Sirena would blame him from start to finish for the relationship between Wren and Weatherly. Sirena van der Rhys never did things in half. No, he would receive full blame, and if she didn't cut him down, then Regan would. Wren was the apple of Regan's eye, and no dandy was going to snap up his little girl. Perhaps they would take mercy on Tyler when he told them he was about to become a father. He blanched as he imagined Sirena's face after she heard the news. How well he knew her. She would say, "Congratulations," and then cut him down. She had style, he must admit. Camilla would be forced to intervene on his behalf, and he would take the coward's way out. God, how could he have been so foolish to let Wren get herself tangled up with Weatherly? How could he have foreseen that a mild flirtation would blossom into an engagement? Why didn't he insist, right now, that she make a quick end of Weatherly? Because the girl could wrap him around her little finger—it was that simple. Women had always been his weakness. Jehovah! He hoped Camilla gave birth to a boy; otherwise he wouldn't have a chance of living to forty. He had to get himself in hand; he couldn't let the girls see how upset he was. He forced a smile to his lips, quickly pecked both of them on the cheek and exited the room, his stomach crawling with fear. Sirena would cut him down in his prime.

Sara's hyacinth eyes were watchful as she and Wren prepared for bed. "Are you really going to take a drive with Mally tomorrow?"

"Sara Ann Stoneham, stop calling Malcolm *Mally*. Yes, I'm going for a carriage ride with the man I'm going to marry. Not another word, Sara Ann," Wren shouted as she dived under the covers, her amber eyes peeping out from behind the satin-edged quilt.

"Very well," Sara acquiesced. "As your infamous Sea Siren would say, 'It's your neck!'"

Chapter Two

The hour was late, the night dark and silent as the hackney carrying Sirena and Regan van der Rhys made its way through the winding, narrow streets devoid of people and noise. As dark and silent as my thoughts, Sirena mused as she peered through the dirty panes of the carriage. The hack was taking the route from the docks to Tyler Sinclair's house, the same route she had taken with Frau Holtz nearly nine years ago when she had come in search of Regan. Bitter memories stained the joy at seeing Wren again. Whenever she thought about the time she had been forced to live in England, she knew a hatred almost as strong as that which she still harbored for the memory of Stephan Langdon. Pressing her shoulder securely on Regan's as he rolled against her in sleep, she felt a small knot of something akin to fear weave its way around her stomach. How did Regan feel about returning to England? Returning not only to England, but to the house of his former wife. What would the flowerlike Camilla be like now that she was married to Tyler? By now, with the lapse of time, childlike Camilla would be a woman fully grown, complete with a woman's wiles. Would she tease and flirt with Regan, and what would be Regan's reaction? Sirena sighed. She wouldn't find out this evening, that was for certain. Dawn would soon be approaching. The Sinclair household would be asleep and unprepared for guests. Surely Tyler wouldn't mind that she and Regan were arriving a week ahead of schedule. Nothing annoyed Tyler.

A smile tugged at the corners of her mouth as she recalled their days in Newgate Prison. In truth, that experience was probably the only thing that had ever annoyed good old Tyler. And if the truth were told, he had probably enjoyed every minute of it.

Sirena sighed again, wearily. That had been so long ago. Another time, another life. Unconsciously, she reached out to touch Regan, to reassure herself that he was still there. How wonderful he felt, so hard and firm. And how vulnerable he looked in sleep. Her bottle-green eyes lighted up momentarily as she realized that Regan was not in the least vulnerable. Well, perhaps in one area, where Wren was concerned. How eager he was to see the girl, to wrap her in his arms and make the sounds all fathers make when they look at their beloved daughters. Even though Regan and Sirena had adopted Wren, they couldn't have loved her more if she had truly been theirs. Was this because they had produced four strapping boys who one day would be like Regan and Caleb? Sirena often wished she had given Regan a daughter of his own. No matter, Wren was their daughter, and that was enough. She carried the van der Rhys name, and Sirena was her mother and Regan was her father. And little Wren had five brothers who loved her dearly. Especially Caleb.

The hackney came to an abrupt halt and Regan was jostled from his comfortable position against her shoulder. "Good God, Sirena, are we finally here?"

Sirena patted his arm. "Now, Regan, remember your promise to me. You won't demand that Wren be

15

awakened. Morning is soon enough. As a matter of fact, it would be wise to insist that neither Camilla nor Tyler be awakened. Your promise, Regan."

Regan grinned. "I must have been drunk when I agreed to such a promise, sweetheart."

"Not drunk, darling, just in a rather compromising position."

"One of these days I'll manage to be one step ahead of you, Sea Witch," he said fondly.

"I miss the children and I want to return to Java as quickly as possible. That was part of the promise."

"You're jealous of Camilla. I've felt it ever since we approached English waters," Regan teased.

"You're a bull, Regan, and I'm not jealous. If she makes one false move in your direction, it's *your* eyes I'll scratch out!"

Regan shuddered. She would do it, too. She might be the mother of four strapping boys and the step-mother of two other children, but she could best him in any way she chose and he knew it, not that he would ever admit it to her. Even now, after all these years, she was still as slim and fast as she had been when he first met her. Little did she know that he was aware that she still practiced daily with her rapier. One day he had by chance overheard her telling Frau Holtz that it was the only way to keep fit. As usual, she was right, he grimaced as his hands found their way to his midsection. Too much good food and rum would ruin the best of men. Not that he overindulged, but it was so easy to throw caution to the winds when a man was happy and contented. Regan was more happy and contented than he had ever been in his life, and now that Wren would be going back to Java with them, his cup would run over. The only thing missing was Caleb. If Cal would only see fit to make his home with them in Java, he swore to all the Gods in Heaven that he would never sin again. What more could a man ask?

"Do try to be quiet, Regan. We don't want to awaken the entire household."

"My dear, I will walk on tiptoe, as though I were walking on eggs. You need to have no fear of my awakening your dear friend Tyler."

"You're baiting me, Regan. Morning is only a few hours away, and sleep is what you need."

"If you're trying to tell me I'm getting old and feeble, you can bite your tongue, young woman. I can still outshine that Sinclair, and well you know it. I'll tell you one thing: I'm not looking forward to seeing either him or Camilla. I gave you my word that we would leave as soon as it was decently possible. I'll keep my word. No noise, I'll sleep in your arms, and you'll wake me at the first early light. I want to see what manner of young lady our Wren has become."

Giggling like two small children, Regan and Sirena followed an aging servant up the curving staircase.

"Reminds me of the time I spent three days in Clarice's brothel." Regan grinned as he pinched Sirena on the thigh.

"If you think I'm going to ask you to tell me about *that* little escapade, dear husband, you're wrong. I'll take it up with you tomorrow," she said, her eyes glinting dangerously.

"A slip of the tongue, sweetheart. You know how boastful I am at times. It was Dykstra who spent three days there. I merely stopped by to see how business was doing."

"You kept that—that—*establishment* in business all by yourself. Don't blame Captain Dykstra," Sirena hissed.

"Well, I do feel a certain responsibility for him. After all, I did take him there, and Clarice . . . what she did . . . actually . . . You're right, we'll discuss it tomorrow. Suddenly I feel so tired I can barely keep my eyes open."

"If I were you, I'd sleep with them open the rest of the night," Sirena warned ominously.

The moment the door closed behind the servant, Regan gathered Sirena in his arms and kissed her passionately. God, how he loved her. He had baited her on purpose just to see her respond with anger. It was his way of proving to himself that she still loved him. He had to see her anger to know for certain that their love had not banked, that it could be rekindled in a moment with a few choice words. Right or wrong, he had to do it, and Sirena understood and played the game right along with him. God, how he loved her. Even more now than on the day he had married her for the second time.

Tyler Sinclair descended the stairs with the same worried expression on his face as he had worn when he had finally drifted off to sleep. He felt his stomach churn as the housekeeper told him that the van der Rhyses had arrived unexpectedly during the night and insisted that the Baron and the Baroness remain undisturbed.

"Is the Baroness ready for breakfast?" the housekeeper asked.

"The Baroness is feeling under the weather this morning. Have one of the maids bring her some mint tea and a sweet roll in about an hour. She will be down for luncheon with our guests."

Good Lord, what am I going to say to Sirena? he wondered as he seated himself at the breakfast table. Perhaps he was worrying about nothing. Both of them might really like Malcolm Weatherly. No one likes Malcolm Weatherly except Wren, he answered himself. Camilla had said that Malcolm could pass muster in a dark room, but this was the bright light of day, and both Sirena and Regan were clear-eyed and as sharp as axes.

Tyler bit into a sweet roll and chewed with a vengeance. Two more rolls and two more cups of coffee laced with rum—or was it three cups of rum laced with coffee?—and he was ready to meet any and all challengers, providing they didn't carry a rapier or a cutlass. Damn it, he was feeling the edges of drunkenness and it was still breakfast time. To be cut down in his prime! "Never mind the coffee, just give me the bottle," he demanded of the cook.

"But, Baron Sinclair, your kippers are ready, and Cook prepared them especially for you."

"Kip, kip, kip," Tyler hiccuped drunkenly. "The child is nothing more than a little kipper, that's what she is."

"Do my eyes deceive me, or are you drunk?" Sirena's melodious voice called out from the doorway. "Two hours past dawn and you're in your cups." Camilla must be up to some of her old tricks to make Tyler resort to spirits so early in the morning, Sirena mused. Tyler was no sot; at least he had never been one before. On the other hand, being married to Camilla should be reason enough to turn to drink. Hadn't Regan tipped the bottle more than usual during his short-lived marriage to that fair petal of flowerhood? A wide smile broke across Sirena's face as she patted a perspiring Tyler on his head. "I can forgive you anything, Tyler, since you've been so generous to give our Wren a home and take care of her."

Tyler extended a shaking hand to grasp Regan's and finally conceded failure when he couldn't establish contact.

"You resemble a fish out of water, Sinclair," Regan said, his eyes narrowed in suspicion. No self-respecting man drank at dawn, or what passed for dawn in this damnable country. Camilla was undoubtedly leading Tyler a merry chase. Suddenly Regan grinned as the thought struck him that, but for the grace of God, he could be walking in Sinclair's

19

boots. Mercifully there was a God, and every day he thanked Him for his good fortune.

Tyler thought the van der Rhyses a striking pair. Regan looked as fit and agile as a man twenty years his junior. Only a slight salting of gray at the temples hinted that it was almost nine years since Tyler had last seen him. He noted happily that Sirena had been treated well by the passage of time. A vague aura of maturity about her belied the sparkle in her extraordinary green eyes, and she wore her hair in a more sedate style, rather than loose and flowing. But her figure was still trim and girlish. Tyler had a vision of Sirena as she had looked aboard her ship, her long, tawny legs revealed by tatter-edged breeches cut up to her curvaceous hips, the salt spray glistening on her skin, her dark hair free to blow in the wind. He knew that beneath her wide skirts and decorous manner still lived the beautiful Sea Siren.

"Tell me, Tyler, how is your business thriving?" Sirena asked.

Tyler flinched. Damn her, she knew something was troubling him, and she hadn't changed a bit. She knew it had something to do with Wren; he could feel it in his bones and see it in her sea-green eyes. There was nothing for him to do but tell both of them the straight of it. With any luck, they would listen with open minds and hear him through. Mentally he squared his shoulders and stood up, his back to the seated couple. He fixed his gaze out the window, on a tree swaying in the early-morning breeze, and watched a sparrow take wing.

Sirena and Regan exchanged glances and waited patiently for him to speak.

"You were never one of my favorite people, van der Rhys," Tyler began, "but you, Sirena, were always like a sister to me. I agreed to look out for Wren and act as her guardian while she was here at the academy. I've done the best I could, but you,

20

Sirena, filled her head with so many tales of the Sea Siren and all that rubbish that there was little I could do when it came to things of that nature. She's devious, something I found very hard to accept. Camilla tells me that all young girls are impressionable and devious; she calls it women's wiles. What I'm trying to say to you is that Wren fancies she is in love with and wants to marry a man named Malcolm Weatherly. She plans to have him ask for her hand. The young man is a dandy, a fop of the worst sort."

"What's this tale you're peddling, Sinclair?" Regan demanded, leaping from his chair. His intentions were clear to Sirena, who reached out for his arm.

"Regan, hear him out," she pleaded.

"Thank you, Sirena," Tyler said quietly, grateful for her interference. All signs of inebriation gone, he proceeded to tell them what he knew. "You see, I was unaware of this affair until very recently, and then I learned about it quite by accident. From what I've been able to gather, Wren met this Weatherly while at the academy. She was shopping in town when she happened to make his acquaintance. She continued to see him without the knowledge of her teachers or the headmistress. This is what I meant about her being devious, or wily, if you prefer. Now that I have the straight of it, I can tell you the whole story. After the nightly bed check made by the dormitory housemother, Wren would slip out and meet Weatherly somewhere on the grounds. It seems that one night the headmistress couldn't sleep and decided to go to the library for a book. It was there that she discovered the two lovers in what she termed a 'shocking embrace.' The headmistress then questioned Wren, who had the good sense to tell the truth. In turn, the matter was brought to my attention with the request to remove Wren from her classes. She came here with a friend of hers, Sara Stoneham, who was a party to the affair. Sara would let Wren back into the dormitory at night after the lovers' tryst. Her parents are due to arrive in London within the next few days to take her home. I'm afraid they're quite shocked by the whole matter. They're Puritans," he added, as if that explained everything.

"Your Wren is a very determined young lady," he went on, "and we've had to allow Weatherly admittance to see her. If we didn't, Wren announced that she would run off with him. What would you have had me do, Sirena? Right or wrong, I thought it best to keep her here till you arrived and took matters in your own . . . capable hands. God only knows what would become of her if she ran off with that fop. That's it," he concluded, turning about, a high flush on his cheeks.

"Damn your eyes, Sinclair!" Regan roared. "I trust you with my daughter and look what happens! One small favor, that was all we asked, and you couldn't handle it! It's a damn good thing you aren't a parent!"

Tyler's eyes were tortured. "I know," he said morosely, "but now I find that in a few short months I will be. All I can say is I'm sorry for this other news."

Sirena leaned back in her chair, her eyes thoughtful. "It's not your fault, Tyler. I see how it happened, and you're right. Wren is an impressionable child—at least she was when she left us. I had hoped she would outgrow that quality as time passed. And it wasn't only I who filled her with tales of the Sea Siren. Frau Holtz allowed the child to cut her teeth on the tales of my derring-do. I place no blame on your shoulders, old friend, nor does Regan. Right now he's a trifle upset, but when he has time to think on the matter, he'll realize you are not responsible. We're at fault. It was a mistake to have sent her here at such an early age. She needed more guidance, more parental love. No, it is Regan and I who are to blame. What we have to do is to look at the matter calmly

22

and arrive at some sort of solution. We cannot alienate Wren; we love her too much. A talk with the man of her choice will be in order, of course. Also a talk with her friend's parents. It is well that we arrived early to put all these matters straight, don't you agree, Regan?" Sirena touched him lightly on the hand.

Her light touch and calm voice worked their soothing magic on the irate Dutchman.

Regan's tone was brisk when he addressed Tyler. "A drink, Sinclair, to show that neither my wife nor I hold you responsible. We both know that Wren is capable of being wily. She's manipulated me on more than one occasion, and she was still a child at the time. I'm afraid that when it comes to women, we men are at their mercy."

"That's damn white of you, van der Rhys," Tyler said in a relieved tone. "If we put our heads together and really talk this out, we should be able to come up with a solution. She can't be permitted to marry that ass. If we start from there, we'll think of something. For now, why don't we enjoy our kippers?"

While Sirena and Regan breakfasted, Wren was getting dressed, her eyes wary as she watched Sara go about her morning ablutions. Sooner or later the articulate Sara would start to chastise her. The sooner she got on with it, the sooner she would be finished. Why did everyone think he or she had to expound on her affairs? The only one who seemed to be on her side was Camilla. Camilla said there was nothing more beautiful than young love. Camilla should know. Hadn't she loved Tyler from the time she was sixteen years old?

"Are you ready, Sara?" Wren asked quietly.

"Yes, and I'm famished. I hope Cook has prepared something extra special this morning."

Evidently the voluble Sara wasn't going to say anything. Wren shrugged. Maybe Sara had finally realized that Wren wasn't going to pay any attention to her vicious comments about Malcolm. What could a straight-laced Puritan know about love anyway?

The two girls descended the wide, circular staircase, which was thickly carpeted in a deep burgundy and muffled their footsteps. Suddenly Wren put a finger to her lips to warn the other girl to be quiet. She frowned. The voices she heard sounded like Regan's and Sirena's. It couldn't be! They weren't due for another week . . . It was! With a sound akin to a war whoop, she raced down the remaining stairs, leaving a wide-eyed Sara behind. Catapulting into the dining room, she threw herself into Sirena's arms and hugged her with all her might. Satisfied that the living, breathing Sirena was no mirage, she extricated herself and turned to Regan.

His anguish of moments ago forgotten, Regan felt his face split into a grin as he clasped the laughing, happy girl to him.

Sirena watched the display of emotion between the two and felt sentimental tears smear her eyes.

"When did you get here? Why didn't you wake me? How long can you stay? Did Tyler tell you about Sara? It's so good to see you! I'm so happy," Wren squealed delightedly. "Look, here is my friend Sara. Come." She beckoned to the girl standing in the doorway.

The introductions completed and the girls seated with plates of food in front of them, Regan leaned back and lighted one of his cheroots, apologizing for smoking at the table. He wanted his cigar, and he didn't want to go into Tyler's library for fear he would miss something.

It was Sirena who took the initiative and spoke first. "Well, little one, it seems that Tyler's duties are coming to an end. Are you ready to return to the Spice Islands and make your home with us again? We've missed you."

24

"Darling Sirena, do we have to discuss that now? I'm so happy just seeing the two of you that I don't want to talk about anything *except* the two of you. Tell me, how are the boys, and have you heard from Caleb?" If Wren noticed the tightness around Regan's mouth, she gave no sign as she filled her mouth with kippers.

"You won't recognize the boys," he said. "They've grown so, I barely recognize them myself. Each is as fair as a staff of wheat, but with their mother's green eyes. Caleb is still shipping cargo for the Dutch East India Company and making a thriving show for his efforts. We have no complaints other than we've all missed our little girl and want her home with us so we can be a family again."

Now, say it now, Wren, Sirena pleaded silently. Don't make it harder for Regan, for if you do, he may never forgive you. Be honest, little one. Do it now; say what has to be said now. Surely you must know that Tyler has told us of your plans.

Wren carefully avoided Sirena's eyes. "You've told me of everyone but Frau Holtz and Jacobus. How are they? How I've missed the Frau," Wren sighed, smiling at Regan.

"You know that the Frau married Jacobus and made an honest man of the old sea salt. They're both well and send their regards and can barely contain themselves till your arrival."

Say it, Sirena continued to beg silently. Wren continued to ignore her mother's silent thoughts.

It was obvious that Sara was embarrassed for her friend. She placed her napkin on the table and directed a pleading look at Tyler. Interpreting her gaze correctly, he rose and held out his hand. "If you'll excuse us, I promised to show Sara a book I purchased yesterday. She wants it as a gift for her father."

Regan rose politely, and Sirena smiled at the departing girl. Wren was on her own, it appeared and would get no help from her friend, which was as it should be.

Silence. Each was waiting for the other to say something. The girl should know that Regan could outwait a tropical storm. Much squirming and downcast eyes did nothing for his disposition. He waited. Sirena waited. Wren swallowed hard and looked squarely at Regan. "I'm sure that Tyler has told you . . ."

"Sirena and I would prefer that you tell us," Regan said quietly. "Both of us are disappointed that you didn't see fit to write of your coming plans."

"A letter wouldn't have reached you in time," Wren cried miserably. "I know that you both must be disappointed, but sometimes these things happen. A woman meets a man and they fall in love. Isn't that what happened between you and Sirena? I can't help how I feel. I didn't want it to happen, but it did. I'm certain you'll both like Malcolm and that he will like you. He loves me dearly, and I think he will make me a fine husband. With your approval, of course," she added hastily.

Sirena sat back and let Regan do the talking. He was so much better at handling Wren than she was. "First of all, young lady, Sirena and I were not boy and girl; we were man and woman. You're but a child compared with Sirena at your age. We sent you here for an education, not to have you fall head over heels for the first dandy who pays you any mind. The world is full of men like Malcolm Weatherly. We had hoped that an education would help you acquire a little judgment. Now we learn the headmistress expelled not only you but also your friend. Tell me, Wren, was it showing good judgment when you involved another in your escapades? Think of how Sara's parents must feel. By helping you, her friend, she earned a black mark against her reputation. It was thoughtless of you. A woman wouldn't do something so foolish, and that's why Sirena and I question your emotions concerning Malcolm Weatherly. It seems that you have more growing up to do. If your swain is bent on asking me for your hand, I am afraid I must deny it."

Wren's eyes narrowed and then flamed. "Sirena was one year older than I when she married you," she said coolly. "And, Regan, you're not my father, so if you do deny my hand to Malcolm, I'll run off with him."

If she had shot him a blow to the heart, she couldn't have wounded Regan more. Sirena wanted to reach out and slap the defiant pout on Wren's mouth. How could she have spoken in that way?

"Regan is the only father you've ever known. How dare you speak to him in such a manner! Apologize this instant!" Sirena demanded furiously.

"And you're not my mother!" Wren cried suddenly as the enormity of what she had said struck her. Never one to back off, she lashed out again. "I never asked you to pick me up off the street. I never asked you for anything. I worked for you and Frau Holtz. I did my share and wanted to do more, but you wouldn't let me. I never wanted to come here and go to that fancy school. You forced me to! I pleaded with you, begged you, and all either of you could say was that it was for my own good. Now you tell me it isn't. Don't I deserve the right to be happy? How can you deny me the one thing I'm asking of you? The one thing I'm asking in all the years you've cared for me. Tell me, Sirena. Can you tell me, Regan?" she all but shouted. "No, I see you can't!" Tears streaming down her cheeks, she ran from the room and made for the front door, almost upsetting a maid carrying a heavy tray.

Sirena's own eyes were as moist as Regan's as they rose to look out the window at Wren's retreating back. Sirena tugged at Regan's arm. "She didn't mean it, I'm sure she didn't. Girls say things they don't mean when they're upset. Right now she thinks she's in

27

love. We have to be patient and let her know we understand, that we pray things will work out for the best. We can't allow ourselves to become angry and say things we don't mean. We're the adults, and we must act like parents. Please don't be hurt, Regan. I couldn't bear it."

Regan gathered her in his arms. "As usual, you're right. We'll do our best to make the right decisions for Wren." His voice faltered.

Tyler, drawn by the commotion, bounded into the room. His heart felt as if it would break when he saw the expressions on Regan's and Sirena's faces. He was powerless to offer words of encouragement; instead, he offered another cup of coffee.

Sirena's eyes went to Regan's granite face, then to Tyler's helpless-looking countenance, and from there to the shimmering silver and crystal on the breakfast table. She knew she should say something to make Regan's sorrow lift. Wren in love! Beautiful, child-like little Wren in love! Impossible! And, according to Tyler, with a bounder, no less!

Her long, slender fingers toyed with an ornate silver spoon as her mind raced. Womanly instinct warned her to be silent, but how could she bear the stricken look on Regan's face? He was wounded to the quick. She was not fooled; in her heart she knew he had harbored a secret hope, a desire actually, that Wren and Caleb would one day find each other. Gossamer dreams. Yet she, too, had hoped for the same thing.

Tyler broke the silence, his voice measured and quiet. "Time. Perhaps time is the answer. When she goes back to Java with you, things will mend."

"Tell me, Tyler, how does one mend a broken heart?" Sirena asked coolly. Regan's eyes remained inscrutable.

"Absence makes the heart . . ."

"Grow fonder," Sirena finished the sentence.

"In her own way Wren is as spirited as Sirena,"

28

Regan declared. "If she fancies herself in love, no amount of talking or cajoling is going to change anything. We have to come up with some sort of . . . plan to make her see this oaf for what he is. Between the three of us, we should be able to think of something. What does Camilla have to say about all this?" Regan demanded of Tyler.

"In all honesty, I don't know, and I haven't had the heart to concern her with the problem. Wait till you see her, Sirena. She's come a far way from the girl you once knew." Tyler's eyes shone as his face split into a proud grin. "However, not to digress. When Camilla's pregnancy became apparent to Weatherly, it was obvious that he was uncomfortable in her presence. In fact, the way his eyes avoided her, it was almost as though he were loath to look at her. At one point I found myself itching to punch his face to a bloody pulp. The only thing that held me back was my affection for Wren. But I tell you, I sensed he thought Camilla an obscenity and he didn't want to sully himself by being in the same room with her. I'm not being dramatic. I observed this for myself. Camilla, on the other hand, blithely happy because of our coming child, was oblivious to his reaction. Her only comment was that Weatherly seemed to behave decidedly coolly to her."

Regan's spine stiffened as he heard Sirena inhale an almost imperceptible breath. He didn't fail to see the narrowing of her bottle-green eyes. If there was one thing that could stir Sirena into action, it was an attack on motherhood. How any man could regard pregnancy as a disfigurement was totally beyond Regan. To him Sirena had never looked more beautiful than when she had carried their children. Even near the end of each term, when she had been heavy and ungainly, the serenity and glow from within had given her the aura of a madonna. Regan's eyes met Sirena's across the table, and he wasn't surprised when he saw hers light like shards of emeralds and burn with warmth. How well they understood each other.

Tyler saw the look that passed between them, and suddenly he felt himself an intruder. Clearing his throat in embarrassment, he pushed his chair back from the table. "There are matters which are clamoring for my attention. Stay and enjoy your breakfast. Perhaps, Regan, you'd like to take Sirena for a walk through the gardens. We try to keep it the way my mother used to. Though she did much of the work herself, Camilla and I rely upon the gardeners."

Sirena smiled. "Tyler, you mustn't feel as though Regan and I require entertaining. Naturally, we can't impose ourselves on you. Besides, we have quite a lot of thinking to do about Wren. We'll excuse you, Tyler. Won't we, Regan?" she asked her husband, kicking him under the table to prompt his response.

Regan wanted to groan aloud from the pressure of her shoe against his shin, but he forced himself to smile. "Of course we will, Sinclair. And you must erase that look of concern from your face. Wren is our daughter, and we'll do the best we can for her. Sirena and I appreciate all you've done for the girl these past three years. We're only sorry that she's caused you and Camilla any worry. We'll take up the reins now and only hope we can do as well as you have."

Sirena beamed approval. She couldn't have said it better. Regan's shins were tender of late, and poor Tyler looked so tortured. Things would work out; she would see to it. And if Weatherly pressed matters for the worse, she would simply cut him down and that would be the end of it. Then Regan's world would be right side up again. No one was going to make Regan look as he had moments after Wren's outburst. And that included her own children. She resolved to do all in her power to prevent that look from ever crossing his face again. Regan belonged to her. No one, save herself, would ever hold the power to make him suffer. She smiled, her face radiant as she gazed deeply into Regan's eyes, hers full of promise and his full of trust.

Their stroll through the baronial garden was aimless, Sirena touching a blossom here and there, basking in Regan's nearness. "There's something I've been wanting to tell you, Regan," she said. "Actually, it's a surprise I've been saving for the right moment. Perhaps it will erase that pained expression from your eyes, and the only person who can do that right now is Caleb. He's here, Regan! He's been here and waiting for us for over a fortnight. He had a cargo to be delivered to England, and he promised to wait for us. Now, tell me I've made you happy with my little surprise!"

Regan grinned. "Of course it makes me happy, but I was saving the same surprise for you. Farrington wrote me that Cal would be stopping to check on his investments, and I was saving his appearance for just the right moment." He gathered her in his arms. "Already I know the way your mind is working. Caleb will arrive on the scene, sweep our little Wren off her feet, and everyone will live happily ever after. Cal may have other plans, sweetheart. I know, I know," he said as she began to protest, "that Cal would do anything you asked, and he probably will do as you want, but remember that you are holding two lives in your hands. You can manipulate to a point; then you must back off and let Heaven take over. Only too well do I recall your words the last time Wren and Caleb were together. You said she was Caleb's destiny. I felt that, too, but Cal is a man now, not a boy."

"And Wren is a young woman now. A beautiful young woman who can turn a man's head with a toss of her curls," Sirena murmured. "She is his destiny. I feel it here," she said, placing her hand over Regan's heart. "At times Heaven needs a gentle nudge."

"I couldn't agree more," Regan laughed.

"Then it's settled. We'll turn Wren over to Caleb and see how matters progress. And if for some reason things don't go the way we want, we'll draw straws to see which of us cuts down that bounder Weatherly." Sirena giggled girlishly.

"I'll say one thing for you, Sirena van der Rhys. Living with you has never, ever been dull," Regan whispered, drawing her close and lifting her off the ground. He kissed her soundly and set her down firmly, his arm around her slim shoulders.

Sirena laughed. "Come, kind sir, we have some planning to do in regard to young Wren and Caleb."

Chapter Three

A cigar clamped between square white teeth, dark eyes smoldering, Caleb van der Rhys strode the deck of the decrepit gambling ship while murderous thoughts raced through his mind. Thank God he had never consented to Lord Farrington's opening the hull of his beloved *Rana* and making her a permanent fixture on the wharf. It would have broken his heart to find her in such total disrepair. And Sirena! What would Sirena have said to find her *Rana,* the ship he had renamed *Sea Siren* after her, little better than a garbage scow? The last time Caleb had been aboard the gambling folly in which he and Farrington were partners, business had been thriving. Carpeted rooms and gleaming wood and brass had accented the gambling tables in the main lounge. Private staterooms, furnished impeccably with satins and brocades, had catered to gentlemen and their club members. At one time the folly had been the most popular casino in England. And now . . . now this!

Slowly and deliberately, his sun-bronzed hand removed the cigar from between his teeth. His dark eyes became cool and calculating as he stared down the dapper Lord Farrington. "While the cat's away, the mouse will play. There'd better be a good answer as to why this establishment is in such sorry condition. Tell me, what lady or gentleman would set foot on this rotting barge? What happened to the money I sent you for improvements? Where did it go? Who frequents this den of iniquity besides longshoremen and cutthroats? Let's take a look at the profit-and-loss statements. Or is it all loss and no profits? Speak up, Farrington! Did that same cat take your tongue? Ah," Caleb said softly, "I see it has." Again the cigar found its way between his gleaming teeth, and he talked around it. "Five minutes, Farrington, and then over the side you go. You'll barely make a splash. The books?" he demanded coldly.

Farrington jumped at the lash of Caleb's temper. His hands twitched nervously as he played with the cuffs of his meticulously laundered shirt. "Cal, my boy," he began hesitantly, pausing to clear his throat, "what you see here is a man fallen on hard times. Money is tight; even the gentry are careful with their sterling. It's all I can do to keep body and soul together," he whined. "True, profits are slim at best. I'm in debt over my head, and there's little to be done

33

for it. If the clientele of this establishment has—er—fallen to the good folk who earn their bread on the wharf, it is merely a sign of the times."

"Cut your flowery speeches," Caleb growled. "Remember, I know you too well."

At Caleb's stony look, Farrington changed his tactics. "After you left England, I couldn't make a go of it. Well, you know, the women came for a night's diversion because of you and your charm," he simpered. "The men came because the ladies prodded, and because they saw in you something they themselves were lacking. Unfortunately, I was a very poor substitute. Oh, in the beginning I lied and said you were away on business, hoping they wouldn't become wise. But that was a foolish mistake on my part. I should have been looking for a replacement to carry on for you. Alas, my heart wasn't in it." Farrington glanced covertly at Caleb, who was close to fuming. He continued rapidly, his eyes carefully watching Caleb's fist for fear it would come crashing down into his face. "It's your fault, Caleb. You left me to fend for myself. Quite a lot to expect of an old man. A tired, old man at that. This was the best I could do. I have a few pounds squirreled away, and if you're in need, I can let you have it." His tone became pleading, his eyes begging as he braved another look at Caleb.

Caleb moved along the deck, his booted foot prodding at loose planks. He felt disgust as his dark eyes raked the ship in her sorry state of disrepair. He felt responsible for the old reprobate following him. He swiveled, his body light and lithe. "Two thousand pounds and that's it. I don't give a damn if you have to do the carpentry work yourself. Hire as many men as you need, and I'll give you exactly one fortnight to get this scow in shape. I'll take care of the printing and have the handbills distributed. You'll have a gala the likes of which you've never seen before. And," he went on ominously, "if my share of this business

34

doesn't improve almost immediately, I'll keep good on my promise. Skinny old men make barely a splash in the cold water of the Thames."

Aubrey Farrington straightened his back and stared at Caleb. "I'll do it, Cal. I'm sick and tired of being a weasel. A man needs his self-respect. You have my word. I do thank you for being so generous. I won't fail you."

"It's a wise man who heeds the first warning," Caleb acknowledged, lighting another cigar. "I'll be back in a few days to see how things are progressing," he tossed over his shoulder as he strode from the deck.

Envy, pure and simple, coursed through the old man's veins. Ah, to be young again and to look like Caleb van der Rhys. His old eyes narrowed as he watched Caleb stroll down the wharf, the eyes of the scurves on his back. He knew if one of them made a move, Caleb would have him by the throat and begging for mercy. There was no more of the boy in Caleb. He was a man and had come into his own. Farrington would have sold his soul at that moment if the devil could promise to turn him into another Caleb van der Rhys. Sold it cheerfully, with no regrets.

Caleb climbed lightly into the hired hack and gave the driver directions to Tyler Sinclair's home on Pall Mall, near Charing Cross Road. He estimated that the drive through London at midday would take more than an hour, and he looked longingly at the Rooster's Tail Pub, where he could be enjoying a cool ale instead of a hot, dusty ride. He sighed, knowing there was no hope for it; he had to contact Tyler for news of Sirena and Regan's arrival.

The route to Tyler's home took him along Thames Street, which ran parallel to the wharves along the river. He pulled at his collar with irritation and wished he were still at sea aboard his *Sea Siren*. Having kept true to a promise she had made him long ago, Sirena had put her ship, the *Rana,* into Caleb's care. Because of his regard for her and for an adventure they had both shared, he had renamed the ship the *Sea Siren.*

Caleb's attention was centered on the view through the grimy windows of the hack. It was always the same, never better, only a little worse now. This was the London of the people. The groomed, tree-lined streets near Charing Cross and Hyde Park were the London of the privileged. These narrow streets and byways and tall buildings leaning heavily on one another, where the shadows seemed darker than anywhere else in the world, represented the people's city.

And yet, for all its ugliness, there was a beauty here, too. London was a polyglot of the ages, old and battered and touched with evil; still, it brimmed with color and a decadent glory. Here was the heart of the city, not behind those beautiful brick edifices of the rich. Here the city teemed with life. The streets were crowded with porters struggling to carry their heavy loads of merchandise as they cried dire curses at any who dared to detain their progress. Merchants and vendors pushed their carts through the narrow alleys, calling out their wares to housewives who swarmed to make their purchases.

Church steeples stabbed the gray sky, which was thick with smoke from the chimneys and rife with the stench from the soap stewers, and through which only the strongest sunlight could penetrate. And each steeple boasted its own melodious bell but only added to the cacophony.

The very center of an Englishman's life was the numerous taprooms and pubs, which were recognized by swinging signs painted in gaudy colors and identified, by those who could not read, by their caricatures of yellow bulls, crimson roosters, goggle-eyed owls and various shields and, most of all, by tankards of ale.

Having seen these sights all too often and feeling stifled by them, Caleb settled back in the hack and

36

thought ahead to his visit with Tyler and Camilla. While Caleb's business in London was infrequent, he did manage to see Tyler on occasion, but never Camilla. Tyler had always met him at his offices on New Queen Street or aboard the *Sea Siren* or at a convenient taproom. It had been years since Caleb had set eyes on Camilla, and he wondered if those years had been kind to her. Each time he was in his company, he had asked Tyler how Camilla fared, always expressing his interest with friendly courtesy, never with any obvious familiarity. He didn't know how knowledgeable Tyler was about his and Camilla's affair while she had been married to Regan, and he didn't wish to dredge up old laundry and leave Camilla to pay the bill with her husband.

Caleb pulled at his collar again. He didn't like having these old memories crop up. He remembered all too well the way he had agonized over his betrayal of Regan with his stepmother. And yet he hadn't been able to help himself. He remembered the way his heart had hammered in his chest and his hand had itched to run his fingers through Camilla's soft golden curls. His involvement with Camilla had tortured him, had stung his conscience to the point where he couldn't face his father. He had felt sick with himself, but there had been no help for it. He had fallen in love with Camilla. She had been so young, so sweet, so tender. And when he had taken her in his arms, despite the prick of his conscience, and she had whispered over and over, "Caleb, I need you, I need you," and offered her lips, he had taken them greedily, feeling her fragile weight in his arms. He had been overcome with emotions of love and desire and protectiveness. And when he had carried her to his bed and she had pulled him down beside her, the scent of her skin and the soft swell of her breasts had exorcised the feelings of deception and betrayal against his father. Camilla had been in his arms and cried that she needed him,

37

and he had closed his mind to any voice of conscience which had told him it was wrong.

Caleb shook himself from his reverie. He assured himself that he was only thinking of Camilla now because he was certain to see her again. It had all washed out in the end, and he was thankful Regan had never needed to know that his own son had cuckolded him. All had worked out for the best. Camilla had found her love in Tyler, and Regan had returned to his one true passion, Sirena.

Assured that the past was well behind him and that he was now in control of his own destiny, Caleb cockily quirked an eyebrow. He was a man now, no longer the boy he had been who had fallen under Camilla's charms. He could certainly take care of himself no matter how urgently Camilla might express her desire for him and her entreaties that they become more than friends. No, this time he would be in full control of himself, even if that meant disappointing Camilla. He had no doubt whatsoever that Camilla would wish to resume their past relationship. After all, she had been married to Tyler Sinclair for almost nine years, and, knowing Camilla, he assumed she had become bored with her role as Tyler's wife.

Humming a tuneless melody, Caleb settled back in the seat and contemplated the steps he would take to keep the ardent Camilla at bay.

Malcolm Weatherly smoothed his richly embroidered dark blue waistcoat and watched with a practiced eye as the groom readied the phaeton for his drive with the shy little bird called Wren. I could do worse, Malcolm thought as he fastidiously brushed a speck of lint from his cuff. After all, Wren was a van der Rhys, and it was well known that her father was one of the wealthiest men in the trades of the Dutch East India Company. Marrying Wren would serve to advance his own station in life, a station, he was loath to admit, that had sorely descended to just above the poverty level.

Wren van der Rhys. Weatherly sneered. An awkward name at best. In no way did it suit the vital, amber-eyed maiden he was intent on making his own. A handsome dowry would certainly be forthcoming—if her father did not take it upon himself to look too closely into Malcolm's credentials.

If the van der Rhyses doted upon their daughter as he had been led to believe, there should be no problem. He shrugged his slim shoulders and glanced down at his boots. He would have to have them resoled very soon. He must remember to keep his feet planted firmly on the ground to avoid discovery of the newsprint which peeked out of the h'penny-size hole in the leather. Style, breeding and class distinction were all-important and if it were not for his wastrel uncle, he wouldn't be in these dire straits.

Malcolm had just returned from a visit to his banker, and the news was worse than he had expected. At his current rate of expenditures, he had only three more months left to him in London. At the end of that time his bills would have caught up with him and his landlady would be tossing him out for unpaid rent—lock, stock and barrel. Yes, Wren would do very nicely indeed for added insurance against that calamity ever happening. And to think he had almost tied himself to Sara Stoneham! The very thought of it terrorized him. Malcolm had assumed that Sara's family was still wealthy and influential. Instead, he had learned, and just in the nick of time, too, that because of the Stonehams' religious views and rash statements against the Crown, their properties were, one by one, being stripped from them. A nice kettle of fish *that* would have been, being saddled with an ex-heiress who was a Puritan to boot!

Wren was another matter entirely. How fortunate it was that he had made acquaintance with her, and so soon after Sara! Luckily, Sara was a wise girl who seemed to know when to keep her mouth shut. Malcolm grinned as he thought of the nights he had made love to Sara, and her passionate responses. That alone was enough to keep her quiet. A wise girl didn't boast that she was no longer a virgin. What Malcolm couldn't quite understand though, was the relationship between Sara and Wren. He shrugged. There was no accounting for women.

He reached into his breast pocket and withdrew a silver snuffbox. Turning it over in his palm, he gazed at his reflection in the polished metal. He never used snuff, considering it a nasty habit which spoiled one's shirt fronts with grains of yellow tobacco. But the box had become an affectation he used to cater to his vanity. It was unseemly for a man to carry a mirror, and the box did just as nicely. He smiled at his reflection, proud of his sterling good looks, his smooth skin and strong chin and bright, intelligent eyes. Women had always turned to stare at him, and he reveled in their attentions. Perhaps his inheritance had been badly handled and stolen from him, but nothing, not even time, would ever steal his handsomeness. He had only to remember his father, whom he resembled. Age had improved his good looks, touching his dark, wavy hair with a feathering of gray at the temples, that added a distinguished air to his boyish charm. And Malcolm was careful with his diet, maintaining the slimness and grace of a dancer. Wren hadn't stood a chance against his charms once he had put them into use. Any more than had Lady Elizabeth Rice, favorite paramour of King Charles. Malcolm laughed aloud. Wonderful, power-hungry, greedy Elizabeth, so ripe for an escapade with an ardent young man who was wise enough to keep their affair to himself rather than boasting about it to add to his own prestige.

It wasn't difficult to understand why King Charles, for all his self-righteous proclamations on the sanctity of marriage, preferred Lady Elizabeth to his dark and homely queen, Henrietta Maria. Lady Elizabeth was as fiery-natured as her flaming hair, and, most important of all, she was discreet, a necessity for a long regime as the King's favorite.

Malcolm had made her acquaintance quite by accident, almost in the same way he had met Wren. Lady Elizabeth had been taking the air in Hyde Park, and he had been so entranced with her beauty that he had boldly initiated a conversation. From there the flirtation had taken wing; when Elizabeth had invited Malcolm to a quiet dinner at her modest apartments on Drury Lane, he had quickly and eagerly accepted. They had been together several times before Malcolm had discovered that the King enjoyed sleeping beneath the same bed linens and between those same alabaster thighs.

Malcolm had thought he had succeeded in keeping his financial difficulties from Elizabeth, but only a few nights ago did he realize this was far from the truth. At first he had feared she would put an end to their affair, but to his surprise she had watched him warily through her azure-blue eyes and told him about a certain collar being fashioned for the King to wear on the anniversary of his son's birthday celebration. Bit by bit, Elizabeth had apprised Malcolm of the situation, carefully avoiding mentioning the name of the goldsmith who was creating the sensational collar. And sensational it would be, according to Elizabeth's description. "Worth a King's ransom," she had declared.

At first Malcolm hadn't understood why she was telling him about it. Finally it had dawned on him that Elizabeth was offering him information that suggested the collar was within reach of someone enterprising enough to relieve the goldsmith of it before its delivery to the King. She had been more than willing to part with the scheme, for a fair share of the profits, of course. Tucking the gleaming snuffbox into his breast pocket, Malcolm nearly chortled out loud. Either way he couldn't lose, so long as he wasn't caught snatching the collar red-handed. If the robbery went off well, as he hoped it would, he wouldn't have to saddle himself with a wife for whom he cared nothing otherwise, failing all else and if the jeweled collar were beyond reach, he would acquire for himself a lovely, rich wife.

Seeing that his hired phaeton was approaching the drive to Baron Sinclair's home, he straightened his cravat and slipped a peppermint into his mouth to sweeten his breath. He stepped lightly from the carriage just as a hackney cab came up the drive and stopped behind him. Malcolm turned, expecting to see Baron and Baroness Sinclair. Instead, a tall, powerfully built man with hair the color of polished mahogany and a complexion like newly minted copper exited the cab, a fragment of a cigar clamped between his teeth. Malcolm watched curiously as the man hooked his thumbs into his vest pockets and looked about, his dark eyes sharply appraising.

Removing the cigar from his mouth, Caleb tossed it into the shrubbery and advanced toward the front door. Malcolm, surprised by the stranger's proprietary air, quickly fell into step behind him. They both reached for the bell pull at the same time, and there was a moment of embarrassed hesitation as they measured each other.

"It seems we are bound for the same place," Malcolm said haughtily. "If you please, sir," he added, pushing his way in front of Caleb and grasping the bell pull firmly.

Caleb took an immediate dislike to the dandy, and his quick eye did not fail to notice that Malcolm's cuff had been ineptly mended.

"Are you expected, sir?" Malcolm asked arrogantly.

"I am," Caleb replied simply, his dislike for the man growing.

"I, too, have an appointment. I frequent the Baron's

home rather regularly, and I'm sorry to say I've never made your acquaintance. Allow me to introduce myself. Malcolm Weatherly," he announced, extending his hand.

"Caleb van der Rhys," Caleb stated, making no move to return the gesture.

Malcolm blinked. Van der Rhys! Surely this man was too young to be Wren's father. He tried to determine if Caleb had recognized his name. He knew only that in appearance he ran a sorry second to van der Rhys. Standing next to this sun-bronzed giant made him feel as though he'd been dipped in milk and hung out to dry.

Caleb seemed completely uninterested in Malcolm. If Tyler counted this dandy among his friends, that was his business. Then, of course, perhaps this Weatherly was a friend of Camilla's. Caleb grinned, his square white teeth gleaming in his tanned face. Perhaps Camilla hadn't changed after all.

Weatherly wondered what the man's private joke was. It seemed to amuse him considerably. He glanced down at Caleb's boots and felt a twinge of envy. Caleb's feet were encased in the finest leather boots Malcolm had ever seen. They were moroccan, from the looks of them, and polished to a high gleam. Van der Rhys was as impeccably dressed as he. But the other man carried himself so effortlessly, with a casual air of superiority that only money could provide. Undoubtedly a woman's man, he thought sourly, yet with a hidden power and a self-assurance that were enviable. In the split second before the maid opened the door, Malcolm decided he would never want to face Caleb van der Rhys in a life-or-death confrontation.

The moment Sally, the dimpled maid, opened the wide oak doors, Caleb grinned and winked at the flustered girl, his manner easy and assured. As if he belonged, Weatherly thought, grimacing.

"Follow me," Sally giggled as she all but ran ahead of the two men, her cheeks flushed and her hands trembling slightly because of the sun god who had entered the house. She skidded to a stop and held open the doors to the morning room for Caleb and Malcolm to enter. "Who shall I say is calling?" she asked Caleb, not even bothering to glance in Malcolm's direction. She *knew* whom he was here to see. Lord love a duck, wait till Miss Wren hooked her eyes on *this* one! Wait till the rest of the staff hooked their eyes, too. All the downstairs maids would be peeking and giggling for weeks, herself included.

"Caleb van der Rhys to see the Baroness." Caleb smiled winningly. He enjoyed the flustered look the little maid wore. He knew the effect he had on women, and it secretly amused him. Until they started playing the little games women play, and then it annoyed him. In that one respect he was most like Regan. He wanted a woman who would be a match for himself and would be honest. He wasn't interested in any weeping and wailing or coy deceptions. A little fire and spirit always made for a worthy encounter.

"Sir," Sally, the maid, said, curtsying low, "the Baroness is indisposed and won't be down till luncheon. Would you care to leave your card, or would you like to see Miss Wren?"

Caleb threw back his head and laughed, making Sally sigh in near ecstasy. "Next to the Baroness, Miss Wren is just the person I'd like to meet. Tell her Caleb is here and to move as fast as her legs will carry her to my arms." He laughed again as the maid cast a puzzled glance at Malcolm and ran from the room.

Wait till the girls in the kitchen hear about this! she told herself. Lordy, I'll be the center of attention for weeks. Morry, the houseboy, will be so impressed with me, he might even ask me for a walk after supper!

Forgetting her training in her excitement, Sally knocked loudly on Wren's door and opened it at the

44

same time. "Miss Wren, Miss Wren, you're to come quick! There's a gentleman downstairs in the morning room. A gentleman to end all gentlemen! Wait till you see him. Lordy, he's the handsomest man my eyes have ever seen! Come," she said, holding out her hand in a girlish fashion.

Wren's lashes drooped. Malcolm was early. She wasn't ready for a confrontation between Regan and him. She would have to plead a headache and hope for the best. How could she face Malcolm now, after the hateful things she had said to Sirena and Regan? Malcolm was so sensitive to her moods that he would immediately know something was wrong. "Tell Mr. Weatherly I've a horrid headache and I'm resting. Give him my apologies and ask him to return at tea-time," Wren begged. "And say that I'm sorry I won't be able to take that drive with him today."

"No, no, Miss Wren," Sally cried in agitation. "His name is Caleb van der Rhys, and he said if he couldn't see the Baroness, then he wanted to see you. Miss Wren, he looks . . . he looks like a—a god," she whispered. "I quite forgot myself in his presence and almost swooned at his feet." As an afterthought, she added impishly, "Your other gentleman friend is in the morning room with him."

Wren's heart fluttered and she felt faint. Caleb! Caleb was downstairs waiting to see her! Caleb was in the morning room with Malcolm! "Damnation!" she muttered under her breath.

The maid frowned. "Miss Wren, for shame. Young ladies never say such words."

"This lady does," Wren said through clenched teeth. "Very well, I'll go down and see my two . . . gentlemen callers." She tossed her dark hair, pinched her cheeks for added color and wiped at her incredibly long lashes with the back of her hand. Why hadn't someone told her Caleb was in England? That was the least Sirena and Regan could have done. They knew how fond she was of Caleb. It must be some sort of trick on their part. Sirena, Regan said, was as tricky as a fox. And for both men to arrive at the same moment was more than a coincidence. "Damnation!" she said aloud, her eyes defying Sally to make any comment. The little maid remained mute, happy that she would get still another glimpse of the sun-darkened giant in the morning room. How she wished she were quality folk with a gentleman caller the likes of Caleb van der Rhys!

"I'm ready, Sally," Wren said, smoothing the skirt of her rose morning gown. One light flick of her fingers to her hair and one last deep breath. Her shoulders squared imperceptibly as she approached the morning room. Sally opened the doors and Wren stepped through. Her amber eyes went immediately to Caleb and she wanted to faint. She forced a smile and, as the good teachers had taught her, walked to the center of the room, both arms extended appealingly in welcome.

Caleb, caught up in Malcolm's boring discussion of London weather, was stunned at her entrance. Merciful God, Sirena was right. What a beauty! Where was the little girl he had known so long ago back in Java? His heart hammered in his chest as he scooped Wren into his arms, ignoring an outraged Malcolm Weatherly.

Tears glistened in the girl's amber eyes as Caleb held her away from him for a moment. "You're all grown up now," he murmured, his voice full of awe. "Who would have believed the little girl who had run barefoot on the wharves could end up like this?" He pointed to her elegant morning gown, then lowered his voice to a bare whisper. "I don't think I care to call you my sister any longer." His dark eyes teased her. "Little sisters should never look as you do."

The amber eyes smoldered momentarily and then became banked fires waiting for another time to be rekindled. Casually, Wren removed herself from Caleb's arms and turned to acknowledge Malcolm Weatherly. "Malcolm, this is my . . . this is my . . . brother Caleb."

"We've met," Malcolm said curtly. Wren had never looked at him in quite the way she looked at van der Rhys, and, supposedly, *he* was her intended. He had never seen a sister look at a brother in just that way, nor had he seen a brother so overcome by a sister's beauty. A small worm of fear crawled around his stomach and then settled down to rest at Wren's next words.

"I'm so glad you arrived early, Malcolm. Sirena and Regan are here; they arrived during the night and are quite eager to meet you. Everything has been arranged for luncheon, when the Baroness will come down to join us. Until then, why don't you and Caleb take a walk through the garden? I'll join you both shortly." She placed a gentle hand on his arm.

"That doesn't sound like one of your better ideas," Caleb said with a grimace. "Now, if you had said, 'Let's remove our shoes and romp through that lush carpet of grass . . . together,' I would be the first one into the garden. However, I guess it's you and me, Weatherly, for a stroll." He turned and grinned wickedly, sending Wren's heart into a quick pounding. "Patience, as you know, is not one of my better qualities."

Wren laughed, the first genuine laugh she had uttered in months. "I remember. If things go well, perhaps we can romp through that meadow of green before you leave for home."

Caleb's dark eyes lightened at her words as he followed Malcolm from the room.

Outside in the spacious marble foyer, Wren leaned against the wall and took several deep breaths. Of all the damn days for Caleb to arrive. "Damn, damn, damn," she cried as she ran through the hall and up the curving stairway.

47

Chapter Four

Unaware of the drama unfolding below, Baroness Camilla Langdon Sinclair slid out from her ruffled, canopied bed and stretched luxuriously, cupped her hands around her protruding stomach and sighed happily. Soon she would be a mother. If someone had told her she would ever welcome this state in her life, she would have laughed. Tyler was so happy, and the way he doted on young Wren was how he would dote on their own child. Even more so. Dear, sweet, wonderful Tyler, who loved her and understood her. Tyler was wonderful. Life was wonderful. The sun was shining and she was glad to be alive. The child growing inside her was the fruit of her and Tyler's deep love. Nothing would ever destroy that love; she wouldn't allow it.

With the help of her maid, she bathed and dressed in a becoming gown of soft gold, cleverly designed to conceal her condition. As if she wanted to hide it. Why had she listened to that prudish seamstress who had said it was unseemly for a "lady-in-waiting" to reveal her condition? *Reveal* it! God! She wanted to *flaunt* it! To shout about it from the rooftops! And all the while to sport her burgeoning belly and milk-heavy breasts in a declaration of womanhood fulfilled. She wanted the whole world to know she was expecting a baby. She would walk with her shoulders thrown back and belly thrust forward in full evidence. She wanted Sirena and Regan to know how happy she was.

Camilla tilted her head and listened. How quiet the house was. By now, with the newly arrived guests, the house should be ringing with Wren's happy laughter and Regan's boisterous good humor. On the other hand, as Tyler had worried, things might not go well once Wren informed them of her intentions. Well, she, for one, wasn't going to worry about it. Nothing was going to spoil her good mood. After all, Wren was already eighteen years old. And hadn't she, Camilla, been secretly married at the same age?

Camilla Sinclair had been little more than sixteen when she had first laid eyes on Tyler Sinclair. Her father, Stephan Langdon, had been distantly related to the late Baron, Tyler's father, through marriage. It had been a sun-kissed summer when she had traveled to Knightsbridge with Stephan to spend a few weeks at the Sinclairs' summer home. It had been no secret to her that Stephan was considered the black sheep of the family and was barely tolerated by the Baroness while the kindly Baron believed in letting bygones be bygones and had warmly welcomed them into his home.

During that glorious summer she and Tyler had fallen madly and impetuously in love, much to Stephan's greedy pleasure and the Baroness's dismay. Even repeated warnings to Tyler that his mother would disinherit him if he continued his dalliance with Camilla had not dampened his ardor. They were in love; that was all that mattered, and later, when it had seemed that the Baroness would have her way and they would be separated, Camilla and Tyler had run off to be married.

At first Stephan Langdon had been overjoyed with the alliance between his only child and the wealthy Sinclair son. But when Tyler had decided to reveal his secret marriage to his parents, Stephan had reconsidered. "Don't do it," he had said. And Tyler, young and still several years away from the time when he would inherit a large part of the Sinclair estate, had heeded his words.

Tyler had thought that it was *his* skin Stephan had been bent on saving. It hadn't taken him long to realize that Stephan Langdon had known the Sinclairs were intractable and that Tyler would most certainly be disinherited, leaving Langdon not only with the burden of a daughter but also with that of an impoverished son-in-law. Tyler would have been disinherited and ostracized, and, along with him, Stephan would have found himself an outcast. He had known the Sinclairs would have avenged themselves on him for his part in the romance and banished him from their society.

The main reason Langdon had been acceptable to his peers was because he had had the Baron's endorsement. Without that, and because of his sullied reputation, he would have been cast like a leper from the fashionable drawing rooms he so coveted.

Innocently, and with Camilla's consent, Tyler had agreed to keep their marriage secret. It had been understood that when he reached his majority, he would lay claim to Camilla. But Stephan had not been able to wait five more years to ease his financial predicaments. When Regan van der Rhys had arrived in London and word of his extraordinary wealth had spread, Stephan had adroitly placed his daughter in conspicuous proximity to the Dutchman. Circumstances, which had been unknown to either Stephan or Camilla at the time, had led to her marriage to Regan.

She had been a girl then, Camilla now reasoned, a

foolish, self-centered girl who had easily been led by her calculating, conniving father. The only honesty she had ever displayed had been her love for Tyler. Everything and everyone else had been a farce. Even in another man's arms—Regan's, Caleb's, little matter whose—it had always been Tyler. Tyler, who knew her for herself, her virtues as well as her faults, especially her faults. Tyler knew them all and loved her in spite of them.

Camilla smiled a self-satisfied smile and patted her swelling abdomen. It had taken quite a few years to become pregnant with this child, but now she had all a woman could ask for. A husband, a child about to be born, and the freedom to be herself and reach out for what she wanted.

While Camilla preened and pampered herself, Wren was pulling one day dress after another from the tall clothespress. This one was disregarded because it wasn't her most becoming color. That one because it didn't suit her mood.

Her eyes spewing amber sparks, she caught a glimpse of herself in the pier glass at the far end of the room. A flush rode high on her ivory cheeks, making her eyes sparkle and snap like a flame and contrasting with the unruly spill of her dark hair. Malcolm Weatherly had never brought her such excitement as had Caleb's arrival. Although infinitely handsome in his own right, Malcolm looked pale beside Caleb.

Now, why did I think that? she questioned herself. Malcolm was one of the most handsome men she had ever seen. And if the way he turned women's heads was any measure of her opinion, she couldn't be more correct. Malcolm had the good looks of an aristocrat blended perfectly with the charm of a rakehell. Women couldn't resist him. His black, crisply curling hair, which tumbled casually over his broad forehead and accented his sleepy-lidded, laughing eyes, gave him a boyish air. And with his sensuous smile and lithe, graceful build, it was little wonder women found him attractive. And not just young women like herself. Older women, too, more sophisticated women, seemed fascinated by him. His grooming was impeccable and his demeanor beyond reproach. Malcolm carried himself with an almost studied affectation, while Caleb just . . . Caleb just moved, effortlessly, with the natural grace of an athlete. Beside Caleb, Malcolm's carriage appeared almost mechanical.

How uncharitable I'm being, Wren scolded herself. Malcolm loved her and she loved him. Hadn't she thrown caution to the winds and practically alienated Sirena and Regan? This was no time to start having doubts about her feelings for Malcolm. Her own impulsive words of anger rang in her ears, and the vision of Regan's pained features swam before her, making the flush on her cheeks burn like fire. I meant every word I said, she defended herself to the mirror. Sirena and Regan have lived their lives, are still living it, and I will do the same, with or without their approval. She jabbed her finger toward the mirror for emphasis and turned with renewed vigor to rummage through the clothespress. She finally settled for a shimmering apricot silk which enhanced her high coloring and set off her flaming eyes to perfection.

"Wren, Wren, I've just come from the garden, and you won't believe whom I saw there!" Sara cried as she closed the door behind her, her blue eyes alight with excitement. "Malcolm and another man, a man to end all men, the kind of man we used to whisper about at the academy. Magnificent! Absolutely magnificent!" She swooned girlishly. "Wren, I swear he makes Malcolm look like a farmer." Unmindful of the cross expression on Wren's face, she burbled on. "I must ask Tyler to introduce him to me. We would go so well together, for he has hair as dark as shadows and skin like bronze. Magnificent! With my fairness, we would compliment each other perfectly!" With a carefully hidden slyness, Sara observed Wren's reaction to her words. She knew if she threw Wren at this stranger, the girl would balk and become more enamored of Malcolm than ever before. But perhaps if she pretended an interest in this man herself, Wren might be persuaded to forget Malcolm and leave him to Sara.

Wren swiveled around and grasped Sara by the arm, her amber eyes shooting sparks. Her mouth set in a grim, tight line, she hissed, "That's my brother you're speaking about, and no, you wouldn't compliment each other. Caleb is a man, not a boy, and you're only a silly, foolish schoolgirl. And if you ever call Malcolm a farmer again, I'll—I'll pull out all your hair! Do you hear me, Sara Stoneham?"

"Mercy sakes, Wren, what's gotten into you? I was only teasing you. You're upset because Sirena and Regan are here, and now all your bad deeds are coming home to roost. Maybe you're what Mother used to call a bad seed," Sara declared loftily.

"Damn your eyes, Sara, I'm not a bad seed and well you know it!"

"Of course not, little bird, ladies always speak profanity. Damn your eyes, indeed! If my mother ever heard you speak like that, she'd forbid me to associate with you. As it is, this will probably be the last you'll see of me once my parents come to save me from your bad influence. It *was* because of you I was expelled from school, wasn't it? And since you've become so sensitive about your brother, as you call him, I'll just wager my pearl comb against your silver bracelet that I can have him falling over his own feet for me within an hour!" Sara turned to hide her smile from Wren. Her ploy just might work. It had been no mere sisterly defense of a brother that had made Wren get her back up. And was she mistaken, or was Wren's defense of Malcolm something of an afterthought?

53

"Don't make me laugh, Sara. Caleb would never find himself smitten with a child like you. And a wager it is. An hour from the time you meet him."

"Wonderful. I'll flirt outrageously. The way you and I used to practice at school. Remember you said I had the longest lashes and would have men falling at my feet the day I made my debut into society?"

"I remember," Wren said through clenched teeth. Why did she have this terrible sinking feeling in the pit of her stomach? Sara was a wonderful friend, who had made living away from home bearable. And here she was, treating Sara like an unwanted piece of baggage. Caleb could do worse, she sniffed. "I'm sorry, Sara. You're my best friend and I shouldn't treat you so shabbily. Please don't be angry with me," she entreated, her tone softening in apology as she touched Sara lightly on the shoulder.

"I'm not angry," Sara said, her smile wide and gentle. "I just don't think Malcolm is the man of your dreams. Caleb, now, seems like a lusty, seafaring man, the kind your infamous Sea Siren would have gone after. He's not your real brother, Wren," she remarked distinctly, to make sure her friend understood what she was saying.

Wren's heart thumped. She herself had thought the same thing the moment she had set eyes on Caleb. He looked just like Regan, except for his dark hair and eyes. Sara was right. Caleb was the kind of man the Sea Siren would want for a lover. Wren sighed. Malcolm was the man she wanted. He was the man she wanted to marry.

"Caleb is a philanderer, Sara. He loves women. All women. I think his sole mission in life is to see how many young virgins he can bed before he takes a wife, if he should ever decide to take a wife, that is. I'm certain he's left a trail of swooning women from one port to the next. Caleb is not the marrying kind, and

54

I want to get married and have children. With Malcolm," she added coolly, her youthful expression composed.

Sara's stomach churned at Wren's words. Not if I can help it, my friend, she thought viciously. She had to do something, anything, to make Malcolm aware of the mistake he was embarking on. Perhaps her first idea was best. She had seen the way Caleb had looked at her in the garden. And hadn't Wren said he was interested in women? It wouldn't hurt to turn her wiles on him and see what effect that had on Malcolm. If Malcolm realized a man such as Caleb van der Rhys was interested in her, he would give up his mad idea of marrying Wren. Sweet, innocent, puritanical Wren. No, that was wrong. She, Sara, was the Puritan. A fallen Puritan. Yes, she would flirt with Caleb, and she would do it as soon as they sat down at the luncheon table.

"Are you ready, Sara? You know how fussy Camilla can be when her meals are late. If we delay any longer, we'll be the last into the dining room, and I want to be the one to introduce Malcolm to Sirena and Regan."

"I'm ready now," Sara said, patting a stray lock of hair into place. She looked every bit as beautiful as Wren, with her delicate good looks and in her pale blue, clinging gown. She would endeavor to stand next to the dashing Caleb so that Malcolm could see how well they looked together. Just like honey and cream, she thought, and smiled secretly.

Regan took one look at Malcolm Weatherly and almost exploded in anger. Sirena laid a gentle hand on his arm to quiet him as she, too, appraised the dandy through narrowed eyes. Then her glance shifted to the tall, dark giant of a man who entered the room. "Caleb!" she cried, rushing to him and throwing her arms about him. "How wonderful to see you!" Suddenly she found herself being lifted from the floor and swung around in a circle.

Caleb laughed. "You're more beautiful than ever, Sirena." He set her down gently, his arm protectively cradling her shoulders as he extended his free arm to his father. "It's good to see you, Father. You look as if the burdens of parenthood haven't been too taxing. Tell me, how are my four brothers?"

"Hale and hearty and looking forward to the day they see you again. When are you coming back to Java? Where are you bound now?" Regan asked, clapping his son on the back.

"Wherever the sea takes me. The affairs of the Dutch East India Company are in capable hands. I told them not to expect me for at least a year."

A momentary twinge tugged at Regan. The boy was free to do what he wanted whenever he wanted to. His own carefree days were long behind him. He felt Sirena grow still beside him. How well she knew him. She, too, had sensed his brief, restless urge. He smiled down into her eyes, all thoughts of envy and freedom forgotten. She was all the pleasure he would ever need.

"So," Regan said jovially to his oldest son, "you haven't cut a wide enough swath with the gentle sex, is that it?"

"From Java to Sumatra," Caleb laughed. "I thought I would take a chance and see what America has to offer."

"They have wild Indians in America," Sirena remarked fearfully.

"And do you think my son is no match for an Indian? For shame, Sirena," Regan chided.

"It might be advisable if you laid back your rapier and took up the bow and arrow. I don't think the women of the world will take to a baldheaded Dutchman." Sirena smiled fondly at Caleb.

Malcolm Weatherly stood on the sidelines, a smile pasted on his face. He thought everyone was displaying incredibly bad manners. Wren's parents hadn't even acknowledged him. The Baroness, despite her bloated condition, had not seen fit to welcome either him or her guests, and Wren was conspicuously absent. And this overgrown clod of a Dutchman was getting all the attention he himself should be getting as Wren's intended. He noticed Caleb's attire, and he admitted to himself that the man's easy elegance annoyed him. No matter how hard he tried, no matter what his tailor did, he would never look like the giant standing in the middle of the room. He watched as father and son lit cigars without offering him one. How long, he wondered, could he keep this ridiculous smile on his face? Peasants, the lot of them! He needed a drink. If these bumpkins could smoke cigars in Baroness Sinclair's parlor, then he could have a drink.

Seeing Malcolm's movement to the liquor cabinet, Sirena turned and smiled winningly, her emerald eyes glowing. "You must excuse our bad manners." Her voice was low, musical—almost seductive, Malcolm thought as his eyes widened in interest. "We haven't seen our son in a long time, and it's just that we're happy to be together again under the same roof. I'm sure you understand and will forgive us. Pour me a glass of wine," she said boldly. "And then let us sit here and have a chat. By the way, I'm Sirena van der Rhys, and the fair-haired man is my husband, Regan, and, of course, you're Malcolm Weatherly. Wren spoke of you this morning." Sirena nodded sweetly as she accepted the glass of wine and downed it in one swallow, to Malcolm's acute discomfort. She wanted to tell him to fill her glass again, because she would need the dulling effect of the wine to get through this luncheon. What a fop he was, she thought with distaste. Oh, Wren, how could you?

"Would you care for another glass of wine?" Malcolm asked quietly. She must be a sot, he thought maliciously.

"If you insist," Sirena said, holding out the goblet. "Fill it to the brim."

To the brim! Malcolm's mind raced. If she drinks, what does van der Rhys do? he wondered as he handed the glass to her, careful not to spill any of the burnished liquid.

Sirena allowed her soft hand to come in contact with Malcolm's long, slender fingers. She glared directly into his eyes and then coyly lowered her lashes. If he was the fool she thought he was, he would take this as a hidden invitation to a deepening friendship, or worse. She preferred not to put a name to whatever he might think it was. She sipped at the wine, the glass held provocatively in her hands as she met his eyes repeatedly.

Regan gave Caleb a gentle nudge. "Another five minutes with Sirena, and the dandy will forget why he's here. A wager, Cal?"

"I may have not learned too much, Father, but I did learn that it's only a fool who would lay odds against Sirena." Both men threw back their heads, the slim cigars clamped between strong white teeth, and laughed uproariously.

Startled, Sirena turned to look at the two men she loved most in her life. She gasped, and then a warm, delicious feeling spread through her entire body. They were hers, Regan by marriage and Caleb by an invisible bond established between them long ago. They belonged to her, for now and forever. The delicious aura stayed with her till Regan and Caleb glanced at her again, each giving her a sly wink. They knew what she was doing with Malcolm, and both of them approved.

This is a woman, Malcolm thought wildly. And I'm

man enough to handle any woman. Women always fell at his feet, begging for his favors. Even Lady Elizabeth Rice, who could count a king among her lovers, was so smitten with him that she had confided the secret of the King's jeweled collar. But Sirena would never beg for favors, nor would she grant any. This woman would never fall at a man's feet, his or anyone else's. Sirena was a woman worthy of a man's challenge.

"What are you thinking, Malcolm?" Sirena purred, her eyes boldly meeting his.

"I was thinking that now I know where Wren acquired her beauty and grace." He smiled broadly, moving a step closer so that he could delight in the delicate, elusive scent of her perfume.

Sirena lowered her eyes to hide their dangerous glitter. Wren had her beauty, indeed! Was it possible that Malcolm didn't know Wren wasn't her and Regan's daughter? As she sipped her wine, Sirena speculated. If Malcolm was a bounder, and from every indication, along with Tyler's word, he was, then he must think he was wooing an heiress. She wondered if his feelings for Wren would be as ardent if he knew that the van der Rhyses were under no obligation to bestow a dowry on Wren or otherwise include her in any inheritance. What would his reaction be if she told him?

Sirena glanced over at Caleb again and was surprised to note that his attention was directed on the doorway behind her instead of on Regan, who was exuberantly describing the "civilization" taking place on Java since Cal had last been there. Curiously, Sirena turned and saw that Tyler had entered the drawing room with Camilla on his arm. She turned back to Caleb, whose expression was something bordering between astonishment and disappointment at Camilla's obvious pregnancy. So, Sirena thought, the young pup half expected that Camilla would be waiting for him to return to her after all these years. Think again, Cal. Camilla has other things on her mind.

Smiling, Sirena made the first move toward Camilla and clasped her in a fond embrace. The old wounds because of Regan had long since healed between them, and Camilla's acceptance of Wren into her household had firmed their friendship. "You're more lovely than ever," Sirena said warmly. "Approaching motherhood certainly becomes you. Doesn't it, Regan?" She turned to her husband, who she knew was waiting to see how she would greet his ex-wife before committing himself to any display of emotion.

Looking at Camilla, Regan was hard pressed to believe he had once been married to her so many years ago. She still looked barely more than the nineteen years of age she had been when they had first met. Yellow-haired and with violet eyes whose look of innocence belied her actual experience, Camilla was still as fetching a woman as he had ever seen, aside from Sirena, of course. He was quick to note the expression on Caleb's face, and it occurred to him to wonder again if there had ever been anything between Camilla and his son. Regan sighed. That was long ago, and he really didn't want to know. However, he couldn't have blamed Caleb for his interest in Camilla. She had been and still was as graceful and winsome as a spring daffodil.

Regan stepped forward and put his arms around Camilla, kissing her soundly on the cheek. "Sirena is right, little one. You've never been lovelier."

Tyler beamed with pride over his wife and inwardly felt greatly relieved that the van der Rhyses seemed to hold no ill will against her, which could have put a strain on his friendship for them. He knew all about Camilla's past, her duping Regan into marriage with her, her affair with Caleb, and none of it meant anything to him. He knew, without a doubt, that he had always been Camilla's one true love.

Only Malcolm stood back from the chatter and bandied compliments. When he did allow his eyes to travel to Camilla, he was careful to avoid looking at her swollen midsection. His lip curled in spite of himself as he mused that pregnant women who displayed themselves in public were as appealing as sows with suckling piglets. He noticed that he had come under Sirena's green gaze and occupied himself with the contents of his wineglass. He hoped she wasn't capable of reading his mind.

Sirena's one glance at Malcolm told her all she needed to know. She had seen that same contempt for women on another man's face, a man she had married to spite Regan. Stephan Langdon, Camilla's father, had died at the point of her own sword for his contempt of women, and her hand now itched for the weight of a rapier to put an end to Malcolm Weatherly. She knew, beyond a doubt, that she would never allow a marriage between him and Wren to take place. If she had had any doubts before, they were all behind her now. Wren, too, had suffered at Stephan's hands, and Sirena wondered why she couldn't see the sadistic similarities between the two men.

As though bidden by her thoughts, Wren and Sara entered the drawing room. Without a glance in Sirena's direction, and ignoring Malcolm completely, Wren moved toward Regan, the silk of her apricot gown rustling softly. Sirena glanced at Caleb, who seemed to have forgotten his disappointment over Camilla and not even to have noticed Sara, whose white-blond hair and pearly complexion was set off by the delicate blue shading of her gown. Caleb's attention was centered on Wren, who by now was firmly within Regan's embrace. Sirena softened toward the daughter of her heart when she saw the barely disguised look of pain leave Regan's eyes.

Malcolm carefully avoided Sara's searching gaze.

He never knew how she had managed to become friends with Wren so soon after he had refused to accede to her pleas to meet her whenever she could slip out of the academy. How fortunate that he had discovered her father's falling from grace with the Crown and his near bankruptcy. Imagine, if he had saddled himself with Sara before he had learned the truth about her family's finances! It was impossible for him to fathom why she had befriended Wren when she knew he had thrown her over for the amber-eyed girl. It really didn't matter to him that Sara was Wren's friend as long as she kept quiet about having been his lover. Malcolm smiled, a churlish lifting of the lip that showed strong white teeth. Sara would never spill that sack of beans; the damage to her reputation would be irreparable. He even doubted that Wren would believe Sara, no matter how convincing her tale might be.

While Camilla drew Sirena aside to exchange news, and Tyler and Regan began to discuss business agreements concerning the handling of certain estates, Wren and Sara gathered about Caleb, leaving Malcolm to entertain himself. Malcolm had never encountered such an inhospitable group of people. He wasn't in the habit of being ignored, especially if there were women present. And what of Sara, so blatantly flirting with the younger van der Rhys? Even Wren seemed to have forgotten his existence as she hung on Caleb's every word. If he hadn't known that Wren was Caleb's sister, he might even become jealous.

Sirena glanced over Camilla's shoulder at Malcolm Weatherly. She didn't fail to notice his chagrin at being excluded from the little celebration. One might think that if he really loved Wren, he would be jealous of the attention she was giving Caleb. Then the truth dawned on Sirena. Weatherly didn't know Wren *wasn't* Caleb's half sister. He couldn't know; otherwise he would feel threatened by Caleb's presence. She almost laughed aloud until it occurred to her that Malcolm thought *she* was old enough to be Wren's mother. Sirena sniffed and threw her head back in a haughty gesture of indignation. Malcolm Weatherly would have a healthy shock coming to him when he discovered that Wren was not the wealthy heiress he thought she was.

Chapter Five

Lunch had been a gay and lively affair, and much to Wren's relief, there had been no mention of her outrage at breakfast. In fact, it appeared as though Malcolm was winning her family over in his own quiet way. Sirena, at least, seemed to hold him in high regard, judging from the way she had directed her attention to him time and time again.

Sara had been totally captivated by Caleb's stories of his adventures in the service of the Dutch East India Company, and Wren had to admit a twinge of resentment over Sara's flirtation with him. But she really couldn't blame her friend; Caleb was charming and extremely handsome. Then again, any envy she might have experienced had been assuaged by Caleb's eyes constantly falling on her, and she hoped Malcolm had noticed Caleb's attentiveness. It pleased her to think Malcolm might be jealous. Then she realized that

Malcolm believed Caleb was her brother and had no grounds for jealousy. That belief was something Wren intended to correct at the first possible opportunity. Malcolm's jealousy was an exciting thought, but first he had to know her true relationship with the van der Rhyses. Perhaps she could get him alone after dinner tonight. She was disappointed that she hadn't been able to go for a drive with him, as she had promised, but the luncheon festivities had lingered far too long into the afternoon. Besides, a few minutes ago Sirena had invited her to go down to the wharves so that Caleb could show his family how he had careened the *Sea Siren,* and she had jumped at the chance. Even in Java, when Caleb had brought the *Sea Siren* into port on his infrequent visits, she had loved to see the warm glow in Sirena's and Regan's eyes whenever they inspected the vessel, and the way they touched each other when they thought no one was looking. The *Sea Siren* was the ship on which Sirena and Regan had first discovered their love for one another, and just the sight of her brought back tender memories for them.

Tying the ribbons of her bonnet beneath her chin, Wren turned from the pier glass to face Sara. "Are you certain you wouldn't like to come along with us? I know Sirena and Regan wouldn't mind."

"No, you go along. I've a terrible headache," Sara whimpered. She was lounging on the high bed.

"Shall I have someone bring you a headache powder or cool cloths?" Wren inquired, moving over to the bed to touch Sara's head. "You do feel warm. Shall I have Camilla send for the doctor?" A note of concern rang in Wren's voice, and worry narrowed her eyes. She had never known Sara to be ill.

"No, no, I'll be fine," Sara assured her. "You go on and have a nice afternoon. Food just doesn't seem to agree with me these days. It's nothing to worry about."

"You do look a little green about the edges," Wren teased. "Are you sure I can't do anything for you?"

Sara groaned and rolled over onto her stomach. "If you don't get away from me with that scent you use, I'll be sick all over the bed! Now go!"

After Wren had closed the door behind her, Sara tried to lie very still. What was wrong with her? She'd never been sick a day in her life. Lately she had had this queasy feeling every day before breakfast and sometimes after lunch. But she had always recovered before dinner. Through her misery she reasoned that the emotional upheaval of Malcolm's rejection and the worry over her parents' financial difficulties, not to mention those concerning her brother's criticism of the King, were causing the butterflies in her stomach. And if those reasons weren't enough, there was always the horror of facing her parents' wrath when they arrived in London.

Sara awakened to a noisy commotion in the main hall below. Greetings wafted upward, and the sound of an autocratic, booming voice brought her fully alert. Her father! There was no other voice as forceful as Jason Stoneham's, except, perhaps, that of his son, Bascom.

Sara's blue eyes snapped open wide, and she quickly rose from the bed. Suddenly the room began to reel about her so violently that she had to sit down again. Her stomach rolled once more, and she dreaded the thought of going downstairs and facing her parents. She considered lying back on the bed and pretending to be asleep.

From the sound of Jason's voice booming up the stairs, it seemed the decision was to be taken out of her hands. "Sara! Where are you! Answer me this minute!"

Then Margaret Stoneham's lighter voice joined his. "Jason! Jason! You'll wake the whole house! We were told the Baroness was napping! Jason!"

"Hush, Margaret! I intend to see my daughter immediately! Sara! Sara, where are you?"

"In here, Father," Sara managed to choke as she braced herself for the confrontation. The door to her room banged open, and through the doorway stepped Jason Stoneham. For a moment Sara almost didn't recognize him. Gone were the meticulously tailored clothes which gave such authority to his deep-chested, slightly portly figure, and in their place were the black frock coat and high-crested hat which had become the popular garb of those of the Puritan sect. Stoneham had even chosen to relinquish the broad white collar that at least offered relief to the somber costume. He removed his hat, placed it carefully on a chair and then came to stand wordlessly in front of his daughter, his hands planted firmly on his hips and a cold glare in his eyes.

"How do you do, Father?" Sara managed to speak. "Well, I trust?"

"Well enough for a man who's learned his own daughter is little less than a trollop!" he boomed at Sara's cowering figure. "How could you shame me this way? I've just come from the academy, where I heard for myself your implication in one of the tawdriest affairs I've ever been told of. The headmistress apprised me of the entire situation, and I've never been so ashamed in my life. To think that a child of mine would involve herself in a—in a—tryst! I can only wonder how long it would have been before *you* had this van der Rhys girl standing watch while *you* slipped away in the dark with some simple-minded idiot who had nothing but lust on his mind!"

"Malcolm is not a simple-minded idiot!" Sara shouted, the words out of her mouth before she knew what she was saying. "I—I mean, I did what I did to help a friend. Wren is going to marry Mr. Weatherly, so you see there was nothing evil about it."

Jason was astounded by her outburst. Neither she

66

nor his wife had ever spoken to him that way. "See here, daughter, remember to whom you are talking—"

"Sara! Sara!" A breathless Margaret Stoneham rushed into the room, still holding her skirts above her ankles from the climb up the stairs.

"Mother! What have you done to yourself!" Sara's mouth dropped open. Margaret Stoneham had always prided herself on her fashionable dress and carefully coiffed hair. Now she looked like an old woman. Her hair was pulled back from her face, revealing streaks of gray beneath the brim of her white cap. The silks and satins she had always worn had been traded for a coarse gown of the deepest black that was relieved only by a white collar and cuffs.

"She has done nothing more than uplift her spirit to the Lord by leaving foolish trappings behind and dedicating her life to Him," Jason expounded. "Something you could have done rather than involving yourself in a scandal, young woman. Well, all that will be behind you when you adopt the dress of our sect. Fripperies are the devil's work, turning young people's heads away from the true Word."

Sara shook her head in disbelief. Her parents had followed the Puritan doctrines for years now, but they had never carried them to extremes. Only Bascom, with his wild eyes and unhealthy gauntness, had worn the somber black costume. "When did all this come about? Surely you haven't gone to such lengths because of what I did at school!"

"Certainly not. Your mother and I have been shown the true path to our eternal rewards. Our dress signifies that we are devoting our lives to the Redeemer."

"You mean ever since you've been condemned by the Crown for upholding Bascom's preachings and because you're close to financial ruin, you can't afford to wear anything else!" Sara stormed hotly, defying her father's masterful gaze. "Mother, where are your lovely clothes, and what have you done to your hair?"

A wistful expression passed over Margaret's face, but when she realized she was under her husband's angry scrutiny, she blanched and said soothingly, "Come, now, Sara, it's not so bad. It's the way to salvation, you know. You'll soon get used to wearing our dress. If nothing else, it solves the problem of what to wear each day."

"I'll soon get— No! Never! I'll never go about looking like a black crow! Not when I've a clothespress full of silks and satins. I've worshipped with you and Father, I've listened to Bascom's preachings, but I will never wear that—that—that!" She pointed at her mother's gown and shuddered.

"You will do as I say, daughter. Margaret, have that servant girl bring up the satchel you packed for Sara. And have a footman sent to remove her things from the clothespress. My daughter will believe as I do, and her behavior will be in keeping with the sister of the leader of our congregation."

"I refuse, Father. I won't wear that nun's habit! I'd sooner go about naked than look like—"

Jason interrupted his daughter's blasphemy with a smart slap on her cheek.

Shocked, Sara gasped and held her hand to her face, too outraged even to cry.

"You will do as I say, Sara," Jason intoned threateningly as he loomed above her. "I have accepted the Baron's hospitality under the condition that I won't have you spend another night in the same apartment with that hellion Wren van der Rhys. You will move your belongings immediately, and they will be few, to your mother's room, where we can keep a watch over you."

Sara gulped back the tears which were choking her. Helplessly she watched her mother open the satchel containing a plain black gown and stiff muslin petticoats.

When Wren returned from the wharf with Regan, Sirena and Caleb, she bounded up the stairs to the apartment she shared with Sara. She wanted to change into something especially beautiful for dinner tonight; then perhaps Malcolm would look at her the way Regan had looked at Sirena aboard the *Sea Siren*. Their past was so romantic, so adventurous, so passionate. Somehow she could imagine Caleb looking at a woman the way his father looked at Sirena, with such love and smoldering hunger, but she couldn't imagine Malcolm doing the same. Maybe she had been foolish to insist that they wait until they were married before consummating their love. Chills danced up Wren's spine when she thought of Malcolm's ardent lovemaking and his protests when she begged him to stop.

"Sara, Sara," she called excitedly as she threw open the door to their sitting room, only to find the upstairs maid in place of Sara.

"Miss Sara's down the hall in Mrs. Stoneham's room," the woman explained.

"Oh, has she already dressed for dinner?" Wren asked, disappointed that she would have to wait until later to tell Sara about her afternoon.

"You might say she's as ready as she'll ever be," the maid answered mysteriously. "Miss Sara will be staying in the same room with her mother," she added.

"With her mother? Won't that be crowding it a little?" Wren's curiosity was piqued. Then she remembered that Sara hadn't been feeling well earlier. "I suppose Mrs. Stoneham wants Sara close by in case she becomes unwell again. Now, do you think you can prepare a bath for me? I've only an hour to dress for dinner. While I'm bathing, you can press my magenta satin gown. I want to look especially nice tonight."

Everyone was gathered in the drawing room, waiting for dinner to be announced. Everyone but Sara.

Wren was concerned for her friend and wanted to ask the Stonehams if Sara was feeling better, but Mr. Stoneham kept throwing her such black looks that she lost her nerve. After the introductions had been made, Wren tried to explain Sara's innocence to the Stonehams, but she was quickly silenced by a scathing look and a curt remark. Caleb came to her rescue and led her to the far side of the room to tell her something about the natives of Brazil, where he had taken his last shipment.

Even Malcolm seemed to fall under Jason Stoneham's loathing, and if Sirena hadn't gone to his rescue, there was no telling how fierce Jason might have become. Only Camilla seemed happily oblivious to the turmoil about her.

Suddenly Sara was standing in the doorway, her eyes downcast and red-rimmed from crying. Wren gasped in spite of herself when she saw what Sara was wearing. The funereal black contrasted dramatically with her skin, making it appear ghostly. Her silky, white-blond hair was drawn into a severe knot at the back of her head, and a white cap perched on top of her head.

Everyone in the room was stunned into silence. Jason stepped over to his daughter and took her arm. "How lovely you are, Sara. So pure and chaste."

Sara could not answer; she kept her eyes downcast, unable to face anyone. She wished Malcolm were not there to see her this way, and when she finally mustered the courage to look at him, all she could see in his eyes was blatant disapproval.

Wren sympathized with her friend. No one, nothing, could ever persuade her to dress herself like a Puritan if she lived to be one hundred.

Sara tiptoed out of her mother's room and closed the door on Margaret's light snores. Hastily buttoning her hated black Puritan's gown over her nightdress, she listened for a moment before moving toward the back stairs, which led down to the kitchen. Thankfully, it was the Stonehams' habit to retire early, and after a rather long session of Jason Stoneham's praying for his daughter's salvation, they had finally settled down for the night.

Jason had held true to his word and had all of Sara's clothes removed. Even her dressing gowns were considered devil's attire and had been taken from her. Now all she had to wear over her nightgown was the black dress.

She brushed her long, silky hair off her face and prayed that Malcolm had not left yet. She prayed even more fervently that her mother would not awaken and alert her father that their daughter was missing. From the front of the house she could hear good-byes being said. Caleb was leaving, and Camilla was complaining to Tyler that she was really quite weary. After a few moments, when she felt it was safe, Sara stole through the back door, into the kitchen garden and over to where the carriages were parked. The last one in line was Malcolm's hired phaeton, the driver fast asleep on his perch. Silently she pried open the door and climbed in. She didn't release her breath until she was safely hidden on the floor between the seats.

After what seemed an eternity, she felt a stirring atop the phaeton when the driver snapped to attention at Malcolm's approach. Her heart was beating so fast she thought it would explode through her breast. At least she would be alone with Malcolm. Within her stirred the faint hope that he would take pity on her and whisk her away. She didn't know how she could face life without being near him, seeing him, hearing his gentle laugh and waiting for the occasional touch of his hand.

The darkness of her gown concealed her in the shadows, and she waited until Malcolm had entered the coach and the driver had pulled away before she revealed her presence. "Malcolm, Malcolm . . ."

He turned his head, his blue-black hair shining in the moonlight. "Sara . . . ! What are you doing here?" he asked, incredulous at her boldness. "What if your father should find out? A fine mess it would be for me to explain to the van der Rhyses why you're with me!"

"Malcolm, Malcolm, please. I had to see you. It may be for the last time! My parents are taking me away somewhere, and they won't tell me where. Malcolm, please," she begged, crawling forward on her knees and placing her hand on his arm.

"Can't you see I'm done with you, Sara? Why won't you leave me be? I'll never understand your sordid attachment to Wren when you knew I had asked her to marry me . . ."

Sara rose and sat beside him. His eyes flashed with fury and she silenced him with her lips. He tried to pull himself away from her, to release her arms from about his neck, but she pressed closer, burdening him with her slender body.

Suddenly his struggles ceased and his lips were clinging to hers. "Sara, Sara, you little fool," he whispered, drawing her closer and burying his face between her breasts. Her flesh tingled where his fingers touched her, and her lips sought his again and again.

The buttons of her gown were quickly undone, and with the ease of familiarity, Malcolm pulled the black garment over her head, leaving Sara in her thin nightdress. The phaeton rocked through the streets, the driver oblivious to what was occurring in the cab beneath him. Sara's hair veiled her nakedness as Malcolm pulled the nightdress down over her shoulders and bared her firm, round breasts. She shivered with uncontrollable desire as her arms closed about him,

72

bringing him down on top of her, relishing the feel of his lithe body pressed against hers.

He whispered her name over and over, filling her with a delight she had never known before. This was Malcolm kissing her, caressing her, penetrating her very soul. This was her love.

His mouth grazed her flesh with a practiced art, his fingers tantalized her skin, his breath was hot upon her cheek and she could feel his muscular back beneath her hands. Surging yearnings locked them together as they rode the dizzy heights and approached the crest. Sara cried out, "Love me, Malcolm, love me!"

She never wanted to leave his embrace. Her heart sang with joy as she rested against him, their passions abated.

"Sara, you must get dressed now. I must get you back to the Baron's home before your absence is discovered."

"No, Malcolm, don't make me go back there. I love you! I know you love me!" she implored, tears spilling from her eyes.

"Don't cry!" Malcolm admonished. "Why must you always cry?"

"How can you be so cruel? I've given myself to you, Malcolm, and you took whatever I had to offer. How can you think of casting me away like trash?" she sniffed.

"Trash is trash, Sara. When something is no longer needed, it becomes either treasure or trash. You, my passionate little Puritan, are no treasure." Malcolm smiled, his lips drawn into a sneer. "This is the last I'll see of you, Sara, unless, of course, you attend my wedding. But perhaps your father will have something to say about that. He seems to consider Wren a bad influence on you." Malcolm laughed aloud, the sound so derisive to Sara that she clamped her hands over her ears to block it out.

The phaeton took the return trip to the Sinclair home while Sara begged and argued and pleaded with Malcolm. But in the end she was left standing at the edge of the drive, near the stables, reluctant to go upstairs for fear her racking sobs would awaken her parents.

Chapter Six

As he had been asked to do, Caleb had come to Tyler's house for an early breakfast with Regan in order to discuss the latest events within the Dutch East India Company, for whom they were both representatives. Caleb sensed that it wasn't business which had inspired Regan to summon him for this quiet breakfast, nor was it a desire for a renewal of their relationship. Regan had something very definite on his mind, and he would take his own good time to reveal it. Whatever it was, Caleb didn't think he was going to like it.

On and on, late into the morning, Regan spoke of the Company, his home on Java, the four young sons who were impatiently awaiting their parents' return. He and Caleb caught up on news of common acquaintances and spoke of the looming civil war in England. Still Regan eluded the point of this meeting with his eldest son.

At last, when the maids kept interrupting them to clear off the table so they could prepare it for luncheon, Regan beckoned Caleb into the library. He poured himself and Caleb a healthy measure of rum and settled into an oversized leather chair. "What do you think of the young man Wren has chosen to spend the rest of her life with, Cal?"

No answer was necessary. Caleb curled his lip and drank deeply from his glass.

Regan laughed. "I thought as much. Sirena and I share your astute opinion, but Wren is another matter. She's positively smitten with him."

"Worse luck for her," Caleb muttered. "Surely you and Sirena aren't going to allow this marriage?"

"Wren is headstrong, as you know. Regardless of Sirena's and my protests, she'll do as she pleases. Sirena is quite distressed." Regan watched for Caleb's reaction on hearing of Sirena's concern. The lad was always sensitive to his stepmother and usually sympathetic to her feelings.

"What do you plan to do?"

"Nothing. What can we do? To forbid her to see him would only make him a more romantic figure in her eyes. Wren has to want to break this off on her own. She's always been sheltered. First with Sirena and myself, living on Java, where, you must admit, society isn't nearly as dazzling as it is here in London; and secondly, at the academy. I think our little Wren has fallen for the first man who has paid her court."

"A likely assumption," Caleb agreed. "You still haven't told me what you plan to do about it."

"What Wren needs," Regan continued, ignoring Caleb's remark, "is to know that she is desirable, beautiful and wanted by men other than this Weatherly."

Caleb raised his brows. "I would say you haven't enough time for that. From what I understand, Wren

75

wants to be married before you and Sirena leave for Java."

"Exactly! And I can't tell you how happy I am that you agree with me. It's settled, then. *You* will be the man to show her that Weatherly isn't the only one who finds her attractive. Wonderful! Sirena will be delighted to hear you've brought yourself into our little scheme."

Caleb nearly choked on his rum. "I haven't agreed to anything! Do you mean to tell me that you and Sirena want me to pay court to Wren so she'll forget about Weatherly?"

"Exactly!" Regan repeated. "It's comforting to know you understand."

"You wily old fox!" Caleb exclaimed. "I never said I would do anything of the kind! Wren's a wonderful girl, a beautiful girl, but she's hardly my kind of woman. I doubt that I could bring it off, Father. And even if I did, then what? I would be the scoundrel who broke her heart."

"Oh, so you admit you could turn her head and take her mind off Weatherly?"

Caleb smiled. "Of course. Don't you know whose son I am? Say, did I ever tell you about that little tavern wench with the unusual appetites whom I happened upon in Cádiz?"

Regan leaned forward in his chair, a proud smile on his face. For the next hour they shared intimate details of the women they had loved and left behind.

Swirling the dark rum in his glass, Regan seemed intent on the burnished liquid when he casually remarked, "So, Cal, all the success you speak of with the fairer sex—it's mostly with tavern wenches and admitted prostitutes, right?"

Caleb raised an inquiring brow and smiled crookedly. "I think it's safe to say that those women are accepted authorities on the matter of what constitutes a man."

"Hmmm. I suppose you could say that; however, that's their business. Let me put it this way: you wouldn't take the word of a horse trader who was interested in your money for his nag, would you?"

"If you're saying that prostitutes always tell their customers what they want to hear because that's the way of business . . ."

"Exactly," Regan said softly, watching Caleb's indignation rise.

"You know perfectly well that women of breeding aren't allowed to associate with seamen, Regan . . . or have you been married so long you don't remember?" Caleb baited.

"I remember . . . I remember," Regan laughed. "And a catastrophe that is. Even when a girl is betrothed, there is always someone peeking over her shoulder and standing guard, not allowing a moment's intimacy. A catastrophe," Regan repeated, shaking his head.

"Come, now! A catastrophe? You're exaggerating. It's just the way things are. Every family wants to protect its daughter from bounders."

"Are you saying you're a bounder, son?" Regan raised his eyebrows and observed his son critically.

"Hell, I hope not. But I haven't had much traffic with the kind of girl I eventually hope to marry. I can't quite see myself with a tavern wench."

"No, I wouldn't imagine so. You've always wanted someone like Sirena, if I remember correctly, from when you were this high." Regan held his hand at waist level.

Caleb laughed uneasily. What was his father aiming at? Had he discovered that Camilla and he had carried on a love affair behind his back?

"What I'm saying, Caleb, is that I know you through and through. You regard marriage seriously. You'd want your wife to be your mistress as well. And you'd be right there. Nothing could be better than for a husband and wife to love each other totally, sharing their bodies as well as their souls, without the slightest hint of reticence. False modesty has been the death of many a marriage. Yet if you persist in your present attitude, you would certainly spoil any chance you have for such a marriage." Regan stared into his glass, his thoughts flying to Wren. How he would hate to think of her locked into a marriage with an unfeeling, self-serving bastard who thought only of his own satisfaction. How much happier Wren would be if she were loved by a man whose main concern was bringing her to a full realization of her passions. He thought of Sirena, his woman, beautiful, self-possessed and without inhibitions when she was with the man she loved.

Caleb laughed again, uneasily. This was by far the most difficult conversation he had ever had with Regan. "First you speak of whores and then you talk about making mistresses out of wives. In that case, what is the difference between a legitimate spouse and a woman who sells her favors?"

"The difference, my son, is between passion and venality. It is the line between inspirations of desire and planned behavior, the wide breach between tenderness and love and promiscuousness."

"God, Father, you really do take me for a bounder, a jackanapes, a whoremonger!" Caleb said hotly, the fine hairs at the back of his neck bristling. "If any other man talked to me in such a way—"

"It's because I care for you," Regan interrupted. "You haven't had the most normal upbringing. Not in the least. You've spent your life among men, aboard ship or in the seaports of the world. Not exactly the kinds of places where a man could learn to appreciate women. All I'm saying is that when the time comes for you to marry, in all likelihood it won't be to one of the doxies on the wharf. She'll be a girl carefully nurtured and watched over by her family. And in that case, her initiation into love will come from her husband, and he must take full responsibility."

Caleb ran a hand through his dark hair. "All right, Father, it seems as though you're not going to let me off without this little talk about the birds and the bees. But you're years late with it. I'll play your little game and listen to what you have to say. You were telling me about a man's responsibility for turning a sheltered, innocent girl into a passionate, responsive wife. What does that responsibility entail?"

"For one thing, a man must understand he is not an animal in a state of rut with only one purpose in mind —to satisfy himself by raping the woman." Regan's voice lowered, and a deep note of sorrow entered his next words. "You saw what rape did to Sirena and how she suffered."

"Father, whatever you may be thinking, I am not a rapist," Caleb said defensively. "I saw what happened to Sirena, I was there, yes. I'll never forget it. I don't consider myself like those scurves who—"

"Don't be so hotheaded. However you look at it, if a woman isn't ready for you, taking her is tantamount to rape. Can you imagine what it's like to be an inexperienced young girl in her first encounter with sex? The nudity of a man, the hugeness of his sex? And to be ridden? I am fully aware that it isn't always horrible to every young woman. I'm speaking of the sensitive, intelligent girl. A girl like Wren, for instance."

"I'll ask again. What responsibility does a man take?"

"Patience. Knowing how to enjoy the awakening of a woman's spirit and passions. Learning how to arouse her and lead her into the mysteries of the flesh. Even if a woman isn't a virgin, if she's been badly used, can you conceive of how frightful it would be to be taken without tenderness? Compare that fear with the delight

79

of a woman overflowing with love for the man hungering for his body, yearning for his caresses."

"And suppose a man finds himself strapped to a woman who is incapable of this sublime passion even after every consideration and patience has been shown her?" Caleb wondered, watching for Regan's reaction.

"Then either she's a goose or the man is a bounder. And since you tell me you're not a bounder, Cal, be careful not to turn the woman you marry into a goose."

Caleb laughed again, this time uproariously, leaving behind the embarrassment he had felt earlier.

Just then the door opened and Sirena appeared. "What's going on in here between you two?" she asked, moving over to Regan, her taffeta petticoats rustling with each step she took. A puzzled expression crossed her face. "Caleb, what in the world is so funny?"

Bringing his laughter under control, Caleb managed to choke, "Nothing, Sirena. Regan was just telling me about goose herding. One more thing, Regan. Where did you learn all this?" His white teeth gleamed in a broad smile.

Regan put his arm about Sirena's waist and kissed her lightly on the cheek. "Everything I told you, son, comes from the best authority. Now, why don't you get your tail out of here so I can learn more about the subject?" he suggested in a husky voice as he gathered Sirena into his arms. "And, Caleb, close the door behind you."

Caleb sat in the garden, a feeling of doom dampening his normally outgoing personality. Why in the world had he promised Regan he would do as he had been asked? Now he wouldn't be his own man until he had resolved this problem with Wren and Malcolm. She was no one's fool. What had made Regan think she would fall for such an age-old trick? Man's vanity, Caleb told himself. He smirked slightly. It was true; he had always been successful with women, and he

could have the pick of the litter, so to speak. And
speaking of picking, he knew he could have little Miss
Stoneham in his bed within the hour if he had a
mind to. Just the thought of all her pink and whiteness
sent a warm, pleasant flush through his body. She reminded him of someone, but who was it? A delicate
flower ready to be plucked. He threw back his head
and laughed. He'd bet his whole cargo that she had
already been plucked by experienced hands, and
quite soundly, too.

Some of the tension between his shoulders eased
with his laughter. He needed a woman. It was that
simple. But there wasn't anything he could do about
it now. He had to put the first part of his father's plan
into motion. Poor Wren. He would sweep her off her
feet, and then what would happen to her? God forbid
he would then be saddled with her. Regan hadn't said
what he should do if that happened. It never occurred
to Caleb that the young woman would find him anything but dashing and irresistible.

Out of the corner of his eye he saw Wren approach
the garden, unaware of his presence. How in the devil
had Regan managed this? Caleb wondered.

Wren continued her walk, her eyes cast downward at the flagstones, completely oblivious of Caleb.
When he spoke, she raised startled eyes and flushed
a deep crimson. "Hello, Caleb," she murmured, her
voice a bare whisper.

"I didn't think anyone but me would be out this
early," Caleb said, getting up from the iron bench
and taking her slim hand in his. How unhappy she
looked. Damnation, if she loved the fop, why couldn't
Regan and Sirena allow her her happiness? Why did
they have to interfere?

"This is my favorite time of day," Wren replied,
smiling slightly. "I love to see the dew on the grass
and feel it between my toes. Look," she cried girlishly,
"I don't have my slippers on."

81

Caleb smiled in spite of himself. "I won't give away your secret. Sit down and let's have a talk. Yesterday was so hectic that we didn't get a chance to say much to each other. You've grown into a remarkable young lady, Wren. You're quite beautiful." He studied her features intently, lingering over her amber eyes and light ivory complexion. Her luxurious dark hair was tied back neatly and he fought the urge to free the pins and run his hands through the thick, silky strands.

"If you can admit I'm a woman, then why can't Sirena and Regan? I'm old enough to choose the man I want to marry." Her eyes and voice were very intense. Caleb's mouth tightened, and he chose his words carefully. "Perhaps it's because they never had a daughter of their own, and they want what is best for you. Once a parent, always a parent. Both Sirena and Regan have taken parenthood very seriously. I myself still talk over plans and decisions with my father. They're older and wiser than both of us. Try to be charitable and fair with them."

Flames shot from her amber eyes. "I should have known you would be on their side. You don't like Malcolm, admit it!"

"The one thing I would never do is take sides," Caleb lied. Damn you, Father, his mind shouted. "And as for my liking or disliking Malcolm, I hardly know the man. If you love him, then that's all I care about. Just be sure you *do* love him and that it's not something else you feel for him."

"And what might that be?"

Caleb decided to shock her. "Lust," he said curtly.

Wren heard the word, jumped up, and then drew back her arm and lashed out, striking him a stinging blow across the cheek. "Lust!" she shrieked. "That's all you or your father ever think about, isn't it? Malcolm is different. What happened to love? Oh, no, with you it's got to be lust. You're dead inside, aren't you, Caleb? You have no feelings, just animal urges that have to be satisfied at the expense of some woman. Animal!"

Taken by surprise with the force of the slap, Caleb stood up and reached for her arm before she could render another attack. He pulled her to him and stared into her eyes. "Don't ever do that again. If you do, I'll forget that I'm a gentleman and give you what for." Wren stared back defiantly, her lips trembling.

Caleb felt a warm flush creep up his thighs, and his heart beat a little faster at her nearness. The sweet scent in her hair was light and tantalizing. He wanted to still the trembling of her quivering lips, to see the thick, sooty lashes close over her flaming eyes and know that he was the man who could make her sigh in delight as she nestled in his arms. She felt something, too. He could sense it in her slim body as she tried to remove herself from his tight embrace. He released her suddenly, applying Caleb's Law: Always leave them wanting more, anticipating what might have been.

His eyes became hooded, barely concealing a decidedly mocking gleam. "There are women, and then there are women. The day I decide that you're a woman, I'll let you know. Run back to your nursery and put on your slippers before Sirena and Regan see you. Grown-up ladies do not wander about barefoot in a gentleman's presence, brother or not."

Wren was infuriated at his derision of her. Childish! Not a woman! She looked almost comical as she swung her arm to strike out. Caleb, anticipating her move, stepped neatly back, and the force of her swing caused her to lose balance, sending her sprawling onto the dew-soaked grass. Caleb made no move to help her to her feet but remained standing, a smile on his face. He shook his head to show her she was indeed not a woman.

Blind with rage and humiliation, Wren reached

out and clutched at his ankle with both hands. Before he knew what had happened, he found himself sprawled next to her on the wet grass. "Pig!" she screeched. "You're no brother of mine! You're nothing but a disgusting animal!"

"Is that so? Let me show you what a disgusting animal I am," he growled, grabbing her by the shoulders and drawing her to him. His mouth came down slowly, his eyes staring deeply into hers. His lips were gentle yet demanding as his arms tightened imperceptibly across her shaking shoulders. His fingers found the pins in her hair and deftly undid them; then her long, flowing hair veiled them both as their lips clung together, neither of them wishing to relinquish the moment.

Some small warning device triggered Caleb's conscience. He had to remember where he was and what he was doing. He was doing his father a favor by kissing Wren and letting her know another man found her desirable. I have to remember that, he told himself as his lips became more demanding, his hands caressing the length of her young body. Why is Regan worried? he wondered inanely as Wren returned his ardor. Somewhere in the deep recess of his mind he heard a soft moan of desire and knew he had won. His lips moved gently and he looked down into her glazed eyes. They were both wrong, Regan and he. Wren was no girl. She was a woman.

His own eyes were dulled with the ecstasy of the kiss, his body relaxed in a warm glow, so that he barely felt Wren move till she was straddling him, her arms pinning his hands to the ground. Struggling with her skirts, she brought up her knee and jabbed him full in the groin. When he wrenched free of her, she doubled her hand into a fist and hit him square on the jaw while he sought to still the spasms in his midsection. "I said you were a pig and I meant it. You're a disgusting animal. You know I plan to marry Malcolm and you try to seduce me. Animal!" she hissed as she drew back for another blow to his face. Through pain-filled eyes Caleb found himself powerless to avoid it. He took the well-aimed stroke right between the eyes and rocked backward, his knees drawn up to his chest with his arms wrapped protectively around them.

"Damn you!" he cursed hoarsely.

"The next time you think to make a fool of me, Caleb van der Rhys, think again." Then she laughed, a light, lilting sound that was somehow devoid of humor. It sent Caleb into a near frenzy. God, how he remembered! Sirena had always laughed like that when she had met the challenge of an enemy and won!

"You can lie here and suffer till the cows come home," Wren said through clenched teeth.

Caleb watched her through a haze of distress as she picked up her skirts and daintily tripped her way back to the house. "Damn you," he called weakly as a fresh roll of pain coursed through him. He tried to struggle to his knees, only to fall backward again; his sun-darkened face whitened and he gasped in agony. His head throbbed in rhythm with the spasms in his lower regions. Christ, how could Regan have asked him for this "one small favor," and where in hell had Wren learned to fight like a longshoreman?

It was Sara who found him when she came out to the garden for one last stroll in the London sunshine before leaving with her family. She would have liked to walk through the streets and stamp the sights and sounds of the city on her memory forever, but the thought of appearing in public in the black, drab costume the Stonehams insisted she wear had dampened her resolve. Somehow she knew in her heart she would never see London again. Or Malcolm either. To have had him see her wearing the somber garb of the Puritan sect had cut bitterly into her heart.

85

Fanatics! That was what Malcolm thought of the followers of Cranmer and Calvin. Zealots! Sara gulped down her bitterness but couldn't swallow it whole. She had no choice but to obey her parents, for now at least. Beset by these unhappy thoughts, she nearly tripped over the figure doubled up on the lawn. She dropped to her knees, her blue eyes brimming with tears, not for the man at her feet, but for herself.

Caleb rolled to one side and opened an eye. Through the swirling red mist which clouded his vision he saw a black, wraithlike figure that seemed to float and come to rest near him. Damnation, he must be dying and the vultures were landing near him for the kill! Damn her soul to Hell and curse that wicked laugh of hers! Just like Sirena's laugh from those long-ago days at sea!

This couldn't be happening to him, not to Caleb van der Rhys. Things like this might happen to other men, but never to him.

"Lie still," the vulture's voice whispered. "I'll go back to the house for help."

With all the strength he could muster, Caleb once again struggled to his knees and held out a shaking arm for Sara to grasp. "No," he croaked, "don't go back to the house. I'll be all right in a few minutes."

Sara helped him to a sitting position and sat back on her heels, her hands folded neatly in her lap. These van der Rhyses were an odd lot. Whoever would have thought a man like Wren's brother would be subject to fits? As she waited for Caleb to get his wits together, her own misery surfaced again. Now what was she going to do?

In just the space of a few hours her whole life had been turned topsy-turvy. After throwing herself at Malcolm and having hope reborn in her heart, they had made wonderful, ecstatic love. And when she was certain that he had put his foolishness with Wren aside and realized that love was more important than marrying into a rich family, he had wrecked her dreams. He had told her in no uncertain terms that they wouldn't be seeing each other again, except perhaps at his wedding to Wren. He had actually held her in his arms and told her that their affair had been a delightful distraction but absolutely over. He was going to marry Wren. And then, most cutting of all, when she had threatened to reveal their affair to Wren, he had laughed. Laughed! He had told her if she wanted to ruin her good name, that was perfectly all right with him, but that it would be foolish on her part and all for nothing. And when she had said she would tell Regan van der Rhys what a bounder Malcolm was, he had claimed that, after all, a man would most certainly understand another man's weakness when a fetching young girl threw herself at him. And besides, a man never bought a cow when the milk was free.

To make matters worse, when she had tried to tell Wren about her and Malcolm's affair, Wren had laughed and laughed until tears rolled down her cheeks. Malcolm, *her* Malcolm, would never look at another woman! Malcolm had little use for Puritans and zealots. And then Wren had spoken in a charitable tone and assured Sara that one day she would find a love such as Wren and Malcolm shared. Malcolm was so wonderful, Wren had said with a smile, to have seen through the wiles of another woman and remain faithful. Malcolm had proved to her the kind of man he was. A good man, a fine man, and a man whom Wren loved.

Lastly, and possibly most humiliating of all, Caleb van der Rhys hadn't seen fit to return any of Sara's flirtations at lunch yesterday. All he had been capable of doing was to stare at Wren, his dark, thickly lashed eyes lighting whenever she had spoken to him.

Sara watched Caleb now with a detached interest as the white blotches on his face ebbed slightly and his breathing became more normal. With her own future so indefinite, she found it impossible to spare a moment's sympathy for his suffering. The only thing she was certain of was that her parents weren't returning home to Surrey, but they wouldn't tell her where she was being taken. Something was wrong. She had never seen her father so agitated, nor her mother so frightened. Whatever was wrong, Tyler Sinclair was somehow involved. Late into the night the Stonehams had been sequestered in his library. At today's early breakfast her mother looked as though she hadn't slept a wink, and her father was curt, almost rude. The most puzzling thing of all was that her father's mood seemed to have nothing to do with her escapade at the academy.

"I think I can stand now," Caleb said, clutching her hand as he rose to his feet. His face blanched with the effort and then regained its natural color.

Sara forced her mind to the present and spoke softly, almost whispering. "Do you have these spells often?"

"Spells?" Caleb muttered through clenched teeth. He combed a strong hand through his dark hair as he tried to comprehend her meaning. Spells! "Only when I walk in gardens before noon," he said, trying to force some sort of smile to his lips.

"I see," Sara replied primly. "Perhaps you should see a physician or take an herbal tea. Can you manage the walk back to the house?"

Fits! Spells! The pain had subsided and Caleb felt better by the minute. He held out his hand to Sara and smiled winningly. "It's been my cross to carry, lo these many years. They just come upon me. It's particularly bad when I'm with a woman. Invariably they take it the wrong way and think my fits are a result of their charms."

Sara's blue eyes narrowed. "You're as stupid and silly as your sister," she snapped, then walked off, knowing that the man behind her had somehow made a fool of her.

At the mention of Wren, Caleb's eyes darkened and he stumbled. No woman had the right to do what she had done to him. He'd wring her skinny neck if it was the last thing he did.

Regan van der Rhys had seen Wren run from the garden, her gown clutched in her hands, her bare feet soundless on the terrace. He had continued to watch, a frown on his face, as she had thrust open the doors and raced through them and up the curving stairs. "God damn it!" he had shouted to no one in particular. What could have gone wrong? "If you botched this up, Caleb, I'll . . . I'll . . . Damn it!"

He sat on the terrace for a long time before he saw Caleb stagger up the wide walkway. He said nothing as his son collapsed next to him on the iron bench, his eyes dulled, his mouth a grim, tight line.

"Don't ever ask me to do you any more favors, Father. Physically, I can't afford you."

Regan suppressed a grin. "So she got the best of you. Shame on you. How could you have allowed it to happen?"

"The same way you allowed Sirena to knee you. I was caught unawares," Caleb said hoarsely. "You can just forget your little plan. I'll have no more part in it. Let Sirena handle it. If you had let her do what she wanted in the beginning, I wouldn't be suffering like this. When are you going to learn that Sirena's the one with the answers?" His tone was bitter as he cast an accusing look at his father.

"Sometimes I forget," Regan replied sadly. "I really thought Wren would be smitten with you. You look just as I did at your age, and women found me irresistible. I had to fight them off with a stick." Regan laughed. "It's not true, like father like son."

"If I had had a stick I would have been better off," Caleb gasped as a twinging ache washed over him.

Regan's eyes held an amused glint. "You'll live through it. I did."

"Thank you, Father, for your words of wisdom, but you'll forgive me if they don't give me much comfort at the moment."

"A hot soak in a tub, a little rest, and you'll be as good as new in a month or so," Regan teased.

Caleb's eyes widened. "A month!"

"Maybe two. It's hard to tell. I wasn't there to see or feel the force of the . . . the impact. It would be best if you set your sights on six weeks, and then if you recover ahead of time, it will be like an extra reward. You'll live, Caleb. Let this be your first lesson. You need eyes in the back of your head when it comes to women. You can't ever let them best you in anything, for if you do, they have you right where they want you, in the crook of their little finger, and you'll be dancing attendance for the rest of your life. You're the master, remember that. It's up to you to tame the woman, not the other way around."

"I can't say I exactly admire your philosophy, knowing your past and how Sirena has had you dancing attendance all these years."

"Ah, you're so young, you don't understand. It just appears that way to you. I *allowed* her to do what she did, *that's* the difference. Of course she doesn't know that, and we'll just keep it our little secret. You have to fool women, lull them into what seems like a false sense of security. For a man of the world, you have much to learn," Regan concluded calmly as he lighted a cigar and leaned back, his manner amused and arrogant.

"Just remember what I said, Father. No more favors. As far as I'm concerned, Wren can do as she pleases. You've heard the phrase 'ill wind'? Well, your little Wren is an ill wind, and don't forget I'm the one who warned you." Caleb rose and made his way from the terrace without a backward glance at his father.

Not for all the nutmegs in Java would Regan have admitted that Caleb was right. He would leave it up to Sirena to take matters in hand. Who could blame him for trying? Poor Caleb. Well, his son would never fall into that trap again. At least he had learned something. The experience had not been a total loss.

Sara Stoneham stood in the dim alcove next to Tyler Sinclair's study, an intense look on her face. Another secret meeting between her father and Tyler? What could it mean? What was going on? She had to find out. Careful lest someone see her, she sidled over to the heavy double doors and pressed her ear against them, hoping against hope that she would hear something that would give her a clue to what was going on.

The voices were faint, almost unintelligible, but she didn't move, knowing that sooner or later her father would raise his voice.

"Time is of the essence, Baron. You promised you would help us, and now you want to go back on your word!" Suddenly, as if remembering his station compared with that of Tyler, Jason Stoneham softened his tone. "I'm afraid I'll have to insist my money be refunded. Immediately. Unfortunately, I cannot wait for money owed me the way I was once able to. Our circumstances have been—er—reduced, to say the least." Stoneham's face bore the pitiable lines of defeat. "Excuse me. I wouldn't ever have spoken to you in such a manner," he apologized, "but my son, Bascom, and his wife have been hiding at a lodging house near the wharves for over a fortnight. Margaret is beside herself with worry and anguish because she doesn't know what's to become of us. Damnation, man! You gave us your word that by noon tomorrow we would all be on our way to the American colonies!" Jason stormed, unable to hold back his fear and discouragement.

Sara, outside the door, could almost see Tyler bristle at her father's tone.

"Listen to me, Jason. The delay, for want of a better word, is not of my doing. There are hundreds, no, thousands of people of your sect seeking passage to the colonies. Unfortunately, for Puritans like your family who are also considered enemies of the Crown, the problem is increased a thousandfold. You, Jason, are not the only man of your religious persuasion who has lost everything he owned. As a matter of fact, I would think it safe to say that the Stonehams are faring much better than most."

"Bah! Easy enough for someone like yourself to say. You don't know what it's like to be hounded and pursued after being stripped of nearly everything you've worked a lifetime to attain." Jason's mouth turned down in a bitter line.

"No, perhaps I don't," soothed Tyler. "But I warned you. I told you to put a stop to your son's constant preaching against the Crown. But you refused to heed my advice. Bascom was a holy man, you insisted. He was appointed by God to speak out for the people. For God's sake, man! We've been friends for as long as I can remember. You were an associate in my father's law practice. Do you think I would cheat you out of a few miserable pounds?"

Jason hung his head in shame. "No, no, of course I don't. It's just that the hounds of Hell are on my trail, and I don't want to see the destruction of my family. Bascom was hasty, unwise, but nevertheless, he is the leader of our congregation. I tell you, Tyler, the change that's been wrought in him is so astounding it can only be called a miracle. Oh, I know you doubt it when he claims to have heavenly visitations. But what else can account for the fact that once he was a wastrel and now he burns with the light of salvation?"

Tyler reached out and laid a comforting hand on Jason's shoulder. "I have no right to disbelieve him. It is enough for me that you believe. I only regret that Bascom was so imprudent as to speak out publicly against the King, and in so doing, he has brought the black name of treason upon your family. However true it may be that King Charles boasts of his 'divine right' to serve as king and upholds his intolerance of the religious reformer, along with his refusal to call together legal sessions of Parliament, Bascom's preachings have wreaked destruction on all of you."

"What's done is done," Jason said weakly. "The fact remains that if I am to save my family and any small measure of my savings, we must leave England now!"

"And everything is being done to insure just that," Tyler assured him. "Already your land holdings have been sold and the money transferred to you. It should be a tidy enough sum to guarantee a pleasant life in the colonies."

"Bah! I had to sell out to the scurrilous Farrington for one-tenth of the true value," Stoneham said disgustedly.

"True. But it is one-tenth more than you would have had if the Crown had been quicker and had confiscated your holdings. As for the price, Farrington takes measurable risks also, and he paid the same as you could have gotten from another broker."

"I never thought I'd see the day when the likes of Farrington would make a fortune from respectable Englishmen," Stoneham moaned. "Once the titles have had a chance to clear, the man stands to reap great wealth by selling the properties at the market price."

"Jason, it's senseless to expound on this. What's done is done, as you said. The important thing right now is to get you and your family out of England."

"Well, what are you doing about it? I came to you for help—I begged you! And now here we sit, cooling our heels, and every moment the King's hounds are closing in on us!"

"Get hold of yourself, man! You sound as if they were on our front step. The Stonehams are not the only fugitives from the Crown. There are hundreds like you, for one reason or another."

"Mark my words, Sinclair. Soon, very soon, Cromwell will force an end to these persecutions. And when that time comes, my family and I will be the first aboard a ship returning to England."

There was a catch in Stoneham's voice that brought a choking response in Tyler's throat. Stoneham was a loyal Englishman, and the thought of leaving his country must be terribly painful to him. Tyler would have liked to pound his fists into Bascom's face and beat the man senseless. Not that he had much sense to begin with. Had it not been for his fanatical exhortations against the King, Stoneham and his family could have lived out their lives quietly and maintained their religious beliefs without interference. He supposed there was no fervor like that of a reformed sinner, which Bascom certainly was. The man actually had an insane look about him, and all Tyler could feel was pity for Stoneham, who, in his joy at Bascom's deliverance, would follow him blindly, all the while believing that his son had been found worthy of heavenly visitations from Christ Himself.

"To get back to the matter at hand," Tyler said with authority. "I explained to you that seeing to your passage would be a risky business. Farrington is also the man who was to arrange that passage. You would be among a group of others emigrating to the colonies. However, Farrington finds himself in bad straits. He's under suspicion and has been watched for the entire fortnight Bascom and his wife have been lodged near the wharves. Contact between them at this time would be foolhardy. I hate to keep reminding you, but you are fugitives from the Crown, unlike so many other

94

Puritans sailing for America. Would you endanger those good people by having the suspicion of conspiracy cast on them?" Tyler waited a moment for the impact of his words to sink in before he resumed speaking. "This delay is only a momentary setback. Good Lord, I don't know why I became involved in this at all. Whatever my sentiments about King Charles, I never wanted to put myself and my own family in jeopardy. For the time being, I've set you up in the same lodging house that your son is in. It is part of a public tavern, as you know, and your presence will not be conspicuous. Farrington will pay for all expenses incurred. What more can I do?"

"I realize I've imposed on our old association, Tyler, and I'm sorry if I've put your family in jeopardy. I'm half out of my mind with worry." Stoneham's voice lowered. "Can you give me any idea how long this will take? When can we sail? A fortnight?" he asked hopefully.

"The best I can say for now is, as soon as Farrington finds himself a new ship's captain. He's got a line on a privateer, he tells me, but there seems to be a holdup. Farrington's reputation depends on his choice of captains and vessels. You wouldn't want to risk a crossing on a leaky old tub at the hands of some drunken fool. Farrington's choice is crucial, and I, for one, wouldn't want to be standing in his shoes. Make up your mind that it's his way or none. The lot of us could end up spending the rest of our lives in Newgate. One experience with Newgate in a lifetime is all I'll ever need."

"We'll repair to the inn where Bascom is staying," Stoneham murmured.

"Jason, you know I would gladly offer you the use of my home, but there is Camilla and our coming child to consider."

"I understand, Tyler, and I would make the same choice if I were in your place. If I don't see you again before we sail . . ." His voice grew husky and he found it impossible to continue speaking. Instead, he extended his hand to Tyler, who put his arms around him and pounded him soundly on the back.

"Write to me when you're situated in America. Camilla and I might just make a journey there someday. And, Jason, between you and me, I hope the day comes soon when you can return to England. If that means we must first have a civil war between Cromwell and the Crown, then so be it."

Outside the library door, Sara blanched. America! The colonies! Indians! Before the door had opened, she raced quickly down the hall and up the stairs to her room. She had to think. She had to make a plan. America was on the other side of the world, and if she sailed with her parents, she would never see Malcolm again.

Flinging herself on the high bed, Sara sobbed uncontrollably. "I hate them all!" she wept. "I hate my father for his radical ways, and I hate my mother for her sanctimonious ways; most of all, I hate Bascom for opening his treasonous mouth and for his so-called heavenly visitations!"

Sirena stood looking out into the blackness, the night breezes blowing gently against the sheer draperies. The lamp beside her outlined her slim body through the gossamer silk of her peach dressing gown. Her dark hair tumbled down her back in charming disarray, and the air was scented with her perfume.

Regan gazed at his wife and remembered another time, long ago, when he had first seen her, outlined by the light from a window. Sirena, although no longer the girl she had been then, was somehow more beautiful, more lovely and exciting, and he knew, by some masculine instinct, that within her beat the heart of that determined, mystical, eighteen-year-old girl he had first seen.

Sirena turned, sensing his presence. Her eyes clouded with questions, but a smile parted her lips. Regan came to stand beside her and took her in his arms. She sighed with pleasure and nestled against his chest, taking delight in his arms wrapped tightly about her.

"What's the problem, sweetheart? Still brooding about Wren?" Regan asked, his lips brushing against her ear.

"At what point does a mother stop worrying about her children? Of course I'm concerned about her. Malcolm Weatherly is not the man for our daughter. Tyler's right, he's a bounder. Even without Tyler's word on it, I would have known that immediately."

"Ah, yes, your feminine intuition," Regan murmured.

Sirena turned in his arms and looked up at him. "Regan, I'm serious! Don't tell me you want to see Wren spend the rest of her life at that dandy's hands."

"No, sweetheart, I don't. But what's to be done for it? We can't tie her to her bed until she comes to her senses. And, knowing Wren, she'd deeply resent any interference by us. That girl can be as headstrong as you are."

"You'd better smile when you say that," Sirena teased, threatening him with a clenched hand.

Regan laughed merrily. "Don't deny it. She took her lessons well from you."

"Bragging or complaining?"

"Bragging, definitely bragging," he laughed.

"Well, pretty compliments don't solve our problem. What's to be done?" Concern clouded Sirena's eyes again, and she turned her head away.

Regan sighed. "I guess I'd better come up with something. I can't have you frowning and creating wrinkles across that pretty face."

"Wrinkles!" Sirena cried. "Where?" She rushed over to the pier glass and scrutinized her face.

97

Regan laughed again, loudly and raucously. "Still vain, eh, pet?"

"Oh, you—you scoundrel!" Her fingers found the hairbrush and Regan artfully dodged the hurled object. Lowering his head, he charged right for her, grabbed her around the waist and tumbled both of them to the soft carpet. His lips found hers and sealed them in an ardent kiss, successfully stifling her protests.

After a moment Regan drew away and looked down at her. "You win, sweetheart. If you want to talk about this situation with Wren, I'm listening."

Sirena smiled. How well this man knew her, and how she loved him. He knew she had to set her feet on a course that would resolve the problem before she could come to him, free and abandoned.

Regan got to his feet and helped her up, holding her for a moment. "Only hurry and work this out in your mind, Sirena. A man can't be expected to wait forever."

Patting him fondly on the cheek, Sirena whispered, "Do you know how much I love you, Regan? You know me so well and love me in spite of myself." She moved away from him and seated herself on a chair that was farthest from the bed. "Tell me what you think of this Weatherly, Regan."

Regan paced, as he always did when he was thinking. "I quite agree with Tyler's opinion. He's a bounder. And from what Tyler has told me, Weatherly is down on his luck. There's not much to be said for his financial status. Which could lead a worried father to suppose that Wren's main attraction for him is money."

"Agreed," Sirena said firmly. "Not that Wren couldn't have any man she wanted. She's certainly beautiful and intelligent, but Weatherly is the first man she's ever become romantic about. We can't allow her to make a mistake she'll have to live with the rest of her life. Regan, can't you go directly to Malcolm and tell him we don't approve of this match and that if Wren insists upon it, we will be forced to disinherit her?"

Regan pondered for a moment, his agate-blue eyes narrowed in thought. "No, Sirena, that wouldn't work. We've already exhibited how dear Wren is to both of us. He'd know that whatever might happen, we could never bear to have Wren live in want of anything we could provide. Naturally, if he were married to her, our beneficence would also fall on him. Any other ideas?"

"We could offer him a sum of money, a large sum. If what Tyler says about his finances is true, he just might jump for it."

"Don't you see that wouldn't work either? We'd be holding ourselves up for blackmail. Yes, Weatherly would take the initial offer, but then he'd bleed us dry while he was contriving little ways to court Wren secretly. Even if Weatherly found himself another woman, he'd still haunt us. And what if Wren were to discover we had paid him off? We'd lose her, Sirena."

When Regan halted his pacing to look at his wife, he was surprised to see Sirena's chin set in a curve of stubborn determination and her eyes flashing green fire. "What is it? You've thought of something, you little witch! Now, give over and tell me what it is!" he demanded.

"It's so simple! It's been right under our noses all the time!" Sirena laughed gaily. "Regan, did you notice the attention Malcolm was paying me this evening?"

"Notice! I noticed, all right! And I don't mind telling you I was keeping a watchful eye. I knew your game, Sirena, but I wasn't certain of his. One false move on his part, and I would have slit his gullet!"

"There, you see! That's the answer!" She went over to the desk, seated herself and withdrew a sheet of stationery from the top drawer. Her pen poised over the paper, she bit her bottom lip and began to write.

"What's that?" Regan asked. "What are you up to?"

"Thank you, darling. You've just given us the answer to Wren's problem with Weatherly. It's safe to say that the only thing more valuable to Malcolm than his fancy clothes and his money is his life. Regan, darling, you are going to threaten Malcolm."

"Threaten to kill him? Sirena, it will never work! Every father threatens murder in some way or another to the man who takes his daughter away from him. Few ever carry out the threat, and Malcolm knows it!"

"Ah, yes. That is true with a daughter. It is quite different with a wife. I've heard of many men who've met their end because they were too attentive to another man's wife. Certainly Malcolm knows of several cases himself. And you, Regan, can be most ferocious when necessary."

Regan thought for a moment and then laughed. "I can see your point. Why, if I ever thought that Weatherly—or any other man, for that matter—were to steal you away from me, he would find destiny at the end of my sword."

"Exactly. All I have to do is write this little note to Malcolm, inviting him to visit me tomorrow. The scene will be set, and you, darling, will find our young dandy in a compromising situation. I'm certain I can rely on you to take it from there."

"With pleasure." Regan made a courtly bow. "Now, hurry and finish that damn note, and I'll have a footman deliver it immediately. It's a fool's idea, but it just might work."

Sirena applied pen to paper, blotted the note and then handed it to Regan. His eyes narrowed.

"Sirena, we're taking a chance here, and, like all schemes, it could backfire on us." At Sirena's questioning look, Regan continued. "We'll have to be very careful. Wren must never know what we've done. She'd hate us, Sirena, but most of all, she'd hate you."

Sirena's eyes became distant. How could she ever bear having Wren hate her? But she knew Regan spoke the truth. "That is a chance I have to take, Regan. I would rather have Wren hate me than leave her to the wiles of a scoundrel." The moment was tense, the air charged with unasked questions. Regan knew Sirena had calculated the odds and decided to live with whatever the outcome would be. Her lips formed a smile, but there were uncharted depths in her eyes. "Regan, give the note to a footman and hurry back," she said softly. "I need you to hold me."

Chapter Seven

As Sirena stepped into the garden, the light breezes caught the ends of her hair and blew them softly against her cheeks. Her face turned to the sun, she bit into her lower lip to keep it from trembling. The scene she was about to play with Malcolm strummed at her nerve endings. She hoped Tyler hadn't noticed her fidgeting at breakfast and the way she had kept asking him the time. Malcolm should be arriving at any moment, and it was only with the help of the heavens themselves that Wren had an appointment with her dressmaker that morning. Otherwise Tyler would have had to be brought into the little plot so that he could keep Wren away from the garden.

Sirena smoothed the folds of her sea-green gown. If she was going to play the part of a seductress, she had decided to look like one. The material matched her eyes perfectly, and she had applied a touch of Spanish paper to her lips and cheeks to heighten her coloring. Trying to find humor in a situation she herself had created, she smiled and hoped she wasn't out of practice. Flirting and seduction were arts that were never lost to a woman. She waved a lace-edged handkerchief in the air; the linen had been liberally doused with scent. Poor Malcolm, she sighed with a touch more confidence. He would hardly be a match for her wiles. Later, much later, years from now, Wren would thank her. If Wren ever found out, God forbid.

Sirena settled herself on a bench near a bed of roses, a long legal paper clutched in one hand. Slowly, sensuously, she swung her foot to and fro, careful that her slim ankle and trim slipper peeked from beneath the hem of her gown. Men liked a show of ankle, and Weatherly would be no exception.

She cast a critical eye at the sun and knew that Malcolm would arrive within minutes. A promise to continue their discussion of the night before in an "intimate setting" was all she had needed to offer him to be certain he would fall prey to the plan.

When she heard his footsteps on the flagstones, she made no move to indicate she knew he was near, but bent her head over the legal paper she had snatched from Tyler's desk at the last minute.

"Mrs. van der Rhys," Malcolm said, bowing low and touching his lips to her hand in a too-familiar and ardent manner. His eyes, however, focused on the legal document in her lap; papers of that nature

102

always represented money in one form or another. It was just possible she was working with Sinclair on the arrangements for Wren's dowry. Commendable, he said to himself, liking Sirena more by the minute.

"Malcolm," Sirena cooed, "how prompt you are. An excellent virtue. A sign of a dependable man. And you Englishmen certainly do have a flair when it comes to dressing. You must give me the name of your tailor, and I'll have Regan stop by and order some new clothes before we leave for Java." She touched the fabric of Malcolm's frock coat, letting her long, slender fingers trail lightly over his chest. "You are simply dashing." Sirena smiled and appraised the man beside her. She could understand Wren's infatuation with him. Any woman might find herself likewise smitten. His dark hair was crisp and curled softly on his well-shaped head, a rakish lock spilling boyishly onto his forehead. His features were handsome, almost pretty, but his strong, square chin lent authority to his face. He had a habit of lowering his chin and looking up through long, spiky lashes, the kind young children have after they've been crying. Only Weatherly's mouth gave a hint to the man within. Well-defined but narrow lips, which Sirena knew could curl with cruelty, were studiously curved into a smile showing gleaming, strong teeth. And beneath the stylish clothes was a sinewy, long-limbed body hardened by years of riding and athletics. Malcolm Weatherly was a vain man, and this trait would provide the key to his undoing.

Malcolm was flattered and his heart beat a little faster at her light—was it also teasing?—touch. "How is your headache this morning?"

"Oh, it's gone," Sirena said airily. "The trick to getting rid of a headache from the night before is to have a glass of wine before you get out of bed the next morning. Actually, Regan is the one who told me about drinking wine on rising. He said something

103

to the effect that sounded like 'a little bit of the hair of the dog that bit you.'" She laughed at the befuddled look on Malcolm's face. "Sometimes Regan can be very crass. Pay it no mind; a gentleman like yourself would never say anything like that, I'm sure."

"Perhaps with another man, but never to a lady or within her hearing," Malcolm simpered.

"Now, Malcolm, there's a little something I want to discuss with you, and I do hope you will give me your word that what we say now will be just between the two of us." Sirena's voice was low and throaty.

"Dear lady, you have my word," Malcolm whispered, his eyes wide and his hands trembling at his sides.

"Now that you've met my husband and stepson, I'm sure you can see they're not . . . not quite like other men. They don't have the flair, the style, that you English have. They're more—how can I say it and not sound disloyal?" Sirena pretended to frown. "Earthy," she declared happily. "Yes, they're earthy. They don't understand young love and romance and things like that, whereas I, being a woman, do. I want you to know that no matter what they say, no matter what they do, I'm on your side." She leaned forward so that her breasts almost spilled from the low-cut gown. "I think that you are the perfect choice for our little Wren." Her slender hand reached up and touched Malcolm's cheek, and she purposely widened her eyes, a look of innocence on her face. "I feel it here," she said, taking his hand and placing it on her bosom, "that you will take care of her and we won't have to concern ourselves with her well-being. I just feel it here," she repeated dramatically, pressing his hand against the soft swell of her breasts.

"And you're right," Malcolm agreed as he tried to loosen his collar. "You can trust me with her life—with your life, too," he babbled, his eyes becoming moist.

Sirena's breath quickened at the hot look in Malcolm's eyes. Fool! her mind shouted. Where is Regan? How long can I keep up this playacting? Regan had promised that he would give her ten minutes alone with Malcolm. Surely it was long past that now.

Her ears picked up the sound of a footfall at the end of the path. At last, Regan! Sirena made her move. Her eyes became heavy-lidded as she licked at her lips, making them wet and inviting. "Come here, closer," she whispered throatily. "I have something I want to say to you, something for your ears alone." She bent forward slightly, one breast almost entirely exposed as Malcolm fought to keep his eyes on her seductive face.

"You can trust me, Sirena, with whatever it is you have to say," he whispered back, quivering at what he knew he shouldn't be seeing.

Sirena was careful not to move. "I wish," she breathed heavily, "that I were the one you were in love with, not Wren. There, I've said it and I'm not ashamed!" She heard Malcolm utter a loud groan and found his head buried in her bosom. "Darling, you feel the same way, I can tell," she murmured, gasping for breath. She clutched his head to her as he burrowed deeper into the soft flesh between her breasts. "I knew you cared for me last evening when you offered me the wine. Stay here forever," she pretended to moan.

"Forever and forever," Malcolm echoed hoarsely, his hands feverishly attacking the beautiful woman's curves.

Sirena's mind raced. Hurry, Regan! Now! Now! The warm wetness of Malcolm's mouth revulsed her. If ever she had any doubt of Malcolm's love for Wren, his actions now were proof of the bounder he was. The footsteps came closer. Hurry, Regan, hurry!

"Of all the despicable tricks!" Wren's voice rang through the garden. "How could you?" she screamed at Sirena. "Aren't you ever satisfied? Isn't Regan enough for you? How could you do this to me, of all people? Whore!" Wren's face was drained of all color, her eyes dull and hard. "I'll never forgive you for this, Sirena. Never!"

Sirena was dumbfounded. Where was Regan? Why wasn't Wren at the dressmaker's? Malcolm was flustered and looking like a plucked peacock. And here was Wren, blaming her, Sirena, not this simpering oaf who was trying to maneuver himself away from Wren's ire. Sirena was being blamed for Malcolm's perfidy. She had to do something, say something to make Wren understand it had been only a ploy to save her from Malcolm. "Wren . . . you don't understand, I wasn't—"

"I don't want to hear a word you have to say. My eyes told me all I needed to know. You have to be the center of attraction. You need men, all men, to throw themselves at your feet and adore you. Regan, Caleb, the boys, they're not enough! No, now you've set your wiles on Malcolm, on my man! Well, it won't work, Sirena, because I know Malcolm loves me! He'll always love me. *Me!* Do you hear me, Sirena? And what's more, I never want to see you again." Wren choked. "I . . . don't . . . *we* don't need you, do we, Malcolm? We don't need anything from her. Not her blessing on our marriage . . . not her money . . . not anything!"

Malcolm's mouth fell open in amazement. This wasn't exactly what he had had in mind when he had begun courting Wren van der Rhys.

"You don't mean that, Wren," Sirena pleaded. "You're my daughter, my child; sometimes I think you are more mine than the children I carried within me . . ."

Wren turned her head away, refusing to face Sirena, feeling betrayed by her. Her heart was near breaking. She wanted to throw herself into Sirena's

106

arms, wanted to listen to any explanation Sirena might offer, yet she couldn't bring herself to do that. If she listened to Sirena, it would mean that Malcolm had betrayed her, and that was the one thing certain to destroy her.

Malcolm gazed in amazement at the two women. What were they saying? What had Sirena meant when she said that Wren was more her child than the children she had carried? Wasn't Wren Sirena's child? "Wren, speak to your father . . ."

Wren turned to face him, her amber eyes sparked with rage. "Regan is no more my father than Sirena is my mother. I only have you, Malcolm," she said with a sudden softness in her voice. "I need you. You must take me away from here—now! Please!"

Speechless, Malcolm followed Wren's lead as she took his arm and pulled him away.

Sirena sensed a presence near her and looked up into Regan's agonized eyes. "We did all we could, Sirena," he said, "and it looks as though we made a botch of it. Wren came home early and must have slipped through the gate near the stables. I was just about to make my grand entrance when she discovered you here."

Wordlessly, Sirena held out her arm and Regan drew her close. "What will we do now, Regan? We've lost her. We've lost our daughter," she murmured through stiff lips, choking back the tears.

"We'll find her again, sweetheart, you'll see."

"But she's leaving, going off with Malcolm."

"No, she won't. I'll bet on it. I heard everything. She told him she wasn't really our child. I doubt he'll have any use for her now that she's decided to quit herself of us. She'll come back, you'll see. Caleb will bring her back."

But Sirena was not to be consoled, and the tears that coursed down her cheeks burned her skin.

107

Outside the garden, Wren waited with Malcolm for the groom to bring his phaeton around. "I'll gather my things and meet you at your apartment," she said softly, still holding back racking sobs. "I imagine it will take no more than a few hours. Hold me, Malcolm, hold me!" she cried, hurling herself into his arms. "I've never spoken to Sirena that way. I've always loved her, always been sure of her love for me. I . . . I don't blame you, Malcolm. Sirena is beautiful, and she threw herself at you."

"I wouldn't do that if I were you, Wren," he said coldly, his tone so stiff and detached that Wren pulled away and looked up at him with bewilderment. "I mean I don't want you to come to my apartment. You've ruined everything with your silly schoolgirl mentality. I'm afraid I have no further use for you, Wren."

"Use for me? Malcolm, what are you saying?" Her voice quivered and her hands trembled. "I love you, Malcolm. I'll always love you."

"Don't say that. Can't you understand? I've enough to do with feeding myself. I can't support you, too. I haven't a farthing to my name, thanks to my wastrel uncle. I've barely enough to keep body and soul together, let alone pay my tailor's bill. Within days my creditors will be hounding me again. I can't afford you, Wren."

"We'll do something. We'll survive. I'll find some work, and you can do so many things—"

"Stop it, Wren. Get it through your head that I can't afford you. Here's my carriage." Barely waiting for the vehicle to come to a stop, Malcolm sprinted inside. "I'm sorry it worked out this way, Wren, but you've only yourself to blame."

"I'll come to you, Malcolm, I will! I'll do anything for you, work my fingers to the bone—"

"Don't, Wren. Don't make this any uglier than it is. Don't come to me. Stay away from me. I can't afford you." Banging the side of the coach with his fist, he shouted at the driver to go faster. Wren was left alone on the drive, tears streaming down her cheeks, a look of confused astonishment in her golden eyes.

Without a backward glance at the girl he had wanted to marry, Malcolm gave his driver instructions to the home of Lady Elizabeth Rice. Now, more than ever, he was interested in listening to what she had to say about the jeweled collar the King was having made for his son's birthday. Now, more than ever, he needed what revenue he could gain from the sale of those jewels. Providing, of course, that he would be successful in acquiring them. Settling back on the leather upholstery, he mentally reviewed a list of all the markets and fences on which he could unload the collar for the top price. The name of Lord Farrington kept cropping up. The Prince's birthday was still two weeks away, which would give Malcolm two days at the very most to relieve the goldsmith of his art work. The first thing he had to do was to contact Farrington. But that would be after he had spoken to Lady Elizabeth. He anticipated her smooth, white limbs welcoming him into an embrace and felt a veil of moisture gather on his upper lip. Sirena van der Rhys had set his blood on fire, and it would take the ministrations of the sensuous redhead to quench his thirst.

The tension in the Sinclair home was unbearable. Wren stayed closeted in her room, refusing to come out even for meals. Sirena snapped and snarled at anyone foolhardy enough to approach her. Regan paced Tyler's study, thinking and shaking his head. He had tried to speak to Wren and been refused entry to her room. Tyler seemed preoccupied with something he refused to share with anyone. Caleb had come to dinner and left early after a long, silent meal. Only Camilla seemed oblivious to the tension in her home. Her thoughts were fixed on her coming child, and that was her only interest now.

Sirena came downstairs after lunch the next day with orders for errands to be made. On her way to the kitchen she passed Camilla in the sitting room, busily stitching what looked like a baby blanket. "The least you can do is say something," Sirena snapped. "Don't you know what's going on in your own home? Haven't you tried to speak to Wren and find out what she's thinking? And the baby hasn't been born who needs seventeen blankets. Don't you ever do anything else?"

Camilla raised her pansy eyes, her needle poised in midair. "Whatever are you talking about, Sirena? Is something wrong with Wren? I mean, is she ill? I already know that you two are having a squabble of some kind. And you're wrong, Sirena, this is the nineteenth blanket I've stitched. England can be quite cold and damp in the winter, and a mother can never have too many blankets."

"Spare me your wisdom, Camilla," Sirena answered curtly as she headed for the kitchen.

Regan had overheard the conversation between Sirena and Camilla and almost found himself ready to make excuses for Sirena's short temper. Wisely, he turned and went in the other direction. He had enough trouble with the women in his family as it was, and he didn't care to have Sirena's rage directed toward him, which was exactly what would happen if she ever discovered him apologizing for her behavior.

Upstairs, Wren paced, wringing her hands and dashing away the tears that continually formed in her eyes. Malcolm. Poor, sweet Malcolm. Pretending he didn't love her to spare her from a life of hardship. Didn't he know she loved him more than life itself and that she would rise above anything just to be with him, to be his wife? Sweet, noble Malcolm. The past two days had been a haze of heartache and tears, and looking ahead to never seeing him again was unbearable beyond belief. It was not to be comprehended. He was her love, her life. His cruelty had been a pose, an act, and he had been driven to it by his love for her. Her love for him became overpowering, and she threw herself on the high bedstead and sobbed into her pillow. "I won't let you do this, Malcolm. I won't let you keep us apart because you think I'm not strong enough to face poverty. I'd face death itself if I could be by your side." With all the aching urgencies of young love, Wren yearned for Malcolm until she thought her heart would break. The nights she had spent in his arms, feeling his lips against hers, hearing him whisper how much he loved her, needed her, rushed back to her. She decried her silly schoolgirl fantasies about walking down the aisle to meet her husband as a virgin. Now she wished she had succumbed to Malcolm, had allowed him to make love to her; then nothing on earth could keep them apart. They would have made themselves one forever.

Suddenly, with a will and a determination she hadn't known she possessed, Wren stumbled from the bed and pushed a chair up to the clothespress. She climbed on the chair, reached for her portmanteau and pulled it down to the floor. Breathing heavily, she flung open the clothespress and searched through her wardrobe, her fingers seeking the most modest gowns she owned, automatically discarding the opulent silks and satins which had always been her vanity. A working girl couldn't wear elaborate clothing, and if she was going to help Malcolm support them, she would take only the most utilitarian items she owned.

The small trunk was heavier than the few belongings stuffed into it, and she had little difficulty carrying it. She was on her way to Malcolm, and she would make him happy, she was certain of that. If Malcolm loved her only half as much as she loved him, their marriage would be made in heaven.

111

Wren didn't look back, for she feared she would falter. Regan and Sirena loved her, but they didn't understand her. She couldn't allow herself to think about them. She was embarking on a new life, and her only concern could be for Malcolm and his happiness.

Wren placed her portmanteau by the door of Malcolm's apartment, then allowed herself a moment to catch her breath. Fortunately, she had been able to slip out of the house unnoticed and had managed to heft the trunk to the corner of the avenue, where she had hired a hack.

Downstairs, Malcolm's landlady had asked her impertinent questions and then snapped her mouth shut when Wren had stabbed her with an icy look. It was obvious the woman knew her betters when she met them. Grudgingly, she had pointed out Malcolm's door and watched as the young girl with the imperious attitude struggled up the stairs with the trunk. Arms folded across her buxom bosom, the landlady shrugged her shoulders. It was none of her business, she thought, as long as the rent was paid. And a long time coming that was, too! Perhaps the young miss would set things aright. If not, the girl's presence at least gave her a lever for having the dashing Malcolm Weatherly thrown out on his elegant ass.

As Wren sat atop her trunk just outside his door, Malcolm stood before his dressing table, holding a package. Gently he unwrapped the cloth. The black velvet slipped through his trembling fingers as he fumbled with the folds. His eyes shone with greed; his lips were slack as he spread out his treasure with tenderness. The light filtering through the worn draperies spun a halo of gold and glitter upon the King's collar. Even as he looked at it he couldn't believe it was here, in his possession. It had almost been too easy.

Because the goldsmith had assumed he was working under great secrecy and hadn't wanted to call attention to his shop until after the collar had been delivered, he had failed to hire a guard. At first Malcolm had been thwarted by the heavy iron bars on the jeweler's windows and door. But the day he had spent studying the small shop on Cheap Street had been worthwhile. Upon first inspection, it had appeared that the shop was self-contained and that the only way to the upper floors of the building was by the outside stairs. Then, shortly after noon, Malcolm had looked up and seen the jeweler pass by one of the windows on the second floor. Having kept himself in full sight of the outside stairs and not having observed the goldsmith use those stairs, he had rightly assumed that there was also an entrance to the second floor from within the shop. And the second floor's door and windows were unbarred. Late that night Malcolm had climbed to the second floor, the lock on the door giving easily under the pressure of his knife. It had been simple thereafter to locate the route to the floor below and help himself to the collar.

Malcolm was mesmerized by it. Made of heavy gold and large enough to go around a man's waist, the piece was intricately wrought and set with precious stones. Fiery diamonds were the largest of these, offset by sapphires and golden topaz. The sunlight caught each facet of the gems and highlighted their brilliance.

The sudden knock on the door made Malcolm start with such force that he found himself trembling. Guilt-ridden, he quickly wrapped the collar in the jeweler's velvet and hastily pushed the cloth into the bottom drawer of the dresser.

"Coming! Who's there?" he called, struggling to keep his voice under control.

"Malcolm! It's me, Wren!"

"Wren!"

113

The door swung open and Wren threw herself into his arms. "I had to come," she cried. "I couldn't stay away any longer. I love you, Malcolm."

"What are you doing here? I told you how it was. Please go home, Wren."

Not to be put aside again, Wren pushed her way into the room. "I won't go away. I came to be with you, for always. No, don't say anything; hear me out first. I know how noble you're being. I know you don't want me to do without the things I've always had. But you're wrong, Malcolm. I haven't always had them. I know what it's like to do without. I know what it's like not to have enough to eat or to pay for lodgings. I didn't always live with Sirena and Regan. I was almost ten years old when Sirena found me and took me to live with her. Before that, I'd been living on the streets or worse. I had to work for my living. Only one person in the world besides Sirena was ever kind to me, and that was Lottie, a foxy old crone. So you see, darling, I haven't always been a spoiled little pet. I knew what life was like for the people in the slums even before I could walk."

Malcolm regarded her with increasing astonishment. Not only had Wren misled him about being the daughter of the van der Rhyses, she'd also lied to him about who she was. An urchin, a street urchin born in the London slums, and now she had the audacity to suppose she might be good enough to wipe his shoes!

Before he could utter a word, Wren was in his arms again. "When will we be married, Malcolm? You can't send me back, you know. I've already told them I was coming to you. I . . . I even told them we were lovers," she lied, hoping he would believe there was no turning back for her, desperate to convince him she had given up everything just to be with him because he was so important to her. She couldn't let him send her back now that they were together again, now that her arms were around him and she was so close to belonging to him forever.

"Did you bring any money with you?" he asked curtly.

"Only my allowance that I've been saving. Thank the Lord I didn't pay my dressmaker's bill. Altogether I've over fifty pounds," she announced proudly. "A very nice start for a married couple. Here," she said, holding out her purse.

"This isn't going to go very far," Malcolm snapped. "The least you could have done was to bring some jewelry or something we could sell."

"Please don't look so upset," she pleaded. "Everything will work out, you'll see. Truly it will."

"Truly it will," he mimicked in a whining voice. "Well, truly it won't. You don't seem to understand, Wren. Go home."

"Don't, Malcolm. Please don't send me away. You said you couldn't afford me. Well, you won't have to. I'll work, I'll do anything, only don't send me home."

"Two days ago I said I couldn't afford you." He glanced covertly at the dresser, where the collar was hidden. "Now I don't want you. I don't need you anymore." He chuckled cruelly, thinking about the price the collar would bring him. "Go home, you silly schoolgirl!"

"No! I won't! I'm not a silly schoolgirl any longer. You need me, Malcolm. You do." She was in his arms, her mouth seeking his, her lips parted, her tongue searching for his. She pressed herself against him, felt his warmth against her, was aware of a rising urgency in him.

His arms came around her, tightening, pulling her toward him. The exhilaration he had experienced over the stolen collar was emphasized by the offerings of this beautiful girl. Yes, she was right. He did need her. For the moment.

"You see, darling," she whispered against his mouth, "you do need me. You want me."

"You're so right, Wren. It's time I learned what you are all about."

The harsh tone of his voice and the rough way he pulled her toward him, crushing her mouth beneath his, startled Wren. This wasn't the Malcolm she knew. That Malcolm had been sweetly passionate, tender, hesitant.

Suddenly fear gripped her as she stared at him. She had expected to see her love mirrored in his eyes; instead, she saw hot, burning coals. His lips tore heedlessly at hers while she stood frozen with terror. His hands worked at the buttons on her dress, and he grasped her breasts in a careless, hurtful way. His breathing was harsh and labored as he bent her backward, his mouth never leaving hers.

Wren knew what was happening and was powerless to stop it. All protests died in her throat, and she fought him with every ounce of strength she could summon. This couldn't be Malcolm. Not the Malcolm she knew and loved. This was someone else, a perverted creature with only lust, not love, on his mind.

The pain he was inflicting on her with his urgent thrusts was hot and searing, unlike any pain she had ever experienced in her life. She wanted to scream till her lungs burst, and yet no sound came forth. His fingers wrenched her flesh, and he sucked at her nipples until Wren prayed she would die. The agony and shame she felt were more than she could bear, but the dull void of love lost engulfed her and rendered her senseless with a force greater than any physical attack.

The torment and degradation continued. Wren's young body was stiff with shock as Malcolm drove into her again and again. Her insides felt hot, swollen, as if they were being torn to shreds by the ceaseless force of the man's deep thrust. Blood seeped between her legs as she tried vainly to beat at him with her small, clenched fists.

Her attempts were futile against his strength as he savored her smallness, savored the fact that she was a virgin no longer, exulted in his possession of Wren and the collar both in the same day. He had always wanted to do this to her, ever since the first night he had kissed her and known that one day she would give herself to him. Malcolm hadn't wanted Wren to give —he had wanted to take! When his passions had gone beyond his bearing them, she would coyly pull away from him and straighten her gown, pleading her stupid virginal morals and saying something about his being naughty. Naughty! When his loins had ached for release and his blood had refused to cool!

Half-conscious from the brutal attack, Wren felt Malcolm go limp, his deep thrusts abating as he remained inside her, his mouth on hers, his saliva merging with hers till she wanted to gag, to rid herself of him.

Malcolm got to his knees and gazed down at her half-naked body, then hurled the final insult at her. "Your friend Sara's body is far more beautiful than yours; her breasts are larger, rounder and softer. She came to me willingly and we were together as one, each of us giving and taking. You're like a lump of clay," he jeered.

Wren lay on the floor, making no move to cover her nakedness. What did it matter now if he saw her or compared her with Sara? Nothing mattered anymore. How could she have thought she loved this cruel, taunting man who was preening before the tarnished mirror, arranging his clothes as though nothing had happened? She wanted to cry, felt the need to shriek and howl, but she couldn't. All she could do was stare at the man who was tying his cravat with a nonchalance that frightened her more than if he had shouted and cursed at her. She saw his booted foot above her, but didn't believe, couldn't believe, he would kick her. She took the blow full in the left breast and rolled over in pain, retching as she did so. He stepped over to the dresser, fumbled in the bottom drawer and withdrew a black bundle.

"I'm going out now to see if I can turn this pittance you gave me into a sizable wad of money. I'm locking you in here; if you aren't here when I return, I'll hunt you down like an animal, do you understand? You wanted to come here and stay with me; now you've got your way. Don't think you can go running off to Regan to tell him how badly I used you. I'd be forced to kill you first. I want no screaming and yelling when I'm gone, or I'll have the landlady call Bedlam and tell them your mind snapped and you should be committed." His toe prodded her in the armpit as he tried to make her roll over. "Tell me you understand what I've just said to you." Wren nodded to show she understood, and Malcolm laughed. "You can't come close to a comparison with Sara," he called over his shoulder as he walked through the door and then locked it.

The sound was final, terminal, as Wren staggered to her knees. She sank down on the lumpy mattress and pulled the spread over her battered body. Had he meant what he had said? Would he do as he had threatened? She admitted she was afraid to find out.

"Please, God, send Regan and Sirena to me. I didn't mean what I said. Please help me," she prayed aloud.

She sat huddled under the spread for what seemed an eternity. Finally she crawled from the bed and searched for her clothes. What time was it? She should light a candle. Was he coming back, and if he did, what would he do? Please, God, help me, she begged over and over as she dressed.

At last she fell into a fitful sleep, only to awaken and cower in a corner of the bed when she heard a key in the lock. The door was thrust open, and Malcolm and four burly seamen entered the room.

"There she is, there's your prize," Malcolm chortled drunkenly. "Get up," he ordered, staggering over to the bed and dragging Wren by the arm to the middle of the floor. "I lost you in a game of cards to these fine gentlemen," he hiccuped. "Take off your clothes so they can see what they're getting."

"Please, Malcolm, you're drunk. You don't know what you're doing. Please don't do this to me," she pleaded tearfully.

"If you won't do it, then I'll do it for you," Malcolm leered, pulling at her gown and ripping it down the front till her body was exposed to the slavering seamen. "There!" Malcolm cried, lunging backward till he fell on the bed.

Wren tried to cover her body with her hands, but the men pulled and jabbed at her, each intent on doing what he wanted with her. She allowed it. She permitted it. She told herself she had no choice. She suffered and survived the onslaught. She knew it was the only way she would live to see another day.

Chapter Eight

Caleb didn't like the speculative looks Aubrey Farrington was bestowing on him. Once before Farrington had favored him with such looks, and he had ended up in a confrontation with Dick Blackheart. However, in all fairness to the gambler, there had also been an expression of deep regret in his eyes at the time. Caleb knew in his gut that if he looked more carefully into the old man's eyes, he would see that same regret now. His gut also told him it was time to cut his losses and let Farrington shift for himself.

If Sirena and Regan could cut their own losses and return to Java without Wren, then he could do the same thing for a few pounds. Farrington wasn't worth the aggravation Caleb was going through.

Cal's eyes traveled the length and beam of the ship and back to Farrington. There was something about the gambler that ate at him. Surely he wasn't getting maudlin about the old rake. If not, then why did this feeling of responsibility hang so heavily on his shoulders?

"If you'd just tell me the straight of it and stop beating around the bush, perhaps I could help you," Caleb said briskly. "I'm wise to your tricks, Aubrey.

You can't get away with what you did to me years ago. I know something's wrong and I want you to tell me what it is. And don't think for one minute I believed you when you swore you were virtually a pauper on the brink of bankruptcy. I made it my business to sniff around and ask questions. I also made it my business to check out your creditors, and do you know what I found out, Aubrey? They told me your credit is magnificent. At first I thought they were talking about someone else, not my old friend Lord Aubrey Farrington."

"Listen, Cal, I had a brief run of good luck and came into a small inheritance, and that helped me clear up a few debts—personal debts," the gambler whined.

"Children whine, fools whine, and you're neither," Caleb said coolly. "This is the last time I'm going to ask you what's going on. If I don't like your answer, you'll end up with a stomach full of bilge water."

"A small, personal business venture. Nothing which need concern you, Cal. Truly, there's no need for you to give it another moment's thought. As a matter of fact, I've been seriously considering the idea of retiring and taking a sea voyage. For my health," he added piously.

"If you're contemplating a sea voyage, that can only mean the law is either hot on your heels or breathing heavily down your skinny neck. It was a mistake on my part to reoutfit this ship, wasn't it? You allowed me to go ahead, make all the arrangements and have the handbills printed, and now you tell me you're considering a sea voyage. Good fortune to you, Aubrey. I'm sailing the *Sea Siren* on the morning tide, so I imagine this is the last time we'll be together. I do wish you well." Caleb nodded curtly and made ready to leave the ship. If ever the old fox is going to talk, now is the time, he thought to himself.

"Where are you heading? Back to Africa or Java?" Farrington asked as he followed Caleb to the gangplank.

"Wherever the sea takes me, I suppose. The *Siren*'s hold is empty, so I'll make good time wherever I go. My business affairs can manage themselves for at least a year, giving me a little time to see the world. Although I must admit I have a hankering to feel the trade winds and see my homeland again." Caleb watched Farrington's reaction to his noncommittal answer with a covert glance.

"Ah! To be young again! To go wherever fortune leads! You are truly blessed, Cal. Would that I were young again and free! The end of my story might be quite different indeed. So you say you might go on to the colonies? I hear America is the gateway to a young man's dreams," Farrington said wistfully, his sharp eyes never leaving Caleb's face.

"No, I didn't say I was going to America, you just did," Caleb answered flatly. "But I have had contact with the Dutch West India Company. Did you know they have fur traders working in their commission in the colonies?"

"No, I hadn't heard," Farrington lied. "Why, did they approach you? Surely they can't suppose you'd be interested in giving up the sea for a life in the woods skinning animals." Farrington gave a mock shudder.

"Not quite, Aubrey," Cal laughed. "At this time they have a small development of Dutch settlers somewhere in a place they call the Connecticut Valley. They're looking for someone to exchange goods and money for the skins. It hardly seems like an adventure to me."

"The colonies, you say?" Aubrey questioned. Then he suddenly held out his hand for Caleb to shake. His eyes turned cloudy and vague. He couldn't involve the boy again, not after what he had done to him the last time, the gambler ruminated. At least then he had had

122

excuse enough. Dick Blackheart had bought up all his debts and held his very life on a thread. Turning Caleb over to the scurvy pirate had been a matter of survival. This time it would be unconscionable. There were ships' masters, men who were operating on the edge of the law, men who would willingly take a chance for a price, men who did not value their reputations and convictions the way Caleb did. After all, Farrington scolded himself, a man must have some pride, some small measure of self-respect. However, Caleb wasn't a boy any longer. He was a man, and capable of looking after himself. Self-respect and pride be damned! He'd ask him. All Cal could do was say no, walk away and call him an old reprobate. Well, he'd been called worse.

"A drink, Cal, before you leave?" Aubrey suggested softly. "A little small talk and another drink. I have something to tell you, something you may find very interesting, a little matter we can both profit from." Aubrey's watery old eyes implored Caleb to accept the offer, and he smiled when the younger man dropped his sea bag in anticipation of Aubrey's fine imported rum.

Caleb settled himself on a tack box and marveled at the beautiful day, a day rare in England as far as he was concerned. He took a long drink from the rum bottle and passed it back to Farrington to show that he was ready for any and all secret confessions on the gambler's part. A gull swept down, screeching and hawing, only to take wing and soar westward. "Amazing wing spread," Caleb remarked, somewhat startled by the intrusion.

"Yes, amazing," Farrington agreed. "However, I detest the things, as I have to clean their droppings from the deck several times a day. I'm not really a bad sort, Cal. In here," he said, placing his hand on his chest, "I am a loyal and conscientious person. I try to do my bit for my country, and if some moneys find

123

their way into my pocket, so much the better. If I don't do it, then someone else will." He took a healthy swig of rum.

"Do what?" Caleb asked curtly.

"I'm getting to it; just give me time to get my thoughts in order. I want you to understand that when I was first approached to do . . . to do this . . . this . . . well, when I was first approached, I said no. I said I didn't want any part of it. Then when Baron Sinclair himself came to me and said what a noble gesture I would be making, I had second thoughts. After all, Cal, the Baron is a highly respected man, and we both know he wouldn't do anything that was . . . illegal. In all fairness to me, though, I did not commit myself on his first visit."

"How many visits did it take till the price was right?" Caleb demanded as the bottle of rum found its way to his lips again. By the looks of things, it was going to take the whole bottle and then some for Aubrey to get to the point.

"Three, four—who remembers?" Farrington said vaguely, reaching for a fresh bottle and uncorking it with a loud plop. He drank greedily, savoring the warmth and fire of the Jamaican rum. Another gull swooped down, emitted its loud, screeching complaint and then left its droppings next to Farrington's booted foot. He pretended not to see them as he inched away to lean more comfortably against a coil of neglected rigging.

"Well?" Caleb prodded impatiently.

Aubrey gulped, swallowed the rum in his mouth and sat up straight. "I've been smuggling, if you like that word, tariff-free supplies and transporting Puritans to the American colonies for a price."

"You what?" Caleb exploded. "You're an ass, Farrington!"

"Among other things." The gambler smiled. "As I said, if I didn't do it, someone else would. Actually, I

124

started out transporting the Puritans and then worked into the smuggling little by little. Sinclair doesn't know about that end of it, and I'd just as soon he never found out. It hasn't been easy. My last captain was hung by the neck at dawn's first light on the last voyage. The passengers were thrown into the sea and my cargo sacked by vicious pirates. The captain had no experience, though he came highly recommended."

"What happened to your ship?"

"Only the good Lord knows. Now, my present problem is this. I have accepted money and given my word that I would have a ship ready to sail. I not only accepted the money, I spent it. My life isn't worth a farthing," he said pitifully. "There's this one zealot who I know is going to do something terrible to me. He's got the fires of Hell burning in his eyes. I need you, Cal, and I need the *Sea Siren* to take these people to the colonies. Whatever you can get for the cargo will be yours free and clear as your fee for the sailing. What do you say, my boy? Will you do this one small favor for an old friend?"

"You don't want much, do you, old friend?" Caleb replied quietly, sobering immediately from the impact of Farrington's words. He wasn't surprised at the man's request; he had known it would be something for which he, Caleb, could swing by the neck.

Seeing Caleb's hesitation, Farrington pressed on. "It's your cup o' tea, my boy. Adventure, profit and women. Why, you could clean up and have the adventure of your life! I have it on fact that the women in the colonies are beautiful beyond compare. And hungry, if you know what I mean." He winked. "Hungry for *real* men, not like those plaster saints who care more for their prayer meetings than they do for warm-fleshed, fair-haired women. A few months of your time, profit from your Dutch company, women, adventure . . . who knows? Perhaps you'll even want to become a partner with Sinclair and me!"

How well the old buzzard knew him. In one breath he had said the two things that appealed to Caleb: adventure and women, and not necessarily in that order.

Farrington, refusing to lose any ground, continued. "You can hold your own against any odds. I've seen you at your best and at your worst. I'd feel very relieved if you'd take on this . . . this mission." He was beyond sobriety and he knew it, but he couldn't relinquish the bottle to Caleb till he heard his answer. "Think of it in terms of helping human beings."

"For a price," Caleb laughed. "You wouldn't surprise me if you sold your soul to the devil. You're an ass, Aubrey."

"Old Horny wouldn't want it, and you're right, I'm an ass, but then most men are in my position. You've agreed, so that makes you an ass, too." He hiccuped drunkenly.

Caleb grinned. He hadn't said yes and he hadn't said no. The old fool had known he would do it; he wouldn't have become so sotted otherwise. "You're right, Aubrey," Cal said, getting to his feet. "I'm going back to the Baron's to say my good-byes to Sirena and Regan, and I'll be back late this evening. At that time you damn well better be sober and have everything in readiness. I'll sail as soon as the *Siren* is outfitted and supplies are aboard."

Farrington waved a limp hand to show he understood and winced as another gull left its droppings, this time on the tip of his shiny boot. He peered at the mess through bleary eyes and shrugged. Loud snores grated on Caleb's ears as he departed the frigate, a wide grin on his face.

He hated going back to the Sinclairs' house. He had heard about the fiasco between Sirena and Malcolm and Wren. When Wren was discovered missing, he had been the first person Regan had come to, hoping that Wren had run to him. Regan and Sirena were in a

126

foul, depressed mood over Wren's departure. If the day ever came when Caleb decided to take a wife, he'd make damn certain she was kept under lock and key with a cloth stuffed in her mouth. How could one little slip of a girl cause so much commotion and heartache?

Well, he couldn't worry about Wren now, especially after what she had done to him. Damn women! For now it might behoove him to stop by Sinclair's offices and announce that he was now a third partner in Tyler's illegal enterprise. He wondered vaguely how stiff the penalty was in this country for privateering. Whatever it was, he wouldn't dwell on it. He had committed himself to Farrington, and he would keep his word. In a few days he would feel the roll of the decks beneath his feet again. What matter if he was going to the new land, America? By picking up his orders from the Dutch West India offices, he could even add to his profit.

An uncomfortable feeling settled between his shoulder blades. By now he should have some definite direction in his life, some goal to work toward, like his father had when he first worked for the Dutch East India Company. It was true he was in his father's employ and that he ran the offices in Africa, but that wasn't his business. A man needed something he could claim as his alone. Something he sweated for sixteen hours a day, so that one day he would have a legacy to leave behind. And here he was, getting ready to take to the sea to transport human cargo to another land. He felt footloose, adrift, aimless. When he returned, he would take a long, hard look at his life and decide where he was going and what he would do.

Caleb considered himself a man, equal to his father, yet Aubrey Farrington constantly referred to him as a boy. Was there something about his makeup that the old man could see and he couldn't? Was there something invisible that marked him as a boy? "Bah!" He spat into the road. He was a man and he knew it. If he were to take a testimonial from every woman he had bedded in his life, each one would vouch for the fact that Caleb van der Rhys was a man.

The late-afternoon sun drifted in through the single window, lighting an array of dancing motes on the worn carpet. The bed loomed large and ominously on the far side of the room, its iron frame gleaming dully against the age-dimmed wall. Wren huddled in a corner, her back against the wall. Her dark, luxuriant hair tumbled down her shoulders and draped her pale face. She was very still, as still as death. Only her eyes were alive, watchful, fearful, burning with horrors known and horrors yet to come.

How could she have let this happen to her? How could she have been so blind? There was no excuse for her. To have thought even for a minute that Malcolm had cared for her, loved her, now seemed to her the height of sublime stupidity. How could she have been such an idiotic, romantic fool? Regan and Sirena had been right when they had said she wasn't ready for marriage, that she really didn't know Malcolm. Oh, God, she moaned to herself, to think I doubted Sirena! Now that she knew the kind of man Malcolm really was, she realized Sirena could never have instigated the little scene she had come upon in the garden. Sirena loved Regan; she would never have encouraged Malcolm to become her lover. And Sara! Why hadn't Wren listened to Sara? If she had only done that now, this very minute, she would be safe with the two people she loved most in the world.

A blue haze of cigar smoke wafted in her direction, causing her to wrinkle her nose and wipe at the tears forming in her eyes. Malcolm and his cronies sat at a small table in the center of the room, playing cards. None of them had glanced in her direction for the last half hour. She toyed with the idea of crawling past them and slipping out the door, but she knew her attempt would be futile, and she was also afraid of Malcolm's booted foot. She had never believed that a man could be so vicious. No, that wasn't true. She had known the evil natures of men. As a child, she had endured the festering alleys and the beatings of men like him, and she had survived. At the age of eight she had fought for food to stay alive and run from the terror that the darkness and the streets had imposed. Only old Lottie had been her friend before Sirena had rescued her. What was it the old woman had said? "Ye need eyes in the back of yer head and yer wits as sharp as a razor's edge." And Wren's wits were sharp, had been sharp, but with the good life Sirena and Regan had provided, she had forgotten, thinking she would never have to use street tactics again. If one wanted to survive, one did what one had to, whatever the cost.

Wren was so deep in her thoughts she almost missed hearing the conversation at the table. "I saw three ships sail at noon," one card player said as he swilled his ale and then wiped the back of his hand across his mouth. "The *Cavalier,* the *Vancouver,* and the *Michaelmas!* What I wouldn't have given to be aboard one of those ships as a passenger!" He laughed raucously.

"In two days' time the wharves will be empty for a while," another offered. "The last to leave will be the *Sea Siren.* She sets sail tomorrow, or so the scuttlebutt goes. There's something fishy there, my friends. That ship is sailing with an empty hold, and that can mean only one thing."

"What's that?" Malcolm asked, his eyes on his unlucky cards.

"She's one of those ships that sets sail empty and then picks up human trade, in a manner of speaking," a third seaman volunteered drunkenly.

"After this round of cards, I'm flat," Malcolm groaned pitifully.

"Mayhap we should sign on the *Sea Siren*. I heard the captain was asking round for good seamen this past day," the burly man closest to Wren said. "I would have added my X, but when he said the port o' call was none of my affair, I changed me mind. It's suspicious, all right. Sailing time is midnight. Under dark of night . . ."

"Dark of night what?" Malcolm demanded, throwing in his cards.

"Where's your mind, Weatherly? When ye be doing something ye ain't supposed to be doing, ye do it under cover of darkness. Seeing as how you're the proper gentleman and all, I can see why you wouldn't know something like that!"

Malcolm let his eyes travel to the corner of the room where Wren was huddled, afraid to move. His drunken mind whirled with triumphant thoughts of the royal collar, and his renewed ego demanded he celebrate his success with a woman. He had to get his hands on Wren, but he knew the seamen would cut him down if he made a move toward her. She was theirs, won by them, and they meant to keep her.

"Look here, Beasley, I have a pound note left. Why don't the lot of you go down to the wharves and do some nosing around and see what you come up with? Bring back some rum, and we'll have a party with the little lady in the corner." Malcolm knew the promise of drink and a party would make them more amenable to his wishes. "I'll have her as docile as a newborn kitten by the time you get back. Get a move on, lads, and let's see which way the wind blows. It's just possible the *Sea Siren* will sail with contraband."

"So what if she does? What use is that to us?" the man on his right demanded. "What can we do with contraband? Where've ye been, man? Smugglin' ain't what it used to be. Now the only thing as what gets smuggled is supplies and fancy yard goods to the colonies that ain't been taxed by yer Royal Highness. They ain't worth the trouble to fence. The only one what makes any profit is the man what's got the ship to sail the stuff over to America."

Malcolm's mind raced. "Yes, but you and I and everyone else knows about the stir that's sweeping the streets. The King's jeweled collar has been stolen. I just wonder if this _Sea Siren_'s departure has anything to do with that. I've heard of the captain—I've even met him. Caleb van der Rhys is his name. He's quite an enterprising gentleman who's been employed by the Dutch East India Company. It wouldn't surprise me in the least if this is a Dutch plot."

The men looked at each other and then at Malcolm. "He could be right," one of them acknowledged. "That's all the talk, the stealing of the King's collar from the goldsmith's. What better place to fence it than in America? I've heard some very rich men live there now and that the colonies are almost civilized."

"From what I've been told about the value of them gems, a man could buy the whole of the colonies and live better than the King himself."

Another seaman spoke up. "Don't go using our prize," he warned Malcolm, jabbing a finger in Wren's direction, "or we'll run you through. You hear me, Weatherly? We'll ask the little lady ourselves when we return. And if there's no talk about gems aboard the _Sea Siren,_ you'd best plan on holding lilies in your hands." His small, beady eyes underlined the menace in his voice.

"You'll see I'm right," Malcolm said with more bravura than he felt. Damn the girl. As soon as they left, he would go out and see about booking passage somewhere. These men were more than he had bargained for. He would have to get an advance on the collar from Farrington. What good was the promise of a fortune to him when he didn't have enough pocket money for food? And what did he care if these toughs ransacked van der Rhys' ship in their search for gems? His collar was safe with Aubrey Farrington.

"Not so fast, Weatherly. Beasley here will say behind just in case you get any funny ideas. If he makes a false move, Beasley, slit his throat," the sailor instructed his cohort.

Well, that takes care of my little plan, Malcolm fumed inwardly. Now I'll have to wait and see what happens on their return. He threw himself on the bed, a morose expression marring his handsome features as he forgot about Wren and his intentions. He knew he had to get away from these ruffians before they killed him. But how? They weren't about to let him out of their sight, because of all the money he owed them. They would keep watch over him, like a cat ready to pounce on a bird, until he took them to his banker. But what would he do in the morning when the banker advised them that his account was bare? He couldn't put them off any longer by saying the man was out of town for a few days. They meant to take him to the bank themselves.

While Malcolm contemplated his dim future, Wren was busily plotting her own. Beasley was sitting with his back to her, seemingly oblivious to her presence as he swilled what was left of the ale. All the tricks and wiles she had used in the dark alleys of London came back to her, and she was once again living in the streets and beneath the bridges, emerging only at night to scavenge for food. When you lived like an animal, you learned to behave like one. And you fought like one. She had to make her mind go back to the alleys and byways and remember what she would do if she were cornered as she was now.

Long moments became minutes, minutes lengthened into an hour, and the room darkened with the setting of the sun. Malcolm was asleep on the bed, snoring peacefully, as though he hadn't a worry in the world. Suddenly, as though being pricked by a thousand pins, Wren raised her head and saw Beasley staring at her. There was no mistaking the look in his eyes or the intention she read therein. He would have her again, would force his burly, stinking body on hers. She had no weapon. All she had were her hands and feet, but she would use them to protect herself, or die trying.

Slowly she rose to her full height, her amber eyes molten and glowing as she watched Beasley's appraisal of her. She moved wordlessly to the rough table, lifted the almost empty pitcher of ale and poured the liquid into a tankard. Taking a sip, she banged the cup down in front of Beasley, noting the marked appreciation in his narrow eyes.

"That's better, wench. I always did like my women friendly," he jeered.

Wren managed a weak smile and sat in the chair opposite him. Lottie's words came back to her as though she were still eight years old and it were yesterday. "Always make do with what ye have, child. If it's only yer own hands, make do. Catch a man unawares and he's little more than yer own size." Still smiling, Wren leaned back in the chair and lifted the hem of her skirt. Extending her leg upward, she slowly began to remove her stocking, allowing Beasley's eyes to linger on the soft flesh of her inner thigh. Then she rose and worked the buttons of her dress, moving around the table to stand near the seaman, close enough to hear his ragged breathing. All the while her mind raced; she could do it, she knew she could. Before she had been frightened, racked with despair because of Malcolm's evil. Not any longer. If her plan failed and she died, then so be it. She would cling to the last breath, but at least she would die knowing she had tried to save herself. She glanced toward Malcolm, still asleep on the bed, his mouth slacked open in an unattractive manner. How could she ever have thought she loved him? If he awoke suddenly, she would have to do to him what she had done to Caleb, what she should have done to Malcolm the instant she entered his room.

Keeping a watchful eye on Beasley, who was draining the last of his ale, she tested her stocking for flexibility. One loop and a knee in his back, careful to stay away from his groping fingers, and it would all be over. The amber eyes were alight as she slipped behind him, and they roared to a blazing fire as she brought up her knee and curved the stocking tightly around his throat. Beasley began to fight, his hands warped into claws stretching backward for a moment before they tore at the silk at his neck. Closing her eyes, terror twisting her mouth into a soundless scream, Wren gave the stocking a vicious yank and choked off the last of Beasley's air.

Malcolm opened his bleary eyes and took in the scene before him. It was the thud of Beasley's body hitting the floor that had brought him to the full awareness of the danger he was in.

Crouching low like a wild animal readying itself for attack, Wren advanced a step, then another as Malcolm, mesmerized by her feral look, tried to back away. Once again the amber eyes breathed flame as she stalked him, aiming for the fire tongs resting near the burning grate. Another step and she would be able to reach them. The moment her hand grasped the metal device, Malcolm's foot shot out; she raised her weapon and slammed it down across the side of his face. Blood spurted profusely from the deep gash. She lifted the tongs and again lashed out, this time rendering him a stinging blow to his head.

Reeling backward, Malcolm could do no more than bring his hands to his wounds, his mouth mewing his agony at what she had done to him. Wren advanced

134

again, this time jabbing the tongs to his midsection. Again and again she attacked him, till he fell to the floor, begging her to stop.

"You took me like an animal, treated me like an animal, and now I'm doing the same to you. Which of us, Malcolm, will survive? *I* will, because I'll be gone when your cutthroat friends return. They'll blame you for what happened to Beasley. Your life will be worth nothing. Nothing, Malcolm." She stood back, her quick, ragged breathing slowly returning to normal, and laughed. The sound was unlike anything Malcolm had ever heard. It frightened him more than the wounds he suffered and more than what he knew would happen to him when the seamen returned.

Through a red mist he saw her remove the stocking from Beasley's thick neck and roll it up her leg. Daintily, she buckled the buttons on her slippers and smoothed down her dress. "I'll be leaving you now, Malcolm. If you ever come near me again, I'll do to you what I just did to your friend." And then she laughed once more. It was her laugh not her threatening words, that made him crawl blindly in search of escape.

Outside, in the cool evening breeze, Wren and the darkness blended as one. She slithered down one narrow alley after another, her old life coming back to her as she made her way. People lived all their lives in dark alleys, leaving their sanctuaries only at night to fight for the very food that would enable them to last one more day. She had done it before and she could do it again. One more day, and then she would sneak aboard Caleb's ship. She couldn't allow herself to think beyond that point. For now, she had to get through the rest of the night and find a place to stay until the *Sea Siren* was ready to sail.

She was no different now, she told herself as she carefully stepped over the cobblestones. She had been beaten, used and abused, but she was still Wren. She had her mind, her heart and her wits, and she had come through the battle intact. It never occurred to her to consider the fact that she had just killed one man and maimed another. To survive, you simply did what you had to do.

Chapter Nine

The velvety darkness was like a shroud cloaking the girl scurrying down a series of crooked alleys. Only once did Wren lift her eyes to get her bearings as she stealthily made her way from Briarthorn Lane into a maze of even narrower alleys and cul-de-sacs. It had to be here, that small doorway with the chipped wood and rotten hinges. Lottie would help her. Lottie would take her in her arms and crush the breath from her slim body, all the while mouthing words of comfort. She would smell the same—sour and dirty. Wren smiled to herself. Lottie would slap her soundly and cuff her behind the ears for her absence all these years. If the old woman was mean enough tonight, Wren might even receive a swift kick on her shinbones to show that Lottie wasn't losing her touch. Lottie was queen of the maze, and every derelict came to her for help at one time or another. If you were on Lottie's good side, you never went hungry and you always had a blanket, even if it was full of bugs. Lottie's philosophy was simple: if the straights saw bugs crawling over you, they left you alone. A few open sores never hurt anyone, and soap and water was a killer.

The maze. Wren turned this way and that, trying to get her bearings. Ten years was a long time. She had to remember. She put her fingers to her temple and forced her mind to quietness. She had just light-fingered a gent and relieved him of his purse, and he was chasing her. Which way had she gone? Memories flooded her weary brain, and she sprinted to the right and then to the left, the gent more than a memory. She ran and ran till the splintered door with its rusty hinges loomed before her. Thank God for the big yellow ball in the sky!

Drawing in a deep breath, she rapped sharply three times at eye level and then gave the door a resounding kick, as she had done years ago. She repeated the process three more times before a raspy voice demanded to know who was beating down the door at this ungodly hour.

"Lottie, it's Wren! I have to see you—please let me in!"

"Ye can't trick me, girl. Me Wren is living with the gentry, lo these many years. Now, give me the straight of it or ye'll be in the arms of the law. Me own law!" the voice said harshly.

"Lottie, it's true. I'm Wren. I ran away and I got myself in trouble and need your help. Listen to me! Remember the time we rolled two drunks we thought were sleeping, and one of them slashed at you with his knife? I came up from behind and kneed him like you taught me. You still carry the scar from the elbow to the wrist on the outside of your left arm. Please, Lottie, let me in. I have nowhere else to go."

Wren waited, her heart pounding, for the old woman to slide first one heavy bolt and then another.

Suddenly she was wrapped in plump arms, the sweet sour smell of the woman's sweat engulfing her. She was safe. Lottie would take care of her.

"Come in here to me parlor," Lottie cackled gleefully. "I knew it was ye all along. I was jest punishing ye for not being in touch with me all these years. But ye came back to old Lottie. Tell me what ye look like. Have ye grown into a beautiful young lady like I said ye would?"

Tears burned Wren's eyes. She couldn't be blind, not old Lottie! "I'm a young lady, but I don't know if you could truthfully say I'm beautiful. What happened, Lottie? How did you lose your eyesight? Who's taking care of the maze if you can't . . ."

"Don't ye fret, girl. I'm still queen of the maze," the old woman said quickly, hearing the anguish in Wren's voice. "But to answer your question, a gent from the other side of town took a torch to me and burned off me hair and blinded me. I've been like this for four years now. Ye ain't asking what happened to the gent."

Wren laughed. "I don't have to ask. He's dead and his body was chopped in two and dumped into the Thames."

"Right ye be, little one. Old Lottie can see more without sight than most people if they had four eyes. Me senses are keen, and the men—they look after me much the same way I looked after you. I can hear a footfall at the beginning of the maze. I heard you, and I heard you stop to get your bearings; and if I know you, my girl, you stood there trying to decide which way to go. I heard every step you took. Any time I wanted I could have had old Bart on ye quick as a whistle. But I didn't. I wanted to see who had the wits to try and come into the maze."

"You have to help me, Lottie. I've gotten myself into some trouble and I don't know what to do. I don't have a shilling to my name and I'm ripe for Newgate. I killed a man tonight!"

If Lottie was surprised at the girl's words, she gave no hint. "Sit here and let me get you some food and ale. Me larder was just stocked today by the generosity of a farmer on his way to market. Bart relieved him of his wares, and we can eat till tomorrow and still have plenty left over. When your belly is full, you can cope with anything." She handed Wren a thick wedge of cheese and a chunk of soft, moist bread. "And for a sweet, we have a basket of honey buns."

"Bless old Bart," Wren sighed, relieved to be among friends.

"I've got some cold mashed turnip if ye want it," Lottie volunteered as she ladled the vegetable into a thick yellow bowl.

"Want it! I'd kill for it," Wren said softly. "I haven't eaten in days. Lottie, if I live to be a hundred, I know that I'll never taste food this good."

"We'll be giving your praise to the farmer the next time we meet up with him," Lottie cackled. "Eat now, till your stomach won't hold another morsel, and then we'll talk."

When she had finished eating and emptied her cup of ale, Wren felt her eyes grow heavy but forced herself to remain awake. She had to talk to Lottie and beg for her help. Lottie would know what to do. In a halting voice that grew stronger with the telling, she repeated what had happened to her, leaving nothing out.

Old Lottie listened to Wren, her sightless eyes focused on a point of past memory. "One thing I'm not understandin'. Why in Heaven's name did ye come here? Not that I don't want ye, understand. My house is always open to my little Wren. Only what about the van der Rhyses? Ye be sayin' how much they love ye and all, so whyn't ye go back to them and tell them what's happened to ye?"

"Oh, Lottie," Wren cried, "I can't. I can't! I couldn't face them now, not after what happened to me and what I've done. And after the way I doubted Sirena? The things I said to her? I wouldn't blame them if they never wanted to lay eyes on me again. Oh, Lottie, I just can't go back!" she sobbed, covering her face with her hands.

"If this Sirena loved ye like a mother, I don't see why not, child. Ah! Yer so young, ye don't know how forgivin' a mother's heart can be."

"Don't make me go back, Lottie. Please. I . . . I've got to get away from London for a while. I can sail with Caleb. When the time's right, he'll take me back to Sirena and Regan. But right now I couldn't face them. I've betrayed their love, their trust!"

"Hush, now, child," Lottie soothed. "We'll do it any way ye like. But ye can't stay here, not that I don't want ye, but now that ye've led the fine life, ye can see this is no place for ye. I'd give ten years off me life if ye'd stay, but ye can't and that's the straight of it. We'll have to think of something. This Malcolm sounds like a proper weasel to me, and what ye did to him was too good for the likes of him. I doubt if the law will be after ye for the killing, and those others ye said went to the wharf will run for cover like the river rats they are. Ye'll sleep now, and I'll have some of the men go to the wharf and see about this *Sea Siren* ye been telling me about. How could yer own brother desert ye like this?" she grumbled.

"He didn't desert me, Lottie. He doesn't know. And he isn't my brother, you know that."

"Thank God for that," Lottie muttered under her breath. She might be old and blind, but she had heard the girl's voice change when she mentioned Caleb's name. "Lie here on this cot, and when ye wake, Old

Lottie will have everything come right for ye. Here," she said, handing Wren a dingy coverlet.

"Is it full of bugs?" Wren asked sleepily.

"Scores of them, and a proper nest or two at the hem. Ye don't bother them . . ."

"And they won't bother you," Wren laughed, rolling over and pulling the filthy rag to her chin.

Lottie waited till Wren's breathing was deep and regular before she clapped her hands sharply. Within minutes three men walked into the room and stood there patiently. From the depths of her shapeless dress Lottie withdrew a pouch of gems and fingered its contents deftly. She spoke softly, urgently, and the men showed no emotion at her orders. They shook their heads to indicate they understood, one of them held out his hand for the ruby she had selected, and they departed as quietly as they had come.

A single tear trickled down one wrinkled cheek as Lottie laid a rough, caloused hand on Wren's sleeping head. She knew the girl was beautiful, as beautiful as she herself had been in her younger days. Out of a hidden pocket she withdrew a comb of sorts and tried to straighten her straggly, ill-kempt hair. Eventually she gave it up as too much of an ordeal, and a colony of head lice scurried down her back. Now, why had she gone and disturbed them? She settled herself in an old, battered cane rocker and waited for the lice to make their way back to her wild mane of hair before she, too, fell asleep.

The wharf was alive with voices and movement and torchlight as Caleb's crew readied the *Siren* for tomorrow's sailing. Men hauled provisions while Aubrey Farrington tapped his elegant cane on the deck, his watery eyes missing nothing. "Thank you, Lord, I knew you'd see it my way," he muttered as a barechested seaman hoisted a wooden crate to his shoulder.

Caleb sat nonchalantly on a tack box, his eyes as alert as Farrington's. If there is a King of Fools, I'm it, he told himself. Any time the old gambler looked as he did now, Caleb knew he was missing something. He'd make damn sure he searched the *Siren* from top to bottom before he sailed. The old fox had something up his sleeve, and it wasn't cards or his arm.

"How many, Aubrey?" he asked, blowing a fragrant cloud of blue-gray smoke in the gambler's direction.

"One hundred or so, give or take a few. You have plenty of room and then some. Don't start fretting, Cal. Everything has been taken care of."

"That's the part that frightens me," Caleb snapped. "When you take care of things, I always wind up on the short end of the stick. It will be dawn soon; we should both get some sleep."

"Sleep!" Aubrey shouted. "And let these men rob us blind! Never! I'll stay right here till dawn. If you feel the need for some sleep, you go right ahead. I'll watch things for you."

"And who is going to watch you? My mistake was not putting a leash around your neck the first time I met you. I'll just stay right here, and if you're half as smart as you think you are, you'll stay within my line of vision."

The gambler nodded agreeably. "Whatever you say, Cal."

"You know, Aubrey, before this ship sails I'm going over her from stem to stern to see what it is you're trying to have me smuggle to the colonies for you." Caleb watched him with narrowed eyes. Farrington wasn't a gambler for nothing. His face remained impassive, even a little sly.

"I'll ignore that insult because we're such good friends. For shame, Cal. How could you think I'd try to pull the wool over your eyes?"

"You said it, Aubrey. *Try.* You can't. I don't want

142

to find myself on the high seas carrying something a bastard bunch of pirates want. I have no intention of getting my throat slit or having my passengers harmed because of some fanciful whim of yours. From stem to stern, remember that."

The desperation on Farrington's face was almost lawless. In the bright moonlight Caleb could see the frenzy in the old rake's eyes. His voice softened unexpectedly, throwing the gambler off guard. "If you'd just tell me what it is you're trying to get me to take, we might come to some kind of terms. Realize, Aubrey, that I'm smarter than you and that you can't get away with anything. If you try your usual tricks, then all these . . . these passengers, as you call them, will be waiting dockside when I set sail—alone."

Farrington took one last look at Caleb's smoldering dark eyes and wavered, straightened his slumped shoulders. "For the last time, I don't know what you're talking about. I'm not hiding anything on your ship, nor do I intend to. I may be old, Cal, but I'm not a fool."

For a minute Caleb almost believed him—until he squinted in the moonlight and saw the same look of desperation in his eyes. He sighed. He would search the ship, as he had said, and woe be to the old man if he found something other than rotting wood and rats.

When the last store of provisions was safely put away in the galley, Caleb strolled on deck, dawn but moments away. He loved the beginning of a new day, but his gut churned at what this day might bring. He had to have been a fool to agree to Aubrey's plans. Well, it was too late now; he had given his word, and he would have to sail for America as promised. He glanced about restlessly, and realized he wanted a woman. He wanted one now. With everything going on around him, he wondered how he could even think about women at a time like this.

He pushed the thought from his mind and settled

himself against a roll of sail. Somewhere, someplace, someday, he would find a woman full of wonder and excitement, a woman who would love him the way he would love her. They would make love the first time to his satisfaction and the second time to the satisfaction of both; each time they would be tantalizing and incomprehensively cruel with each other, yet gentle, so very gentle, as if their lovemaking were an assault and a confession at the same time, as if it had to illustrate a confusion in themselves that was imperative for both to understand. If he sailed the world over, he wondered if he would ever find such a woman and if he would recognize her for what he wanted her to be, needed her to be, in order to make him complete. I'll know, he told himself, a touch of arrogance on his face. I'll know.

Malcolm Weatherly stood in the lavender shadows of early dawn, his torn and ragged cheek throbbing painfully. He couldn't see at all out of his left eye. He was afraid. More afraid than he'd ever been in his entire life. More afraid than when he had heisted the jeweled collar right from under the King's nose. What would become of him now that his handsome face had been ruined by that bitch Wren? If he ever got his hands on her, he'd be certain to do the same thing to her, so that she would have to hide out for the rest of her life. He'd make certain no man ever looked at her again.

He glanced around to get his bearing. For a moment he was confused. Somehow he thought he had come farther, was closer to the wharf and Farrington's derelict gambling ship. The deep, black fear rose in him again as he realized the sky was getting brighter by the minute. He forced himself to think and to take stock of his situation. He looked no worse than some of the water rats who frequented the seamy wharves and the taverns scattered along the rancid alleyways.

In his condition he doubted if any of his acquaintances would recognize him, and the rats would take him as one of their own. The worst that could happen to him was that he would get rolled and beaten as just another drunk. He raised his good eye to the east and quickly closed it. Christ, he must have pulled the muscles in the injured side of his face, and now it was bleeding again, the blood seeping into his eye. Rage at his circumstances swept through him, and in that moment he swore to himself that if Farrington gave him one false look or word, he'd kill him on the spot and take back his booty. If he got caught, then that would be that. He was ruined in society now, so nothing really mattered anymore.

He moved crablike, his injured shoulder slumping, along the grime-infested walls flanking the alley. When he came to the end of the cul-de-sac, he blinked at all the activity down on the docks. There was young van der Rhys, shouting at Farrington in a harsh voice. Malcolm was too far away to make out the words, but even from this distance the gambler looked afraid. That's good, good for me, Malcolm told himself. Farrington was leaving, his elegant walking stick making quick, light taps on the rough boards. Malcolm would give him just enough time to clear the wharf and then would follow him and take matters into his own hands. The gambler was a spry old gent, crafty and cunning, but he would meet his match in Malcolm Weatherly.

The moment the old man made his way onto the deserted open street, Malcolm shouted hoarsely and waited. Aubrey Farrington turned, his blank look quickly dissolving into one of fear when he saw the dandy's injured face. "Lord luv a duck. Weatherly, what happened to you?"

"Never mind what happened to me. I want to talk to you in your rooms and get myself taken care of. Help me."

"And why should I be helping the likes of you? We had a business deal and it's over. I owe you nothing except your share of the gems, and you agreed to wait till they were sold. I owe you nothing," he repeated firmly, making a move to walk away.

"You bastard," Malcolm gritted through clenched teeth. "Either you help me or I swear I'll find my own way to your rooms and set fire to them and roast you like a chicken."

Aubrey Farrington abhorred violence and threats, especially those made against his person. "Very well," he said coolly, "but let me tell you that I am no doctor and the sight of blood makes me ill. I can't tend to your wounds; I know nothing about them and I have no intention of learning. A physician is what you need. From the looks of things, you might lose that eye if you aren't careful."

"It's my eye, and if I'm not worried, then you need not be, either. You'll take care of me, you old sinner, or you'll never set foot outside your rooms again. I mean it, Farrington."

The gambler knew this was true. Weatherly was worse than Cal. His faded eyes went skyward and he begged silently, Why me? All I did was cut a few corners. I take a little from here to pay there, and if it weren't for me, those poor souls, the Puritans, would be sitting here waiting for the ax to fall. Remember that when You judge me. He lowered his eyes, careful to note that Weatherly's feet were just behind him. Even if he managed to shake loose of him, where would he go? Best to get on with it and rid himself of the vermin.

Inside his comfortable quarters, Aubrey fetched a basin of water and set to work. His touch was not gentle as he poked and prodded Malcolm's slashed cheek. His tone was cold and clinical as he spoke. "There's a smart cut on your eyeball and your face needs to be sewn. I can't do it."

146

"What happens if it isn't sewn up?"

Farrington treated him to a disgusted look. "I told you, I'm no doctor. The wound will heal the way it is if it's kept clean, but your face will be distorted. Forget the eye—it's gone. If the cheek wound is taken care of and sutured, you might end up with a red welt running from your eyebrow to your chin. In time it may fade, and then again, it may not. For God's sake, man, I told you I know nothing about these things." As he carried the basin to a table in the corner of the room he couldn't resist a parting shot. "You just might secure employment in Newgate or Bedlam and scare the prisoners and patients into obedience."

Malcolm ignored the callous words. The next time he peered into a mirror would be time enough to determine the state of his looks. For now, with his wound clean and bandaged, he had other matters to attend to. "Is it true that van der Rhys' ship is sailing today? No lies, Farrington."

"Yes," Aubrey said, returning to the center of the room, "his ship sails tonight with a full hold of passengers. Why?"

"Because you're going to get me on that ship. It's not safe for me here any longer. What's her destination?"

Farrington drew in his breath sharply. "The colonies, and then on to Martinique to sell our little . . . prize." He cast a quizzical glance in Weatherly's direction, uncertain whether he should have told him the collar would be leaving England with the *Sea Siren*. "What's the matter, man? You're white enough to have seen a ghost."

"I . . . I didn't know van der Rhys would have any part of this." He thought of the toughs he had sent down to the wharf to nose around the ship for any hint of jewels. If he were to lose the collar now, he would be left with nothing.

"The captain of the *Sea Siren* knows nothing about

the King's collar. He thinks he's on a mercy mission to help some Puritans escape the country. And you can rest at ease; the collar has not yet boarded the ship. Why your sudden concern?" Farrington asked uneasily.

"It's just some talk I heard. You're certain no one else knows about the jewels?"

"As certain as I am of my own name," Farrington assured him. "However, if you think for one minute that you're going to 'guard' the prize, you're mistaken. You're a thief." the old man exclaimed.

"And just what the hell does that make you?" Malcolm spat.

"A fence. And an honorable profession it is. I just make sure everyone gets what he wants, and then I take my commission. Thievery," he continued in a pious tone, "is the work of the devil. My hands are clean. I deal only in honorable professions."

Malcolm tried to sneer but gave it up and let his facial muscles relax. "And I suppose gambling is an honorable profession?"

"What's a man to do? If people want to throw their money away, can I stop them? I'm an honorable man dealing in honorable professions." Farrington's tone was virtuous, his eyes sly as he observed the effect of his words on the wounded, suffering man.

"Bah! You talk like an old fool, and I'm losing my patience. I want to be on that ship when she sails. Arrange it, Farrington. I don't care how you do it. Just do it. You'd be wise if you smuggled me aboard without van der Rhys' knowledge. I know I can trust you, Farrington, to do whatever is necessary." Malcolm's voice was cold, his face deadly with its disfigurement.

"You're insane, Weatherly. Van der Rhys has the sailing list, and there's no way an extra person can be smuggled aboard in broad daylight."

"You'll think of something. Arrange for some food

for me, get me some decent clothes and put it all on my tab."

Aubrey's mind raced. What in the hell was he supposed to do? Cal was breathing down his neck; this vulture was threatening to kill him. Even if he managed, somehow, to smuggle Weatherly aboard the *Sea Siren,* he knew he would never see his share of the profits from the King's jeweled collar. His contact in Martinique would pay over the vast sum to Weatherly, and that would be the end of Farrington. If there was one thing he hated, it was missing out on the final result of anything, especially if he had been in at the beginning. The only thing he hated worse was an empty pocket or purse. He had no choice but to make the crossing with Cal to protect his investment. He would confide in Cal to be certain he didn't find himself dead. A three-way split was better than no split at all. As long as he retained possession of the collar, he could call the shots. Yes, he would confide in Cal and then figure out a way to smuggle Weatherly aboard. Cal's cabin, a few greased palms—well-greased—and the matter should be settled to his and Weatherly's satisfaction.

I must be getting old, he mouthed silently as he made his way down the narrow stairwell to see the landlady, who, for a few flowery words and a quick peck on the cheek, would supply him with food for the vermin resting upstairs in his favorite chair. The things he had to do to stay alive in this cruel, heartless world! He sighed heavily as he knocked on the landlady's door and flinched when she opened it and said, "Coo! And if it isn't himself this beautiful day."

The things he had to do!

Chapter Ten

Lydia Stoneham woke up and lay perfectly still. She always woke up with fear in her throat. She went to bed with fear churning throughout her body, she ate in fear and she existed in fear, as she had done every day of her life since she had married Bascom Stoneham at her parents' insistence. She was afraid of everything—if she ate too much or if she didn't, if she spoke too much or too little, if she soiled her dress or kept it spotless—which meant, in Bascom's eyes, that she did nothing, even though her hands were red and cracked from the harsh lye soap he made her use. Cleanliness, he enjoyed repeating, was next to godliness. But most of all, she was afraid of her husband, Bascom. Of what he was and what he made her do. Obscene, filthy things that he insisted she perform in the name of the Lord so that she would be purged. How, she wondered anew, could those disgusting acts ever purge her? They were degradations matched only by the ugliness contained in his gaunt face and needle-thin body. She admitted to herself that she hated him with a passion she had never known in love.

As always when she thought of her deep aversion

to him, like now in the early hours of the morning, she trembled and shook, and tears welled in her hyacinth-blue eyes. They were tears of self-pity and remorse, for herself and for others like her who were forced to live out this farce of a life.

She squeezed her eyes shut to stop the tears, when Bascom's skinny leg reached out to touch her foot. He would feel her trembling and, like the insane person he was, assume it was a trembling based on sexual desire. If she lived to be a hundred and protested every hour of the day that she trembled from fear and not from any sexual desire, he would never believe her. He was convinced that she lusted after him even in her sleeping hours. And, wonderful husband that he was, first he would allow her to give in to her bodily urges, at his insistence, and then he would force her to pray to God for forgiveness. If there was a God, why didn't He intervene? Why did He permit her to be subjected to Bascom's madness?

She had to stop her trembling, had to force herself to get up and dress. Once she was fully clothed, Bascom couldn't see or feel her quaking body. But it was too late. His clawlike hands were working their way up under the thin nightdress. She wanted to scream as one bony hand cupped her full breast and the other stroked her flat stomach. She fought back a retch and lay still, hoping that he would tire and fall asleep again. That had never happened yet, but she always hoped and sometimes even prayed.

Bascom's head moved slowly toward the back of Lydia's neck, and then his tongue flicked out to lick at the warm spot at the nape. His head burrowed into her skin, her bright red hair shielding him from the sunlight filtering into the room. His tongue worked slowly while his hands were feverish in their pursuit of her soft, yielding flesh. Roughly, never releasing his hold on her breast, he rolled her over onto her stomach. Her eyes were closed. That is good, he told himself. She is begging for forgiveness, as I have taught her, while allowing me, her beloved husband, to have my way with her and to bestow on her unparalleled delight. Every muscle in her body was quivering, and behind her closed lids he knew her eyes were burning, fervently for him, and for the sexual pleasure he could give her.

He played with her, fondling each breast till its rosy crest became taut and erect. His hands moved slowly downward and began to explore the soft, warm place between her thighs until her tightly closed mouth opened and she moaned . . . in desire . . . for him. Always for him. His mouth found its way to the hollow in her throat and again his tongue flicked this way and that, traveling to the cleft between her breasts and then to the taut tips, which he licked and sucked on greedily, her moans ringing in his ears. He removed her nightdress and his own nightshirt and edged closer to her, the sharp, protruding bones of his emaciated body digging mercilessly into her. He was behind her, his organ between her thighs, his hand crushing the softness of her breasts. "It's time, Lydia. Say it now."

"Forgive me, Lord, for lusting after my husband's body. Deny me that which my body seeks for fulfillment. Forgive me, Lord, for my weak flesh," Lydia intoned loudly to be sure Bascom heard and did not make her repeat the words.

"I hear you, child, and I shall deny that which you ask. I am your lord and your savior!" Bascom shouted, his voice dramatic in the quiet of the room, as he thrust his throbbing manhood into her.

It is true . . . my flesh is weak, Lydia sobbed silently. If only he would . . . just once . . . How can he do this to me day in and day out? She felt him move away and knew what was coming. He got out of bed and stood by the edge, pulling her upright toward him. His skull-shaped head, its stringy hanks of hair falling over his eyes, bent to her breasts and he nipped at their pink erect circles. His hands caressed her haunches and then slid slowly upward till they rested on her shoulders, forcing her to her knees till her mouth was level with his manly pride. He lowered his eyes and watched her open her mouth. How obscene she looked. How could a woman degrade herself this way? He would make her do penance for this. He would make her kneel and pray till her knees were raw and bleeding and she was hoarse from her entreaties. Disgusting harlot! His eyes became glazed and a convulsive urgency seized him, causing him to shudder and cry out repeatedly. He was in agony because of what she had forced him to do in the name of God.

Lydia sat back on her haunches, her eyes downcast and full of shame. She took the blow squarely on the side of her face and didn't flinch. She had to pay for what she had done, what she had made Bascom do in order to save her soul from the devil.

Bascom reached for his Bible on the night table and opened it. "We must pray now for your wantonness. We will both ask God to spare us of more of these doings. He knows you for the harlot you are, and He will come to me in a vision and tell me what to do with you. Pray, Lydia," he commanded.

"Dear Lord, I am the harlot Your disciple says I am. I am full of lust, which must be driven from my body to purify it so I may serve You in any way You choose. Forgive me my weakness and make my husband strong of mind and body so he can bear my defects. Spare me, God, from Your wrath, but take pity on me and show me mercy." Her voice was flat and dull, and she repeated the words over and over until Bascom was fully clothed.

"You may get dressed now. Tonight, aboard ship, we'll pray again for your soul. Tell me that you want me to pray for your soul, Lydia."

"Yes, Bascom, I want you to pray for my soul," Lydia said tonelessly.

"My parents and my sister, Sara, are waiting for us downstairs. When we go into the dining hall, be sure to keep your eyes lowered, or everyone will know what you've just done. They'll all see you for the obscene harlot you are, and then they'll be forced to pity me. Pity me!" he screeched, his eyes burning madly. "If that happens, God will punish both of us. It is only you, Lydia, who need to be punished. It is you who must constantly fight these bodily urges and conquer them. Perhaps one day, if you pray long enough and hard enough, you will be saved from yourself and will relieve me of this cross I bear."

"Yes, Bascom, I will do as you say," she agreed, pulling her petticoat over her head and tying the laces across her bosom. I know there must be another God besides the one you pray to, she said silently, and to that God she dropped to her knees and prayed, tearfully, not for forgiveness, but for help in ridding herself of the insane zealot who was her husband.

Lottie opened the door leading to the maze, tilted her head to one side and listened. Three pairs of footsteps. The men were returning. Quietly she closed the door and sat down in the cane rocker. A scrawny yellow cat leapt into her lap and purred loudly. Lottie's dirty fingers, their nails cracked and split, stroked the cat gently, her unseeing eyes on the sleeping girl. What was going to happen to her? In her heart Lottie had known that one day Wren would escape the maze and marry a fine gentleman who would love her devotedly for all his days.

Three quick knocks on the stout door, the low-placed kick, and Lottie was off the chair, the yellow cat spitting his outrage at being dumped so unceremoniously on the hard floor.

"No wasted words, just the quick of it," Lottie commanded the men.

"The *Sea Siren* sails at midnight. The ship carries no cargo, only passengers to the American colonies. Puritans. We managed, at great expense, to purchase this outfit." Bart handed Lottie a parcel. "The girl should be able to slip aboard and go unnoticed. If they have an accurate head count, then we'll have to divert a woman passenger. Lucas here has agreed to that little task. Either way, the girl will be aboard when the ship sails. Seth pawned the ruby and got nearly two hundred pounds by holding a knife to the pawnbroker's throat. Did we do well, Lottie?"

"Very well, Bart. I couldn't have done better myself," Lottie said, laying a hand on his arm to show she was proud of his accomplishments. How well these thieves looked after her since she lost her eyesight. Why, even old Seth gave her a bath twice a year and never once paid attention to her flabby body. He soaped her like a baby and dried her off as if she were his own mother. These little things made life bearable.

"I left breakfast for ye in the other room," Lottie said happily. "Eat hearty, old friends. I'll wake the child now and ready her for her journey."

Lottie stroked the sleeping girl's tangled hair and ran her gnarled hand over one smooth cheek. She showed no emotion when she felt her wet cheeks. The child was crying in her sleep. "Come, Wren, it's time to rise and make ready for a new day. Come." She shook her gently, and when Wren sat up, she gave her the parcel. Quickly she explained what Wren was to do and where she was going, and patted her fondly on the head. Wren retired to a curtained-off section of the room to change her clothes. When she had finished dressing herself in the black Puritan garb, her hair pinned beneath the starched white cap, she came back and sat down next to Lottie at the table. She

155

ate her breakfast quickly, ravenously, licking her fingers to indicate her appreciation of the food.

"Listen to me, child," Lottie said, holding out a pouch. "Here is a hundred pounds. This other little sack is full of gems. Guard them both well, for it's all ye'll have when ye get to America. God only knows what ye'll be finding there, and this will be all ye'll have between starvation and survival. I'd give ye more if I had it, but I have the men to look after."

Wren's eyes widened. "It's too much, Lottie. I can't take it all. Half will do nicely. I'm strong and I can find work when I get there. You may need this for yourself and the others."

"Nonsense, child. We can always get more. This is to be yer nest egg against the future. Ye don't know what that strange land is like, and it might not be a fit place for a woman lookin' for work. Ye keep it and use it wisely."

"I wish I weren't going, Lottie, but I know I can't stay here. To do so would be to place all of you in danger. I'll never be able to repay you for your kindness."

"I need no payment. Seeing ye safely aboard ship will be payment enough. However, if ye have a mind to, ye can be doing me one small favor—if the opportunity presents itself, that is."

"Anything. Just tell me what it is," Wren urged.

"Seth said a man named Aubrey Farrington will be aboard the Dutchman's ship. He's known as the foxiest cardsharp in these here parts. A day or so before ye get to yer port, seek him out and engage him in a game of cards. Use every trick I ever taught ye. Fleece the old gent for every cent ye can. And after ye win, tell him the win was for Lottie. He'll know what yer talking about. Will ye do that for me?"

Wren nodded, a wide grin splitting her gaminlike face. "Every trick, Lottie?"

"Every trick," Lottie repeated firmly. "Seth overheard him talkin' with young van der Rhys, and that's how I know he'll be aboard. It's an old, private score ye'll be settling for me. It was the one and only time in me life I got fleeced, and it still don't sit well. I want ye to even up the odds for me."

"I'll do it, and as soon as I get to America I'll post a letter to you with your winnings or send them on the next ship that sails for England."

"Child, I don't want no winnings. Keep them. I just want him to know I ain't forgot and that I don't need 'em. I want to see him bested. To do that, ye'll be using this deck of cards." Lottie dug into one of the pockets of her tattered gown. "Whatever ye do, don't lose them. Ye remember the markings, don't ye? Seth was the best forger in all of England, and his steady hand has no equal. Just look at the tail feathers of them peacocks and ye'll see the markings clear as a bell."

"I remember, Lottie. You have my word."

The three men entered the parlor with smiles on their faces for Wren. "Me and Lucas will be leaving for the wharf, and Seth will be back for Wren when it's time," Bart said quietly. Lottie nodded and the thieves went out, the yellow cat at their heels.

Aubrey Farrington stationed himself near a porthole in Caleb's cabin so that he could observe Malcolm Weatherly being brought aboard. Van der Rhys had eyes in the back of his head and the instincts of a cat. Keep him occupied and his mind clacking away, Aubrey told himself, and hopefully he won't get suspicious. When Cal learned of the gambler's little coup, he would be bug-eyed.

"All right, Cal, I can see that the gig is up and there's nothing to do but 'fess up to you," Aubrey rattled away. "It's simple, really. With you gone and the gambling fever at a low, I found myself hard pressed for a little cash, so I agreed to—to put a

157

friend of mine in touch with a . . . lady I once knew, and then he—"

"Heisted the King's jewels," Caleb finished flatly. "I knew you were behind that caper the minute I heard the news. You might as well have drawn a road map, Farrington. It smacked of your devious hand. The only thing that surprises me is that you haven't been caught yet." Caleb's face was tight and grim, but his eyes were speculative. "How much, Aubrey, on the black market?"

"Nothing less than a king's ransom!" Aubrey crowed smugly. "I've arranged for the transfer of the collar in Martinique. I'm sailing with you, Cal, to protect my investment."

"Nice of you to tell me," Caleb remarked coolly. "Somehow I knew you would. Now, tell me where the jewels are, in case one of my men decides you're taking up space and need to be eliminated. I wouldn't want this little trip to be for nothing."

"You disappoint me, Cal. You know the rules a gambler lives by. I never reveal my hand."

"If that hand's about to be cut off, you will. For now, though, I'll let you keep your little secret; but remember, the day I decide I want an answer is the day you'll babble like a court fool."

"That seems to be a fair bargain," Farrington replied blandly as he twirled his elegant Cavalier hat between his fingers. "Very generous of you indeed, Cal." He turned to go, his uneasy stomach quieting to a purr. By now, Weatherly was safely ensconced in the bowels of the ship, securely sequestered in the locker box.

"One last thing, Aubrey. Even shares. Agreed?"

"Anything you say. You can trust me. Even shares it is."

"Then you'll have no objection to signing this little document in the proper place," Caleb went on, extending a piece of paper and a quill. "Cutthroat pirates aren't the only ones who have walked the plank, remember that. This is my ship and I'm the captain. Do we understand each other, Aubrey . . . old friend?"

"Perfectly." Farrington smiled, put his signature to paper and strode from the cabin. A pity he had never learned to swim as a youth. He hated cold black water. But it will never come to that, he assured himself as he made his way to what would be his new home for the balance of the journey. He needed a drink, maybe two or three, to settle his stomach. Two-way splits were for fools. Three-way splits were for the feebleminded. Winner-take-all was the way it would be. All he had to do was figure out how to eliminate Weatherly and give Cal the slip, and he would be the winner.

The minute Farrington had left, a broad smile creased Caleb's face. Whom did he think he was fooling? He could have had the jewels in a minute if he had wanted them. Aubrey had lived by his wits too long. Where besides on his person would he keep them? And that rakish hat with its plume! What better place to hide something than the most obvious one of all?

Wren sat quietly while Lottie dozed in the cane rocker. Her mind whirled. She felt nothing, no emotion whatsoever. She should be feeling something, anything, to prove she was still alive and the same person she had been. She was sailing under an assumed name, in clothes stolen from God knows where, on a ship captained by her stepbrother, who was not to know she was aboard. She had a deck of marked cards that would enable her to cheat, and a hundred pounds and a cache of gems stashed next to her bosom. She had misjudged Malcolm, been raped and almost killed by his hand and his friends, and Sirena and Regan, those dearest to her heart, were lost to her forever.

She was going to a new land overrun with savage Indians. How had all this happened? she questioned herself. Because I was a fool, she answered as tears trickled down her cheeks. She felt a small measure of comfort in knowing that if anything terrible did occur on the sailing, she could always plead with Caleb to intervene. Surely he wouldn't desert her. She wiped at her eyes with the back of her hand and looked around the squalid room.

She had lived like this as a child; actually, she had lived under worse conditions until Lottie had found her and taken her in. The days when she had slept in alleys with garbage keeping her warm were behind her. She didn't have to think about them any longer. They were lost to her forever, and now she was going to a new land and a new life. She would have to survive on her own. She had learned her lesson well. Never trust anyone. Trust was for fools. She had believed and trusted Sara and Malcolm, and look what had happened to her! Sirena and Regan had trusted her, and see what she had done to them! And that bastard, Caleb, trying to seduce her in the garden. She hoped she had crippled him for life so that he could never take advantage of another young woman. Mentally she placed him in the same category with Malcolm and then wiped him from her mind. She would survive or die trying, and if the latter happened, she would endure it by her own hand—no one else's.

The stool Wren was sitting on teetered suddenly as she tried to make herself more comfortable till Seth returned. She wished she could see outside. She knew the moon was full, but layers of grease and dirt covered the windows with a smudgy grayness, eliminating all signs of moonlight. She blinked as she saw a parade of roaches cross the table and envelop a chunk of bread lying on a cracked plate. Within seconds the bread looked as if it were alive as it shriveled to nothing but crumbs. They have to eat, too, she told herself; they have to live just as I do. The spindly legs of the stool creaked again as she looked at Lottie. How could her old friend live like this? "Because she's never known anything else," Wren muttered aloud. Bart and the others, they never knew anything else either. You did what you had to do to keep body and soul together; if something better came along, then you were lucky enough to taste the cream on top of the crock. "Damnation!" she spit through clenched teeth. She had lived with the garbage, slept under it and tasted the cream. She had no taste for garbage and swill and from now on she would have only cream.

The door opened silently this time, and the yellow cat was first through the opening. He leapt onto Lottie's lap and snuggled down in her filthy skirts. Seth nodded slightly. Wren rose first, and then Lottie. Neither woman said a word. Wren turned and followed the man through the doorway without a backward glance. She knew Lottie was crying silent tears as she cradled the cat in the crook of her arm. There were no tears left for Wren van der Rhys to cry.

"I'll be givin' ye me good-luck charm," Seth said, holding out a portion of a sow's ear as they hurried down the alley. Wren accepted the offering of the silken talisman with a smile.

"I'll take good care of it and pray that it brings me as much good fortune as it has brought you." It was all he had to give, and both knew it brought no luck, for if it had, Seth wouldn't be living like Lottie and taking care of her.

"Step lively, little one, and as soon as ye see a cluster of those black and white birds, mingle with them and make your way up the gangplank like ye belong with them. Don't look about, and keep your eyes down like the women do." He squeezed her arm lightly and whispered, "Good luck, lass."

Wren nodded and moved ahead quickly. She

161

spotted a family of Puritans gathering near the frigate and slipped in among them, her head and eyes downcast. She knew every nook and cranny of the *Sea Siren* from the times Caleb had sailed to Java, and she could outwit anyone who might get in her way on board. Sirena had pointed out various hiding places to her and how she could dart from one to the other if a hunt were on for a stowaway.

She saw Caleb's boots first and realized she had to pass him. Her head lowered, she scuttled by him and knew from his stance that he hadn't given her more than a casual glance—if he had done even that. Cattle, animals, that was all they were to him. Human beings didn't sleep in the confines of a ship's hold. Human beings lived in houses, ate proper food and slept in proper beds. How many of these people would survive the trip? The older ones, with their pale skin and brittle bones, would never last it out. The dampness of the hold and the lack of fresh air would make them develop coughs, and they would be buried at sea before the voyage ended. Regan had told her this and she believed him. She wondered if Caleb had explained these facts to the people before he had agreed to captain the ship. Not likely. Why should he care, as long as he got what he wanted? Men were all alike. If they couldn't get what they wanted with their charm, they took it by force. Whatever she had left she wasn't giving up, either by charm or by force. If there was any charming to be done, she would do it; and if it came to exerting force, she could do that, too.

A pole jabbed her cruelly in the side. "Move on, now, you're holding up the line," a harsh voice demanded, prodding her again. An angry retort rose to her lips, but she stifled it. Not now. She looked up to see who had jabbed her. Satisfied that she would remember the man's face, she quickened her pace and climbed down the ladder into the dark hold.

The *Sea Siren* secure, Caleb gave the order to weigh anchor. He cast a critical eye at the moon, measuring the stiff wind that bracketed the vessel. It was good sailing weather, better than he could have hoped for. His gut churned as the ship slid from her berth into the open water of the Thames. Six weeks with that ragtag passel of religious fanatics! In his eyes they all looked like somber penguins, intent only on converting souls and preaching fire and brimstone. Especially Bascom Stoneham, with his blazing eyes and self-righteous rantings and ravings. "Spare me from his daily visitations from the Lord," he muttered under his breath. Did Puritans ever do anything else but pray? he wondered. A vision of Sara in her black garb flashed before him as he gave the wheel a hard turn. She wasn't so docile, and her brother's teachings looked as though they had fallen on deaf ears as far as she was concerned. Without her clothes, he imagined she would be a fine figure of a woman. It was going to be a long sailing, and what better way to while away a few hours every now and then? He would have Farrington suffer with Bascom's prayers and preachings. That would keep Bascom occupied and at the same time do the old reprobate some good. Aubrey could benefit from exposure to religion. It was time somebody made an effort to save that curmudgeon's soul.

With the ship sailing almost of her own free will because of the strong sea breeze, Caleb let his thoughts wander, as he always did the moment the *Siren* and he felt as one. He hoped that when Sirena and Regan found Wren, they would have a safe journey back to Java and the sons they loved so deeply. And Wren, where was she? His lips tightened and an imaginary pain attacked his midsection. Wherever she was, he knew she was in trouble. Trouble followed her, settled around her, and if he was any judge, it was her middle name. The grim set of his jaw lessened when he remembered how warm and soft she had felt in his arms, how ardently she had returned his kiss with the promise of more to come. Sweet, virginal Wren. "Spitfire" was more like it. His lips tightened again when he recalled how he had rolled on the ground in pain, his groin on fire. Suddenly he laughed. Sara's face had just swum before him, and she was asking him if he had spells. He'd show her the kind of spells he had before this trip was over! But where had Wren gone? Was she with that fop Weatherly? Surely she wouldn't be foolish enough to marry him. But just for spite she might. She had learned too much from Sirena. Wren was strong-willed, and had an ungovernable temper and a tongue that should have been forked. Yes, Sirena had taught her well. In his gut he knew they would cross paths again, and when they did, she wouldn't be a schoolgirl any longer.

Aubrey Farrington, resplendent in his sea attire, as he called it, marched on wavering legs to the wheelhouse, his face pale and his hands trembling. Caleb took one look at him and pointed to the railing. He listened as Farrington retched while holding his stomach as if it were going to drop to the deck.

"Whatever you do, don't eat today, Aubrey," Caleb advised with a chuckle. "Serves you right for coming along. God's punishing you for not trusting me. You might have this miserable sickness for the entire length of the journey. Seek out Bascom Stoneham and ask him to pray for your relief."

"Bastard," Farrington hissed as he once again leaned over the rail. "I've lost today's breakfast, lunch and dinner. There's nothing left in my stomach."

"You're being punished, Aubrey," Caleb continued to taunt the gambler. "If you should waste away entirely or find you can't maneuver around, what shall I do with your body? You'd better tell me now where your prize is."

164

"I'm not going to die, so don't concern yourself, you insufferable bastard. You're enjoying my agony, aren't you?" Farrington said weakly as a fresh wave of nausea swept over him.

"Couldn't happen to a nicer person. Go below and lie down. Sooner or later dizziness will overtake you, and you might fall and get hurt. I've no mind for setting bones this trip, and yours are so old I doubt if they could be mended. Splinters. There's no hope for you, Aubrey."

The gambler was too weak to retort and gladly took the arm of a seaman named Peter, who helped him to his cabin. He barely reached the rough bunk before renewed attacks of nausea overcame him.

The Puritans settled themselves in the hold, three yellow smoking lamps lighting the darkness. Wren glanced around, trying to see if Sara was aboard. The blond girl was sitting next to her mother, an unhappy look on her face. Mrs. Stoneham looked as if she were praying. Wren carefully inched her way to a dim corner and sat down, drawing her knees up to her chin. She lowered her head and fell asleep almost immediately.

In what seemed like only moments later she was jarred awake by a prod to her leg. "Wake, sister, we're about to pray." Wren blinked. She thought she had just seen the devil. She swallowed hard and got to her knees and bowed her head with the others. An hour later she fought the urge to laugh at the preaching man whose eyes were blazing with a vision of the Lord. She lifted her head defiantly and stared at him. She had had enough, and her knees hurt.

Bascom Stoneham stared back at her and said, "Lower your eyes, sister, while I pray for your soul. Never look upon me as I preach, for I am the Lord's emissary. You are but a poor sinner and have no right to gaze upon me as I spell out God's Word. Sinner!" he shouted. "You're all sinners, and I've been sent to save your souls! And I will save them! Pray with me now and ask for forgiveness. Sister, I won't tell you again to lower your eyes. If you don't, you'll be punished at day's end."

Wren giggled. How could the likes of him punish her? Such a skinny, scrawny, ugly man! How could the Lord pick such a man to do His work? Evidently his mother was wondering the same thing, for she raised her eyes and met Wren's. If she recognized the girl, she gave no sign but lowered her eyes again, a look of outrage and disgust on her face.

"Now," Bascom continued, "repeat after me: We are all sinners and must ask for forgiveness and also for punishment so that our souls can be purged and we can walk among decent people and do God's work."

Wren was beside herself. This time she raised her head and spoke loudly. "What if we haven't sinned, but have been sinned against?"

"Who is that who dares to speak while I say the Lord's words?"

No voice answered the preacher's question. Wren lowered her head and folded her hands into a pyramid, a smile parting her lips. Hypocrite, she said silently. Punish me, will he? Damnation, her knees hurt. If this was what this trip was going to be like, she had best get herself out of there, and quickly. She would ask the next seaman she saw to send Caleb to her. She'd rather deal with Caleb than with this devil standing before her.

"Every sinner in this room, stand up and tell the Lord what you've done, and I'll forgive you and pray for your soul!" Bascom shouted, his eyes blazing and spittle forming in droplets on his mouth. Wren looked up. Everyone was standing but her. She knew in her heart she wasn't a sinner, and she'd be damned if she'd stand up. And if that insane man took it into his head to punish her, she'd give him what for in a hurry, just like she had given Caleb, although, from the looks of things, he wasn't endowed with Caleb's manly attributes. She giggled at the thought and felt a viselike grip on her arm.

"You dare to laugh when I'm preaching the Lord's words and asking for purging? You dare to make a mockery of what I'm doing for these poor souls who have sinned against the Lord? Just this noon the Lord favored me with another visitation. He told me to be wary of those who refused to repent and to cast my eye upon them. You are a sinner, sister," Bascom declared loudly. "By the set of your jaw and the defiant look in your eyes I can see that you were the one the Lord was talking about. You must repent now, before it's too late. Together"—he waved his arms around the hold—"we will save you."

"I haven't done anything, and I don't need to be saved. I'm here by mistake. Captain van der Rhys is my brother. I'm Wren van der Rhys. I was expelled from school along with your sister, Sara."

Every head in the room turned and then immediately snapped back; all eyes were downcast. Wren ripped off the white cap and her hair tumbled free. She swirled the dark tresses about her shoulders and shook his arm away. "I've decided I don't like it here, and I'm leaving. Now," she said adamantly.

"Every sinner says he's done nothing and has no need to be saved. Yes, I recognize your name, and that's why I'm going to devote myself entirely to saving your soul. The others are well on their way to being purged through my mighty efforts and my daily visitations. And we'll hear no more of your going topside. You'll go on deck only when I say so. For now, you will do penance and ask the Lord to forgive you for talking to me in such a manner. But first," he said, dragging her to the front of the flock, "you will tell your brothers and sisters what your sin is. Then we will all pray for you."

"Damnation!" Wren spit. "Well, if you must know, I play cards." As an afterthought, she added, "On Sunday."

"Heathen woman!" Bascom admonished, aghast at her words. "If you promise to mend your ways now, this moment, in front of my flock, I will not have you punished at day's end."

"But why should I do that? I always win. I don't want to give up my evil ways. I enjoy a good game of cards and a glass of wine. That doesn't make me a sinner and I don't wish to repent. Call my brother and let me out of here," she demanded.

"All in good time. All in good time." Bascom rubbed his hands together. "For now, you will kneel and pray. I shall go on deck and speak to your brother myself. I shall tell him of your wicked ways and that I'm going to purge your very soul and welcome you into the Lord's hands."

The moment the hatch had closed on Bascom, Sara was at Wren's side, her mother with her. "I see you and I hear you, but I don't believe it," Sara said coolly. "How could you hold me up for ridicule before everyone and say I was expelled from school? What are you doing here and why are you dressed that way? I thought by now you'd be married to Malcolm and that both of you would be living the life of leisure and luxury." She felt ill as she waited for Wren's reply. She had to know what had happened to Malcolm.

"Malcolm is . . . was . . . actually, Malcolm is . . . dead," Wren began lowering her eyes in chaste Puritan fashion "He developed some sort of . . . of pox and just . . . he just died. In my arms," she added hastily. "I decided it was time for a little adventure, and the . . . opportunity to sail on Caleb's ship came up and I jumped at it. As for these clothes, I've always had a secret desire to dress like this. Is there anything else you want to know, Sara Stoneham?"

Not for the world or for every ounce of silver in all of England would she tell what had really happened. She wouldn't bare her soul to anyone. Sirena had always told her to carry her hurt in her gut and maintain a serene face. That way you could look at the world and let it look at you, and only that deep core within knew how wounded and hurt you really were. And she was wounded and she was hurt, but she couldn't dwell on it; otherwise it would eat her alive.

"That's a baldfaced lie if I ever heard one," Sara snapped. "Malcolm was all right several days ago. How could he have developed a pox and died?" Please, God, don't let it be true, she cried inwardly.

"And you called *me* a scatterbrain! I loved Malcolm, you know that, with all my heart. Do you think I would be sitting in this rotten hold dressed the way I am and listening to that—that—ass of a brother of yours if my dear Malcolm were alive? Well, do you?" Wren shrilled.

"Malcolm couldn't die like that. I know him—he would have fought the disease, had the best physicians Why are you doing this to me? I thought we were friends!"

"He did fight it . . . like the man he was, and I am your friend; that's why I'm telling you what happened." Wren forced a tear to her eye and let it trickle down her cheek. "I've lost him forever."

Sara wasn't about to give up. "I heard no word of an epidemic before we boarded. Poxes are passed from one person to another. Bascom would have said something. Your brother wouldn't have let us sail if there was a chance any of us might catch the disease. After all, Malcolm was in contact with all of us at the Sinclairs'."

"I know. You shouldn't sit so close to me, Sara. I held Malcolm in my arms before he . . . before he . . ." Another tear found its way to her eye and dribbled unchecked down her cheek.

169

Sara rocked back on her heels, her face ashen. "It can't be . . . it just can't be. Someone so alive as Malcolm can't be . . . dead."

Wren felt a brief stab of remorse, but it was short-lived when she remembered what Sara had said about her affair with Malcolm. While she hadn't believed it at the time, she knew now that it was the truth. "You'll live, Sara. I'm living with my grief, and if you ask that dotty brother of yours to pray for you, he will. He loves to pray for all us sinners. And you're a sinner, Sara," Wren said virtuously.

Oh, God, it can't be true, it simply can't be, Sara repeated to herself. Wren wouldn't lie to me. She must be telling the truth. Why else would she be on this Godforsaken ship bound for America? Now, what was *she* going to do? And what if her suspicions were right and she was pregnant? That was all Bascom needed to know. He would have her cast out of the community, a marked, evil woman.

Wren watched Sara and her mother return to their former places and lie down on the plank floor. Her eyes closed, almost as if she were praying. She leaned against the wall and waited for Caleb to come down the ladder to take her topside.

While Wren waited, Bascom sought out Caleb in the wheelhouse and promptly told him of his sister's plight.

Caleb was stunned. "Let me be sure I have the straight of it, Stoneham. Are you telling me my sister is in the hold, dressed like a Puritan and claiming she plays cards and cheats at them—on Sunday? And that she's tired of her devious little trick, so she says, and wants to come topside? You think you can save her from her evil ways with prayer, and you don't want me to intervene? Now, is that the straight of it?"

"Every last word, Captain van der Rhys. I know I can save her. It will take time, but I'm confident

170

that when the Lord visits me tomorrow, He'll have answers for me. Answers for your sister, too."

Caleb threw back his head and laughed. Bascom was shocked at the captain's mirth. This was certainly no laughing matter. Sara had told him van der Rhys was prone to fits, so what could he expect?

"Very well, Stoneham, I will not intervene. If my sister has embraced your religion, then she should be free to make her own decisions. You're probably right, and all she needs is prayer, an abundance of it. As for that wicked card playing, you have to break her of that. Why, her whole life could be ruined!"

"She said she wins all the time," Bascom declared piously.

"I'm sure she does, and she probably cheats, too. You have to keep a sharp eye on women these days. You're right, prayer is the answer. Good luck to you, Stoneham, and if there's anything I can do, just call on me. Give my sister my warm regards and tell her I hope she mends her wicked ways before the journey's end."

Caleb watched Bascom wind his skinny body down the ladder to the hold, and then he doubled over in laughter. "Well, Preacher," he addressed Stoneham's back, "I don't know which of you has met your match, but this should prove to be interesting, if nothing else." He laughed again, his white teeth gleaming.

In the hold, Wren sensed Bascom's presence before she opened her eyes. "Why are you standing there?" she demanded. "Take me topside to my brother."

"Your brother has asked me to deliver a message to you. He said to give you his warm regards, and since you have embraced our faith, he knows you will mend your wicked ways with prayer. Your brother is a sensible man, even if he takes fits."

"Fits! What are you saying? Take me topside or I'll go myself!" Wren shouted, getting to her feet, only to be pushed back onto the hard planks.

"Don't you understand? You aren't going topside at all. You're to remain here with us so we can pray for you and purge your soul. Your brother does not want you up above. Now, do you understand?"

"I understand, all right. It's you who doesn't understand. Isn't it time for the Lord to pay you another visit? You better get ready while I leave. You can pray and purge someone else."

"You're worse off than I thought. Make up your mind that you aren't leaving here. If necessary, I'll have you tied up by some of the men."

For the first time since boarding the ship, Wren felt a stab of fear. This crazy man meant every word he said. Perhaps when he slept, she could sneak up the ladder. After all, her passage had been paid for; she wasn't a prisoner. That's what I'll do, she decided. I'll give in to him now, and as soon as he falls asleep, I'll leave.

Almost as if he could read her mind, Bascom told her, "If you have any thoughts of sneaking away while I sleep, you can cast them from your mind. Members of my flock will guard you. This is for your own good, and your brother agrees, so you might as well come to terms with our decision. Now, let me get my Bible and we'll read aloud—together."

Angry beyond words, Wren lashed out with her arm, which was immediately pinned to her side, Bascom's face within inches of hers. She smelled his stale breath and saw his limp, stringy hair hanging down his cheeks as if through a magnifying glass. His eyes took on a glassy look, like that of the card players to whom Malcolm had lost her. She felt his hand move up her arm to her shoulder and then down to the swell of her breasts. He moaned slightly as his breath caught in his throat. "Are you a fallen woman, too?" he asked hoarsely, saliva moistening the corners of his mouth.

"Not till now," Wren said through clenched teeth as

she forced his hand from her bosom. "I think your calling is prayer, and you can leave the lovemaking to those who know how to go about it."

The blow Wren received was hard and fast, coming straight across her face. Her head reeled as she tried to bring her eyes into focus, and she was amazed to see that not one of the preacher's flock was looking at them. They were like trained animals, she thought wildly as she again fought off his searching hands. No one would ever touch her body again unless she permitted it, and this perverted man of God was not going to lay a finger on her. She cupped her hands together into one large fist, and aiming directly at his chin, sent him sprawling backward. Like a cat, she crouched quickly over him. "If you ever touch me again with so much as a finger, I'll kill you." She lowered her voice to a bare whisper. "I've killed before, and I'll have no qualms about doing it again. Now, do *we* understand, Preacher? If my brother doesn't want me topside, that's all right, but that doesn't give you the right to think you can take liberties with my person. You can pray till the moon is full, but don't expect me to do the same. And as for your flock members, remember this. Once you kill one person, it's easy with the others. Now, if you'll excuse me." She grimaced, then made her way back to her own secluded corner. When she sat down, she was trembling from head to foot. God in Heaven, what had she gotten herself into? Damn you, Caleb, she muttered to herself, all the while keeping her eyes on Bascom Stoneham. Her stomach churned and her breathing was rapid, her pulse quick. Old Lottie had told her about men like Bascom when she was a child, and she had never forgotten. They were sick in their heads, Lottie had said. Visits from the Lord, indeed! Wren sniffed.

Bascom's eyes were dangerously cold when he stumbled to his feet. As cold and malignant as a

173

snake's. It was just as well Wren couldn't see them from this distance. If she had, she would not have slept a wink that night.

One day ran into the next, with Wren becoming more hostile toward the ranting preacher. He forbade her to go topside with the others for the usual afternoon airing; instead, he made her kneel for hours on end, although she refused to pray aloud. If it were the last thing she did before she died, she would make Caleb pay for the humiliation Bascom was making her suffer. It wasn't as if she didn't believe in God—she did—and she prayed daily in her own way. Unfortunately, she thought morosely, He wasn't seeing fit to answer her prayers. She would have to take matters into her own hands, as she had done in Malcolm's room when she had killed the card player and wounded Malcolm.

The body stench in the close confines of the hold was making her nauseous, and she had seen Sara vomit more than once. Bad weather had prevented Bascom from taking his flock topside for its daily allotment of fresh air. Wren was sick of it all. She was sick of Bascom, sick of Sara with her vacant eyes, sick of Mrs. Stoneham and her simpering expression. Only Lydia, Bascom's wife, appeared to be normal —or what passed for normal, Wren thought. Lydia had given up her airing three days ago and knelt with Wren in the position of prayer. Later she had tried to explain her husband to Wren, who had scoffed at her. Tears had gathered in Lydia's hyacinth eyes and she had gone on to say Bascom was different and that one had to get used to his strange ways.

"Never!" Wren had exploded. "He's insane. Why do you put up with him?"

Lydia had cried, great heart-rending sobs, and said she had nowhere to go and no one to turn to. Bascom

174

provided a roof over her head and food for her stomach.

"But there's more to life than a roof and food," Wren had protested. "You're young and healthy and strong. There are other men who would take care of you and love you. Take Peter, for instance. I've seen the way he looks at you when he brings us food."

When Lydia had returned to the other side of their quarters to see to Sara, who was retching wildly, Wren had sighed and blessed herself. "The devil made me do it, God. She deserves better than that fanatic. Help her. If You can't see Your way to helping me, then help Lydia."

Now, satisfied with repeating these same prayers, Wren settled back into a sitting position, withdrew her deck of cards and looked at the colorful squares. Damnation. Here she had the tools to win a fortune, and she was locked up like a common criminal. If she could just figure out a way to get her hands on Bascom's hoard of money, she would be set for life. The heavy pouch of gold he kept tied around his waist was the only thing that prevented him from going over the side of the quarterdeck rail in a strong wind. He was so thin and brittle that he would have taken to the wind like a dry leaf. Besides getting even with Caleb, Wren promised herself that somehow she would leave the ship with Bascom's cache. Lydia had said that as soon as he reached America he was going to have a stonemason carve his likeness for his new church. America didn't need a likeness of Bascom, not if she had the real thing. If Wren could persuade Lydia to bolt, she would share Bascom's wealth with her. The idea seemed more than fair to Wren, and she smirked to herself as she slid the deck of cards into her pocket.

Chapter Eleven

The *Sea Siren* rode high on the waves as she dipped and rocked amid the white-capped peaks. Although it was high noon, the sky was black and threatening, the wind buffeting wildly. Caleb cast an anxious eye at the crow's-nest and the man in it trying valiantly to gain a secure hold on the rigging. All hands kept their eyes peeled on Caleb, knowing instinctively by a nod, a shrug, a movement of his leg, what he wanted them to do, since his voice couldn't carry over the wind.

All thoughts fled from Caleb's mind as the storm gained in intensity. He felt strangely exhilarated by the force of the elements and knew he had a battle on his hands. The tang of the salt air was like a balm as he gripped the wheel, the wind howling through the rigging and the close-reefed sails. Gigantic swells, whipped into curly white combers by the gale, rolled in continuously from the north. Spindrift flew in flakes, stinging his face as he fought to master the wheel. Hands gripping the slick, stout mechanism, which was nearly as tall as he, Caleb stood erect, man and ship brazening nature. Lightning flashed, illuminating the dark, spectral clouds scudding across the sky. Rain had not yet begun to pelt the decks, but it was out there, waiting. Making ready for the onslaught, Caleb lashed himself to the wheel as Sirena had taught him to do.

Minutes seemed hours and hours an eternity. The storm now raged in full fury. Blinded by the savage downpour, Caleb kept the ship true to her heading. His body was battered by the elements; his hair beat against his face and twisted about his neck like insistent, strangling fingers. When his physical strength began to ebb, an iron determination to survive became his mainstay. Nothing would stop him from conquering this storm. He had ridden out worse in the *Siren* and always lived to sail another day.

Below decks, Bascom braced himself in the confines of the hold, the wind and rain pounding in his ears. His flock was kneeling in prayer of its own accord. Most of the Puritans had never been on a ship before or been exposed to this monster that was howling and shrieking above. They held on to each other, secure in another's touch. Bascom himself was elated, and his eyes gleamed in the flickering light. This was God's way of punishing all sinners. And the biggest sinner in his flock was Wren van der Rhys. He would take her topside in the storm, and if she survived, then she would know that she was one of God's chosen few and that He forgave her her sins. Bascom knew she was a harlot, a jezebel, a tainted woman. She had probably lain with a hundred men. He knew it as sure as he knew his name was Bascom Stoneham, messenger of the Lord.

He would drag her forcibly by the scruff of the neck, if necessary, to the quarterdeck and make her kneel there, her eyes and head raised to Heaven, and if she still refused to pray to the Lord, he would do it for her.

A vision was coming to him and he closed his eyes. He saw Wren kneeling on the slippery deck, her arms reaching out . . . to him . . . to help her. Her clothes were ripped and tattered, her breasts bared, one long leg and thigh silken from the slick rain. He was helping her . . . His breathing became ragged and his eyes narrowed to slits as the ache in his loins grew more pronounced. When he felt the exquisite release of pain, he would know the Lord had purged her soul.

Wren flailed out with both fists when Bascom bent down to drag her to her feet. "Take your hands off me. Help me, somebody!" she shrieked to be heard over the crashing waves that beat against the ship. "I'll kill you, you lecherous bastard!" she screamed as she lashed out with her foot to give Bascom's stick-thin leg a vicious kick. No one made a move to help her. All of them would merely stand by and allow this crazy person to take her topside in the storm. She screamed her protests and continued her struggles, to no avail.

She was almost comical in her entreaty as she prayed to the real God to help her. "Please, God, don't forsake me now; deliver me from this madman who is bent on killing me." Bascom was shouting for his God to purge her soul, that he was doing everything in his power to follow the instructions of his visitation.

Caleb was stunned when he saw the two figures hurl themselves onto the deck. Now, what in the name of holy hell was going on? He tried vainly to see if any of his men were about, but all were secure in their posts and following his previous orders. He couldn't leave the wheel. All he could do was watch the macabre scene below. His ears rang with Wren's cries for help, and for the first time in his life he felt powerless. His heart hammered in his chest, not from the storm, but from fear for Wren.

Bascom lost his hold on the screaming girl when a wave leapt the side and crashed down upon them.

Wren struck out and grabbed at a water barrel standing next to a heavy tack box. She managed, amid the vicious downpour, to wedge herself between them and at the same time loop the thick ropes around her wrists. She hung on for dear life, the waves and the rain beating against her like a drum.

Bascom was shouting words and prayers to his God, words and prayers which sounded obscene to Wren's dulled mind.

Lightning raced across the sky like a fleet-footed runner, and Caleb saw a swell coming and groaned. She would drown or be washed over the side by the force of the water. He drew in his breath as the rain lashed against him, beating him, clutching at him, trying to claim him, trying to claim Wren. Caleb wasn't a religious man, calling on God only when he felt the need, and those times had been few and far between, but he prayed now. Please save her. Surely He would hear that it wasn't a prayer for himself.

Wren had seen the wave at the same time Caleb had, and she drew in a mighty breath. She had to hold on. She wedged herself tighter between the barrel and the tack box till the rough wood cut into her ribs. It was all she could do. The rest was in His hands. Her eyes were tightly closed, and so she missed Bascom's departure from the quarterdeck to the stern rail as the elements washed him from her sight.

Caleb watched helplessly from his position at the wheel. He saw Bascom being swept along and saw Wren's indrawn breath. If she could just hold on long enough and not lose her grip, she might make it. The tightness in his shoulders was the scaring pain of a branding iron.

The ship heaved with the force of the swells; the masts groaned with the weight of the saturated rigging. Rhythmically, the *Siren* rose and fell as she rode the turbulent waves. Caleb guided the vessel from the trough to the crest of each gigantic wave. For moments the *Siren* would balance dizzily on the crest, then plunge steeply into the next trough as though dropping off the edge of the world.

For hours the storm persisted, each hour an eternity that took his toll on Wren and Caleb. He couldn't see her, didn't know if she was alive or dead. She could have been washed overboard. As for that preaching emissary of the Lord, he had to be dead. Nobody that evil—and Caleb had decided he was evil—deserved to live. But Caleb had never lost a man at sea. How would he explain to Sirena and Regan that he had let Wren go overboard? They would never understand, nor would they ever forgive him. Especially Regan, who loved Wren as if she were his own flesh and blood. Regan would pierce him accusingly with those agate eyes of his. Regan would never forgive him.

He experienced a loss that he had never known before. Wren. How well he remembered the feel of her, the warmth of her slim body. Even then he had realized he wanted to know her better, the way a man knows a woman. The way Regan knew Sirena.

He felt helpless. He was more tired than he'd ever been in his life. There was no sign of the storm's abating. How much longer could he take this torture? As long as necessary, an inner voice answered. His shoulders slumped and his head rested on his chest. He couldn't be beaten, wouldn't be. Imperceptibly his shoulders straightened, and with every ounce of willpower he possessed, he raised his dark head. His body leaning against the wheel, he could feel the burn marks on his rib cage from the lines holding him, and he knew that when he removed his hands from the wheel, his skin would be torn and bloody. He could bear the physical pain, but he would carry the hurt in his soul for the rest of his life. The thought of Wren's body being hurled about beneath the relentless tides was more than he could bear. A single, lone tear formed in his eye and clung to the lash. Only once

180

before could he ever remember a tear coming to his eye, and that had been when Sirena had told him Regan was his father. The tear had clung precariously to his thick lash and somehow, miraculously, found its way back into his eye. No one had even seen that tear; no one had known his gut-searing joy on hearing those words. His great head slumped and he felt the tear drop from his lash. He had shed his first tear. And he had shed it for a woman. No one would ever know that except him. In that moment he understood he would have given his life if Wren could have been saved. He couldn't love her, could he? He barely knew her, but in some strange way he had always been drawn to her. Ever since the first time he had seen her.

Caleb had gone to visit Sirena and had been in the library of her London town house when Frau Holtz had entered with an enchanting little girl at her side, dressed all in pink. The first time he had ever heard her name, Sirena had said it. "Come here, Wren. There's someone I want you to meet. He comes from the Spice Islands and his name is Caleb. He is Mynheer van der Rhys' son."

Wren had been staring at him, oblivious of the new frock she wanted to model for Sirena. She had moved toward him slowly and asked softly, in her little girl's voice, "Do you know the Sea Siren?" Her brown-gold eyes had been lit from within like tapering candle flames.

Caleb had laughed, his strong, white teeth catching the light. "I know the story very well. She was a beautiful lady." He had taken a step closer and dropped to his knee. "I think she was almost as beautiful as you are," he had said, taking her hand and bringing it to his lips. His smiling eyes had sobered as he had gazed at her.

When she had spoken, it had been quietly, and her

words had startled both Frau Holtz and Sirena. "I hope the man the Sea Siren loved looked like you."

Caleb had temporarily torn his gaze away from Wren and glanced at Sirena. After a brief period he had whispered, "I hope he looked like me. I would be proud to have someone like the Sea Siren love me."

Wren had smiled, a knowing smile, adult beyond her years. "When I grow up, I'm going to be like the Sea Siren. Then I can . . ." She had hesitated. "Will you wait for me to grow up?"

Wait for me . . . wait for me . . . The words echoed in his head, words said by a little girl, in a little girl's voice; yet, as they gathered in intensity, they became the words of a young woman with a woman's voice, and they resounded over and over in his head. *Wait for me . . . wait for me . . .* And the words became the song of the sirens who beckoned to sailors at sea.

The storm persisted in its outrageous assault on the *Sea Siren* for another twelve hours. Caleb had long since slumped against the wheel, believing he was half dead. Yet his numb arms continued to steer the ship to a safe course through the swells and stinging spray.

An hour before dawn the storm wore itself out and the waters calmed to a mere boil. Peter, the first mate, and Harkin, the second mate, untied Caleb from the shoulder-high wheel and carried him to his cabin. Farrington was called in. He looked at Caleb with awe and pity and immediately set to work. No matter what he had ever said or done, the old man loved Caleb like a son. He performed healing ministrations to the best of his ability and sat back to wait.

When Harkin next appeared in the captain's quarters, he was carrying Wren's limp body. Farrington raised his gray brows in astonishment. The second mate gently placed Wren on the bunk opposite Caleb and spoke in a somber tone. "I don't know if she's even alive. I found her half in and half out of the tack box. Her shoulder's been wrenched by the rigging and has to be snapped back in. I've seen it done, but I could never be the one to make her suffer that pain. And while she's lying here more dead than alive, that preacher's out on deck, hale and hearty, praying for our souls. He's saying we're all going to Hell and it's up to him to save us from the devil's clutches. I want permission from someone, now that the captain is laid up, to throw him overboard."

Farrington waved Harkin away, his gaze intent on Wren. He peered down at her white face and noticed that the bodice of her gown was torn, revealing deep red welts peppering her sides. Her ribs were bruised at best, if not broken. Harkin was right. She was more dead than alive, her breathing ragged and raspy. Yet if her shoulder was to be snapped to, no better time to do it than when she didn't know what was happening to her.

"Harkin, come over here and help me with her. And if you're not man enough to make a good job of it, send me someone who is. I'll hold her neck and shoulder, you do what must be done with her arm. And make a good job of it, man, or it's the captain you'll be answering to." Aubrey's voice was gruff and revealed little of the pity he was feeling for Wren. His knowledge of medicine was limited, and he relied on common-sense remedies. Warm blankets, hot tea, bindings for the wounds and tender, loving care.

Farrington was unwavering in his care of the young couple as he tended and mended their battered bodies as best he could. Both spoke in delirium from time to time. Wren would cry out pitifully, "Caleb, help me!" And the man in the next bunk seemed to answer her. "Wren! I'll wait for you . . . Wren!" his cries tortured and heart-rending.

Though exhausted from bathing their fevers and changing the dressings on their wounds, Farrington refused the help of the crew and spurned the suggestion that one of the women from below assist him in his care of Caleb and Wren. He would allow no one to touch them save himself, and he spent the long hours stretched out on the floor between their bunks.

By the end of the third day Caleb was lucid but in severe pain. Aubrey grew fearful. "Cal, it is I, Aubrey. You must lie still. You've been ill for days with a raging fever. I'm almost sure your ribs are broken, but I couldn't chance taping you up for fear I would do something wrong and pierce a lung. I'll do it now, but you must remain still. Cal, do you understand me? Just nod your head." Caleb nodded weakly. Sensing his need to talk, Aubrey warned him not to make the effort till he was bandaged and resting comfortably. Again Caleb nodded.

He was as weak as a newborn infant and barely had the strength to lift his head. Aubrey had to balance his shoulder and neck as he wrapped strips of cloth around his rib cage. The effort left Caleb exhausted, and he fell into his first natural sleep. The old dandy sighed. Caleb would be hale and hearty in good time. It was the girl who worried him. By now she should have come around. There were periods when she was so still, so pale, locked in the embrace of a deep, unnatural sleep, and other times when she would cry out for Caleb to help her.

When Caleb awoke the following day, the first thing he heard was Wren's voice calling to him. For a moment he was back in the thick of the storm, lashed to the wheel, hearing her cries for help. His tortured eyes sought out Farrington's. The old gambler pointed a finger at the other bunk, and Caleb's eyes widened in shock. The enormity of what he was seeing hit him full force. She was alive—and calling for him! He struggled weakly to get up, and the pain that shot through him brought him back down on the hard bedding. "Tell me, Aubrey, how bad is she?" he rasped faintly.

Farrington shrugged. "I'm no physician, Cal. I

think she may be dying. She's been calling your name, but that's all she says. Her fever's been raging, just like yours was, but you met your crisis and conquered it. Her ribs are bruised and her shoulder was dislocated, though not too severely. Harkin and I saw to setting it, but I can't say we didn't do her any harm. She's been developing chills these past few hours, and I've covered her with as many blankets as I could lay my hands on. Harkin keeps me supplied with heated bricks from the galley, but nothing seems to help. There isn't much more I can do. I'm sorry, Caleb."

"It's my fault. I never should have let that preacher get his hands on her. There must be *something* you can do," he pleaded.

"All we can do is wait," Farrington said miserably.

"To wait is to see her die," Caleb moaned. Then he remembered when Sirena's son Mikel had been ill and had violent chills. She had taken his small form into the bed with her and held him close. Her body warmth had been all the small boy had needed, and the chills had soon ended. His mind refused to remember that little Mikel had died two days later. Wren wouldn't die! She couldn't die!

"Bring her here, Aubrey, and place her beside me. Don't look at me like that, you old fox. My body warmth is all we have. Strip her down. I can't get her warm if she's wrapped in those sweat-dampened rags. Be gentle and be careful, Aubrey."

Ignoring his pain, Caleb slid over close to the wall to make room for Wren. The effort of his movement left him breathless and lightheaded.

Aubrey gently laid the girl beside Caleb and discreetly looked the other way while Caleb enfolded her in his arms. He cradled her next to him and murmured soft words which were indistinguishable to Farrington. The gambler decided it was time to go topside; he wouldn't watch what wasn't meant for his eyes. Only men hopelessly in love looked as Caleb had when he had taken the shivering girl in his arms.

"Caleb, help me," It was the barest whisper, and he almost failed to hear it. He held her closer, careful of her injuries.

"I'm here, Wren, I'm here."

Throughout the long, endless day Wren cried out for Caleb and he would answer, his mouth pressed against her ear. His strong, sinewy arms enfolded her, and from time to time he kissed her cheek in tenderness.

During the night, as her chills began to abate and her sleep became lighter, her words became clearer as she cried for Caleb. He listened to them, his heart breaking for her as, bit by bit, the episode concerning Malcolm came to light. At first he hadn't understood when she had whimpered with fear. But as the night wore on and he continued to whisper words of comfort, she told him about Malcolm's losing her in a card game to the rough and surly seamen. Her eyes squeezed shut as though she were reliving the horror of the rape; she breathed the words over and over. Only the sound of Caleb's voice seemed to assuage her as he gentled away her tremors. Toward dawn, Wren seemed disposed to answering simple questions, and Caleb knew without a doubt that the horror she had described was much more than a nightmare. It was the horror of truth.

Hatred boiled in his heart when he thought of Malcolm and what perfidy he had enacted upon Wren's innocence. The desire to kill, crush, destroy, throbbed through his veins. He tried to tell himself he was experiencing the reaction of any brother who has learned that his sister was used and raped. But as Wren settled into a more natural sleep and nestled her body closer to his, drawing strength from the warmth he offered, he realized his pain went much deeper than that of a brother. With very little persuasion, he could love

186

Wren. He could erase the tortures she had undergone in her first physical contact with a man. The inner strength of Wren's ability to live with that violence filled him with awe and respect. He himself had witnessed the devastation that rape could have on a woman. He had been with Sirena through the worst of her trials, and he was familiar with the courage and resiliency that were necessary to go on with life.

Remembering what had been enacted upon Sirena and imagining what had been done to Wren, Caleb wrapped his arms more protectively about the girl who slept so trustingly in his arms, a haze of moisture in his eyes making a nimbus of the single lantern light flickering in the darkness.

By midafternoon of the following day Wren's fever had broken. Caleb climbed gingerly from the bunk, careful not to disturb her. She was sleeping her first natural sleep since the storm. He held his bruised sides carefully and motioned Farrington, who had peered in to check on them, to go topside.

After dressing, Caleb stood looking down at Wren, a great lump in his throat threatening to choke off his air as he remembered the things she had told him the night before. Again a surge of protectiveness swept over him, existing simultaneously with the hatred he felt for Malcolm Weatherly. His hand reached out to brush away a stray lock of hair that had fallen over her cheek, but he quickly withdrew it. He wouldn't allow himself to feel anything other than brotherly toward her. Wren needed time to heal, not to find herself thrown into the midst of another love affair. After what she had suffered, how could she ever learn to trust another man? It had taken Sirena what had seemed a lifetime to overcome the memories of what she had suffered before she could admit her love for Regan and go into his arms with trust and confidence.

Caleb told himself he had no time for waiting

games. Wren was his sister, or close to it, he amended. He would find his satisfaction with a woman who would understand his need was just for that. For satisfaction. If Wren wanted someone to talk with, he would be there for her. He couldn't allow his feelings for her, which were dangerously beyond those of a friend or a brother, to get the better of him.

Once out on deck, Caleb walked on wobbly legs to the wheelhouse to see how his first mate was faring. Satisfied that the ship was still keeping a true course, he made his way with Farrington to the quarterdeck. In a voice the gambler had never heard before, Caleb thanked him for his aid and for ministering to Wren.

"There's no need for thanks, Cal. I saw my duty and I did it. You would have done the same for me," Aubrey said offhandedly.

"What you say is true, Aubrey. But this is the second time you've stepped in and come to my rescue. The first time was in the Owl's Eye Inn, when I was about to be rolled by the doxie's accomplices. I'm in your debt."

"Just get me to Martinique, where I can unload this store of riches that has fallen into my hands. That's all I want from you, Cal. You've been like a son to me. Oh, I know you lose patience with me, and sometimes I'm insufferable, but if there's one thing you must believe, it's that you are truly like a son." There was an almost humble note in the old man's voice, and Caleb was surprised. Just when he thought he had the old fox figured out, Farrington did something that cancelled all his previous wrongs.

Well, he didn't have time to worry about Farrington now. Now he had to concern himself with Wren and how he was going to get her back to Sirena and Regan. And then, he thought to himself murderously, I'll get that bastard Stoneham and wring his goddamn skinny neck till he looks like a dead chicken! There was little he could do about Weatherly until he returned to England, but he swore he would seek him out if it took a lifetime. And when he found him, Weatherly would curse the day he had ever set eyes on Wren.

Back in his quarters, he leaned over the sleeping girl till he had assured himself her breathing was deep and normal. She had a little coloring in her cheeks and he knew she would mend, perhaps not as quickly as he had, but she was alive and would continue to stay that way if he had anything to do with the matter.

Slowly he descended the ladder into the hold of the ship and found himself in the midst of a prayer meeting. Rage coursed through him at the fanatical look on Bascom Stoneham's face. Without stopping to think, he reached for the prayer book Bascom was reading from and flung it across the wooden floor. Gasps and sharp exclamations of horror rang in his ears.

"I've met fools in my day, but none your equal," Caleb growled. "Do you realize you could have killed Wren by taking her topside during a storm? It's a miracle either of you is alive! From now on, you and the others will stay here in the hold. It matters little to me if you like it or not. I've given orders to my men to report to me immediately the first time one of you sets foot on deck. Do we understand each other, Stoneham?"

"Heathen unbeliever!" Bascom cried piously. "Your sister needed to be purged for her wrongdoings, and what better time than during one of the Lord's miracles of nature? You yourself just said it was a miracle we both survived, and that's exactly what it was—a miracle! If you no longer wish us to go on deck, then we will stay below with the rats. But I want to implore you to take pity on my sister and allow her a little fresh air daily. She's been ailing since the start of the voyage, and nothing we do seems to help. Sara," he called, "come here."

Sara rose to her feet and walked slowly toward her brother and Caleb. She tried to smile, but her stomach

189

felt so queasy she gave it up and grimaced as though in pain. Caleb frowned. If he did what the preacher asked, he would be running a damn nursery. Sara did look ill, though. He couldn't leave her down here with her brother and not feel guilty.

"Very well, she goes topside with me." There was no need to tell Bascom that he would quarter her in his cabin with Wren. The less that God-fearing gentleman knew, the better off everyone would be.

Sara followed Caleb docilely up the ladder and trailed him to his cabin. She showed no emotion at the sight of Wren asleep in the bunk, and Caleb thought it strange that she, as Wren's friend, did not inquire after her health. It seemed as if Sara had blindly accepted whatever story Bascom had told his congregation regarding Wren and the storm and his part in her near death.

Caleb watched Sara slide into the empty bunk and pull the cover up to her chin. The dark hollows around her eyes and the decidedly green cast to her complexion evoked in him a thread of pity for her mal de mer. The girl looked almost gaunt, and he found himself hoping it was only seasickness that was troubling her. The last thing he needed aboard ship was an outbreak of typhoid or the plague. He was about to reconsider the judiciousness of placing Sara in the same cabin with Wren when he saw her eyes close in a kind of painful sleep. Unable to bring himself to disturb her again, Caleb settled himself on a tack box and thrust his legs out before him, careful not to place undue pressure on his bound midsection. A little warm air, a mug of rum and a dash of sunshine were all he needed, and before long he would be in fine fettle.

Chapter Twelve

Aubrey Farrington was fast losing his patience with Malcolm Weatherly. "You'll live," he said callously. "You have no choice; you knew that when I made the arrangements to bring you aboard. You agreed; it's as simple as that."

"Listen to me, you weasel. I've had about all of this that I can stand. I need some hot food and fresh air. This locker box is like a hellish pit, and if you don't figure some way to get me out at night and filch me some decent food, I'll kill you," Malcolm threatened. "It's as simple as that."

A chill washed over Farrington. Weatherly was brutally ugly. Gone were his dashing good looks and his debonair manner. Now he was scarred, his eye blinded and a vicious, crusting scab running the length of his face. His once elegant manners were now those of a hunted animal. "I'll see what I can do, but I'll make no promises. Caleb is resting on deck. If the opportunity presents itself, I'll smuggle you some hot food. As for the fresh air, it depends on who is about and standing watch. I told you all this in the beginning and warned you there would be days when you would go hungry. You agreed. If you want to jeopardize all of our efforts, do it. Cal will have you shackled down here, and then where will you be? In case you aren't familiar with the nautical mind, let me tell you that this locker box is a brig when the occasion demands it."

Weatherly's lip curled and he stifled the urge to lash out at the old man. He couldn't allow him to have the last word. "Then see to getting me some clean clothes. These rags aren't fit for the likes of me. They smell," he said curtly.

Aubrey Farrington did not reply as he walked out the door. Some people were ignorant beyond insult, he muttered to himself as he threw the heavy iron bolt on the outside door. He smiled at the terminal sound. If he had his way, that sod would rot in there and no one would be the wiser. Only he would know. Himself and his maker, and as his years were drawing to a close, he knew he had better stay on the straight and narrow if he wished a seat in Heaven. He wasn't exactly a religious man, calling on his God only in times of stress—acute stress. He was, however, superstitious, as were most gamblers. He smiled and wrinkled his nose. Weatherly was right. Rotten fish smelled better than he did.

Back on deck, Farrington approached Caleb and was told about Sara.

"I'll be taking over your cabin; that means you move in with the crew," Caleb said firmly, disregarding Farrington's look of displeasure at being ousted from his small, comfortable cabin. "And if you see that bastard Stoneham step one foot off that ladder, call me immediately. I've already alerted the crew. And, Aubrey, I want you to see to the women's wellbeing. Take their food to them and keep an eye on Wren. It will be a couple of days before she can walk the decks. I'm placing their care in your hands. I don't know what ails the Stoneham girl, but I'm sure you'll find a remedy."

Farrington heard the ring of iron in Cal's voice and knew better than to protest. He had seen the tired look in his dark eyes and realized his friend was in pain. But now Aubrey had to be both a jailer and a wet nurse!

Later that evening, while Sara was out on deck, Caleb let himself into his former cabin to look in on Wren. She was lying on the bunk, her slight form barely making a mound beneath the coverlets, her face pale and wan against the pillows. Yet she gathered her strength and smiled up at him, the gratitude in her eyes magically kindling them to flames.

"I'm glad to see you looking alive. How does your shoulder feel?" he asked her, tenderness in his voice.

"Much better, thank you," she whispered, her eyes never leaving his face.

"Have you everything you want? Are you thirsty?"

Wren nodded in affirmation. He lifted her gently to a half-raised position and placed a glass near her lips. She sipped slowly, barely having the strength to swallow. "You shouldn't be alone; I'll have someone come and stay with you." Just as gently he lowered her to the pillow and moved toward the door.

"Caleb, wait," she said hoarsely, her voice weak and thready.

Almost as though he knew what she was going to say, he hesitated in returning to her side. He crossed the cabin slowly, trying to assume some of his old swagger in spite of his injuries. But he realized it would be better to have it said than to keep running from it. If anything, it would be more painful for her than for him.

"Caleb, I . . . I have the feeling that I've . . . did I say anything to you about . . . about . . ." It seemed impossible for her to voice the words. It was unnecessary. From the pain in his eyes she knew she hadn't been dreaming. She had told him everything about

Malcolm, or at least enough for him to put the pieces together to comprehend what had happened to her.

"Caleb, I couldn't bear it if you turned away from me. Do I disgust you?" she asked weakly, the effort of speaking nearly taking her breath away.

Instantly he was down on one knee, his face close to hers. "Never," he assured her, his voice threatening to break. "I think you are the bravest, most courageous girl . . ." It was impossible to continue.

"I know what happened to the Sea Siren. Frau Holtz told me. And I knew that if she could go on with her life, so could I. But I couldn't bear to have you look at me with pity, Caleb. That is all I ask of you."

"Never, Wren, only with admiration. And I promise you something else. When I get back to England, I'll search out that bastard and make him pay for what he's done to you. I swear it. He'll never draw another breath once I find him, no matter what it takes." The vindictiveness in his voice frightened her, and she calmed him with a light touch to his cheek.

"Hush. There's no need for that. Every time Malcolm looks into a mirror he'll remember what his lust cost him." Slowly, and with great effort, she insisted on telling him what she had done to escape the seamen and Malcolm. She admitted killing the ruffian and waited breathlessly for a look of horror to fill Caleb's eyes. When she saw only respect and admiration mirrored there, she relaxed and felt cleansed by her confession.

"Sleep now, little one," he told her, placing a gentle hand on her forehead, afraid that the strain of their conversation would mean the return of her fever.

Obediently she closed her eyes. Just before he stepped out of the cabin, she called to him. "Will you come and see me again?"

In that long moment before he answered her, sleep

claimed her, and her face became peaceful and serene.

Two days short of a fortnight found both Sara and
Wren up and about. Caleb, completely mended, had
resumed his duties as captain of the *Sea Siren.*

It was an hour past noon when Wren looked deeply
into Aubrey Farrington's eyes and said, "Thank you
for saving my life. I'll never forget it. I don't know
how I can ever repay you for what you've done and
for the care you've given me."

Aubrey blinked and frowned slightly at her words,
and at that precise moment Wren won a permanent
place in his heart. She looked different to him somehow. More womanly, more sure of herself. He hadn't
known her before, but she had had the face of a girl
when Harkin had carried her into Caleb's cabin. He
couldn't explain it, and he was probably thinking
through his hat, as Caleb called it. So he would mark
it down to a foolish old man's wandering mind. Or
did he have some preconceived opinions of her because Caleb had said she was flighty, irresponsible,
spoiled, and had a tongue as sharp as any shrew on
the wharf?

"You owe me no thanks. I did what anyone else
would have done. You owe your true thanks to Caleb.
He is the one who saved your life and knew what to
do when your fever reached a peak. I was out of my
depth, but he wasn't. You should be talking to him
and not me."

Sara sat quietly and listened to the exchange between Wren and the gambler. She was puzzled. She
and Wren had spoken very little since the day Caleb
had brought her up here. Wren slept for long periods,
and when she did awaken, she seemed to prefer her
own company and to remain quiet. Sara didn't really
feel like talking either, and, at best, the long silences
were companionable. She wondered if she should

confide in Wren, tell her what she feared. Sometimes it helped to talk to someone, even stupid, frivolous Wren. Once she had tried and been stunned at the look in Wren's eyes. But Wren wasn't a silly schoolgirl any longer. She seemed different now, more assured . . . more womanly. Besides, what could Wren do except listen and then make a cutting remark, as had been her custom when she didn't like something? But Sara didn't think she could bring herself to tell Wren that the child she carried was Malcolm Weatherly's child. She couldn't. Then what was she to do? If Bascom ever found out, God in his Heaven couldn't save her.

She shuddered, and Farrington was immediately concerned, thinking she was having another attack of mal de mer. She smiled and said she was fine. He looked relieved. Taking care of two ailing women appeared to have bested the old man. Perhaps he would help her when they got to America. He was experienced, wise to the ways of the world. And old men liked young women. If she approached him carefully, she might be able to wrap him around her little finger and have him dancing to her tune. There was Caleb to consider also. After all, hadn't he taken pity on her and brought her to his very own quarters so that she could recuperate from her malaise? Caleb and the gambler seemed to be fast friends, and if she remembered correctly, at one time Wren had said they were partners. If she behaved smartly, perhaps she could pit one against the other and come out the winner. Tomorrow she would put her ideas into action and get the feel of things. Tomorrow was a new day. She needed this long night to map out a plan that would guarantee her safety from Bascom when they reached America. A plan whereby she and the child growing in her womb would have sufficient funds to enable them never to want for anything. All she needed to achieve her goal was a sound plan.

One day ran into the next, the mid-May weather becoming softer and more inviting. Sara and Wren barely spoke to each other, with Wren alternating between periods of depression and anger when she realized Caleb had made no move in her direction since she had explained what had happened to her. He had come to see her on several occasions, that was true, but only when Sara or Farrington had been in the cabin. Since she had recovered, her attempts to seek him out had not been successful. Each time she ventured near the wheelhouse, one of the crew would hurry her back to the deck, telling her the captain had no time for women's chitchat.

If it was the last thing she did before she left the ship, she would give him a piece of her mind for letting her rot in that dreadful hold with Bascom Stoneham. And if Caleb thought that helping her pass her feverish crisis served as his atonement, he was sadly mistaken. He couldn't face her. That was just like a man. He does his dirty work and then runs and hides, afraid to stand up and get his comeuppance. Well, she wouldn't let him get away with *that!*

Gulping back a well of tears, Wren hated to admit that Caleb's avoidance of her had begun just after she had told him she had killed the seaman and maimed Malcolm. How the sight of her must repel him! She had driven him away with her confession just as surely as if she'd hefted a club in his direction.

She sat in her hard wooden chair on the deck and idly played with the deck of cards Lottie had given her. Since the order had been given that none of Bascom's flock could come above, the decks were painfully absent of people walking about, conversing in hopeful voices about the new lives they were going to lead in America. Even Bascom's fire-and-brimstone preachings were missed. "Like a stone removed from my shoe," Wren muttered, refocusing her attention on the thin cards which slipped through her fingers.

She hated the idea of tricking Aubrey Farrington into a game of chance now that she had gotten to know him so well. He treated her kindly, like a grandfather, and she liked his sly smile and disarming wit. How could she bring herself to cheat him after all he had done for her? Damnation! But there was still the promise she had made to Lottie to settle an old score with Lord Farrington. She decided she would make it up to him later.

Sara appeared on deck, her sea legs making her movements graceful and unhurried. Every hand working with the rigging or sheets stopped what he was doing to watch her as she tossed her long, silvery-blond hair over her shoulders and pretended not to see the flirting looks cast her way.

Vain bitch! Wren thought uncharitably. I know she's going by the wheelhouse, I know she's going to wave to Caleb and I know he's going to wave back. The crew never stopped Sara from visiting the wheelhouse, just Wren. "Damn you, Caleb," she said viciously just as Aubrey Farrington sat down next to her, his eyes on her playing cards.

"What have we here?" he asked, a surprised look on his face.

"Aubrey!" Wren cried in surprise. "Sit down and talk to me for a while. I feel like such an outcast on this damn ship. Sara looks at me as if she's blaming me for her brother's insane behavior, and Caleb hasn't come near me since I managed to get up and walk. You're the only one who will talk to me. Sara mutters from time to time, but it's not the same as talking." Then she laughed. "I see you're looking at these cards. I like to shuffle them; it keeps my fingers limber. For when I play the spinet," she added hastily. "And I like to look at the birds on the back and imagine where they come from." At Farrington's skeptical glance, she continued. "When I was in school we studied nature and the woodland creatures, and I quite fell in love with plumed birds. So colorful and bright, they take your breath away. Don't you agree?"

"To be sure, to be sure," Aubrey said. His skepticism had changed to amusement. "Do you know how to play? Cards, I mean."

"Yes, but not very well. Ladies don't play cards. I just like the pictures of the birds. But if you want to pass some time, perhaps you could teach me what you know, and then later on we could play a real game for . . . for money. I have five pounds I could wager."

An hour later Aubrey rose and stared down at Wren. "My dear, you have a natural talent for this game. For someone who just likes to look at the backs of the cards, you did remarkably well. If we had been playing for money, you would have skinned my purse."

"Beginner's luck, Aubrey. If we had been playing for money, I doubt I could have been so lucky. Are you sure you taught me all you know? Somehow I thought card playing was more difficult."

"It's only difficult when you cheat at the game. And I would never do that," he said virtuously, raising his eyes to the heavens.

"Nor I," Wren echoed just as virtuously. "Being a cardsharp is the same as being a thief."

"You're so right, my dear. What do you say to a short stroll on deck before dinner?"

They chatted companionably as they made their rounds. When Wren saw Sara enter the wheelhouse, she faltered in her step and her eyes smoldered and sparked angrily. Then she turned abruptly, anxious to get back to her quarters, and left Farrington standing there perplexedly.

Aubrey saw Caleb nod to Sara and motion her to sit down. "It's the wrong choice, Cal," he said quietly, and wandered off.

Sara seated herself and folded her hands primly into the folds of her thick black skirts. How pale her hands looked, she thought, with their delicate tracing of blue veins. She was thin, much too thin, unable to eat for fear the rocking of the ship would make her vomit. Her liquid-blue eyes appeared to Caleb to be gentle, yet sad. What was she doing here? he wondered.

She knew she had to say something or he would begin to think her as addlepated as Bascom. "Captain van der Rhys, I've come to thank you for allowing me to stay on deck. I feel much better now that I've gotten my sea legs, and if you wish, I can return to my . . . my brother and the others."

Caleb watched her closely. Captain van der Rhys, she called him. In Tyler Sinclair's house she had called him Caleb quite freely and had openly flirted with him. Women! His voice was soft, barely above a whisper, as he replied, "I was planning on seeking you out later to see how you were faring. I feel reassured to hear you are on the mend and have your sea legs. For a while I thought I was captaining a hospital ship."

Sara moistened her lips with the tip of her tongue and gazed up at him. She was annoyed at the way he was staring at her. His eyes traveled from her mouth to her throat and down to her breasts. His face wore an amused look and his eyes were openly mocking as he made no effort to conceal his approval. It had been a long time since he had had a woman. He made a mental wager with himself that he could have her in bed within the hour.

"It's time for me to turn the wheel over to my first mate. Would you like me to show you around the *Sea Siren?*"

Sara's eyes lowered. "I'd like that very much, Captain van der Rhys."

Caleb's expression continued to be amused as he

handed over the wheel to Peter, who grinned at him knowingly.

As they strolled along the deck, Sara spoke quietly. "Does this invitation to walk with you mean you no longer find me unattractive?" It was a bold, blatant question, and Caleb answered in kind.

"I found you very attractive back in England, and I find you very attractive now. But I like to be the one who does the pursuing. I've found over the years that when a woman sets out to snare a man, she usually has some use for him. Do you, Sara Stoneham, find me useful in some way?"

Sara laughed, the first genuine laugh she had uttered in months. "And if I did, do you think I would admit it? Why don't we agree that if we were to find a convenient room with a bed, I would find you useful?"

Caleb laughed also. "I guess that means you no longer fear my fits."

Sara raised her eyes and smiled happily. "I've learned to live with many things not to my liking over the past months. I think I can learn to live with your fits." Out of the corner of her eye she noticed the openly speculative looks the seamen were giving her and Caleb. It was good that they noticed. Later she would need them to bear witness that she had lain with the captain.

Caleb's shoulders tensed as he approached Peter's cabin. His gut told him he would be sorry for this little adventure, and he almost made an excuse to turn back. But it was too late. They were already through the door, and Sara kicked it shut with her foot and leaned against it, her eyes wide with invitation. Caleb took her in his arms and she flung her arms around his neck, her lips slightly parted. He kissed her savagely, his tongue exploring the sweetness of her mouth. Then he drew away and carefully chose the words he wanted to say. "This means nothing other than what it is." His sun-bronzed hand tilted her chin upward, bringing her face to his.

"But of course. A moment of passion, of bodily release, nothing more. I understand, Caleb," she said, moving toward him and locking him in a tight embrace. The pulsating throbbing in her breasts made her cry out as she returned his ardor with total wantonness.

Their clothing in a tangled heap on the floor, Caleb lay down next to Sara and pulled her close. His movements were slow, almost lazy, as he played with her body. His mouth was brutal in its intensity as he brushed and teased her silken skin till the rosy crests became taut and erect.

Sara's tongue became a live serpent as it traced the outline of Caleb's mouth, darting inside, treasuring its warm moistness.

He kissed her eyes and neck and the hollow of her throat, where her pulse beat so wildly she thought she would faint. His hands were demanding as they swept across her thighs and found the warmth between her legs, sending her into a breathless frenzy of desire with each caress of his fingertips. When she thought she could no longer bear the feverish pitch to which he had brought her, he drove into her, again and again. Crashing waves of fire coursed through her as she cried out his name over and over.

Later, lying side by side, she stroked his cheek with gentle fingers. Perhaps now she could live again, love again and find some kind of happiness, regardless of Malcolm. Her body had responded to his passions, and that was all she needed to know for the moment. She watched Caleb's eyes close, his face content in the aftermath of their lovemaking. How well he had enjoyed her, crying out her name as she had forced his from her lips.

When sleep had overtaken him and his breathing had become deep and regular, Sara crept from the bunk and dressed quietly. She paused for a moment to stare down at him and admitted regretfully to herself that she had no feeling for Caleb other than that of physical satisfaction. He was an artful lover, demanding, overpowering, exciting, yet Malcolm would always be the man she wanted, the man she hungered for and craved. However far away from her Malcolm was in death, she would always remember the urgency of his hands, his mouth, his entire body. Her need for him went beyond the physical boundaries of sex, hers was the need of love.

Perhaps, Sara thought, in time she could learn to love Caleb van der Rhys. The next time she joined him in bed she would practice all the things Malcolm had taught her. Today was too soon. As it was, the Dutchman had been surprised to discover she was not a virgin. What would he say when he found out she was pregnant and claiming him as the father of her unborn child? It didn't matter what he thought. It mattered only what he did. Caleb van der Rhys was an honorable man. And honorable men always did what clever women said they should do.

Caleb woke, immediately aware of where he was and what had occurred between him and Sara Stoneham. He stretched his long-muscled limbs and felt them come to life. There was no denying he was much better, recovering nicely from the injuries he had sustained during the storm. A man had to be in fine fettle to satisfy a woman the way he had just satisfied Sara. He could still hear the sound of his name on her lips as one wave of passion had followed another. He smiled, self-assured that his injuries had in no way affected his performance in bed.

He supposed he should be feeling somewhat guilty about Sara. He knew he entertained no thoughts of a deeper attachment to her, except perhaps another encounter beneath the sheets. He had no desire to play

203

the part of a love-sick puppy. It had been a pleasurable interlude, and somehow he had the impression that little Miss Stoneham was more versed in the arts of love than she had let on. And he hadn't been disappointed to discover that she wasn't a virgin. Virgins, he told himself, are bothersome creatures. He was tired of breaking them in for some other man to enjoy. He'd take a woman of experience any day.

As happened so often lately, whenever his thoughts were on women, somehow they traveled to Wren. He would have to seek her out and explain to her that his plans included taking her back to Sirena and Regan, even if that meant bringing her all the way to Java. And the sooner the better. Why did he keep postponing the inevitable? Before long he would have to face her, something he had been avoiding to keep from remembering how she had felt beside him in the bunk, his arms wrapped protectively about her. How she had called his name and how he had answered. How he had buried his face in her wealth of dark hair and groaned at his inadequacy to make her well. She couldn't mean anything to him, he wouldn't allow it. She was a sister of sorts. A street urchin whom Sirena had defended and generously adopted. His only obligation to her was that of a brother bent on avenging his sister, regardless of her insistence that she had avenged herself. Then why did you give orders to the crew to bar her from the wheelhouse? a niggling voice questioned.

How well he remembered the first day he had seen Wren. The image of her as a child was almost impossible to keep from his thoughts. As well as the sound of Sirena's hushed murmur to Frau Holtz that Wren was his destiny. Why did those words persist in revolving around his head? He must not have heard correctly. How could a woman be a man's destiny? Bah! he snorted as he swung his legs over the side of the bunk.

204

One leg in his trousers, he stopped and almost fell to the floor. Sirena had been Regan's destiny. He had known it before either of them. "God, help me," he muttered as he shoved his other leg into his trousers and hastily donned his shirt. He needed fresh air and the deck beneath his feet. He needed to look at the ocean and see the breakers. The sea was his destiny, not some two-legged creature with eyes like tapered candle flames.

While Sara had whiled away her idle hours with Caleb in the first mate's bunk, her brother had been telling his flock that the sinners above deck were the devil's handiwork and he would save them all. His prayer book clutched in his bony hands, he called for each member to stand in front of him so that he could personally convince them, just by the touch of his hand, that he was the Lord's chosen messenger and, as such, would drive the devil from this ship. If necessary, he exhorted, he would captain the ship himself.

Lydia Stoneham was the first to stand before him and hold out her hand. "Please, Bascom, speak with Captain van der Rhys and ask if the women might not go on deck just for a few moments. The heat down here is unbearable and the stench is terrible. Tell him you're sorry and beg his forgiveness, if necessary." Her voice rose till it was a shrill shriek. "Damn you, ask him!"

Bascom raised his hand and hit her on the side of the head with the prayer book, stunning her briefly. "Profanity! You dare to use profanity in the presence of a messenger of the Lord! My own wife! Down on your knees, woman, and if the Lord doesn't strike you dead, you can consider yourself fortunate. My own wife! And in front of my flock!"

Lydia was beyond caring, beyond feeling. He was insane, and if he was a messenger of the Lord, then she was his disciple. "I've had enough of you and your mealy-mouthed mutterings. I can't bear another minute of it, not another minute. I'm going up that ladder and I'm never coming down again. Did you hear me, Bascom? If I have to leap overboard, I will. I'll do anything to get away from you. You're insane!" she shot over her shoulder as she gathered up her skirts and raced up the wooden ladder.

When she emerged through the hatch and stepped onto the deck above, the seaman standing guard could only regard her with surprise, unsure of what he should do. He couldn't push a woman back down the ladder. Captain van der Rhys hadn't said what he should do if a woman came up the ladder and tried to escape. Before he could decide what course of action to take, Lydia was running down the deck, sobbing heartbrokenly. She would throw herself over the rail and it would be over. Better to die than to live out her life with Bascom.

Blinded by tears, she paid no heed to where she was running and didn't see a pair of strong arms reach out for her. She shrieked as though in pain, thinking it was Bascom who had trapped her.

But these strong arms weren't Bascom's. And the square face with the strong chin weren't Bascom's either. This face had dark eyes full of concern and belonged to the first mate, Peter. "Easy, now . . . easy, now," he said softly. "What seems to be the matter? How did you get up here and where are you going?"

"Over the rail," Lydia gulped as she dabbed at the tears glistening in her eyes. "I hate him—I've always hated him," she blurted defiantly. "He's insane, and I'd rather die than go back down there. If you make me go back, I'll find a way to get up here again. Please," she implored, "don't make me go back down there."

"I won't make you go back, but I think we'd better

206

have a little talk with the captain." So she hated her husband and thought him insane, did she? It was the first sensible thing Peter had heard in weeks. She should know about the preacher, being married to him, he thought happily. She certainly was a pretty woman, and he did admire a pretty face.

When Peter ushered Lydia into the wheelhouse, Caleb groaned aloud. He was being overrun by females. "All right, the straight of it. What did *she* do?"

Peter suppressed a grin, his eyes twinkling merrily at Caleb's discomfort. "She said she was going over the side. She said she hated her husband and she refused to go back to the hold. She said if we made her go back, she'd find a way to get out again, and she also said she'd rather die than go back. The matter is in your hands, Captain," he concluded smartly, turning on his heel and leaving the wheelhouse.

"Mrs. Stoneham, it isn't easy operating a ship," Caleb began warily. "It takes one's full attention to navigate and stay true to the course. I have no time to settle marital disputes. Whatever your problem, it will have to be settled by you and your husband. There's no room topside for another female. I'm ordering you to go below to your husband."

"I suppose you're going to tell me you're a messenger of the Lord, too. Is that it? Well, I'm not interested in hearing any more messages. I've had enough to last me a lifetime. I meant what I said. I would rather be dead than go back down there to him. He's no messenger of the Lord. He's the devil himself. He's evil. He makes me do terrible things, makes the others do terrible things, too. He tried to make Wren obey him and she wouldn't. You can't send me back. I won't go," Lydia declared firmly, settling herself on a round stool near Caleb and the wheel.

Damn fool woman. Now what was he to do? "I'm the captain and you must obey me," he said, frown-

207

ing at her docile look. She wasn't going to budge, he could feel it in his bones.

"It was your very own sister who gave me the courage to rebel at last. What kind of man are you to make me go back there so he can force me to do all those terrible things?"

"My dear woman, there are worse things in life than praying for forgiveness."

"I didn't do anything for God to forgive!" Lydia shrieked. "Weren't you listening to me?" Merciful God, was this strange person who was carrying on in such a state really Lydia Stoneham? Where had she gotten the courage to say something as bizarre as that she would jump over the rail? She couldn't swim and would go straight to the bottom! Belatedly, she covered her mouth and groaned inwardly. Who would blame the captain if he thought she was as dotty as her husband?

Caleb didn't want to ask her, but he did, almost knowing what her response would be. "What things, Mrs. Stoneham?"

Her face a bright crimson, Lydia spoke hesitantly, gathering courage as she went along, leaving out nothing, not even her own scorching humiliation, finally ending with, "I meant it, Captain. I'll leap over the side if you try to make me go back there."

Aubrey, you bastard, where are you when I need you? Caleb swore silently. He felt out of his depth with this woman seated before him. He couldn't send her back. What man in his right mind would subject a woman to such degradation? The only name that came to his lips was Bascom Stoneham.

Caleb whistled between his teeth, a shrill, sharp note that brought Peter on the run. "Take Mrs. Stoneham to my quarters and arrange sleeping accommodations for her with the other two women. They can take turns with the bunks. I don't care how you do it, just do it."

"Aye, Captain." Peter grinned as he gallantly escorted Lydia from the wheelhouse.

Whoever had said that men needed women was a fool, Caleb thought with a grimace. Or else that person hadn't known the women on his ship.

Chapter Thirteen

Bascom Stoneham felt the eyes of his flock on him. For the first time since he had become a preacher, he knew the emotion of fear. If he couldn't control his wife, how could he minister to and aid his followers? He had to do something, say something, and it had to be now, before the mass in front of him revolted. Even his parents were looking at him strangely. He cleared his throat loudly and opened his prayer book. Deliberately, he lowered his eyes and read the printed words in a somber tone. The thick book closed with barely a sound. His eyes were hooded and his mouth grim when he began to address his congregation.

"I see now that all my prayers, all of your prayers, were not enough to drive the devil from my wife, Lydia. Sometimes the Lord works in strange ways. It has come to me that Lydia's fate is to be an example to all of us. Just this day I've perceived a vision.

Lydia is lost to us and can never return. But," he said, opening his eyes wide till the pupils were bare pinpoints, "we will continue to pray for her soul. Even though she is lost to us, we must never forget her. Now we are in a tunnel of darkness, but there is light at the end, and we will all walk toward that light while Lydia remains forever in the darkness with the devil at her heels."

If the devil was indeed at Lydia Stoneham's heels, she paid him no heed as she blurted her tale to a sympathetic Wren. "I'm so frightened. When we get to America, what will I do? How will I survive? What's to become of me?" she cried pitifully.

Emotion welled in Wren's throat. What *would* become of this gentle creature in a new land? What would become of Wren van der Rhys in the new land? It was her fault that Lydia had defied her husband and was now sitting next to her with no future before her.

She squared her slim shoulders and spoke confidently. "I'll take care of you, Lydia. I have some money, and we'll manage somehow. We're young and strong and we can surely find something to do in America. Something that will pay us enough money to live on. You must not worry, Lydia, promise me."

Lydia smiled and threw her arms around Wren. "I feel so good. So free for the first time in my life. I could sleep on the floor with the sleep of pure joy. And when I wake, I'll thank the Lord, *my* Lord, for giving me the courage to do what I did, and I'll thank Him for sending you to me to show me the way."

Damnation! Now what had Wren gone and done? She had saddled herself with another responsibility when, according to Caleb, she couldn't even take care of herself. Money. She had to get money for Lydia. If need be, she would badger Caleb to take her back to Java. How he would love to see her come crawling to him for help. She quailed at the thought. She'd make her own way and the devil take the hindmost!

It always came down to money. Aubrey Farrington had money, she was convinced of that. Bascom Stoneham had money. Bascom Stoneham had a lot of money. All the Puritans had entrusted their life savings to him. He had a fortune and she had a deck of cards. A deck of marked cards. And Caleb had money, probably more than Farrington. All she had to do was figure out a way to relieve each one of his hoard, and then she could set Lydia up in America and not have to worry about her. All she needed was a foolproof plan, and she herself would be comfortable indefinitely. It never occurred to her that she would not come out the winner. After all, she was the one with the marked deck, and even a professional gambler like Aubrey hadn't been able to spot the markings. By the time they reached America, Lydia would have so much money she would need someone to help her carry it off the ship.

Sara entered the cabin, her eyes widening when she spotted Lydia talking to Wren. She looked at both women and said nothing. The flush that rode high on Sara's cheeks didn't escape Wren's notice, and her jaw tightened. She knew where Sara had been recently and what she had done. Her heart pounded in her chest at the thought. Sara looked like the cat that had sat in the cream crock.

Lydia walked over to her sister-in-law and put her arms around the girl's shoulders. "I want to be the one to tell you that I've renounced your brother. It's better you hear it from me. I hope it doesn't upset you, Sara," Lydia said softly.

Sara grimaced. "Why should it upset me? Bascom is insane; we both know it. I'm just surprised that you had the courage to leave him. I could never understand how you tolerated him from the day you married him. Speaking personally, I think he's the devil reborn. I applaud you, Lydia."

211

Lydia tightened her hold on Sara and laughed. "It seems the three of us have the same opinion of Bascom. I'm glad to see that you're feeling better, Sara. I was truly worried about you when we were both in the hold. The sea air has worked its magic on you, and for that I'm glad."

"Sea air, my foot!" Wren snapped. "You can stop all this needless pretense, Sara Stoneham. I know what you've been doing and with whom, and you should be ashamed of yourself. Dallying with Caleb will get you nowhere, and it only cheapens you. He's a womanizer of the worst sort!" Her upper lip curled in distaste.

"Is that a note of jealousy I hear ringing in your tone?" Sara asked coolly. "Caleb isn't your real brother and you're simply jealous. Just the way you were with Malcolm because it was *me* he loved, not you. I told you, tried to warn you, but you wouldn't listen. It was only the van der Rhys' money Malcolm found alluring, Wren, not you!"

Wren's eyes glittered dangerously, sparks of fury lightening their depths. "Think what you will. I know Caleb, and if you have any serious plans, you might as well forget them. Caleb isn't the marrying kind. He plays with women the way children play with toys. Don't say I didn't warn you."

The slim blond girl faced Wren defiantly, the naked truth of her hatred for Wren written on her features. "I'm glad Malcolm is dead! Glad, do you hear!" she shrilled. "Now you will never have him! I told you he belonged to me! He was mine, and now he'll always be mine! Just the way Caleb is mine! I only wish you had caught the pox, too. I only wish you *were* with Malcolm—in his grave!"

Wren nearly staggered beneath the hatred in Sara's voice. Lydia, too, was aghast at what she had just heard. Sara, with a smirk on her face, lay down on the bunk and turned her back on the two women.

Wren felt the need to breathe clean air, to be away

from the stifling contempt which Sara exuded. She stumbled toward the door and Lydia followed, her hand ready to steady her new friend. Out on deck, leaning against the rail, Wren braced herself against the wind, the color slowly returning to her features. Lydia watched her anxiously, her own vivid red hair coming loose from its pins and whipping against her face. "I don't know what's come over that girl," she said tonelessly.

"What comes over a woman when she's been spurned by a man she loves?" Wren said, her words more a statement than a question. "Lydia, it's not true that Malcolm is dead. When last I saw him, he was very much alive, although somewhat the worse for wear. I told Sara he was dead only out of cruelty. I should go back in there and admit I had lied."

Lydia placed her hand on Wren's arm. "No, don't. It will do her little good. Better she thinks he's dead, for all the good he can do her. She has greater problems on her mind right now. Sara is with child."

"Do you know what you're saying?" Wren asked in a shocked voice, the terrible implications dawning on her instantly.

"It's true. A woman can always tell. It also explains the sickness she had below. I'm familiar enough with women when they're bearing a child. My own mother brought nine besides me into the world. I feel sorry for Sara when Bascom discovers it. He'll kill Captain van der Rhys for taking advantage of his sister."

"What makes you think Caleb is the father?" Wren demanded indignantly. "Caleb cannot be the father of her child, if she is in truth carrying a child."

"Then who?" Lydia asked quietly, watching Wren's face.

"Who?" Wren repeated. "I don't know who. I just can't believe it's Caleb." Damnation, it couldn't be Caleb, it just couldn't be! Wren's thoughts raced. There hadn't been enough time, the journey was

213

barely two weeks gone. An unbidden memory of Sara and herself in their room at Tyler's house, and Sara's boasting that she could have Caleb madly in love with her before dinner was over that evening, came to Wren's mind.

Will you wait for me to grow up? How often those words came back to haunt her. She had said them to Caleb the minute she had laid eyes on him in England, so long ago. *Will you wait for me to grow up?* Caleb had laughed and stared deeply into her eyes and said, "I may just do that." Damn liar, just like all men. Why could a woman speak with another woman and pour out her heart and be completely understood, whereas a man had to lie and twist the truth? Did that make him feel more manly, more worldly? Her lip curled as she muttered, "I may just do that." Damn liar. Caleb van der Rhys was a liar, and he had probably learned his trade from Regan.

Too bad dear old Caleb doesn't know what dear, sweet Sara has planned for him, Wren fumed inwardly. Instant fatherhood. Well, he can just stew in his own masculine juices for all I care!

Later, lying in her bunk, Wren admitted to herself that she was jealous of Sara. At the very least Caleb could have given her the opportunity to reject him. And reject him she would. Damnation, it was her inalienable right! He was making a fool out of her and she was allowing it. She would cut him down to size if it was the last thing she did.

"If you'll excuse me, ladies, I think I'll take a turn on the deck and see who's afoot," Sara said, looking from Wren to Lydia, defying either of them to make a comment. Neither said a word as she walked through the door.

"Twice in one day is a bit much," Lydia said pontifically. "She's like a harlot on the prowl."

Wren shrugged as jealousy once again coursed

214

through her. Damn you, Caleb van der Rhys, she thought murderously.

On deck, Sara carefully looked around and waited for Aubrey Farrington to make his appearance. For three days now she had seen him stuff leftover bread and cheese in his coat pockets. What did he do with it? If she could find out what Farrington was up to, she could go to Caleb and deepen his trust in her. She would say she wanted to help him and that whatever the old gambler was up to, Caleb should know about it.

Dressed in her Puritan garb, a black scarf around her bright hair, she stood waiting for the moon to take cloud cover. The spindly-legged gambler was late this evening. Perhaps he wasn't coming, she thought nervously. A footstep, another, and Aubrey Farrington came into view just as the moon ducked behind a dark cloud. She removed her stout shoes and pursued him stealthily.

Once Farrington stopped and looked over his shoulder to see if he was being observed. Sara crouched behind a thick roll of canvas and held her breath. Had he seen her? No. He was continuing his silent trek, and she was but a few steps behind him. She followed his cautious progress down the ladder of the fore hatch, her stockinged feet hesitantly finding the ladder rungs, and she dreaded stepping into the shallow pool of bilge water that sloshed rhythmically with the rise and fall of the ship. Plunging her feet into the murky, ankle-high depths and refusing to give her imagination free reign as to what unspeakable creatures might attack her from beneath the dark surface, she listened attentively for the sound of Farrington's treading water. Heeding her instincts, she caught up with him and winced from the light as he struck a flint to a tallow candle.

She stopped in midstride as she saw his arm reach out and slide back a bolt. After he had closed the wooden door, she tapped her stockinged foot impatiently on the planks. Who was inside that room, and what was Farrington doing in there?

Crouching low, she crept over to the door and pressed her ear against it, trying to hear what was being said. A chair scraped on the floor, and the words spoken within were muffled, as though the people talking didn't want anyone to overhear them. She would have to wait; when Farrington left, she would open the door to see for herself, but first she would have to arm herself with some sort of weapon. God only knew whom the gambler was harboring inside. A cutthroat, a pirate, a murderer. She crept cautiously back to the dim recesses and fumbled around for something that would serve as a weapon. Her fingers fastened on a stout piece of board, and she clutched at it like at a lifeline. Now all she had to do was wait for Farrington to leave. Her stomach churned at the thought of what she might find behind the door, but she had to do it. She had to do it so that Caleb would be indebted to her and trust her. Lovemaking was one thing, but this was something else entirely. Men didn't like to be made fools of, especially by other men. Malcolm had taught her that at the very beginning of their relationship. Yes, Caleb would thank her.

What seemed like an eternity later, the door of the locker box opened and Aubrey Farrington exited, but not before he had looked to the right and then to the left, a wry expression on his face. Satisfied that no one was about, he slid the heavy iron bolt into place and quickly walked away, his pockets noticeably lighter.

Sara drew in her breath and tiptoed over to the thick wooden door. Surprise would be on her side. Whoever or whatever was on the other side of the door would think the gambler had forgotten something and was returning. Slowly she slid back the bolt, the stout board clutched between her knees. The moment the bolt slid back, she grasped the club and flung open the door. Lantern light cast an oily, yellow glow over the small area. A rough bunk stood against one wall, bare of mattress or bedding. On it lay a man who was slowly getting to his feet, muttering, "Well, what did you forget to tell me, Farrington?"

Sara gasped, all senses frozen, her breath locked in her lungs. It couldn't be! Her mind was playing tricks on her! "Malcolm! Is that you?" she cried in a shocked voice. "Malcolm, how can you be here? Wren said you were dead!" At last believing her senses, she rushed toward him. "Malcolm, Malcolm!" Her arms locked around his neck, and she buried her face in his chest. "Oh, Malcolm, I thought you were dead. My love, we've found each other, and I'll never let you go. Never!" she cried vehemently as she clung to him.

Malcolm was stunned. "Sara! How did you get here? Darling child!" he exclaimed, his mind working furiously to determine what advantage she could serve him. Suddenly he remembered his disfigurement. "Don't look at me, Sara," he pleaded. "I've suffered a misfortune that's seriously altered my appearance. That's why I left England, thinking I would never see you again. I'd rather suffer the fate of an outcast than bear the pain of having you see me as I am now." His words and tone were carefully calculated to elicit her pity. "It was always you I loved, darling Sara. Never Wren. Wren did this to me—to us," he added meaningfully. "I told her it was you I loved and would cherish for the rest of my days. She turned wild and took a hot poker to my face, saying if she couldn't have me, no other woman would. She tried to kill me, and there are days I wish she had. Anything rather than have you see me this way. I broke your heart and knew in my own you would never have me after the way I had made you suffer. Now I'm disfigured, a horror, and it's too late, my darling Sara. Please forgive me."

"Malcolm, darling, I love you, and a little scar couldn't change my devotion to you. If it did, what would that say for my love? Let me look at you, please, darling."

Slowly Malcolm turned the left side of his face toward the light, his anxious eyes willing her to tell him that his disfigurement wasn't as hopeless as he imagined. Sara's face whitened as a gorge rose in her throat. God! What had she just promised to this monster? Fighting to regain control of herself and to hold in check the trembling that had seized her, she wrapped her arms about him, pity for his condition and fresh hatred for Wren consuming her. Wren had done this to him—purposely, vindictively, with malice. Wren had reduced Malcolm to hiding in the depths of a ship, afraid to show his face in public, nearly maddened by the loss of the one thing which had been his mainstay besides herself—his good looks.

Her mind rambled and raced, jumping from the past and then into the future. A future with a man who resembled a gargoyle. The scab on his face was crusted; his forehead was puckered from the burn; his blinded eye stared sightlessly from behind a contorted eyelid that would never close again. Never again would Sara dream of being the envy of other women when they saw her sported on Malcolm's arm. She would be the object of their pity. Women would run away from Malcolm in terror instead of pursuing him. Oh, God! she thought wildly. Why had she followed Aubrey Farrington down into the reaches of Hell?

Malcolm's hands tightened about her, seeking, pressing, attempting to arouse.

"You smell, Malcolm. Poor darling," she added hastily, "doesn't that old man provide you with soap and water?" There was no way Malcolm was going to seduce her in this stench-filled room, smelling like a rutting pig. She had to get out of here before he overpowered her. Merciful God, she didn't know which eye to look into.

"Did you hear what I said to you, Sara? Your friend, Wren, did this to me. What are you going to do about it? I know from Farrington that she's aboard this ship. If I could get out of here, I'd finish her off myself."

"What would you have me do with her, Malcolm? Why did she do this to you? I don't for one minute believe that story you just told me. Wren's not violent, excepting her tongue. She is aboard ship, that's true. As a matter of fact, my sister-in-law, Wren and I share Captain van der Rhys' cabin." Her voice took on a sudden lilt when she mentioned Caleb, which didn't escape Malcolm's attention.

He sensed her withdrawal and was engulfed with rage. "Say it, Sara. My face offends you. Suddenly you find you no longer love me. You're comparing me with your Captain van der Rhys, and I come out a poor second. Say it!"

Sara suddenly felt very powerful, more powerful than she had ever felt in her life. "Actually, Malcolm, you sicken me. You're right, I no longer love you. I doubt if I ever did love you. And yes, Caleb does come out first. Any day now I expect a proposal of marriage. It's over between us, Malcolm. It was over the day you decided you wanted Wren van der Rhys and her dowry. I wasn't good enough for you, and now I've decided that you aren't good enough for me. Good fortune to you, Malcolm. When we get to America, perhaps they'll employ you to frighten off those savage Indians." She enjoyed her cruelty toward him. "And don't worry, I won't give away your secret. I'll tell no one that you're hiding down here with the rats. By the way, why *are* you hiding? Passage for this voyage was very cheap. It wouldn't have anything to do with the captain's seeking retribution for something you've done to his sister, would it?" Seeing her suspi-

219

cions confirmed in Malcolm's expression, she laughed, the sound mirthless and harsh in the stillness of the locker box.

Malcolm wanted to slap her, to hit her till her teeth rattled, but he knew she would fight back, and he had already had a taste of what a woman would do to protect herself. He no longer had any control over Sara, and the realization frightened and emasculated him. All he needed was another jab to his good eye, and he might as well lie down and die. Women were the root of all evil. He had heard that Sara's brother was always spouting off about the evil that festered in a woman's breast. How right Bascom was.

"Ta-ta, darling," Sara cooed as she slammed the door behind her and quickly shot the bolt home.

The darkness of the ship and the soft lap of the water against the sides was like a balm to Sara's uneasiness. She felt as though a mountain had been lifted from her shoulders. She was free of Malcolm, free of Bascom and free to go to Caleb. Caleb was her answer, her salvation.

Sara's feet took her up the fore ladder, through the hatch and onto the deck. There was no one about, only the seaman on watch in the wheelhouse. Vaguely she wondered where Caleb was and if he knew of the fugitive hiding belowdecks near the bow of his ship.

As she walked quietly toward the cabin she shared with Wren and Lydia, a queer feeling within her body made her hesitate. She waited, as women had from time immemorial, for the featherlike quickening to occur again. The child. Her and Malcolm's child. Sudden fear struck her. God! What if seeing Malcolm the way he was now had marked the child? Heaven forbid it be born with a hideous disfigurement brought about by its mother seeing its father! Suddenly Sara began to giggle, a light chortle at first, which built to ringing peals of laughter that brought tears to her eyes. Even now Malcolm could not allow himself to be honest with her. He had tried to use her again, to win her over with pity, to lie to her and think her stupid enough to believe him, pity him and even love him. But she had been smarter this time, craftier.

How ugly Malcolm was now. Gone were the abundant good looks which had always attracted women to him. Now his glance was sly, feral. His words seemed slick and well rehearsed. Never again would he be a strikingly handsome man who could win a woman's heart just by the grace of his looks alone. What could he have done to Wren to make her take a poker to his face? That was the only thing Malcolm had said that Sara could believe. The only thing that would move Wren to violence was an attack on her person. Sara laughed again, the sound ringing out over the water, the note of hysteria rising to a shrillness. So Wren was no longer a virgin. That was the only thing she would protect with her life; Sara knew it in her heart. Malcolm must have tried to seduce her before the wedding and Wren had refused. Malcolm, not used to refusal, had become violent, and Wren had reacted in the only way she could. Dirty scum, Sara thought, he deserved whatever he got.

It never occurred to Sara that just hours before she had lain in her bunk dreaming of Malcolm. Now she had to concentrate on Caleb, definitely the better man of the two. Her child needed a father and she needed a husband to save her from the outraged scorn of the community of Puritans. She sniffed delicately and continued with her stroll as if it were something she did in the middle of every night. Her hand caressed her burgeoning belly and her thoughts whirled in crazy circles. No one would stand in the way of what she meant to have for herself. Slowly, her footsteps led her in a circular course around the deck.

A seaman was coming on duty to take the watch, and in the darkness he bumped into her. He lifted his lantern to identify the woman and was perplexed when he saw the expression in Sara's eyes.

"Can I help you to your cabin?" he asked politely. "You shouldn't be out here this time of night. It's too easy to fall overboard—" He broke off his words, the flesh on his back rising as though a goose had just walked on his grave. In the dim light of the lantern Sara's eyes were wild and staring, her lips drawn back over her teeth in a soundless, mirthless laugh. When she at last seemed to notice him and the light, he had the feeling that a sly, demonic creature was peering out from behind her eyes. The seaman backed away, unable to take his gaze from her face, remembering the time he had taken a ha'penny tour of Bedlam and seen the stark raving madness on the faces of the inmates. His hackles still rising in warning, he backed away still further and broke into a run. As he ran he could hear the woman's laughter, demonic in its intensity, leaving the ranks of saneness and breaking into a possessed howl.

Back in her quarters, Sara stood looking down at the sleeping women, her thoughts vaguely disoriented. Ever since she had seen Malcolm, she felt somehow different. Her brain seemed fuzzy and her thoughts weren't clear. She stared down at Wren, moving closer to her bunk. There was something about Wren, something she should do, but what was it? Was it a secret? She had to think, to clear her head so that she would know what to do. She would talk to Bascom in the morning; he would know what to do about the problem. Perhaps if she slept, she would be able to remember what it was she was supposed to do in the morning. If she couldn't remember then, she would go to Bascom anyway.

Wren was not asleep. She watched Sara out of the corner of her eye, her heart thudding in her chest. Something was wrong with Sara. The girl's eyes were peculiar, and the way she was hovering over the bunk

222

made Wren nervous. How pale Sara looked with the moonlight streaming through the porthole and casting a silvery aura around her, as if she were a ghostly specter. But it was Sara's eyes that frightened Wren.

Once Sara had settled herself in her own bunk, Wren realized there was no point in trying to sleep. The air in the cabin was very close, and she was fearful that her tossing and turning would disturb Lydia's sleep. A walk on the deck might help her sort out her thoughts. There would be no one about except the man on watch, and she doubted if he would pay her much notice. She had to think. The time had come to face a few truths.

The night air was brisk, yet it held the promise of the coming summer. She leaned against the rail and pondered the happenings in her life since Sirena and Regan had returned to England to take her back to Java. Why had she been so stubborn? Why hadn't she trusted their love and listened to them and done what they wanted? Now look at me, she wailed silently. What's to become of me? She also had Lydia to worry about, and the way Sara was behaving, it wouldn't be long before she would be saddled with her, too. She watched the dancing waves, eerie in the moonlight, as she pondered her problems. If she went over the side, she wouldn't have anything to worry about, she thought morbidly, but then that was the coward's way out. She had gotten herself into this situation, and she would have to extricate herself as best she could.

She was so deep in thought that she didn't hear the footsteps till a dark shadow caused her to turn her head. Caleb! She said nothing but returned her gaze to the water. Her heart pounded in her chest at his nearness.

How fragile she looked in the moonlight, Caleb thought. He said nothing but folded his arms and stared out across the water.

Wren wanted to shout at him and tell him what she

223

thought of him, but the words wouldn't come. Was she finally growing up? If so, it was a painful business indeed. She didn't have to be so physically aware of his presence if she didn't want to be. Then why was she? How close he was. Wasn't he ever going to say anything? Was he waiting for her to say something? She gulped and wet her lips, her knees trembling madly. What did he want? He wanted Sara. Her back stiffened at the thought and her jaw tightened. Well, he could have her, with her wild eyes, and he could have Bascom, too. The lot of them could sail off to the end of the world, for all she cared!

His voice, when he spoke, was soft, yet husky. "It's not wise for you to walk the deck at this hour of the night."

Her own voice matched his for softness. "I couldn't sleep, and the room was too warm. I wanted to feel the spindrift on my face." Was that soft, purring voice hers?

"How long have you been standing here?"

"Not long. If my being here upsets you, then I'll go back to my quarters. Caleb, I—"

Caleb touched her lips gently with his finger. "It doesn't upset me. I just don't want anything to happen to you." How soft her skin felt beneath his fingertip.

Wren moved slightly, his touch searing her mouth. She had to say something. "I guess I haven't done so well with things. I seem to have botched everything up. I'm sorry, Caleb." She looked up into his face, her features composed in the moonlight, belying the torrent of emotions that churned through her breast.

Caleb drew in his breath sharply. This beautiful creature standing before him couldn't be the same fire-breathing Wren who had so deftly defended herself when he had kissed her in Tyler Sinclair's garden. Nor the same girl who would have him believe she had killed a seaman and disfigured a man in self-defense.

He had to say the right words so as not to frighten

224

her and cause her to run off. "It's all right," he said gruffly. "Isn't that what a brother is for?" The moment the words were out he knew he had said the wrong thing. He wasn't her brother, didn't want to be her brother. That was the last thing he wanted. The vision of her as a child, staring up at him, flashed before his eyes. *Will you wait for me to grow up?*

Wren backed off a step and lowered her eyes. Her voice was so soft he had to strain to hear it. "Somehow, Caleb, I never thought of you as my brother. I'm certain you don't remember, but a long time ago, the first time I ever saw you, I fell in love with you, the way a little girl does with her schoolmaster. I remember . . . remember asking you if you would wait for me to grow up."

"And I said, 'I may just do that.' "

Wren's eyes widened and she smiled. Suddenly a brisk wind came up and penetrated her cloak and thin nightdress.

"You're cold," Caleb said, wrapping her cloak closer about her chin. "I don't want you getting chilled, not after what we all went through to make you well." He took her by the hand and led her across the deck. "Come into my cabin. I have a bottle of brandy, and it will warm you."

Obediently she followed his lead into the small cabin he had taken since giving the women his. It was lit by a dim, glowing candle, and when his hand reached out to lengthen the wick, she stopped him. "No, don't. It's so pleasant as it is."

He filled two snifters with brandy and handed her one. "Drink up. It'll ward off the chill. Then back you go to your bed."

"Don't treat me as though I were still a child," she pretended to pout. "I'm grown up, Caleb, or haven't you noticed?"

Caleb threw back his head and laughed. "I've noticed."

225

At his words a delicious tingle worked its way through Wren's veins, mingling with the warmth from the brandy. She felt drawn to him, yearned to have his arms encircle her as they had when he had helped her through her illness.

Caleb reached out and drew her to him. Her body seemed to have a will of its own as she moved into his embrace. Tenderly he covered her mouth with his and felt her lips tremble. His breath was warm upon her cheek, and his lips coaxed hers into a lingering kiss.

Wren felt his arms tighten around her, pulling her close against his lean, muscular body. She was aware of the warmth he offered and the tenderness of his arms. She knew without a doubt that he could have crushed her in a bone-breaking embrace, but his arms were gentle, holding, persuading, not brutal and forceful, as Malcolm's had been. The stubble on his chin scratched her cheek, making the soft contact between their mouths more gentle by comparison. This is Caleb, she told herself—Caleb, who would never hurt or degrade me. Yet the memory of what she had suffered at Malcolm's possessive, hurting hands and the indignities she had undergone at the hands of the seamen pervaded her consciousness.

Caleb held her, soothing away her tremblings with his lips, encouraging hers to part. He felt the slimness of her body through the light material of her nightdress, and the dual provocation of her high, full breasts against his chest. He slid his hands along her hips and pressed her firmly against his loins, taking pleasure from the warmth of her body against his rising desire. Her lips were soft and tasted of the brandy she had drunk. Her arms tightened around his back and her fingers lightly traced a path along his muscles. She felt so small, so pliable. He grew dizzy with his urgent need for her, a dizziness that climbed from his loins to his head. His desire for her became overwhelming, and his fingers found the opening to her nightdress. He wanted to rip the cloth from her body, to touch her flesh, to drink in her beauty, to be naked with her and make love to her.

Wren pulled her lips from his. In the frightened astonishment in her eyes he could read the lusty savageness on his own face. He felt himself beyond the point of judgment. No other woman had ever excited him this way, tantalizing him with her lips, teasing him with the pressure of her body against his. He knew only that he wanted, needed, intended to have the woman who had driven him to such passionate heights.

Indifferent to her terror, he picked her up and carried her over to the bunk. Dropping her down onto the mattress, he threw himself beside her, seeking her mouth with his own, his hands tearing at her flimsy nightdress in his eagerness for her silky skin and the place protected by her tightly clenched thighs.

Wren attempted to fight him off, making unintelligible sounds of protest, but he overpowered her by twining one leg around hers and pressing himself over her, reveling in the feel of her breasts against his chest. From deep inside him he growled, "I want you. I mean to have you."

Wren struggled, images of Malcolm and the seamen heightening her terror. She raised herself up in a sudden movement and crawled down the length of the bed. He caught her by the ankle and pulled her backward, attempting to cover her with his weight. She drove her fingernails into his wrist, savagely slashing at him, her other hand reaching for his face to tear at it. Their eyes met, each staring at the other—the friend and the foe, the trapper and the trapped, the predator and the prey.

Two tears welled in Wren's eyes and coursed down her cheeks, and from her throat came a desperately pleading voice. "Not you, Caleb. Please, I beg you," she whispered. "Never you!"

Caleb looked into her eyes for a long moment. Suddenly he reached for her and brought her into his arms, kissing her tenderly and brushing the tears from her face. She buried her head in his chest, her body trembling with unshed tears and remembered terror. "I don't think I could ever have forgiven you," she sobbed, the hot tears scalding his flesh.

From out the mullioned windows of the sterncastle, the moon could be seen dipping into the ocean. Soon it would be light.

Like two abandoned children, they huddled together on the bunk, one forgiving, the other begging forgiveness. The hours passed and Wren's tears were dry; yet still she hid against his neck, and from time to time, at long intervals, she sobbed.

Caleb's desire had completely subsided, even to the point that he was indifferent to Wren's hand which had slipped between his legs. The weight of what he had nearly done to her lay heavily on him. He realized that he had almost brutalized her, and he was deeply saddened. Knowing that she had been raped and abused and denigrated, he considered his brutality and unquenchable lust unpardonable. And yet, she had pardoned him. She was holding him tightly and taking comfort from him. He cradled her, feeling the warmth return to her body, knowing that, above all else, he loved her. He wanted her, but he wanted her to desire him, to seek him as her lover. Bewildering thoughts rampaged through his head. How could she desire him when the very thought of giving herself to a man filled her with terror?

When the sun's first golden light stained the sky at dawn, Caleb remembered Regan's words. Patience, he had said. Nuzzling against Wren's fragrant drape of dark hair, Caleb once again tightened his protective embrace. Closing his eyes as a smile came to his lips, he repeated the word to himself. *Patience.*

Chapter Fourteen

The *Sea Siren* kept true to her course, rollicking amid the low swells, her sails full of wind and promise. The sun was just lifting over the horizon and glinted gold off the starboard porthole. Sara lay in her bunk, watching the progression of light as it cascaded through the mist-sprayed glass. At the sound of the door opening, she quickly closed her eyes and pretended to be asleep.

Hours before, she had awakened and noticed that only one figure occupied the adjoining bunk. Wren had gone out, and now she was returning. A rustle of whispers reached Sara's ears, and she recognized the other person's voice before Wren had shut the cabin door. Wren had spent the night with Caleb.

With an animalistic keenness, Sara knew that their meeting had been less than innocent. She could feel the heat coming from Wren's body across the room; she could almost smell the aura of sexuality surrounding her. For one instant she knew a sense of futility. She would bear her child, a bastard, a fatherless, nameless creature who would never have the advantages of honor attached to its name. Her fingers rode over the barely perceptible swelling of her belly, imag-

229

ining she could perceive the life within. She herself would be an outcast, branded with the mark of an adulteress, an embarrassment to her family and the object of derision.

No! she screamed silently. Never! She would have her way yet. Regardless of what she had to do, Sara Stoneham would become Mrs. Caleb van der Rhys, and the devil take the hindmost.

A corrosive jealousy burned through her soul. Wren! Wren had always had the best of everything. The best clothes, the best family, the most love . . . even Malcolm! Well, she wouldn't have Caleb. No matter what Sara had to do to stop her, Wren would never have Caleb!

Later that morning Sara descended the ladder into the hold to see Bascom. She tolerated her mother's inquiries about her health and felt herself rebel against her father's black looks. His expression seemed to accuse her of having left the flock for the conveniences and luxuries topside. Facing down his paternal disapproval, Sara drew her brother aside.

"I knew you would see the error of your ways and come back to your family," Bascom told her as he followed her over to the ladder, where no one could hear their conversation. "Come, it is time for our morning prayers."

Sara stared at him with unseeing eyes. "I have to tell you something. And you must listen to me and forget your silly prejudices."

Bascom peered at his sister and frowned. She looked peculiar. Perhaps the Lord was going to take her to Him. If it had to be someone's time, Bascom was glad it was Sara's. She was a foolish girl and served no real purpose in the world. Besides, the Lord willing, that way Sara would not live to disgrace the family. Now that he headed a congregation, his good standing and good name were all-important.

"What is it, sister?" he asked, his haunted eyes

scrutinizing her face. "Have you done an evil thing and want to pray for forgiveness?"

"Of course I've sinned. Everyone sins!" she answered impatiently. Her eyes were bright and almost feverish, glaring at the hard lines of his face. "I want to tell you a secret. Promise me you'll keep my secret till the ship docks in America. Give me your promise as a messenger of the Lord; I'll accept nothing less, Bascom."

"You have my word, sister. What troubles you? Confess to me, and we'll pray together to make it right."

"We could both pray till the cows come home, Bascom, and it wouldn't make my problem come right. I'm with child, brother. The father of my unborn child is being kept prisoner in the locker box of this ship. Wren maimed him horribly and he's disfigured. I thought him dead till I followed Lord Farrington, who was bringing him food in the middle of the night." Her eyes turned cunning as she watched Bascom pale and then flush a rosy hue. "This is your chance to get back at Wren for humiliating you in front of your flock. Trick her into the locker box and leave her with the animal who rests inside. She wants to take Caleb from me now. Captain van der Rhys," she amended. "Don't you see, Bascom? If I can trick the captain into thinking the baby is his, he'll marry me, and you won't be saddled with me or lose face with your flock. You can't afford another mistake; after all, your very own wife left you and is spreading all manner of lies around the top deck. Wren wants Captain van der Rhys for herself. She ruined the first man I loved, and now she wants to ruin Caleb, too. Say something, Bascom," she insisted.

"Merciful God, forgive this poor sinner . . ."

"Forget your merciful God and say you'll help me."

"Very well, sister. Tell me what it is you want me to do."

Sara whirled on him suddenly. Her eyes were blazing in her pale face. "I don't want you to do anything, you miserable excuse for a man! I'll do what has to be done myself! I just came down here to tell you to pray that I succeed!"

For the first time in his life Bascom Stoneham was speechless. He completely forgot it was time for morning worship. Somehow the devil had taken possession of Sara's soul, and that was almost more than he could comprehend.

While Sara sunned herself on deck and Bascom preached the horrors of sin to his congregation, Wren joked with and teased Lydia as she proceeded to teach her the basics of cards. Lydia teased and joked in return, delighted that Wren had returned to her normal, cheerful self. She suspected that Captain van der Rhys had a great deal to do with Wren's uplifted attitude, but she kept her own counsel.

Wren was bent on teaching her new friend how to act the foil for her own cheating, and Lydia proved to be an apt pupil. "But what if we're caught?" she asked fearfully of her teacher.

Wren sniffed disdainfully. "We're sailing the high seas. Caleb is the only authority we have to contend with. The worst thing that could happen to us is that he would throw us in the brig. Somehow I don't think he'll do that. Now, this is what we'll do. After lunch we'll entice Farrington into a simple game of whist, and when we see that he thinks we're not keen card players, one of us will suggest playing for money—and then we'll take all of his! Do you think you can do it, Lydia?" Wren asked anxiously. "I'm doing this for you, you know. When we get to America, you're going to need a great deal of money to live on."

Lydia's blue eyes were wide and incredulous. Her life had certainly changed since she had met Wren. She had divested herself of one husband, found the first mate to her liking and openly flirted with him, become a card shark in a matter of a few hours and was now ready to fleece, with her accomplice's help, one professional gambler. She giggled. She was having the time of her life. "Of course I can do it," she replied confidently.

"Just keep your wits about you. Aubrey Farrington has the eyes of a hawk and knows every card trick and then some. Remember, look dumb, and always be surprised when you win. Tomorrow we'll have to think of a way to get Bascom up here so we can relieve him of his hoard. Today will be a sort of practice session. Just keep flexing your fingers so you can handle the cards with no wasted motion. Don't be nervous," Wren warned. "If either of us appears jittery, Farrington will become suspicious. Gamblers are a suspicious lot."

Lydia's eyes boggled. Wren was the most fascinating woman she had ever met. What a pity the captain didn't think so. Lydia shrugged. Wren was right—all men were bastards. She would reserve her judgment of the first mate, Peter, until she knew him better.

As Wren had suggested, the card game began after lunch and was still in progress as the afternoon wore on. Caleb, from his position in the wheelhouse, watched it with narrowed eyes. Aubrey was taking a beating, and it looked as if his bank roll was being depleted. Squeals of merriment from the girls every time they won made Caleb wince. Wren had never once looked in his direction all afternoon, and soon it would be sundown. He could feel in his bones that trouble was brewing and that somehow she would be at the bottom of it. Any minute now he expected Bascom Stoneham to charge up the ladder and drag his card-playing wife below, praying loudly all the while.

His shoulders tensed as he watched Wren, her dark hair flying wildly in the stiff breeze. Her laugh, each time she won, chilled him to the bone. It was a damn good thing Aubrey had no vested interest in the *Sea Siren,* or he would truly have cause for worry. He saw the gambler rise and excuse himself with a motion indicating he would return—with more money, Caleb assumed.

A short while later Farrington appeared, his brow furrowed in deep thought, his hands clenched tightly into fists. Casually, he placed a gemstone next to the girls and nodded. Even from this distance Caleb could see Wren's eyes widen, and he heard Lydia giggle. Wren tilted her head and picked up the stone. She turned it this way and that in the dimming light, finally putting it between her teeth and biting down hard. For Christ's sake, Caleb fumed, she acts as if she knows what she's doing! She nodded to Farrington to show she accepted the gem as his bid. The gambler bit into his lower lip and threw down his cards. Wren's trill of delight was blood-chilling.

In the course of the next few hours, with the aid of lantern light, Aubrey Farrington tossed nine more gems into the center of the small ring and managed to lose each one of them.

Caleb knew in his gut, in every bone of his body, that Wren and Lydia were literally cheating the pants off Aubrey, and he was powerless to stop it. Serves the old fox right for gambling, he told himself, and to be done in by two women would be more than Aubrey could bear.

The game wore on long into the night, with both women winning consistently. The moon rode high in the sky when Farrington tossed what he said was his last gem into the ring. He looked at his cards, spat over the rail with uncanny accuracy and staggered to his feet. He was less than gracious as he stared down at the laughing women and said, "You two . . . ladies have got to be the smartest or the dumbest card players I've ever had the pleasure to come across. I know that you cheated me, but I don't know how. I'd appreciate it if someday you'd tell me how you did it."

Wren gurgled deep in her throat and Lydia smiled beatifically. "For shame, Lord Farrington," Lydia admonished. "We played fair and square and trounced you soundly. Let's not hear any evil talk of cheating, or we'll be forced to call you out. How would that look—two ladies dueling with a gambler? For shame, thinking such a thing!"

Caleb winced again and groaned aloud. "Women!"

Back in their quarters, Wren threw her arms around Lydia and both of them laughed hysterically. "We have a fortune here," Wren said, opening the palm of her hand. "We have to keep them safe, but where?"

"Perhaps Captain van der Rhys would keep them safe for us until we dock," Lydia replied hesitantly.

"You can just forget that idea, Lydia. We have to come up with a hiding place ourselves. The crewmen know we won all these gems, and some of them didn't look as if they would be above cutting either of us down for this little treasure."

Just after lunch the next day, Caleb knocked on the door to the cabin he had given over to the women. Hearing a bid to enter, he opened the door and found Wren and Lydia intent on a game of cards. Apparently Wren was teaching Lydia the finer points of the game. Sara sat sullenly on her bunk, repairing a ribbon on some feminine undergarment. He saw her eyes light when he stepped into the cabin, but he carefully paid her no attention. If Sara were one to kiss and tell, she would have done so by now, and Wren seemingly had no knowledge of what had transpired between the blonde and himself. So much the better.

Caleb signaled Wren, who left her cards on the table and moved toward him, a question in her eyes. He was planning to draw her outside on the deck to say what he had come to say, but then he decided there was little use in trying to be secretive. Shipboard was the last place to keep a secret, since everyone lived so closely together. Even with the Puritans, whom he had allowed to come above once again, everyone's business was everyone else's.

"I'd be honored if you'd share my dinner with me this evening, Wren. Gustave has promised something special from the galley." His eyes were warm as they rested on her, and Wren felt her heart skip a beat.

"When and where?" She smiled, relieving him of the formality of his invitation.

"Eight bells, my cabin. I'll just have come off watch."

When Wren turned back to her game with Lydia, neither woman had seen the burning hatred that banked in Sara's eyes. After taking her place at the table, Wren turned only once to glance at the blue-eyed blonde. Sara's stare was pointed enough to bore holes through her back.

Caleb watched the door close behind Gustave and turned to scrutinize the table which had been set for Wren and himself. It had been a long watch, and he looked forward to a leisurely dinner with her. A bottle of wine and two glasses dominated the center of the cloth-draped table, and he decided he would struggle with the cork before Wren appeared.

A light, tapping sound at the door announced her arrival. He bade her enter and was pleasantly surprised when he saw her. Her long sable hair was coiled around her head, emphasizing the graceful length of her neck and the feminine slope of her shoulders. She wore several layers of petticoats and a prettily laced chemise.

"Once before you came to this cabin without benefit of a dress," Caleb said softly, his voice husky as

236

he took in the ivory tones of her complexion and the womanly softness swelling above the top of her chemise. "Good God, woman, where are your clothes?"

"The Puritan garb is so dull and unfeminine," she pouted. "Lydia and I thought this would do me as well as a gown, and at least I feel pretty in it."

"You're beautiful tonight." His voice was low and his eyes enveloped her in an aura of rekindled desire.

Attempting to lighten the mood, Wren curtsied and played the grand duchess. "Thank you, kind sir. Would you care to kiss my hand?"

Caleb's eyes didn't brighten at her little jest. He was conscious of the long sweep of her neck rising above her nearly bare shoulders and the deep cut of her chemise, which brought into prominence the soft curve of her breasts. Remembering the last time he had kissed her and his dangerous responses, he didn't dare play her little game.

Sensing his reticence, Wren seated herself at the table and began to serve the dinner of chicken and precious potatoes. She proceeded to put on airs like an affected duchess and sought to make him laugh. Her humor rang false in his ears and clashed with his silence. They picked at their food without interest; only the wine was totally consumed.

Wren watched Caleb through lowered lids, feeling his tension. "Caleb," she began hesitantly, not certain where her words would lead, only knowing they had to be said in order to erase that terrible look of guilt from his eyes. "I want to confess that I don't regret anything that happened between us. Not a single action on your part. Since then, you have been extremely delicate . . ." She paused. "If I didn't know firsthand what a passionate man you are, I could never appreciate your consideration of my fears." Her voice was softly tender, her eyes pleading with him to understand her. "I feel I know you so much better,

237

and that you understand me and that my feelings are important to you."

Caleb looked into her eyes, saw the pleading and confusion there, and felt his heart beat rapidly within his chest. She was trying to tell him that she wanted him, desired him, yet she was also trying to conquer the fears that Malcolm had instilled in her. Once again the deep heat of hatred rose inside Caleb, until he knew that if Weatherly were standing there before him, he would cheerfully kill him for what he had done to Wren.

Seeing Caleb's mouth tighten into a thin line and his eyes harden into gleaming chips of jet, Wren immediately regretted having reminded him of Malcolm's cruelty. Jumping to her feet, she rounded the table and placed her hands on his shoulders, feeling the knots of tension beneath the muscles in his neck. "Don't, Caleb. What's done is done."

He gazed into her eyes and saw the same understanding he had once seen in Sirena's eyes, the same concern. She, too, had once said the same words to him. "What's done is done, and where we go from here is what matters." He had marveled at the Siren's resiliency, and now he was finding it again in Wren.

Still gazing into the amber depths of her eyes, aware of her slim body and the scent she wore, Caleb pulled her wordlessly onto his lap, holding her against him as if she were a small child who had been frightened by a nightmare. Wren lifted her face for his kiss, allowing her lips to part beneath his.

He was aware of the pressure of her thighs and the thinness of her petticoats and the rising urgency of his own desires. The softness of her mouth and the delicate scent of her skin awakened a similar throb in his temples. His arm made a support for her while his free hand pressed her legs against him; he consciously resisted the impulse to touch her neck and the silky swell of her breasts, which were tantalizingly accessible beneath her low-cut chemise.

Their kisses became more passionate, more searching, and Wren responded by parting her lips still further. Tenderly, he advanced his tongue and was immediately regretful when he felt her stiffen and draw back. But suddenly her lips opened to him again and she returned his kiss. While he caressed her offered lips, slowly and lightly, she seized the hand that had been resting on her knees and raised it with a gentle movement until it lay against her breast. Beneath the thin cambric, he could perceive the perfection of her form and the stiffening of the coral tip beneath his palm.

Hardly daring to breathe for fear of frightening her, he allowed his hand to maintain its delicate contact with her breast. His thoughts were becoming unfocused and blurred because of the heady sensation of her lips greedily seeking his and the heat forming between her breast and his hand. Had he understood her action? Had Wren been making a conscious appeal for more intimate caresses, or had the placing of his hand upon her breast been merely a tender reflex?

Wren arched her back, her body extended toward him in an unmistakable offering. She felt his hand tremble where it touched her, and when he drew down the lace of her chemise, she was aware of a sudden burst of heat throbbing through her, igniting her senses to a flame of desire.

The pure, womanly curve of her breasts was bared to Caleb's view, and he was astonished by the silky whiteness of her skin, a whiteness all the more alluring in contrast to her throat and arms, which had been tanned by the sun.

His lips grazed her exposed skin tenderly, longingly, and with a sigh of pleasure she stretched herself in his arms, relishing the intimacy between them, aware of his desire for her, responding to him in a succession of undulating tremors which she knew were repeated within him.

For long moments their lips touched, their mouths searched, each straining toward the other as their desires mounted. Delicately, Wren detached herself from his arms and rose from his lap. She led him silently to his bunk, where she lay down and drew him close beside her, nestling her face into the hollow of his neck and tasting the salt tang from the spindrift which had misted over him during his watch at the wheel.

"Kiss me," she whispered, her voice barely audible in the cabin.

Responsive to her demands, he put his arms around her and sought her mouth. Edging slightly away from him, she tugged at the straps of her chemise until her breasts were completely bare to him. Fearing to surrender to his own wants, he hesitated to understand her action. Thoughts of the violence she had suffered at Malcolm's hands and his own vow of patience muddled his thinking. With a shy yet determined gesture, she lowered his head toward her bosom, offering herself to him, arching her back to bring her body into contact with his mouth.

Usually a demanding, impatient lover, Caleb acted with supreme tenderness, and instead of covering her breast with his mouth, he merely caressed the coral tip with a light flick of his tongue.

Wren issued a cry of surprise and delight, murmuring over and over, "Again, again."

Her demand freed him, allowing him to express his passion in a multitude of caresses with his lips and tongue, each more varied and intoxicating than the other.

Beneath the pressure of his hips, her legs had unconsciously parted and her petticoats had gradually rucked up, disclosing first a silk-stockinged leg and

240

then a firm-fleshed white thigh. Caleb closed his eyes to blot out the unexpected temptation, telling himself that he had promised patience with her, fearing he would be overcome with passion and force himself upon her. Yet he was aware of the close contact of their bodies, and his imagination was set afire as he pictured the nudity of her thighs and the center of her womanliness which was so near.

Wren jerked her head back, thrilled by the myriad caresses he was bestowing on her, oblivious to the temptation her parted legs offered, innocent of the nearly uncontrollable passions pounding through his veins.

To quell the desire to throw himself between her thighs and ravish her, Caleb slid from the bed and rested against the low side, his mouth teasing Wren's in a variety of warm, voluptuous caresses while his hands never strayed from her breasts. He murmured words of love and stirred her senses with his appreciation of her beauty. Her fingers tore at his fine lawn shirt, her lips seeking the hollow of his throat where she could feel his pulses throb. In a husky, impatient voice, she pleaded with him to remove his shirt. In his haste to obey her, he tore at the lacings, pulling the fabric over his head and tossing it to the other side of the cabin. Wren glided to the edge of the bed, turning toward him, her arms ready to enfold him, her eyes eagerly searching his newly bared midsection.

A wild temptation seized him . . . to outstrip her thoughts, remove what remained of his clothing and bring his urgent desire before her. Although he was increasingly aroused by this imagined gesture, his tender consideration for her sensibilities made him hesitate risking her alienation from him.

Wren allowed him no time for further reflection. She enclosed him in her arms and pressed herself against him, reveling in the sensation of her naked breasts molded to his bared chest. Her need to be close to him bordered upon a hunger, a yearning, an all-consuming desire to make herself a part of him. Her lips traced a pattern of a thousand interlaced designs; her fingers explored the finely honed muscles of his back and made a tentative survey of the hardness of his midsection.

His hands played in her hair, tangling the long sable strands through his fingers, grazing the soft skin of her cheek and stroking her lips as they came into fragile contact with his flesh. He gave himself up completely to her gentle ministrations and allowed himself to be transported beyond the threshold of mere physical satisfaction, finding he was able to contain his desires because of his most tender consideration for her needs and wants. He experienced heights of voluptuousness he had never known existed, and he marveled that he had discovered them at her shyly innocent, tentative touch.

He pulled back a little, away from her kisses, and in her hunger for him she drew him close again, making room beside her on the bed and fitting the curves of her body tightly against the long, lean length of him. Petticoats already rucked up above her knees, her motions pushed them still higher, displaying the harmonious roundness of her hips and the elegant stretch of her thighs, revealed in the dim lantern light.

Caleb was astonished to find his hand covering a portion of her bare thigh. His passion flared and his mouth sought hers with a deeper yearning, the sharp intake of his breath and the low sound of a moan coming from deep within his chest exciting her own heightened sensations, and she found herself exalting in his desire for her.

Prudently, he advanced his hand, wishing to prolong this unexpected contact without causing her to associate his intentions with the violence and degradation she had experienced at those other men's hands.

He knew in his heart and without a doubt that what was most important to him was not the conquest of her flesh but the conquest of her heart. He loved her without reservation, and the thought of doing anything which would destroy her trust in him was more devastating than an arrow shooting through his chest.

She was pleased by the touch of his hand on her thigh, and she too, sought to prolong that contact. Yet when her petticoats uncovered the whole length of her as far as the delicate line between leg and hip, she made an instinctive movement to drape herself beneath the lace skirts. But she didn't complete the gesture, and as though wanting to lose herself and erase her inhibitions in the rapture of his kiss, she moved her legs toward him.

Still Caleb hesitated, not wishing to alarm her, yet hungering for her, unable to draw her close enough, know her well enough.

His touch was light as he caressed her gently, stroking the inside of her thigh with a movement so soft, so gentle, that she relinquished herself to the delight she was experiencing.

Her acceptance of his caress provoked him toward further raptures. Their lips met, their tongues touched, her body molded itself against his, but when his fingers grazed the warm secret of her femininity, she instinctively closed her thighs, refusing him additional intimacy. Then, feeling him about to draw away, she seized his hand and stayed it in the place where her thighs met. He could feel the tension ripple through her body, the involuntary rigidness in her arms and neck, the sudden tightening of her mouth as it rested against his. Immediately regretful that he had initiated this resistance in her, he attempted to remove his hand, seeking to reassure her that he had no intention of submitting her to ravagement.

She demonstrated her reluctance to end this embrace by holding firm to his hand until her thighs relaxed their grip. With a deep, sensuous kiss, she offered him a victory over her constraints. A succession of tremors, long and passionate, coursed through her body beneath the warm contact of his hand, culminating in the blending of their lips as one.

The quiet night was broken only by the creaking of the ship and the low sound of his voice as he whispered lovers' words, telling her of her beauty, of the need he had for her, of his love. He spoke and she believed. His love was evident in the tenderness of his touch, in the adoration of his lips and in the emotion in his eyes when he looked into hers. She knew he would always keep her trust, knew the price his consideration of her was extracting. He worshipped her with his hands, protected her with his arms and loved her with his heart.

And, in return, Wren responded with her heart and soul. Loving him, being loved by him, knowing he understood her, appreciated her and intuitively perceived the woman behind the flesh, the soul beneath the intellect. The loving and the giving were enhanced by their mutual joy; their passions flamed by tender devotion, the treasure of their love cherished more fervently than a kingly prize. Wren had found Caleb and Caleb had found Wren; prophetically, each had found his destiny.

They were still; no words needed to be spoken; no kiss could demonstrate the emotions within them. Her voice was whisper-light, threaded with happiness; her words posed a question which was already answered in her heart. "Why did you stop, Caleb?"

He held her in his arms, his mouth pressed lightly against her brow. "Because, sweetheart, I will take you only when you ask me to."

"I couldn't have stopped you, and I would even have forgiven you. But I love you so much more, so much more completely, because you didn't insist . . ."

"Shhh. Hush, sweetheart. You needn't tell me. Don't you know, can't you feel, that our hearts speak to each other and make words unnecessary? Now hurry, fix yourself up. It's time I brought you back to your own bed. For now," he amended, his voice throbbing with a meaning that made her pulses dance.

Chapter Fifteen

She should have been one of the happiest women alive, Wren thought miserably as she leaned over the rail. *Should have been!* The last time she had been alone with Caleb, she had been certain she had found love. But in the two days since then, Caleb seemed to have little time for her, and watching Sara manipulate him fed Wren's jealousy as if it were a festering sore.

Caleb's face was grim as he made his way from the galley to the deck. His ship was infested with women! Every time he wanted to take a brief rest on deck, there was a woman occupying his favorite seat. The captain of a ship could expect certain calamities, but one of them wasn't a covey of squabbling women. Between Wren's arrogant hostility and Sara's persistent offerings to him, he was ready to pull out his hair. There was no reason for Wren's aloofness. What did she want from him? He had thought she loved him, but when he remembered their last night together, he had to face the fact that it was *he* who had professed his love, not Wren! Was she playing him for a fool? Damn! he cursed, realizing a dull aching in his loins. And he had been so considerate of her, of her fears, of her hesitancy to make love. How fitting! he laughed bitterly to himself, wincing from the uncomfortable ache. I denied myself and now she despises me for it!

He strode rapidly, hoping to avoid Sara and another one of her half-tearful pleadings to take her to his bed. He was fast running out of excuses. But he was too late. Sara was lying in wait, about to pounce on him. At least Wren was not around to witness this little maneuver of Sara's. He steeled himself in anticipation, hoping he presented a stern, forbidding manner.

"Caleb," Sara cooed, "how nice to see you on deck. You look tired. Was the watch strenuous this day?" Not waiting for a reply, she looked up at him and parted her lips in an inviting manner. Slowly, she let her tongue trace the outline of her mouth while she raised a hand to smooth a path on his cheek. "I have nothing to do, and I was wondering if we could have a talk." She paused briefly. "You see, it's about Bascom, and . . . well, it's just too difficult to stand here and try to explain. You have such a—what I mean is, you're so forceful and masculine—so unlike Bascom. I just need someone to talk to. Please," she pleaded, tears gathering in her eyes.

Damn it to Hell. He didn't want to talk to her in his cabin or to . . . he didn't want her in his cabin at all. Did she think him a fool? Evidently she did. He felt his face flush slightly and turned just in time to see Wren whirl on her heel and march out of sight. Son of a bitch! he almost howled. Once again Wren had misinterpreted what she had seen. Only this time there was no wounded expression, no hurt eyes. This time there was a piercing look of hatred shooting from those glowing eyes. She had wanted to kill him on the spot.

Sara had also seen the expression on Wren's face, and she smiled. She could care less how Wren felt. Wren was merely a silly child who was inexperienced in the ways of men and the world, while she, Sara, knew just how to entice a man. Hadn't she just convinced Caleb to go to his quarters? Men like Caleb didn't talk when they had a woman behind closed doors. Men like Caleb did what was expected of them. Caleb would never admit to Wren or to anyone else that they had only "talked." With men like Caleb, the less said the better. It was enough that Sara made trips to his cabin. Let the others think what they wanted.

Damn brazen jezebel! Wren cursed all the way back to her cabin. Damn brazen womanizer, that's all Caleb van der Rhys is. If he couldn't get what he wanted from me, Sara will do just as well. Does he think I am stupid? The *very* next morning after *I* was with him, I saw *Sara* leaving his cabin. If he's going to take Sara to his bed, the least he can do is to do it in the dark. Oh, no, not Caleb! Broad daylight, for all the world to see! Dirty rotten womanizer—all he thinks of is one thing!

She threw herself on her bunk, a lone tear trickling down her cheek. One tear for Caleb. He wasn't worth more. Just one tear. She was so glad she hadn't given in to his lust! At least she could comfort herself that she hadn't allowed her flesh to weaken! Damn herself! She sniffed and blew her nose loudly as she got up from the bunk, banging her head sharply on the top board. She cursed again, long and loud, using every filthy expression she knew. Well, he could make a fool out of her only if she permitted it.

She sat for hours, perched like a bird ready for flight, figuring out how to destroy Caleb. She finally settled on the method of castration and racked her brain trying to remember how the Sea Siren had done in Chaezar Alvarez. It would come to her, and then she would do something. She swallowed as she recalled that Sirena had said there had been a river of blood. She hated blood. She would have to think of something else, some other way to make Caleb pay for all her sufferings. And I am suffering, she told herself. I can't eat, I can't sleep, she whined silently as she bit into a chunk of cheese and chewed rapidly. I'll hack off his leg at the knee, that's it, and then let's see if that jezebel wants a one-legged lover! And I'll chop off all of his fingers so he can't fondle Sara's pink-and-white flesh, she added as an afterthought.

She felt better. Once a decision had been made, the whole world looked brighter.

She was just stuffing another chunk of cheese in her mouth when Sara danced her way into the cabin, her dress buttoned sloppily and her long golden hair tangled and matted. Her lips looked bruised; her cheeks were flushed and her eyes sparkling. No woman had the right to look so . . . so alive and contented, Wren thought spitefully. She was the one who should be looking like the cat who had swallowed the canary. She would hack off all his toes—no, only five, because he would have only one leg, Wren added fiercely to herself. It seemed fair to her, ten fingers, five toes and one leg for making her suffer and putting her aside for Sara. Damn you, Caleb van der Rhys! She felt suddenly weak at the thought of what she was going to do to him.

"Wren, Caleb is so wonderful! Your brother is such a gentleman! I was so foolish not to have believed you all those times you told me how gallant he was. He knows how to make a woman feel like a woman." Sara eyed Wren suspiciously, wondering if she had noticed her clumsily fastened dress and disheveled hair. To her own disappointment, Caleb hadn't laid a finger on her. He had demanded she speak what was on her mind and leave him to tend to his duties. Certain that Wren would think she had spent the last hour in Caleb's cabin, she had made herself scarce by hiding on the afterdeck, behind several crates of chickens. When enough time had passed, she had returned to the cabin she shared with Lydia and Wren, hastily rebuttoning her gown, tearing the pins from her hair and biting hard on her lips to redden them and give them a passion-bruised glow.

"Shut up, Sara. I don't want to hear anything about Caleb and how marvelous he is. Just tell me one thing. How would you like him if he only had one leg, five toes and no fingers? Just tell me that."

"I think your jealousy has left you tetched in the head," Sara said loftily. "Is it my fault that your brother finds himself enamored of me? Well, is it?"

"You're a slut, Sara Stoneham! You throw yourself at him! Any man becomes an animal when a bitch in heat wags her tail!"

"The pot calling the kettle black!" Sara spit. "If you want to think I'm a slut, then go ahead and think it. Caleb, however, doesn't share your opinion, and that's all that matters."

"How could he know any differently? All he's ever known are sluts like you!" Wren shot back defensively. "But you're right. Caleb's opinion is all that counts, and if he loves you, then I wish you both well."

Sara yawned, stretching her arms above her head. "I think I'll take a little nap before the dinner hour." She fixed a sleepy eye on Wren and added, "Somehow your good wishes don't ring quite true. Is it my fault, dear little Wren, if Caleb prefers me?" Her voice dropped an octave and became sly. "It must be difficult to be rejected by a man, and doubly hard when you have been rejected by two men!"

Wren wanted to reach out and wring her neck or, at the very least, put her fist through Sara's sensuous mouth. Instead, she seethed inwardly till her stomach felt on fire. She had to get away from Sara, away from this cabin. Could she go on deck and chance running into Caleb? Never. She would go to the galley and talk to Gustave.

Out of the corner of her eye Wren saw Peter relieve Caleb from the watch. Damn! She had dallied on deck too long. Now she would have another confrontation with him, one she couldn't afford emotionally. Caleb worked his magic on her, and she was quicksilver in his hands. But not this time. Enough was enough.

A quick look over her shoulder proved that her long-legged gait was no match for Caleb's determined stride. He was just another womanizer, like Regan used to be. Like father, like son! Well, she wasn't going to be one of his "women." She felt his warm breath on her neck as he grasped her shoulder and spun her around. "Take your lecherous hands off me," she gritted. Shaking free of him, she proceeded to walk away.

Angered at her attitude, Caleb blasted out. "Just a goddamn minute, Wren. I want to know what's going on. Don't think you're going to pull one of your pouting acts on me like you do with Regan and assume it will work. If you have something to say, say it. Act like a woman!"

Grow up! Act like a woman! Didn't he know any other words? She whirled around, her eyes spewing fire, her small hands clenched into fists. Before she knew what she was doing or could even think about it, she had clasped both hands together and brought them up under Caleb's chin with every ounce of strength in her body. "I *am* grown up, or hadn't you noticed? I am a woman. As a matter of fact," she said viciously, "I think I'm too much woman for you to handle. You need someone like Sara to mew and weep on your shoulder. That," she spit, "is the only thing that makes

250

you feel like a man!" An angry, hurt sob caught in her throat as she turned and raced down the deck.

Caleb rocked, stunned from her blow and at her words. Then he sprinted after her and this time pulled her to him from the waist. He held her in a viselike grip, his strong fingers digging into her shoulders. His eyes were mocking and full of devilment as he stared down into her flushed face. "You're jealous of Sara. My little bird is jealous of Sara." His marveling tone was more than Wren could bear.

She forced all emotion from her voice and spoke slowly and distinctly. "On the contrary, Mr. van der Rhys." She made his name sound like an obscenity, and Caleb gritted his teeth. "If the bed-hopping Sara is what you want, then she is what you shall have. Stay away from me before you end up giving me one of the social diseases that Sara is so fond of sharing with her . . . friends."

Caleb's face drained of all color at her words. Jesus Christ, that was all he needed, a good dose of the clap! Damn her eyes, was she lying? She certainly sounded as if she knew what she was talking about. Christ, was that subject something women spoke of? How many men they had— The thought was so horrendous that Caleb backed off a step and had to fight to get his breath. Damn her to Hell. He should have taken her by force when he had had the chance. He was less than a man, and, by God, if he did have the clap, she would have it by now, too. When a van der Rhys fouled up, he fouled up all the way. She had to be lying. Sara was a Puritan, and Puritans just didn't have things like that. Or did they? Sara certainly was knowledgeable, almost as professional as some of the whores he had known.

If he could have seen the wicked smirk on Wren's face, he would have killed her then and there. He stormed into his quarters. Before this voyage was over, he would have Wren in his bed with or without his social disease, and this time he wouldn't be a gentle-man about her and her damn fears. This time he would act like the man he was. And then he'd wring her goddamn skinny neck and laugh while he was doing it. And he'd wring Sara's neck right along with hers. Women!

Sara wanted to strike out at Wren when she returned to her bunk. In the dim light Sara imagined she saw a warm smile on her face, a satisfied look a woman wears when she has just made love. The same warm, contented look she herself had worn so many times with Malcolm. She watched Wren with deep hatred as the girl snuggled between the covers and drifted off to sleep. She couldn't let Wren steal Caleb away from her. Caleb was hers. After all, he was the father of her child. How easy the words fitted once she had decided in her mind that Caleb was to become her unborn child's father. She had decreed it, and that was all that mattered. In time Caleb would come to accept it without reservation, if he thought of it at all. Caleb was an honorable man. Honorable men always did what they were supposed to do, and he was supposed to marry her. Men were also stupid. They believed what they wanted to believe. Men always liked to know that their seeds had sprouted. That made them feel manly and protective. And if there was one thing Sara needed now, it was protection. She couldn't allow Wren to steal Caleb from her. She had to do something and do it soon.

She lay for hours formulating one plan after another and then rejecting each of them for various reasons. Aubrey Farrington was close to Caleb, a confidant and good friend. Wren was in love with Caleb, any fool could see that. Farrington and Wren stood between "her" Caleb and "their" child. Therefore, they would have to be eliminated. A smile tugged at the corners of Sara's mouth, and her eyes took on a glazed, faraway look. She rolled over and slept, satisfied that she had at last decided on a plan of action.

On his way to the wheelhouse the following morning, Caleb's face was black with rage at his circumstances. All through the morning he watched the three women sun themselves on deck. Each time his eyes fell on Wren, his heart lurched. When he looked at Sara, his eyes became speculative and brooding. Lydia, on the other hand, brought a soft smile to his lips. When he saw Wren lean over the rail, an alien feeling washed over him. She tripped on the hem of her skirt and almost fell into the churning water. He gasped as his throat tightened. If she had gone over, it would be the end for him. How could that be? he questioned himself. The answer was simple. He, Caleb van der Rhys, loved Wren. Totally. As he had professed to her their last time together. Since the beginning of time, men had loved women. Why had he thought he could go through life and never truly experience that feeling? Because, since the beginning of time, women had been wily and devious and manipulative in regard to men, and he hadn't wanted to be trapped into those circumstances.

He wanted her. He needed her. God, how he needed her! Wanting her was selfish; needing her was as necessary as having to draw another breath. Would she listen to him? Not likely. Wren never listened. Then he would have to show her. Regan always said actions proved more than words. Some women liked the words, like Sara. Pretty words, lies really, pleased Sara. But then, Sara was a fool. Wren was not. He could tell her all the pretty lies and she would turn around and match him word for word, lie for lie, and where would he be then? Back where he had started.

He seemed to be having difficulty breathing as he gazed at her from time to time, and his loins took on a suspicious ache that only one thing could relieve, but he would die before he made another advance to Wren. A goddamn pity if he should die at sea within the next few days and go to his watery grave in a semicelibate state.

He forced his mind and eyes back to the endless expanse of water. When Peter relieved him after the noon meal, he would seek out Wren and try to convince her. Convince her of what? his mind shouted. He refused to answer his own question.

When Wren had tripped on the torn hem of her dark gown, Sara had thought to herself, Now, why couldn't she have gone over the side and saved me the trouble of— No, she wouldn't even think about that here in the bright sunshine. That thought was for her dim cabin during the velvety night. She glanced toward the sun and swiftly calculated how much longer Caleb would be on watch. A little more than an hour. By that time she would have contrived a way to meet him and throw herself into his arms for the benefit of Wren's watchful eyes. Her face was almost feral in the golden light, and Lydia nudged Wren, who refused to look in Sara's direction.

From time to time Wren allowed herself to be tortured as she gazed at Caleb's muscular body behind the wheel. How could he prefer Sara to her? She loved him, couldn't he tell? Why was he making a fool of her in front of the crew and everyone else? Because he was a hateful man, and that was what men did. Why did they think women were good for only one thing? And who taught them such things? Another man, of course. If Caleb wanted Sara, he could have her, with Wren's blessing. Never with my blessing, she sobbed inwardly. Oh, God, I love him so, she wanted to cry out for everyone to hear. I can't let him do this to me; I can't show him how he's hurt me. I can't bear it. Tears of anger and frustration gathered in her eyes, and she brushed them away impatiently. She would be damned if she would cry over Caleb van der

Rhys. Never! The man hadn't been born who was worth her tears. Her mind refused to listen to her heart, and she closed her eyes wearily, visions of herself lying in Caleb's arms and responding to his tender touches flashing suddenly before her. She leapt off her chair and strode down the deck as if the hounds of Hell were on her heels.

As she passed the wheelhouse she sent Caleb such a scathing, scorching look that he blanched. Now, what in the hell had gotten into her? he wondered. She was just like Sirena—all mouth and legs. His lean jaw hardened as he remembered how she had felt in his arms, how her long legs had pressed against his. Christ, he couldn't think of that now! Yes, he could. He wanted to bury his face in her wealth of dark hair and then twine it through his fingers as he drew her face to his in a long, passionate kiss that she returned with equal ardor. "Peter!" He'd be goddamned if he would wait another minute. He would go to her now, tell her now, and then drag her off to his quarters whether she liked it or not. She would like it! He would make her love it and him at the same time!

Peter loped into the wheelhouse, breathing heavily and wondering why the sound of his name had the ring of iron in it. Seeing the look on Caleb's face, he merely grasped the wheel and thought better of the question he had been about to ask.

Caleb took to the deck at a dead run, his bare feet barely touching the polished planks. He saw a wisp of black round the corner and increased his speed. He was upon her within seconds and had her pinned in his arms. His eyes were closed, his breathing heavy, as he forced her body close to his. She felt different. He had expected her to stiffen at his touch, and here she was, soft and pliant. *Aaah.* He opened his eyes and almost choked on his own saliva. At the moment his stunned eyes accepted that it was Sara in his arms, Wren came into view and saw them locked together.

255

Caleb would have sold his soul to the devil if he could have erased the wounded look from her face. But it was not to be. He knew in his gut that no matter what he said or how he said it, she would look right through him and not hear a word. Wren was lost to him forever. God in His Heaven would never be able to convince him otherwise.

Wren heard Sara say, "Darling Caleb, how wonderful of you to take time away from your watch to be with me," as she continued on her way. She would bleed later, in the privacy of her bunk, but not here for all to see.

Caleb stared down into Sara's eyes. "What are you doing here?" he demanded harshly, his eyes hard and cold.

"I'm standing here with you, in your arms. What a foolish question," she purred softly. While her tone was soft, her insides churned. She had seen the look on Wren's face as well as the horror in Caleb's eyes when he had realized just who was in his arms. Her mind raced as she squirmed, rubbing her body against his in an almost sensuous rhythm. She would make him forget Wren. He didn't need Wren; he needed her and their baby. He would be so happy when she told him that soon they would be parents. He would love her then. Caleb was an honorable man, and honorable men always loved their wives and families. Caleb wouldn't be any different. "Darling, shall we go to your quarters?" she asked breathlessly.

Caleb's terse "No," slashed through her like a whip. She recovered quickly and smiled at him, her eyes lowered demurely. "I understand. Daylight does pose its problems. I'll come to you tonight, after the moon is high. I'll spend the rest of the day thinking of you."

Before Caleb could reply, she had gone. For a moment he was puzzled. Her eyes had reminded him of something. Or was it someone? He couldn't think now; it would come to him later.

Two days passed with Caleb, according to Aubrey Farrington, acting like the devil himself. He was torn, anguished over the fact that he couldn't get near Wren. Each time he came within eyesight of her, she put as much distance as possible between them, and always her face mirrored that same wounded look and then deep hatred. The situation was eating him alive, and for the first time in his life he didn't know what to do. He was being boxed into a corner with his emotions running high for Wren, and at the same time he was fighting off Sara's bold advances, which were becoming increasingly more blatant. He knew he had always been desirable to women, but Sara was something he had not counted on, unlike any woman he had ever come across. She wanted him, desired him and intended to have him. He would have to tell her, and the sooner the better, that she could never mean anything to him.

Sara had been deliberately stalking Caleb for two days, and was horrified to discover that all her suspicions were correct. Caleb was lost to her. He wanted Wren, desired her and was fighting the way a man fights for a woman. Like a fool, Sara thought angrily. And stupid, silly Wren was playing right into her hands by running from him. Sara was wise to Wren. She knew Wren was running from Caleb in the hope that her unavailability would drive him mad with desire. Now, where had the silly little fool learned *that* trick? It doesn't really matter, Sara told herself calmly. Caleb is falling for it and making an ass of himself in front of his crew and the others. Wren will have Caleb in the palm of her hand in another day. Sara knew that just by looking into Caleb's eyes. Well, Caleb might love Wren, but he would be honorbound to her, Sara, when she told him of "their" baby. Caleb would then fall *out of* love with Wren and fall *in* love with her. She would make him love her. And to insure that happy occurrence, she would do away with the only two people in the world who meant anything to him. In his sorrow and grief he would turn to her and "their" child for comfort. Her eyes were sly as she watched the crew go about its duties. Sly and furtive and not quite seeing.

By noon of the following day Wren felt as though she were possessed by the devil. She wanted to wreak havoc, to kill Sara, to lash out at Caleb for his uncaring attitude toward her and for the humiliation she suffered at his hands. And, God help her, she loved him. Another day or so and they would touch land, and she would put as much distance between her and Caleb van der Rhys as possible. She would cut him out of her heart and make a new life, she and Lydia. She knew she was lying to herself. She could never forget Caleb, not ever. He was in her blood for now and for always. She amended the thought: she would *try* to forget him.

Lydia's heart ached for the sorrowing girl. She wanted to comfort her, but she knew that Wren preferred to be alone with her thoughts. She felt she should say something but didn't know the proper words. When she tried to speak to her, Wren's face closed like a book. She would suggest a stroll around the deck and then, when the moment was right, say something comforting. Wren refused the offer of a walk, pleading fatigue.

"Wren, my dear, has it occurred to you that you may well be doing Caleb an injustice? You haven't given him a chance to explain or to set matters straight. You aren't certain of all the facts. If things are as bad as you seem to think, then why has the captain been trying to talk to you?"

"Talk, my foot," Wren shrilled. "I know what I saw and heard. He's nothing but a damnable womanizer, and all he wants is another notch in his belt. He's mean and rotten through and through." Wren kicked out viciously at the bunk.

"No, he isn't, and you know it," Lydia defended the captain. "He's a fine man who loves you very much. I'm not wise like you, Wren, but I know what I read in his eyes. You are the one who is being mean and rotten. Forgive me for speaking to you like this, but someone must make you understand the man whom you're tormenting."

"Save your breath, Lydia. I saw him with Sara and heard the words she spoke to him. That meeting was prearranged, and every night she goes to him. She can have him. I wouldn't take him if he were offered to me on a silver platter. And you're wrong, Lydia. If Caleb loved me, as you said, he would keep the greatest distance between Sara and himself. Every time I turn around I see her draped over him in some fashion. I no longer care," Wren concluded loftily.

Disgusted, Lydia picked up some mending to while away the time. "Since you're an authority on the subject, I refuse to waste my breath, as you put it. However," she added, striving for the last and final word, "you're wrong about Captain van der Rhys. The day will come when you realize this, and then it will be too late."

"If that day should ever come, you'll be the first to hear of it, for I won't be around," Wren said wretchedly. If only what Lydia said were true, she would be the happiest woman in the world.

Why, why, *why* hadn't she proved the full extent of her love for him? Damn herself and her little girl's fears! Caleb had wanted to make love to her, the kind of love a man gives to a woman, and, Heaven knew, she had wanted him to. But after Malcolm and the seamen, she had been afraid. If only she'd been able to conquer her fears and behaved like the woman she longed to be. The kind of woman Caleb wanted and needed.

The afternoon hours crawled on tortoise legs toward evening and darkness. Sara was nervous and irritable, ignoring Lydia's feeble attempts at conversation. She ignored Wren completely. Wren was the root of all her problems. Ever since Wren had spent the entire night with Caleb, Sara had been rebuffed by him, and none too nicely either. This evening might be her last chance to make him want her again. Once she had told him of "their" child, things would be different. Things *had* to be different!

Unable to sit still after dinner, Wren went on deck for a breath of fresh air. As she glanced about her, she realized a storm was brewing from the west; from the looks of things, it was going to be a bad one. Already the crew was busy securing the ship for the onslaught of winds and rain that would pour down on her. She wondered what Caleb was doing and where he was at this exact minute. Had Lydia been right? Did Caleb really love her? Was he simply playing with Sara to make Wren jealous enough to crawl to him, as all his other women had done? If that was so, he was certainly going to have a long wait. She'd crawl for no man, especially Caleb van der Rhys.

What she could do was walk. She didn't have to crawl. Worms crawled. She had pride and Caleb had injured it, either knowingly or unknowingly. She could go to him and at least listen to what he had to say. Listening couldn't hurt anything. She could listen and walk away and ponder the matter, then make a decision later as to what he had had to say. Surely that couldn't hurt, and maybe she would be able to sleep peacefully and not have her dreams tormented by him. But before she did that, she would have to calm herself and collect her wits. She clung to the mizzen-mast as her heart began to pound at the thought of being near Caleb again.

While Wren considered her actions, Sara left the cabin and made her way directly to Caleb's quarters. She knew she had picked the right time. For some reason, when a storm was approaching or in progress, a person's emotions ran high. Caleb would be in fine fettle, and so would she. She could barely balance herself as she went along, holding her arms out against the bulkheads. She could almost feel his arms around her in his cabin as the storm raged outside. Caleb would protect her and keep her safe because he was an honorable man.

She reached his cabin, knocked on the door and waited. Realizing he couldn't have heard that feeble little sound with the wind howling the way it was, she opened the door cautiously and was almost blown inside.

Caleb looked up, startled, at the open door, which she didn't bother to close. He dropped the boot he was about to pull on and stood up, his face becoming mottled because of her uninvited intrusion. "What are you doing here?" he demanded harshly.

"That's a silly question for you to ask me, Caleb. You know very well what I'm doing here. Actually, I'm here for two reasons. One, to make love to you, and two, to make you the happiest man in the world. So far I'm the only one who knows the secret, but because it involves you, I'm going to share it with you. It's the secret that will make you the happiest man in the world. Sit down, Caleb, and let me help you with your boot," she singsonged, sending chills up Caleb's spine.

His mouth tightened. "Sara, a storm is approaching and I have to take the wheel. Look, I don't want to hurt you, but this . . . this lovemaking is not going to work. I don't love you; I never did. I love Wren, and I think you know that. I'm sorry, but I told you in the beginning that it was just a—"

"Fling," Sara again singsonged. "But," she said, wagging a playful finger under his nose, "that little fling has made me pregnant, and now what are we going to do?"

Caleb had bent down to pull on his boot, and when

he raised his eyes, stunned at her words, he saw Wren standing in the doorway. She, too, wore a stunned, unbelieving expression. Then she vanished. Sweet, merciful God. Of all the goddamned, ill-timed luck! Rage boiled in him as he pulled on his boot and got to his feet. He took Sara by the shoulders and shook her wildly. "Do you know what you just said? Do you know or care, for that matter, that Wren heard your lie? No, I see that you don't. I can count, Sara, and it's impossible for me to be your child's father—if there is a child. Your trick won't work, Sara. I'm not the father, and well you know it. I'm ordering you to go below and tell Wren that what she overheard was a lie! What you've done is despicable, and I can never forgive you for it. What we had was nothing more than a physical encounter. We both spoke of it that way, if you remember. No promises were made by either of us. I took you to be a worldly woman; you certainly acted like one. It was never my intention to deceive you in any way, and if you misunderstood me, then that becomes your problem. Not mine, never mine. You would be wise if you'd go below before the storm worsens. In the morning you can talk this matter over with your brother and seek your best course of action. I can't. I won't allow you to ruin my life with this false accusation."

Sara heard the words, understood them and nodded. "If Wren weren't here, you would love me—I know it. You would love me and our baby. You don't need me now that you have Wren and Aubrey Farrington. If you don't want to have anything to do with our baby, then I will do as you suggest. I will go to Bascom and have him help me. I don't want you to worry about our child. Somehow I will manage without your help. In later years, if you have the desire to see your child, I will not stand in your way."

Caleb stared at her, not quite believing what he was hearing. He knew damn well he wasn't the father of her child. What was wrong with her? And, for Christ's sake, why was he standing here wasting time worrying about what she was saying, when he should be concerned with the coming storm and Wren? Of all the damnable luck! He couldn't waste any more time; he had to get on watch. "See yourself out and be careful on deck," he called over his shoulder.

"Of course I'll be careful. I know that you're just upset now because it is difficult for a man to know he's going to become a father and that he'll have to put his wild ways behind him and settle down to a domestic life. Have no fear, Caleb. I'll walk with great care to protect our child."

It wasn't her words that sent a chill down Caleb's spine, it was the vulturelike look in her eyes and the singsong way she spoke.

After he had left, Sara sat for a long time on Caleb's bunk. Thoughts skittered through her brain like wildfire. She smiled as she picked up a shirt Caleb had discarded, and a brush. She held them against her cheek and then hid them beneath her petticoats. Her child would have these articles as remembrances of his father. They weren't much, but they were something. She looked around for an item for herself and picked up a pair of faded trousers. These few mementos would prove to her child that he did have a father.

She trotted happily out of the cabin, singing softly under her breath. The strong wind almost lifted her off her feet, but she held on to the masts with a firm grip. She had already made up her mind to ignore Wren, so there would be no problem. All she had to do now was wait.

263

Chapter Sixteen

A jagged streak of lightning danced across the sky, followed by a low, threatening roll of thunder. Sara drew her knees up and locked her arms around them, frightened of the ominous sounds coming from the heavens. Did she have the courage to carry out her plan? The idea of going anywhere near the locker box again terrified her, as did the idea of being near Malcolm again. I must do what must be done, she told herself, or else Wren will have Caleb and I will be an outcast with a child.

Almost as soon as the blackness overhead was silent, she moved on cat's feet toward Wren's bunk and shook her awake. "Shhh," she cautioned, a finger to her lips. "Come with me. There's something I have to show you. Be very quiet and follow me," she implored, "and don't awaken Lydia."

Startled by Sara's intrusion on her sleep, and even more apprehensive about the girl's strange behavior, Wren crept from the bunk and her place beside Lydia. Sara's glassy-eyed expression was the same one she had worn the night Wren had found her standing over the bunk she shared with Lydia. A flutter of fear tugged at Wren, but she disregarded it as Sara led her through the darkness, nimble as a cat.

Their trek took them below, into the belly of the ship, and they turned to the right, toward the bow. Sara had lit a candle stub and carried it in front of her, her hand protecting the feeble flame. Finally she came to a halt and put her finger to her lips to indicate silence. "I want you to see what's inside."

"Sara, are you all right? You don't look well to me." Now Wren's skin was crawling with fear, the hackles rising on the back of her neck, and she felt as though her hair were standing on end. This was crazy! Sara was crazy! What were they doing here in the belly of the ship, below the waterline with the rats? Wren wanted to turn tail and run, but she had come this far, and her curiosity was heightened by Sara's furtive attitude. She decided to humor Sara for the moment and then take her back to bed.

"Don't make a sound," Sara warned. "You're never going to believe what I'm going to show you! Be careful, now. When I open the door, we'll walk through and stand to the right. Stand perfectly still, and you'll see what I'm talking about."

Wren reached for Sara's hand, holding it tightly, feeling the pressure returned to her own fingers. As Sara slowly and silently slid the bolt and swung open the door, Wren's flesh crawled at the thought of what might lie behind it. Together they moved from the darkness into a room Wren recognized as the locker box, which was sometimes used as the brig. She moved to the right, as Sara had instructed, still holding the girl's hand. Before she had felt Sara wrest her hand free and heard her slip outside the door, she knew what was going to happen. The terminal sound of the bolt sliding across the iron flange greeted her ears.

She whirled, her fists beating against the stout door, screaming at Sara to set her free.

265

"It won't do you any good, my dear," said an oily, ugly voice.

At the familiar tone, the blood froze in Wren's veins and she slowly backed off, her arms held straight in front of her for protection. "Stay away from me."

"Oh, no, my little bird. I want you to see what you did to me." Malcolm turned and picked up the lantern and held it high over his head. Wren gasped and edged away a few more steps till her back was against the damp wall. "Do I frighten you? Ah, I see I do. Look at your handiwork and know that I'm going to return the favor. When I finish with you, there won't be a man who will look at you."

Wren tried to breathe through her mouth to avoid smelling the rotten stench that was everywhere.

"Come here, little bird, kiss me the way you used to and whisper all those pretty words. Damn you, come here! Scream, I see you want to. No one can hear you in the storm. Scream if you want to, I won't stop you."

Abruptly she was in his arms, his foul breath on her cheek, his hot, moist lips crushing hers. She stiffened and tried to free herself from his grasp. He was harsh and brutal in his handling of her as he tore at her clothing, exposing her breasts to his greedy mouth. Overcome with revulsion, she struggled vainly as his mouth moved again to hers. His lips were avid, searching, and she felt his tongue force her lips apart. The harder she struggled, the tighter his embrace became. He freed his mouth and let his lips travel down to her throat, and again they touched her silky skin. When his viselike hand grasped her breast, her eyes widened in fear and her breathing grew ragged. Loathing him, loathing herself because she was in this situation, she continued her struggles, which only made him more demanding. Cruelly, he twisted the soft flesh of her breasts until it stung. She whimpered with the pain and felt scalding tears course down her cheeks, knowing that no matter what she did, the inevitable was certain to happen.

Malcolm laughed lewdly as he taunted her with filthy phrases of what he was going to do to her and what he was going to make her do to him.

He threw her roughly to the dirty floor and was atop her in seconds. Holding her shoulders pinned to the floor, he kicked off his trousers and freed himself for his attack. He drove into her and smiled sadistically at her cries of pain and shame. Again and again he used her, each time more brutally than the last.

When he had finished with her, he pushed her against the wall and laughed. "When I'm through with you, that's all you'll be good for. To service men."

Wren lowered her head and vomited at her feet, adding to the stench in the room. God, help me, she prayed silently.

Back on deck, Sara found her way to Aubrey Farrington's quarters and tiptoed inside. Her eyes gleaming wickedly, she lifted the club she carried high above her and brought it down on Farrington's head.

Without a backward glance, she walked through the door and out to the deck. The night was velvet black, the only light a streak of lightning frolicking across the ebony sky. Quickly she tossed the bloody club overboard and stood back to wait for the driving rain that would thunder down on the decks. Her eyes were blank, her body limp. When she felt she had been sufficiently soaked from the heavy downpour, she ran screaming to the wheelhouse. Caleb looked at her in shock. He heard the words but couldn't believe his ears. Wren had jumped overboard and Sara couldn't save her. Christ!

"All hands!" he shouted to be heard over the storm. "Man overboard!" What in the goddamn hell was *that* going to do? All around him was inky blackness and torrents of rain. The swells were higher than the ship. She didn't have a chance. No one, no matter

267

how excellent a swimmer, could survive those waters during a storm. "All hands!" he repeated hoarsely.

The first mate looked at him and shook his head. "Captain, there's no way. You know that better than anyone. Go below. I'll take the wheel."

Caleb left the wheelhouse in a daze, Sara on his heels. "What happened?" he asked, his gut on fire with the effort of his words.

"I don't know. She said she wanted to go out for a breath of air. I told her not to go, that there was a storm. I begged her, pleaded with her," Sara babbled as she brushed her wet hair from her forehead. "She's dead, isn't she? I should have tried harder, but she was so strong and I'm so weak. I tried, truly I did. Please tell me it isn't my fault. You know how strong-willed Wren always was. Once she got an idea into her head, no one could shake it loose. Something was bothering her. She had acted peculiar all evening. Say it wasn't my fault, Caleb, please say it wasn't my fault. I refuse to believe Wren would kill herself because she had seen me and heard what I said in your cabin."

Wren was gone. Dead. She had said she was grown up and had looked at him the way a woman looks at a man whom she loves, and now she was gone. Dead. Given over to the sea. He groaned and buried his head in his hands.

"Caleb, say it wasn't my fault," Sara cried wretchedly.

"Go below, Sara. We'll talk later. I want to be alone."

She couldn't be dead. Not Wren.

The storm raged far into the night. Caleb watched it and listened to it with unseeing eyes and unhearing ears. His thoughts were only on Wren. Torrents of rain beat against him. He felt nothing, numb to his surroundings. The crew, intent on keeping the ship secure, could offer him no aid. He needed his time alone to accept what had happened. It was his fault, and he would have to live with it for the rest of his life. Thoughts of Sirena and Regan crept into his mind from time to time, and he quickly rejected them. He would have to deal with them some other time and in another place. If he were lucky, the storm would claim him, too. He couldn't go back. By now God only knew where Wren's lifeless body would be. He wondered how long she had fought the turbulent waters before she had finally succumbed to the inevitable. Why?

A vicious bolt of thunder ripped down and rolled out to sea as the question entered his mind. Why? Why would Wren leap overboard in the middle of a storm? In her own way she was as feisty and fiery as Sirena had been. Their meeting on deck a few days before was hardly reason for her to go overboard tonight and end her life. She had eaten a hearty dinner, too; he himself had seen the empty plates. It was Sara and her damnable lie!

He rubbed his temples with unsteady hands and then felt the stubble on his chin and cheeks. He should go below and change his sodden clothing and shave. When the seas calmed, he would have to assemble the crew and officiate at a makeshift service of sorts for Wren. He couldn't do it. But as captain of the ship, he had to. Why? The question tormented him. Over and over he repeated the same question. Why?

His legs stiff and cramped, he stood and stretched his aching arms. Empty arms. Again he felt the stubble on his chin. Why? He would ask Aubrey if he had noticed anything. Perhaps Wren had said something to him. He had a keen, if not slick, mind, and sometimes he was damn intuitive. Aubrey might know something.

In his cabin, Caleb shed his water-soaked clothing and donned dry clothes. He shaved and gave himself a wicked gash across his cheek to which he applied a dab of alum and then flinched. Why?

His shoulders slumped as he made his way to Farrington's quarters. If Aubrey didn't have an answer for him, what would he do? Sara claimed she knew nothing. Lydia might know something. That was unlikely, or she would have made her way to him during the storm. She seemed a sensible, forthright woman and genuinely fond of Wren. Perhaps she didn't know anything. But that was also unlikely, since Wren shared the same cabin with her.

He didn't bother to knock but opened the door, calling Aubrey's name as he entered. As he made his way to the bunk, he drew back in horror when he saw why Farrington hadn't answered. The old gambler's mouth was agape in a soundless cry. His dead eyes stared out from beneath a lethal wound. Caleb swallowed hard as he bent his ear to the gambler's mouth. Nothing, not even a faint breath. His fingers sought the pulse in Farrington's throat. No faint beat. Aubrey Farrington was dead. Caleb's mind refused to recognize what his eyes were seeing. Tears stung him at the injustice of it all. What was happening on his ship? Who would do such a dastardly thing? Farrington had never hurt a soul, and when it came down to the wire, he could always be counted on to do the right thing. Who? Why? Tears filled Caleb's eyes for the old man who had no one but Caleb to mourn him.

A white-hot fire took possession of his mind and body as he stormed his way to the main deck, cursing and bellowing so that the hands needed no call to report to their captain. Caleb was like the devil incarnate as he told the drenched crew of Aubrey's death and Wren's going overboard. "It's too much of a coincidence, and before we dock in America, I promise you the guilty party will hang by the neck. Now search this goddamn ship from stem to stern and see if there's a stowaway we don't know about. I want that bastard brought before me so I can stare into his eyes and know why he did this. Peter," he shouted hoarsely, "bring that son of a bitch Stoneham here. Now!" The order was thunderous.

Minutes later Bascom Stoneham was standing before him, a prayer book clutched in his bony hands. He waited, a feral look on his face, for Caleb to make his intentions known. If he was shocked at the captain's words, he gave no sign. "We can all attest to the fact that none of us left the hold. Your own man, guarding the ladder, will bear this out. You must look elsewhere for your guilty party," he said arrogantly.

Caleb took a step forward and grasped Bascom's shirt in his fist. "You might have been in the hold, but somehow, some way, you're responsible; I feel it in my gut. Get him the hell out of my sight before I kill him!" Caleb shouted.

Sara stood next to a weeping Lydia, watching the confrontation with wide eyes. She felt her legs go weak with relief when Bascom was dragged off to the hold. Now she had only one problem to contend with, the search. She had to get below and somehow waylay any intruders in the locker-box area. She would offer her services in the search, saying she couldn't stand by and do nothing. She would cry and plead if she had to. She couldn't let one of the men find Malcolm and Wren. She had killed once and felt no remorse. She could do it again!

Her eyes took on a fanatical gleam as she watched Lydia weep and wail. "Blow your nose," she said curtly. "I can't stand your sniveling. Go back down to your quarters and cry there. You're doing no good here. I'm going to help in the search, and you're only getting in the way."

Lydia, used to obeying orders, turned and walked away, crying loudly and dabbing at her eyes with the hem of her skirt. She had lost the only friend she had ever had. Now what was she to do? And who had killed Aubrey Farrington and why? Why would Wren jump overboard? Why? Lydia might not be as smart or worldly as a man or more experienced than some women, but she knew one thing for a certainty. Wren van der Rhys would never kill herself. She knew this as well as she knew she needed to take another breath in order to live. Someone on this ship had killed Aubrey Farrington and caused Wren to go overboard. Who? Why?

The *Sea Siren*'s rain-swept decks, fore, aft and below, were alive with activity as the crew began the search the captain had ordered. Sara picked up a lantern and joined the men down the slippery deck, her long, heavy skirt caught in her fingers. She was intent on getting to the confines of the deepest regions of the ship before anyone else did. She held the lantern out in front of her, pretending to search in the darkest corners below decks. When she reached the locker-box area, she halted in her tracks and began to swing the lantern to and fro, humming to herself some senseless ditty that pleased her for the moment. Wouldn't silly old Wren be in her glory if she knew she was indirectly responsible for the activity aboard ship?

When her soft humming began to irritate her, Sara began to move about again, fighting the temptation to slide back the iron bolt and look inside. Let them rot, both of them. They deserved to die, eaten alive by the rats that scurried in the darkness.

Gustave, the galley cook, held his lantern high as he made his way to the locker box. Seeing Sara standing there carrying her own lantern aloft, he stopped short, his mouth agape.

"I've already looked in there, and there isn't anything inside but enormous rats," she said. "I've looked all over this area," she whined pitifully. "Aubrey Farrington was my friend, a dear friend, and I felt I had to do my bit by helping with the search." She moved closer so that Gustave could see the tears trickling down her cheeks. "I'm so tired from all this searching that I feel faint. Please help me."

272

Gustave, only too glad to take a rest, gallantly escorted her to a stack of wooden crates. Carefully, as though he were handling eggs, he eased her down and set his lantern on the floor at her feet.

"Oh, my, that does make me feel better," Sara sighed as she opened the buttons of her dress and fanned herself with a handkerchief. "It certainly is sweltering in here," she went on, opening another button and bending forward slightly. Her cleavage had the desired effect, and the cook forgot why he was in the depths of the ship, intent only on a better look at Sara's ample endowments.

"Dear lady, you must let me help you back to the deck," Gustave said huskily.

"In a moment. First I have to catch my breath. While I'm doing that, why don't you look over there?" she suggested, pointing to a dark corner. "I've looked everywhere else, but whatever you do, please don't open that door. I couldn't bear to see those big old rats run by me. Why, a dozen of them ran right by me when I opened it before. But I didn't let that bother me. I looked all over that room and saw nothing but more rats. I swear to you, it was more than I could bear, but I forced myself for the sake of my friend Aubrey Farrington," she declared breathlessly, leaning over again to peer at her dusty shoe. "Mercy me," she continued to babble, "a person just isn't safe anywhere anymore, and I had put so much trust in Captain van der Rhys." Sara watched the cook carefully to see how he was taking her blatherings; she was confident that she had indeed pulled the wool over his eyes. "Just keep looking," she trilled to the startled Gustave. "We do want to tell Captain van der Rhys that we searched every inch of this blasted ship, as he ordered."

"Yes, ma'am," Gustave said happily. After he had satisfied himself that nothing or no one was lurking in the dark corner, he made his way back among the heaving packing crates and settled himself at Sara's feet to wait. For what he didn't know. She certainly looked like a lady, a distraught lady. His eyes went to the opening of her gown and her heaving breasts. How he wished he could reach inside that gown and touch her silky skin. Ladies like Miss Stoneham always had silky skin.

Sara watched him through sulky eyes and finally got up. "I think I feel strong enough to go back, if you'll just let me hold on to your arm." Deftly she buttoned her dress and stared primly ahead.

"Yes, ma'am," Gustave agreed dutifully. What had ever made him think a real lady like Miss Stoneham would be interested in the likes of him? She was the next thing to a saint, as his old mother used to say. Imagine a lady the likes of her coming all the way down here to help find the murderer of her friend. A genuine lady, there was no mistake about that.

Caleb's mouth became a tight white line when his crew stood before him and reported there was no stowaway on board. The *Sea Siren* was secure. He had known in his gut that the men would find nothing on the ship, but he had had to try. Now he would have to look elsewhere for the murderer of Aubrey Farrington. The crew understood what he was thinking, and each of them, save Gustave, wore a sullen look. Each had automatically become suspect.

His eyes on the sea, now calmed after the storm had spent itself, Caleb dismissed the crew and let his mind race. Wren must have been thrown overboard because of the gems. Whoever had done it must have thought Aubrey had more precious stones in his possession, and therefore had killed him. This solution was the only one that made sense.

The killer had to be a member of his crew. All the hands had watched the card game, making their own side bets on who was going to win, the ladies or the gambler. They had seen Wren and Lydia wrest a fortune in gems from Farrington, and Wren carry the stones away. Two lives for a pouch of colorful jewels. How Caleb wished that the murderer had been Bascom Stoneham; then he could wring that bastard's skinny neck.

As the night faded into the light of day, he drove himself and the crew unmercifully. He felt no need for a woman and turned Sara away when she offered to comfort him. As if there were any comfort for him anywhere. He only wanted to do his penance so he could live with himself. Comfort was the one thing he didn't need or want.

Chapter Seventeen

Sara stood against the rail and made her final plans. When the Puritans, the crew and Caleb left the ship, she would slip below and slide the bolt. It wouldn't matter then, for afterward she would be long gone. Caleb would be busy on land with the funeral service for Aubrey Farrington, and no one would miss her. If she unbolted the door silently, she would not have to make a penance. She had decided hours ago that she couldn't leave the pair locked in, no matter how she felt about them. After all, Malcolm was the true father of her child, and she simply couldn't kill him. If he chose to die by not opening the door, then that would be his decision. As long as she left it unlocked, God couldn't punish her.

The *Sea Siren* was like a ghost ship. The crew kept to itself, each man suspecting the other and fearful to be caught alone at any time of the day without someone close by. While Sara was amused, Lydia was quiet and withdrawn, silent tears streaming down her cheeks. The small pouch of gemstones she carried between her breasts—Wren's legacy to her—was becoming worrisome. She would give it to Captain van der Rhys for safekeeping and reclaim the gems when she needed them. She might as well do it now and get it over with. Sara was growing more peculiar by the hour, and that constant humming of hers was about to drive Lydia mad.

She approached the wheelhouse hesitantly, but when she entered, her stance was firm.

"Captain van der Rhys," she said quietly, "I would like to speak with you for a moment." She withdrew the pouch from her bodice and handed it to him. "Will you keep this for me till we make port?" Tears gathered in her eyes as she added, "It's Wren's legacy to me."

Caleb was stunned and his back stiffened. "Are these the gems you and Wren won from Aubrey Farrington?"

"Yes, Captain. Wren gave them to me. She said I would need them to make a new life when I got to America. She only played cards with Aubrey Farrington so I could have what she called a stake to make a new life. She did it for me, and I can't bear it." She began to sob.

"When did she give them to you?" Caleb asked harshly.

"Right after the card game, Captain. The following day she said she was going to try to figure out a way

276

to get Lord Farrington and Bascom into another game. She said these gems wouldn't last me too long and that I would need gold and Bascom had gold."

"Mrs. Stoneham, are you sure of what you're saying?" Caleb demanded.

"Of course I'm sure, Captain. I'm not a fool, as some people seem to think." She dried her eyes and glared angrily at Caleb. "It was someone on this ship, and I can't forgive you for not finding out who it was. And if you think it was my husband, you're mistaken. He's a coward, not a murderer."

Caleb's eyes were anguished and torn with guilt. Lydia felt sorry the moment she uttered the words, but they were true, she knew that. It was his duty to find the murderer. After all, he *was* the captain.

Long after Lydia Stoneham had returned to her quarters, Caleb sat hefting the small pouch in the palm of his hands. He was right back where he had started. If Wren and Aubrey hadn't been killed for the gems, then why had they been killed at all? Had they known something? Had they seen something? As always, his thoughts went to Bascom. According to the preacher's flock and to the guard on duty, Bascom Stoneham was as pure as an angel's wing. Caleb would just have to put him from his mind and concentrate somewhere else. The question was where? There was little time left. If the weather held, they would reach America in a few hours.

The *Sea Siren* straight on her course and secure, Peter herded the crew into Gustave's galley and motioned for silence. "It's time we had a few words," he said, not bothering to raise his voice. "I'm tired of looking at all of you with suspicion, just as you're tired of looking at me in a like manner. This ship will dock in a few hours, and we're no closer to finding out who killed Farrington than when we first began searching. Now, I'm not against our captain, because we've all done our jobs and haven't come up with anything better than he has. I'm casting my vote now that I don't sail the *Sea Siren* on her return journey until the murderer is caught. Those in favor say aye; those not in favor, nay."

A chorus of "Ayes" rang in his ears.

"If there's one among you who has an idea, a clue, something to go on, spit it out and we'll talk it over, and perhaps we'll come up with an answer. I've sailed with the lot of you, and it's my opinion none of you is guilty. We've crewed together for a long number of years, and this is the first trouble to hit us. Speak up."

"Peter is right," Jacques, a Frenchman, said loudly. "I would have placed my life with the lot of you and never thought twice. I don't think it's any of us."

"The Puritans in the hold, that divine preacher they have—what about him?" a seaman named Claude asked.

"The hold has been under guard at all times by one of us. Religious people like the preacher and his flock don't lie," Peter volunteered.

"There's a first time for everything," Jacques snapped.

"If what you say is true, that places the blame right square on one of us. Someone bludgeoned the old man and tossed the girl over the side."

Diego Sanchez stood up, resplendent in his brilliant scarlet shirt, and spoke softly. "It is bad luck to sail a ship with women aboard." He looked around to see the effect his words would have on the others.

The crew looked at one another and then at Peter, who was frowning.

"Diego is right," Claude said sourly. "Women are unlucky. Wherever they go there is trouble, and that's all we've had on this bloody ship since we set sail."

Heads nodded and sharp mutterings were heard as one man jostled another to make his point. All seemed in agreement that somehow a woman was involved. They were also in silent agreement that it couldn't be Miss van der Rhys, who had met her own untimely end, so therefore, it must be the preacher's wife.

"I disagree," Peter declared firmly. "Lydia Stoneham is a timid little thing and wouldn't have the strength to do Farrington in. It took strength to kill him." Heads nodded while the men mentally evaluated the only other woman who enjoyed the freedom of the ship—Sara Stoneham. She was tall, well fleshed and had muscular, long arms. Again there were vague mutterings and ominous curses. Only Gustave looked puzzled, out of his depth. How could they say such things about so fine a lady? he wondered. Why, she had been so distraught she had barely been able to walk, and still she had helped in the search. He should say something, make the men shut their filthy mouths. What did they know of fine ladies and how gentle they were? He sighed. Why waste his breath? All they would do was mock him. What did an old cook know?

Below decks, Sara paced the cabin, humming her sad little tune, her eyes burning feverishly. From time to time she cast anxious glances at Lydia, who sat quietly on her bunk, idly flipping Wren's playing cards.

Lydia watched Sara out of the corner of her eye, feeling her flesh crawl as the girl's nervous pacings seemed to take on an increased urgency. The humming sounded a trifle shrill, and she didn't like the way Sara was knotting and unknotting her hands. If only she had the nerve to tell Captain van der Rhys of her suspicions. He would think her dotty and perhaps blame her somehow, or, worse yet, make her go

279

back into the hold with Bascom. Yet the captain seemed a fair man, and he had listened to her before and done what was right. Perhaps he would listen now, but would he understand and believe her? She could only try.

Sara, tiring of her pacing and humming, lay down on her bunk and closed her eyes. Lydia was off her bunk and out the door before Sara had time to open them. She made straight for the wheelhouse and waited for Caleb to motion her forward. Christ, he groaned to himself, now what? He forced a look of interest on his face as Lydia began to speak.

"Captain van der Rhys, I've anguished over this second visit today and decided that once I talk with you and tell you what I suspect, I will breathe easier. I may well be wrong, but then again I may be right, and you really should know. I'm saying this badly because . . . I don't want you to discount what I'm going to say because of Bascom. I'm not like him and the others. It's just that . . . what I mean is . . ."

Caleb was puzzled. He liked Lydia; she was a sensible woman who had shown great courage in her stand against her husband. He knew she had meant it when she said she would go over the rail if forced to return to her husband. He wouldn't admit it openly, but he admired her. He gave her his full attention and waited for her to get her thoughts in order.

Lydia squared her shoulders and primly folded her hands in her lap. "It's my sister-in-law, Sara, Captain. I know that she's . . . that she . . . is . . . is your lady, and that's why it is so difficult for me to say what I have to say. She's been acting very strange of late. She hums to herself, a nonsense tune, and her eyes are . . . are like Bascom's when he gets carried away, almost as if he's in some other world. Sara prowls the decks in the middle of the night, and she . . . she paces the cabin like a caged animal. May God have mercy on me, but I think she killed Aubrey

Farrington." She waited breathlessly for Caleb's eyes to lose their look of shock. "I feel it here," she said, placing her hand over her heart. "I don't know why she killed Aubrey Farrington, but I do know that she hated Wren. I see that surprises you. Sara had no love for Wren, and Wren barely tolerated Sara. Women know things like that." A ring of authority entered her voice. "It's up to you to find out the why of it all. Oh, one other thing. Sara is pregnant. She never said so, but the signs are unmistakable. I don't expect you to be aware of such things, and I don't know if it's important, but I felt I should mention it. Sometimes a woman will become crazed when she finds herself in that . . . delicate condition and without a husband."

Caleb almost choked in his attempt to get his words out. He wet his lips before speaking, and his voice sounded far away to his ears. "Tell me, Mrs. Stoneham, when did you notice Sara's . . . condition?"

Lydia flushed. "In the hold, shortly after coming aboard. She was nauseous every morning, which, of course, could have had something to do with the rocking of the ship, but again, a woman knows these things. Also, she has gotten a . . . little thick around the middle." The flush ran down to her throat and she closed her eyes. "Please, Captain, forgive me for being so forward and so blunt. I know a lady doesn't speak like this in front of a man, but I felt you should know. I don't want to stay in that cabin with her anymore," she blurted. "She frightens me."

Caleb felt as if the weight of the world had been removed from his shoulders. "Dear lady, whatever you want on this ship is yours, you have but to ask. You have just saved my life in more ways than one. If it won't cause you any anguish, you can have Farrington's quarters. One more thing, Mrs. Stoneham. In your opinion, why do you think Sara did this thing, if indeed she did do it?"

Lydia grimaced. She tapped her head lightly with

her fingers and said, "She's fey, unstable. I don't like speaking ill of my husband, but he is her brother, and perhaps it's a trait they were both born with. It happens sometimes," she insisted defensively, fearful that he didn't believe her. "Do you think, Captain, that what I said has any merit?"

"More than you know, dear lady. I don't want you to be afraid. I'll have the crew keep an eye on you. There's no cause for you to be alarmed."

Relief flooded through Lydia. He believed her, she could see it in the grimness of his face and the set of his jaw. Thank God she had had the courage to come and tell him!

Caleb watched her leave the wheelhouse with a lightened heart. How fitting it was that a woman had caused so much havoc and that another woman had set it to rights. He grinned and stared out across the great expanse of water. Very fitting indeed.

A nod of his head and Peter came loping into the wheelhouse. They held a long, low-voiced conversation. Peter's eyes widened, and then his face also became grim. He nodded several times and left to follow his orders. Perhaps the lady called the *Sea Siren* wasn't cursed after all, he thought.

Sara wasn't surprised when the first mate came to get her. She rose from the bed and followed him docilely to the hatch, where she descended the ladder to the hold. She was conscious of her surroundings, but her eyes were glazed and staring. Nothing mattered anymore. Her family could take care of her; she was too tired to care what became of her.

Settling herself next to her mother, who ignored her completely, she narrowed her eyes and watched the first mate and Bascom carry on a quiet conversation. She would tell Bascom it was all Lydia's fault that she had been returned to his keeping. That should set his hackles to rising, and perhaps he would leave her alone. All she had to do was ignore him the way her very own mother was ignoring her. Nothing mattered anymore. Not Wren, not Malcolm, not Caleb, and least of all Bascom.

Something niggled at her brain. Wren. It always came back to Wren. Of course, Wren would starve if she didn't take her food. Malcolm would starve, too.

"I'll take care of her," Bascom said curtly to Peter. "You can tell your captain that he's wrong about my sister. If he thinks she's acting strange, it's because of the fever she had. There's nothing wrong with her mind. She is as sane as I am." At Peter's skeptical look, he hastened to continue. "My sister doesn't know the meaning of the word 'violence.' Be sure to relay that message to Captain van der Rhys. If he fears for his crew, assure him that she's safe below with her family. Now, if you'll excuse me, we have a prayer meeting scheduled, and unless you're ready to become one of us, I suggest you go topside and leave us to our Lord."

Peter needed no second urging. He was up the ladder and gulping deep breaths of salt air in a matter of moments. Then he bounded into the wheelhouse and gave Bascom's message to Caleb. Caleb listened, his face granite-hard. He nodded and dismissed Peter and let his eyes drift back to the sea. What he hoped to see, to find, he didn't know. Before him lay only an endless expanse of blue-green water.

While Caleb scanned the vastness before him and Sara slept, Wren sat huddled in one corner of the locker box. How long have I been here? she wondered. Ever since the lantern had gone out, she had no way of knowing. She couldn't decide which was worse—staring at Malcolm's mutilated face in the light or having the rats play around her feet in the darkness. Isn't anyone ever going to check this damnable hole in which I'm being held a prisoner? What did Sara tell the others about my whereabouts? By now Caleb should have turned this ship upside down looking for me, she thought miserably. And where the devil is Farrington? Malcolm said he usually brought him food late at night and then took him out for an airing. Where *is* the old man?

After his initial brutal attack on her, Malcolm had left her alone, saying she wasn't worth what little effort he had to expend. To assure himself that Wren wouldn't cry out and reveal his hiding place, he had torn his shirt and bound and gagged her.

The bindings cut her wrists, and the foul, linty rag he had stuffed in her objecting mouth was rancid with the smell of him and choked her. She felt a fresh flurry of tremors ripple through her body, tremors of rage and fear, and in her heart she knew she was approaching the edges of despair. She began to pray.

Chapter Eighteen

As the *Sea Siren* tacked gracefully toward port at the mouth of the Connecticut River, Gustave completed the list of supplies he would need for the return trip to England. The galley had been scoured to his satisfaction, and he poured himself a large mug of coffee and went up on deck to view the approaching verdant landscape. His friend Diego meandered over and reached for the mug, helping himself to a long drink. They sat together companionably, neither talking.

Diego reached for the mug again, and after taking a few more swallows, began to tell Gustave of the plans for disembarking and dissembling the Puritans, who were gathering the last of their belongings in the hold before coming up on deck for their first glimpse of their new home. The conversation turned to Sara Stoneham.

"She's below with that preacher brother of hers," Diego stated, his mouth curling at the aftertaste of the bitter brew. "Just as well. That's one lady who could make me feel as though a goose were walking over my grave. Did you ever notice her eyes, Gustave? She looks like she's here, but the rest of her is out there." He waved his arms to indicate the vast reaches of Long Island Sound.

"I thought her to be a lady," Gustave said hesitantly.

Diego touched his temple and shook his head. "I had a sister who got like that once when she couldn't take her husband's carousing with other women. She died," he said bluntly.

Gustave rolled the words around on his tongue and decided he needed more clarification. "She died because her husband tossed in the covers with other women?"

Diego looked at the cook with disgust. "Yes and no. Something snapped in her mind, and she was never the same again. My sister was a lady, too," he said defensively. "One day she was fine and the next— poof!" He snapped his fingers. "It was terrible. Her husband cried for eleven days. He cried each day with a different child. They had eleven children," he explained to Gustave.

For some strange reason Gustave felt sick to his stomach. Miss Stoneham seemed like such a lady. But Diego seemed to know what he was talking about. He looked at the Spaniard craftily and asked, "Did your

sister ever do strange things, go strange places and ...
you know ... do things ladies don't normally do?"

"Like what?"

"Like would she ever go about at night with a lantern to places that were dark and full of rats?"

"I thought you said this was coffee," Diego remarked, peering at the dregs at the bottom of the mug. "I told you my sister was a lady. *No* lady, dotty or not, does things like that. You're disgusting, Gustave, even to think my sister would do such a thing. I'll wager you've been cooking with rum again, haven't you?"

"I was just asking," Gustave replied heatedly. "I didn't mean your *sister* did those things; I just asked if *women* did those kinds of things, other women. I would never say anything bad about your sister. If you say she was a lady, then she was a lady."

"Damn right she was a lady. She was a good mother, too." Diego cast a withering look in Gustave's direction, handed him back his cup and proceeded to change his boots.

Gustave sat in silence for a long time. Women were known to make fools out of men. He looked around to see if Diego had noticed his changed status from cook to fool. Diego was concerned only with his feet, so that had to mean Gustave was safe; he was the only one who knew what a fool he was. He sucked in his plump cheeks and began to whistle tonelessly as he made his way back to the galley. The first chance he got, he would take another look down in the bowels of the ship. Yes, that was what he'd do. It wouldn't hurt to take another look at all.

In the black darkness, in the deepest, most forward compartment of the *Sea Siren*'s hull, Wren and Malcolm waited. All motion of the ship had ceased, and the stillness was ominous. The slow rocking without the slight drag and pull of the force of the waves warned them that the vessel was either becalmed or at anchor.

Tears streaked down Wren's cheeks. They had been only a day away from land when Sara had tricked her into this hellish place with Malcolm. The *Sea Siren* had made port. She would rot in the stench-filled dungeon. She would die. Here, alone with the one man who hated her most in the world. Bound and gagged like the trapped animal she was. There was nothing, no word, no prayer, no hope, that could save her.

Above decks, Sara prepared to leave the ship in the last jolly boat. Several of the crew and two Puritans with whom she was not familiar waited alongside her for the jolly to beat the shore-rushing waves and follow the current back to the *Siren*.

Sara's thoughts were intent on the locker box holding her prisoners. Somehow she had to find the courage to sneak below and unbolt the door before she disembarked. No one was paying any attention to her; every eye was intent upon the slowly approaching jolly. Fear pervaded her body and chills danced up her spine. If she was to unbolt the door, she would have to be quick about it in order to return to the deck and leave in the last jolly. She was terrified at the thought of being alone aboard ship with a recently freed, half-crazed Malcolm.

She backed up a step, then two, and scurried to the hatch on the forward deck. After crawling rapidly down the ladder, careful not to make a sound, she inched across the keel line through the hull and made her way to the locker box by touch alone. It was as though her fever-bright eyes could penetrate the dark and perceive distinguishing touch marks. She had traveled the length of the hull a thousand times in her mind. Her fingers groped for the familiar outline of the door, searching for the bolt like a blind man's fingers searching for a tossed coin. Holding her breath, not daring to breathe, she silently eased the bolt free.

Immediately relief flooded through her. She had done it. She had freed them. They could walk out of the cell any time they wanted. She wasn't murdering them; she wasn't killing the father of her child. She had set them free!

Soundlessly she retraced her steps, her back hunched in a similar manner to those of the rats who existed in the dank darkness.

Hours later, Wren tried to ease her cramped position and stretch her legs. Malcolm must have heard her movement, because she sensed he was moving toward her. She cringed from him, dreading his touch, then felt him work the knots in her bindings. He loosened the gag from around her face and she spit it out. She was parched and dry, her mouth foul-tasting. She forced her lips to work, her jaw aching and sore.

"Don't touch me, Malcolm," she managed to utter hoarsely. "Don't touch me!"

"As if I'd want you," he sneered. "I won't waste my strength on a dead woman."

The truth of his words reconfirmed her worst fears. She would die here alone with Malcolm. "The door," she croaked. "Damn you, Malcolm, try the door. Beat it down! Don't you understand we'll die in here?"

"We'll wait for Farrington. And don't try to scream. You'll have that rag stuffed back in your mouth before you can get out one syllable."

Wren shook her head, not realizing he couldn't see her in the blackness.

"Do you understand me?" he threatened harshly, his fingers digging into the soft flesh of her shoulder.

"Yes . . . I understand . . . What you don't seem to understand, Malcolm, is that we've put in at port. When I was thrown in here with you, we were only a day or two away from reaching land. We're trapped in here! Trapped!" Her voice rose. "Lord Farrington isn't coming back for you. He'll never find me!"

The intensity of her words struck Malcolm with an unbidden fear that she was right. Farrington would sooner see him dead than alive. Then the gems would be his.

Wren scrambled to her feet, rubbing her wrists where the bindings had cut into them. She was unfamiliar with the cell, and her searching, outstretched hands discovered it was even smaller than she'd imagined.

"Damn you, Malcolm, help me find the door. Get up and find it! Beat against it! There's always a watch aboard ship—he might hear us!"

"One more word out of you and I'll strangle you," Malcolm warned, alarmed by the strength she was suddenly exhibiting.

Wren's fingers found the hinges flanging the door, then groped for the crack between door and bulkhead. The edges of her fingers felt a cool draft blowing through the minuscule space. She began to hit the bulkhead, her hands clenched into fists, her throat aching to realize a scream. Her poundings met with resistance but still she beat with all her might. She moved to the left and heard her poundings sound hollow as she found the center of the door.

Malcolm seemed suddenly to realize what she was doing and began fumbling for her in the darkness to quiet her hysteria.

Soundlessly the door swung open, revealing a glimmer of gray light. Both Malcolm and Wren fell back, mouths agape.

"Sweet Christ, the door was open," Malcolm whispered in shock. "All this time the door was open."

Wren lowered her head into her hands. She could not take in the reality confronting her. She had spent eternal hours in Malcolm's presence, and all the while the door had been open. Sara had never locked it, and neither of them had thought to try it, accepting their prison sentence like a final judgment. "We're free?" she asked in amazement.

"Will you shut up!" Malcolm ordered. "We're free. All we have to do is walk out of here."

"Let me go, please let me go!" she pleaded, struggling to wrest herself from his grasp.

"Not so fast, little bird. I'm not done with you yet. I'll still get some use out of you. But never fear, we'll leave here together."

"Where? Where can we go? Please let me go!"

"Shut up," he commanded. He knocked her down to the floor, pinned her beneath his weight and covered her mouth with his hand. He felt around the floor with his free hand and found that for which he searched. Quickly he had her bound again, the gag choking off her air and rendering her silent.

Wren's eyes were wild with fury and she kicked out at him with her foot.

"Try that again and I'll leave you here, and this time I'll lock the door myself." Wren was immediately docile, fearing he would carry out his threat. "All I need are the jewels from Farrington and a little cash money, and I'll be set for life," Malcolm plotted, his voice low and calculating. "And you, my little bird, will bring a nice ransom. Sara told me your brother captains this ship."

Tears coursed down Wren's cheeks. She was lost and totally alone. Caleb wouldn't give a tinker's damn about her. He had Sara and their coming child to occupy his mind.

"It'll be interesting to find out what your brother thinks you're worth. I'm going topside to see what's about and if I can find some food and water. I'll come back for you."

He whirled around and disappeared out the door. Several minutes later he was slowly climbing the ladder to the forward hatch, which he lifted cautiously. He took great gulps of air, and the stiff breeze whipping about nearly made him dizzy.

The sun was low in the sky; there was no sign of

anyone on deck. Straining his neck, he peered over the hatch side, across the deck and through the rail. Land. Green, inviting land. It would be another hour till dark. He spied the two-man dinghy which swung from lines over the starboard bow. He would take Wren with him in the boat. Upriver. When the time was right and he had her secure, he would seek out van der Rhys and name his price.

Malcolm waited, almost fearfully, for darkness to descend. He had to take care of the man on watch— kill him, if necessary—before he could lower the dinghy and head upriver. Well, he had proved that he was good at waiting; as a matter of fact, he excelled at that. Another hour, perhaps a little less, and he could set out on what he considered the last leg of his journey that would lead him to God only knew what. If it was the last thing he did, he would get those jewels from Farrington and a handsome ransom for Wren. He would set himself up like a king on one of the islands and have people wait on him hand and foot. He would have a different woman for every night of the week. If his scarred face troubled those about him, he would simply kill them. In time they would learn that he was a power, a force to be reckoned with. Money could buy anything. It could buy people; it could buy whatever service he required. It could even buy physical love.

He tilted his head upward. The dark clouds rode the new moon like a novice rider on horseback, and he crept toward the wheelhouse. He smirked to himself. The stupid guard would probably be drunk, relying on the man in the crow's-nest to warn of any approaching intruders. On silent feet he attacked the guard from the rear, grasping him around the neck and jerking him off balance. Then he smashed the seaman's head against the stout wheel before he let the guard crumble to the deck. The man wouldn't be doing anything for a long while. By the time he woke up, if ever, Mal-

291

colm and Wren would be long gone, armed and gone.

Malcolm went to the galley for some food, which he threw into a sack, and then made his way to the dinghy, which he lowered into the water. He sat down to rest for a moment and get his bearings. Satisfied that everything had gone the way he had planned it, he relaxed and sighed deeply. A few hours of hard rowing and he would be far enough upriver. He would find a safe place to secure the dinghy and then take to the woods on foot. He'd keep Wren tied so she couldn't escape, and then he'd rest himself. By nightfall he could return to port with his ransom demand for Wren. Everything was working out just the way he had planned it.

There was no fear in Wren, just white-hot fury. She knew now that Malcolm wouldn't kill her, but he could make things so miserable for her, she might wish she were dead. There was nothing she could do, and that only added to her rage. When the door was flung open, she let her eyes do all her talking. If the hatred that burned from them could kill, Malcolm Weatherly would have fallen lifeless before her. He pulled her roughly to her feet and pushed her ahead of him. She didn't balk; there was no point in angering him further.

"Down the ladder, and one false move out of you, and your face will be ugly in comparison to mine," Malcolm said, untying her hands. "I'll be right behind you," he added ominously.

Wren rubbed at her wrists and did as she was told, the gag almost suffocating her.

Malcolm wasted no time putting the dinghy into motion, dipping the oars deep and pulling back, every muscle in his back bunching into knots.

Wren cursed him with her eyes every time the oar struck the water. God, how she hated him! She had to try to get away from him somehow. Bound and gagged like she was, she knew there was little chance he would take his one good eye off her, let alone free her. As soon as he had tossed her into the dinghy, he had bound not only her hands but her ankles as well. If he fell into a fit of rage and decided to toss her overboard, she would be dead within seconds. It would be to her advantage to lie perfectly quiet and not antagonize him in any way.

Every muscle in her body stilled as Caleb's face swam before her tired eyes. How clearly she could see him, and if she willed it, she could remember the feel of him next to her. How good had he felt, so hard and so warm. She had fitted so perfectly in the cradle of his arm, and he had told her that in gentle whispers. She had felt as though she had come home, home to Caleb, where she belonged. Always Caleb. How gentle and warm, so very warm, he was. She had been a fool and was still a fool. She could have fought Sara for him, could have asserted herself. Instead, she had taken the coward's way out and run. She always ran instead of facing up to her problems. She should have gone to Caleb and poured out her heart; he would have listened and understood. And now he was lost to her forever. He would marry Sara because she was pregnant, and part of Wren's life would be over. Wren could never love anyone the way she loved Caleb. Caleb was part of her. He was her destiny. Sirena had known that, just as she herself had known. Why hadn't Caleb been able to recognize it, too? He had said they were as one, but that already seemed a long time ago. From the beginning she had been like an open wound to him, and she had merely made matters worse for herself. She was stupid and silly, just as Sara had always claimed.

As Caleb stood near the open gravesite, his glance was drawn to his ship anchored offshore. A feeling washed over him that, if he looked hard enough, he would see Wren. Calling himself a fool, he redirected his attention to the ceremony taking place.

Aubrey, Lord Farrington, was being laid to his final rest. Caleb had insisted that burial be on land, knowing how much his old partner had disliked the sea.

The crewmen were present, and their heads bowed as they waited for Caleb to find the proper words. Clearing his throat, he managed to say simply, "He was my friend. His only sin was his love for life and adventure, and for that I ask forgiveness in his name."

His hand shook slightly as he threw a clod of dirt into the yawning grave. Tears misted in his eyes and he turned away, unable to watch as the crew heaped the black, rich earth onto the simple coffin.

"Captain, I have to go back to the galley before I take shore leave," Gustave said somberly, respectful of Caleb's grief. "Can I leave you a plate for supper? Peter said you would be spending the night aboard ship."

"I'll see to my own supper, Gustave. Don't put yourself out. Join the men and have a drink for Aubrey. He'd like that."

"Aye, Captain, as soon as me and Diego get back."

The sleek, three-masted frigate dipped and rose at anchor in the gentle swells of the Sound as Gustave made his cautious way across the deck. From time to time he cast an anxious glance over his shoulder, even though he knew no one would be watching him. They were alone on board, he and Diego and Claude, the watchman. Still, he had the feeling someone or something was peering at him through the dark. Yellow lanterns lit the perimeters of the deck and he stood a moment at the rail, relishing the breeze on his leathery cheeks and sparse gray hair.

Why do old men make fools of themselves over a pretty face? he questioned himself. The captain would have his hide nailed to the mizzenmast in short order if there was anything in the locker box besides the rats. He shuddered in the warm June breeze as he pointed his feet in the direction of the forward hatch. He couldn't put it off any longer; he had to go below and see what the locker box held.

His bare feet were soundless as he continued his trek below decks. He stopped once and drew in his breath, feeling unseen eyes boring into the back of his skull. He cocked his head to the side like an inquisitive sparrow but could see nothing in the ghostly shadows. Still the feeling persisted. He swallowed hard, the thin knob in his neck bobbing up and down as if to a lively tune. He was almost at the locker but still couldn't shake the impression of unseen eyes. "Who's there?" he demanded, and half jumped out of his skin when Diego's voice shot back at him.

"What in holy hell are you doing down here? Don't tell me that swill you've been cooking has finally gotten to your brain and rendered you senseless!"

Although Diego's tone was gruff, Gustave knew immediately that something was terribly wrong. He held up his lantern and looked into his friend's face.

"We've got to get off the ship and back to the captain," Diego said in a lower voice. "I was just above and found Claude. He was hit over the head. He'll be all right in a few days, but he never seen who done it. Another thing—the two-man dinghy is missing. I know we didn't use it to go ashore. It's supposed to be hanging over the starboard bow in case of an emergency." The hairs on the back of Gustave's neck stood on end. His gaze left the cook's face and centered on the locker-box door. "What in hell are you doing down here, anyway?" he added.

Gustave debated a moment, then motioned Diego to come closer. Quickly he explained why he was going to the locker box.

Diego's eyes widened and he shook his head. "You're right, my friend, the captain will nail your hide to the mizzenmast in short order. The captain is a great one for setting an example," he muttered in sympathy as he followed Gustave and his bobbing lantern. "How about a few short snorts before you throw open that door?" he suggested as he withdrew a rum bottle from his baggy shirt front.

Gustave accepted greedily and drank as if he had been parched for months. He handed back the bottle, which was now nearly empty.

"I said a few short snorts, not half the damn bottle. Do you know what I had to go through to steal this?" Diego grumped as he brought the bottle to his lips and finished it off. Then he picked up a stout board which could have smashed the skulls of ten men with one wicked swipe. "A man should be prepared for any and all emergencies."

Gustave nervously wiped his sweating palms on his tattered trousers. "Let's get it over with. I'll throw the bolt and you go in first, with the board straight in front of you. I'll be right behind you with the lantern held high."

"Why is it every time you get yourself into some kind of mess, I'm the one who has to get you out or go first so you don't get yourself beaten to a pulp?" Diego grumbled as he hefted the board in anticipation of Gustave's arm movement with the bolt.

The cook sucked in his breath and threw the bolt on the third try. "Because you're my friend and I pulled you from shark-infested waters when you were but a wee lad, that's why, and you owe me your life," he replied.

"That was over thirty years ago, and I've more than paid my debt," Diego snorted, charging into the foul-smelling room, Gustave at his heels.

"Son of a bitch! I was sure. I was so sure." Gustave held his lantern high, the light filling the shadowy depths of the empty locker box.

The simple funeral service over, Caleb's mood darkened. Farrington had been laid to his final resting place, and now that the others were settled, he had nothing more to do but return to the ship. He knew he would feel better if he could instigate a real fist-pounding, no-holds-barred fight with someone and get himself beaten to a pulp. He was alive and Farrington was dead. His eyes grew wild as he looked at the soft mound of earth and then at Peter, who was shuffling his feet. "It seems that we should be doing something else, saying something else. This is so . . . so final."

"Death is always final," Peter mumbled. He, too, was grieving for the lively gambler. Many a long talk had passed between them, and he had genuinely liked the man, as had the rest of the crew. Death always left the living in agony. He had never seen Caleb in such straits before, and in his heart he knew the captain was grieving more for Wren than for the gambler. There should have been another body to bury. Caleb was grieving twofold.

Peter stepped aside. He didn't want to intrude on Caleb's grief, and yet he didn't know what action to take. He couldn't just leave him standing there with nothing to do and nowhere to go except back to the lonely ship. He would give up his liberty and return with his captain and Lydia, who, because of her desertion of Bascom, was no longer welcome in the Puritan community. They would have something to eat and a little rum, and after a good night's sleep Caleb would feel better. At least Peter hoped so.

"Come, Captain," Lydia said gently. "It's time to go back to the ship. It's been a long day, and it has taken its toll on all of us." Carefully, so as not to startle him, she took his arm, and Peter took the other. They made their way back to the dock and climbed into the jolly. All was quiet on their path across the water; no sound permeated the ebony, star-filled night.

Once back on board the *Siren,* Caleb was surprised to find Gustave and Diego waiting for him. Gustave's leathery face was tormented and the old man picked nervously at his hands.

"What's troubling you, Gustave?" Caleb asked. "Didn't burn down the galley, did you?"

Haltingly, and glancing at Diego for support, Gustave told the captain about the incident with Sara and the locker box, the subsequent attack on Claude and the missing dinghy.

Within minutes they were at Claude's side, and Lydia began ministering to him as he lay on his bunk. Water, clean cloths and a medicine box were before her as she set to work. Caleb and Peter hovered, offering advice and help. "I think," she said firmly, "that it would be better if you left me to my chores and went topside." Her tone was gentle but firm. "Better still, go to the galley and see if Gustave left any broth in the larder, and if he didn't, make some." It was an order. Caleb looked at Peter and Peter looked at Caleb. Both men shrugged and headed for the galley.

Peter struggled to collect his wits. What kind of order had that been? An order from a woman, no less! The captain and his first mate didn't make broth in the galley. The cook made the broth. Where in the hell was Gustave? Then Peter remembered the captain had dismissed both Gustave and Diego to pursue their liberty. And quick they had been to leave the captain's sight after confessing about the locker box! So he would make the broth and maybe a sweet, too, while he was at it. He hoped Caleb didn't have two left hands when it came to measuring, like Gustave had.

In less than an hour Gustave's spit-and-polish galley was a disaster, and Caleb and Peter were no closer to a simmering broth than when they had first started.

"Begging your pardon, Captain, but this tastes like water with a fishy taste. I think you're supposed to put in bones or dried meat and then let it cook."

298

"I did that," Caleb said belligerently, a fine bead of perspiration dotting his brow and upper lip.

"All I can say, Captain, and I say it with all due respect, is that if the patient drinks this 'broth,' it will kill him. I never tasted such vile stuff in my life. It's worse than Gustave's swill!"

"What do you suggest?" Caleb demanded.

"I'm no cook and neither are you. I think we should have a drink and ponder the matter. Maybe it will taste better if it cooks longer," Peter said, uncorking a bottle of rum. "Gustave cooks everything from sun-up to sundown. I've decided it just has to cook longer." His face darkened to that of a thundercloud. "And another thing, Captain. If you botch up this broth, Miss Lydia is going to blame me, and then where will I be?" He took a deep gurgle from the bottle and continued. "I've had my eye on that fair lady for a long while now, and whatever you do in this galley is going to come home to roost on my shoulders. Add some rum," he suggested, handing the bottle to Caleb.

"So that's the way the wind is blowing." Caleb grinned and added a dollop of rum to the pot.

"Pour, Captain, pour, don't trickle it," Peter said, tilting the bottle with a heavy hand. "Yes, that's the way the wind is blowing. She's a fair-looking woman, and she would fit real nice right here." He indicated the crook of his arm. "Any woman don't fit here, well, then she's not my kind of woman." He shook his head decisively.

"I know just what you mean." Caleb remembered how Wren had fitted into his arms and how wonderful she had felt next to him. He drank deeply, relieved now that half his burdens had been lifted from his broad shoulders. He handed the bottle back to Peter, but not before he had added another "dollop" to the simmering pot of broth. While Peter finished off the rum, Caleb was busily uncorking not one but two additional bottles.

"One for you and one for me," Peter hiccuped.

"Well, don't think I'm putting mine in the pot," Caleb protested indignantly.

"You're the captain. I'm only the first mate. Rank always fills the pot." Peter smirked.

"Who told you a thing like that?" Caleb demanded.

"Gustave, that's who," Peter lied as he brought the bottle to his lips, missing his mouth. He cursed loudly as he wiped at his bare chest.

"That sounds right to me," Caleb agreed drunkenly, now lacing the pot liberally. "You're right, I am the captain of this ship."

"And a damn good captain you are. You're the first captain I ever sailed with who knows how to make broth. Even the damn cook doesn't know how to cook," Peter laughed happily.

"I know, and it's a damn shame, too. I pay good wages and the crew expects to eat hearty and all we get is slop. My provisions are the best money can buy. Gustave ruins everything. This will be the first decent meal we've had in days."

Both of them peered into the pot.

"I thought this broth was for the guards. Why are your eyes watering, Captain?" Peter asked, staggering back from the strong fumes rising from the pot.

"Damned if I know. Must be from the onion I put in there," Caleb said, wiping at his eyes.

"That was no onion, it was a potato. Gustave ran out of onions days ago." Peter uncorked another bottle of rum and passed it to Caleb. "That's for the pot. You're the captain, and you shouldn't have to put yours in the pot. I'm the first mate, and it wouldn't look right if I did, so let's just use this bottle for the pot and forget about sharing."

"That sounds right to me," Caleb said, dumping the contents of the third bottle into the pot. "We seem to

300

have quite a bit here, Peter, enough for an army. We'll eat hearty tonight."

"You're a good man, Captain, even if you did get off to a bad start with all those . . . those . . . holy people on board."

"I know. I can't stand them," Caleb whispered confidentially. "They've been nothing but trouble, and now you tell me you have designs on the preacher's wife. The question is, does the preacher's wife have designs on you?" he chortled, waving his rum bottle in the air and narrowly missing Peter's head.

Peter nodded sagely. "She looks at me and then looks at the floor."

"That means she likes you, and yes, she does have designs. I'm an authority." At Peter's look of disbelief, he laughed loudly. "Even Regan says I'm an authority. Married ladies can be trouble, especially when they have husbands."

Peter nodded again. "I'm expecting the worst," he said slowly and distinctly. "The very worst."

"That makes sense. That way you won't be disappointed if the preacher doesn't give you trouble. Bottle's empty," Caleb announced, flinging it across the room.

Peter laughed as the glass shattered in all directions. "You broke it, and Gustave goes barefoot in the galley. Now you have to clean it up."

"I'm the captain. All I do is steer this damn ship and cook broth. You have to wield the mop."

"Sounds fair to me." Peter peered into the pot again and reeled back, his hands to his face. He stumbled, righted himself and stared into Caleb's dark eyes. "I think, Captain, that you put just a little too much rum in the broth."

"How can you tell? Too much is never enough. If you're worried because the fumes unclog your nose and burn your throat, that doesn't mean anything. It's cooking away. See how thick it's getting?" He backed

301

away from the cookstove and fell heavily against the doorframe.

Two hours later, her patient resting comfortably, Lydia set out for the galley to see how Peter and the captain were faring.

The fumes from the cooking pot drove her back into the passageway. Cautiously, she poked her head around the corner of the door, all the while dabbing at her eyes. Caleb was sprawled on the floor, snoring loudly, a rum bottle clutched in one hand, the other shielding his eyes. The first mate was trying, unsuccessfully, to wield a mop over what looked like broken glass. He wore a look of disgust as he scattered the fragments and drank from his bottle at the same time.

"And what do you think you're doing? Who made this mess? Who's going to clean it up?" Lydia demanded.

At her words, Peter dropped the bottle and the mop and clapped his hands over his ears. "Isn't it bad enough I can't keep my eyes open? Do you want to make me deaf, too, with your caterwauling? Don't look at me for this mess!" He smirked as he pointed a shaking finger at the prone captain. "He did what you ordered, and he's the one who made this mess. All I did was watch. I think it's going to be the best damn broth you ever ate." He nudged Caleb gently with his toe. "Pity he won't be awake to try it." He took one step and then another toward the rum-laden pot and crumpled to the floor. Loud, lusty snores permeated the galley as Lydia threw her hands helplessly in the air.

What did she have to lose? All the while wiping at her eyes, she ladled out a generous portion of broth for her patient. It would either kill him or cure him. If the captain cooked it himself, it had to be worth something. It looked like pure, undiluted, hot rum to her inexperienced eye.

Even through his rum-induced sleep Caleb was aware of a deep-seated restlessness, and he tossed and turned in his bunk—the same bunk he had shared with Wren when she had been beset by feverish chills and he had wrapped her in his arms and shared the warmth from his body. In his grief-tormented dreams he heard her cry out, "Caleb! Help me!"

Wren tossed fitfully in her sleep, her mind screaming Caleb's name over and over. Hours later, Malcolm shook her roughly and pulled her to her feet. He loosened her bonds, and Wren stumbled as the blood rushed through her veins. Her feet on dry land gave her no comfort. She looked around but could see only inky blackness and dark, spectral-looking trees. She was standing in mud and slime up to her ankles. There was no means of escaping the man who was securing the dinghy to an enormous tree on the shoreline. Where would she run to in this infernal darkness? With the way her luck had been of late, she would run straight into some wild animal's lair and be chewed alive for her intrusion. She gulped and decided to take her chances with Malcolm.

Malcolm pushed her ahead of him and pretended to look around. If she couldn't see in the dark, what could he see with one eye? she wondered nastily. She was about to voice her opinion and then thought better of it. "I'm hungry and you damn well better feed me," she snapped. "If you think Captain van der Rhys is going to pay out good money for me, I better be hale and hearty or the price will go down."

"Shut up," Malcolm grated. "Get over there by that tree. I'm going to tie you to it, around the waist. You can maneuver your hands and feet. And if you don't shut that mouth of yours, I'll gag you again."

"You want me to shut up? I'll shut up, but not before I tell you that you are without a doubt a ring-tailed son of a bitch!" She felt better for expressing her opinion of him, coining Sirena's favorite phrase for an insufferable bastard.

Malcolm ignored her words and dragged her toward the tree. "I won't tell you again to shut that mouth of yours. This is your final warning. Once I gag you, that means no food. It's immaterial to me if you die. I can get the ransom from your brother even if you're dead. Dutchmen like bodies to bury."

Satisfied with the tight knot on the rope that bound Wren to the tree, he handed her some cheese and bread. "No more until tomorrow evening, so you better make it last," he said coldly as he gave the rope a vicious twist. It cut into her ribs, but she didn't flinch.

Wren bit off a piece of the rancid-smelling cheese and devoured it. She would eat the bread and cheese now; for all she knew, he might decide to kill her within the hour. That remark about the Dutch liking bodies to bury bothered her. If she was going to die, she would rather die on a semifull stomach.

She cast a critical eye toward the sky. Soon it would be dawn. What was going to happen then? Would he leave her here tied to the tree? Of course he would; he had no other choice. Then he would go back down-river, seek out Caleb and demand the ransom. That meant she would be tied here for another day. Already she could feel the pull of the rope around her waist. If she kept perspiring, the rope would tighten more cruelly. She wished she had more clothes on to protect her from the burning sensation she was beginning to feel. It was impossible to remain perfectly still. Fidgeting was a habit she had been born with.

Malcolm toiled to start a small fire within the

304

cluster of trees, more for light than for warmth. The balmy June weather was holding, and the studding of stars in the black velvet sky abated the threat of rain.

The moment the flint sparked, he sat back on his haunches and glanced about him. This was as good a place as any, he thought. Far enough away from the water to be safe from discovery by a passing boat. The woods were dense here, a shield from observing eyes.

Soon he would approach van der Rhys and find Farrington. For now, he had to sleep, to regain his strength. A few more days wouldn't alter his course and would only serve to increase van der Rhys' anxiety for Wren. Malcolm knew he would need all his strength to face a man as formidable as Caleb van der Rhys.

Chapter Nineteen

Leaving Peter and Lydia to tend the wounded crewman, Caleb had come ashore to make a cursory tour of the fortress settlement of Saybrook town, which rested at the mouth of the Connecticut River, in the heart of Pequot Indian territory. Owing to his colossal hangover from the night before, it had nearly been dusk when he left the *Sea Siren,* and the great gold ball in the sky was dipping rapidly into the thick tree line on the west as Caleb made his way down the hard, dusty road inside the protective walls of the fort to the office of the Dutch West India Company, as it was known in the New World.

Caleb had been in Saybrook two years before when he had arranged for tobacco, the "Imperial Weed," to be transferred from the Virginia colony to the office at Saybrook for shipment and distribution through the Company. The progress made by the settlers since he had last been here was at once visible. A wide expanse of forest surrounding the fortress, had been cleared, a precaution that aided visibility in case of an Indian attack. Several hundred people now lived in Saybrook town, many of them merchants and skilled craftsmen. Farms flanked the territory, the boundaries of their property lines hugging one another for security, and all roads led to the fort.

Caleb quietly opened the rough wooden door of the Dutch West India office and immediately upon entering knew something was wrong—very wrong. He could see it and he could smell it. The office was dingy and bare of everything save a primitive desk and a stool. A map, tattered and ragged at the edges, was hanging by one nail on the far wall. A lantern, empty of oil, was carelessly flung into a corner. A man Caleb had never seen before lolled drunkenly on the stool, his feet propped on the desk. Loud snores resounded through the room. Caleb raised one booted foot and knocked the man's moccasined feet to the floor. His anger was immeasurable. Was everything concerning this voyage destined to go amiss? A familiar heaviness swelled in his chest as fleeting thoughts of Wren and Aubrey Farrington crossed his mind.

"What . . . who?" the man muttered, trying to orient himself and failing miserably.

"What the hell do you call this?" Caleb shouted.

"You're a disgrace to the Company. Where's Galt?" he demanded.

"And who the hell are you to be asking me any questions at all?" the man retorted angrily as he wiped at the spittle drooling from his mouth with the back of a filthy hand.

"I'm Captain Caleb van der Rhys, and I'm here for the yearly report and to take the furs and tobacco back to England on my return voyage. Where have you been storing them? But first I want you to tell me where Galt is and explain this sorry mess!"

The man swallowed hard. He had known that sooner or later this day of reckoning would come. He only wished he had been better prepared. The man standing in front of him didn't look as though he would listen to an explanation, much less an excuse. But why should he give a damn? His wages were already a month late in arriving. By rights he owed this bastard nothing.

"I'm waiting," Caleb said through clenched teeth, fighting the urge to strike out at this slovenly figure.

"My name's Conrad. Galt is dead, attacked by a small band of renegade Indians months ago. The furs were stolen, the storehouse emptied, and this is all that's left. If you think I'm going into those Indian camps to make your bastard burghers rich and me dead, you have another think coming. The raid was long overdue and everyone knew it was coming. Those thieving Indians stole everything they could get their hands on. They emptied the storehouses, plundered—they even took two of the women!"

"Why?" Caleb shot out, remembering the good relations between red men and whites which had existed two years before.

"How the living hell should I know? Who knows why an Indian does anything? They're savages and don't think like humans," Conrad grumbled, his eyes avoiding Caleb's.

"I asked you why and I expect an answer!" Caleb grabbed Conrad by his shirt front and pulled him to his feet, staring down into the older man's eyes with contempt.

A new respect for Caleb dawned in Conrad. This was the first white man, besides the stray Jesuit priests who sometimes wandered through Saybrook on their way to the upper reaches of the Hudson Valley, who had ever admitted the Indians had a reason for committing their ruthless acts. Conrad could understand the prejudice against the Indians. The settlers were taking land which belonged to the tribes, pushing the Indian out, a subject which was defended with a heated self-righteousness but was nevertheless a cause for guilt. And, too, it wasn't easy to live under constant threat of attack. That was reason enough for the settlers to hate the red man. But Conrad himself had no such stake in the New World. Once his contract was completed with the Dutch West India Company, he would go home to Holland, hopefully richer than when he had left.

Now, with Caleb's inquiry as to why the Indians were prompted to pit themselves against the colonists, Conrad decided he deserved an answer. "On second thought, Captain van der Rhys, I'm going to tell you why the unrest exists between white and red. But you won't like the answer, and there's nothing that can be done about it. The Dutch West India Company is responsible." Conrad curled his lip in distaste and ran a hand through his sparse hair. "We, the pragmatic Dutch, with our 'Christian' approach to the aborigines. Bah! Lip service! The burghers of the Dutch West India Company are more interested in making money!"

As Caleb listened to Conrad's now mostly sober words, a colorful and true picture of the circumstances emerged.

At first arrival in the New World, the Dutch

company had established friendly relations with the Indians and managed to make its home base in the wonderful, deep harbor of Manhattan Island. Within a relatively short time the thriving colony of New Netherland and its capital, New Amsterdam, had become one of the most powerful footholds in the New World. This productive tranquility, however, was short-lived. Two years before, just after Caleb's last voyage to America, the incompetent Wouter Van Twiller had been replaced as governor of New Netherland and as regional head of the Company by a man named Willem Kiefft. Kiefft was a bigger thief and an even worse administrator than Van Twiller had been. The new governor's way of dealing with the Indians was to extort from them levies of corn, wampum and especially furs for the "protection" afforded by New Amsterdam.

"So you see why the Indians stole back the furs and emptied the granaries," Conrad concluded. "They stole to give the booty to the fat governor, Kiefft. I'm no Indian lover, but they have to live, too! It's extortion, pure and simple. Pay up or be decimated. That's the message our humble governor puts out."

Caleb shook his head, trying to absorb what Conrad was telling him, knowing that no matter how much rum the man had consumed, he was speaking the truth.

"The Indian traps his furs honestly, sells them to the Dutch West India Company and then has to turn over one hundred percent profits to Kiefft in New Amsterdam. Their women and children are hungry. I don't blame them for stealing, and that's why you see me here—drunk. I can't stand seeing another Indian come in here begging for food for his children. If I had any to give, by God, I'd give it! And to hell with your fancy burghers in Holland just waiting for their profits. Hand over my wages and the place

309

is yours," Conrad said, hitching up his trousers. "And you're welcome to it!"

"On whose authority does Kiefft extort these levies?"

Conrad laughed. "How would I be knowing?" he sneered. "The likes of the governor don't see fit to confide in the likes of me. So if you'll just hand over my wages, I'll be departing your premises."

Caleb counted out the man's wages, his face a mottled mask of rage. The first order of the day would be to get a replacement for Conrad and then pay the governor a visit, an unexpected visit. Tomorrow, after sunup, he would find a horse and set out for a look at the governor's ledgers. It would be interesting to see how Willem Kiefft had prospered.

Caleb sat down on the wooden chair, propped his feet on the flimsy desk and then dropped them to the floor. He had seen a strongbox beneath the desk, full of papers. The Company's records, no doubt, for the trading post. He would take them back to the ship and go over them later. Now he had to think about what he had to do and how he was going to do it. He was one man, alone in a strange new world. The fact that he had been here when the trading post had first been established didn't alter the reality of the present situation.

During that trip he had spent his time wisely and to good advantage. He had established friendly relations with the chief of the Pequot tribe and smoked a pipe with him and his council members on the agreements between them. His relations had been so friendly, in fact, that on his departure the chief had offered him a gift of one of the young tribal maidens. Caleb had been hard pressed to decline the generous offer tactfully, and with tears streaming down Wildflower's face, he had sailed away with a brisk wave of his hand and a sly wink for the aging chief.

Now he had been told that the Pequots had rebelled and taken women hostages and stolen their own furs, furs meant for rich, elegant ladies in Europe. Something besides the levies must have stirred up the old chief. He had proclaimed that he was a peaceful man who only wanted to live out his days in his village and watch the young bucks grow to manhood. The men of his tribe were not warriors and were as peaceful as their chief.

When unrest settled in, everyone involved was threatened. Christ, what if the Indians decided to stage a war? Caleb mused. These settlers didn't know the first thing about fighting. They would be no match for the revenge-seeking Pequots. He shuddered when he remembered having heard that New Amsterdam matrons had used the severed heads of Indian men, women and children for a grisly game of kickball on the dusty streets. And the chief had remarked sadly, "Your governor laughed heartily. We did not go to war but turned our backs. Fence a dog or drive him into a corner, and sooner or later he will strike back." Those had been the only ominous words mentioned on the day Caleb had sailed back to Holland. Had that day come and gone? Were the Indians preparing for another attack, and would it be an all-out war against the ill-equipped settlers?

He groaned aloud at the thought of Bascom Stoneham wielding a weapon to ward off an Indian attack. Prayer wouldn't help Bascom if the Indians decided they wanted his scalp. Caleb seriously doubted that anything would help Bascom. But Bascom wasn't his worry any longer. The preacher would live here with his people and help build the church of his dreams. This was no time for Caleb to saddle himself with worrying about the good people settling this lush new land. The Dutch West India Company was of the utmost importance. The burghers had told Regan they expected and would accept nothing less than that New Netherland would attain the most powerful

311

position in the New World. Regan had agreed to their plan and sent Caleb to arrange matters. And Caleb had done what he had been told to do, and now everything was in a shambles.

First he would see the governor, and then he would go up the river to the Mystic fort of the Pequots and get the straight of it. Thoughts of renegade Indians with their deadly bows and arrows made him flinch. His hand went to his thick head of ebony hair and his mouth tightened. He was going in peace and would fly the white flag if necessary, along with the emblem of the Dutch West India Company. It was unfortunate he couldn't carry Kiefft's head on a pike to show his good faith. Kiefft had been installed as governor by the Dutch West India Company, but now, since Caleb's authority superseded Kiefft's, the governor's days were numbered as regional head of the Company in the New World.

Darkness enveloped Saybrook when Caleb closed the door behind him, the strongbox containing the piles of business papers riding on his shoulder. Great bonfires raged toward the sky, and women bustled about smaller cookfires, preparing the evening meal for their men.

From his position on the road Caleb could see Bascom leading his people toward the center compound, where the largest fire burned, for a prayer meeting before dinner. He frowned when he saw Sara walking behind her mother. A stab of guilt and remorse pierced him but was short-lived when he remembered that Sara's lies had most likely prompted Wren to go overboard.

Grief ripped through him. *Wren.* His loneliness was tangible and his sorrow weighed him down. How was he to live without her?

His feet directed him to the river and the jolly that would take him back to the ship, but his thoughts were centered on the last time he had been alone with Wren, when they had vowed their love to each other. How could she have believed Sara was carrying his child, regardless of what she had overheard? A flush of shame coursed through his veins. If he hadn't prided himself on being such a womanizer, and if he'd kept his hands to himself instead of on Sara, there would have been no recriminations. Guiltily, he recalled that even he had considered the possibility that he could have fathered Sara's child.

Choking back the taste of bitter gall, he broke through the clearing to the river. Wren was lost to him. He knew it in his head, but he would never accept it in his heart.

Chapter Twenty

Shortly after dawn, when only the earliest rising inhabitants of Saybrook were stirring, Caleb rowed ashore in the jolly and made his way around the back of the rustic Company building to the stables. One glance at the poorly fed, ill-kempt horses filled him with contempt for Conrad's inefficient handling of Company property.

After watering and feeding the three mounts, he finally chose one he thought would withstand the trip to New Amsterdam without mishap. After saddling his horse he led it from the stable and called to a small boy who was playing in the street. He reached in his pocket tossed the youth several coins and told him to curry the other two horses and lead them around the stable yard for exercise.

The boy, whose name was Sammy, was delighted with the coins and bobbed his head agreeably as he looked up at the tall man with the shiny boots. "I'll have to tell my mum, sir, and hand over the coins. Will that be all right?"

Caleb smiled. "It will be fine. Do a good job and you can do it every day. How old are you, son?"

"I'm seven, sir, but I'm big for my age and strong, too!" he said enthusiastically. "Could I be your ostler? My da' taught me everything about horses. And my family would be real pleased if I had the job. My da' has just about used up all our savings, and the store won't be giving out credit to the farmers. Governor's orders." The small face darkened with the injustice of the order and then brightened as he saw Caleb give his request deep thought.

"Governor's orders, is it? You're hired as long as you can do the job and your family gives permission. When I get back, we'll settle on a wage agreeable to your dad." So there was another matter to settle with the new governor. What right had he to claim that no credit be given to farmers?

Caleb sat tall in the saddle, urging his mount forward with a gentle hand and a firm pressure of his knees. He handled the animal with the same confident persuasion with which he mastered the *Sea Siren*. The steed surrendered to its rider, followed the well-traveled road out of Saybrook and turned west along the shoreline of the Sound.

Caleb squinted up at the sky and estimated he would find himself at the ferry landing well before dark. There he would take a ferryboat across the river to

Manhattan Island. As he rode his mind wandered away from the governor and dwelled more and more upon Wren. No matter how he tried to discipline his thoughts, they kept returning to her. At times he could see her so clearly in his mind's eye that he believed he could reach out and touch her.

Traveling along the tree-lined roads, he felt the salt breeze from the Sound freshen his cheeks. And always he thought of her, felt her amber-lit eyes following him, imagined he could hear the sound of her voice, low and husky as she called his name. Wren would always be with him wherever he journeyed. And always his heart would cry out for her and his arms would be empty without her, and for the rest of his life, and possibly beyond, he would know he had met his destiny and lost it.

Two hours before dusk found Caleb disembarking from the ferry which had taken him across the water to Manhattan Island. He thought of Peter Minuit, the first director general of New Netherland. Now that good man was building colonies in New Sweden, along the Delaware River to the southwest.

Regardless of his quarrel with Governor Kiefft's policies concerning the outposts and the Indians, Caleb could find no fault with his attentions to the burgeoning colony of New Amsterdam. The streets were in the process of being paved with the cobblestones many ships used for ballast, and the people looked well fed and prosperous. Construction had been accomplished at an alarming rate, and Caleb had to ask for directions to the Governor's Manse.

Skirting around the center of New Amsterdam to avoid the clutter of carriages and people, Caleb took a side road, prodding his nearly exhausted mount with his heels and encouraging it with his voice. Coming around a bend, Caleb saw a group of men riding toward him, accompanied by a two-wheeled cart into which was built a cage. He immediately recognized the yellow cockade of Dutch militiamen and was curious to see whom or what they had caged in the cart. As he passed them, he glanced into the cart and saw two Indians who were rail-thin from lack of food and had suffered a severe beating, no doubt from the hands of the militiamen.

"What've they done?" Caleb asked the leader of the party in an offhand manner, careful to keep any note of pity from his voice. He was aware of his own vulnerability, being alone on a back road with eleven or more men who were apparently proud of having captured the unfortunate Indians.

"Thieves is what they are!" came the fast reply, accompanied by a bitter, self-satisfied smile.

"We had reports of poaching and stealing from several farmers, and we caught the devils in the act!" another offered.

"What were they stealing?" Caleb asked.

"What else? Grain and food, and they were poaching the sheep and cattle. There was a band of 'em, and all got away except these two. We'll make a fine example of them, we will. When their friends see their heads on pikes, they'll begin to think twice about coming over here to do their dirty work."

Caleb again looked into the cage and was saddened by the apathetic expressions on the captives' faces. These red men were a far cry from the dignified, proud and noble Indians he was familiar with, and little wonder why. They were half starved and more than half dead from their beating.

"What's their tribe?" he asked, unable to distinguish any markings on them.

"Wappinger! And a fine bounty they'll bring."

"Wappinger! I've heard they were a friendly tribe."

"Maybe. But there's about a hundred of 'em stowed out on Staten Island, running away from marauding Mohawks. The governor don't care much about that, but canoeing over here and poaching is something else again. Indeed, these are the first we've captured, and we'll receive a nice purse for them, I can tell you that."

Rage against this sort of injustice filled Caleb, and he kneed his horse sharply and continued down the road, eager now to come face to face with Kiefft.

The long, tree-lined stone drive leading to the expansive Governor's Manse was well tended and landscaped. Politics must be paying well, Caleb told himself as his weary mount plodded up the drive at a slow pace. Huge tubs of flowers and evergreens dotted the wide veranda, and lanterns were strategically placed near the potted plants. Caleb knew it would be a magnificent sight at night. Whom did the governor welcome that he needed all these expensive trappings? The house and everything inside and out belonged to the Dutch West India Company. Things had certainly improved from the profits, just as he knew they had the moment he had opened the ledger he had found in Saybrook and poured over the spidery column of almost nonexistent figures.

Caleb tethered his horse and stomped to the front door. He smirked. Solid mahogany. Must have cost a king's ransom in this part of the world. He gave the silver knocker a vicious tug and stood back, waiting to be admitted.

He wasn't surprised when a liveried footman opened the door, making Caleb think for a moment he was back in England, where pomp and ceremony were a daily occurrence. "Captain Caleb van der Rhys to see Governor Kiefft," he said curtly.

"The governor retired early. His office in town would be happy to make an appointment for you, Captain. His lordship never sees anyone until after lunch." The footman's tone was haughty, and with the firm, no-nonsense hand of a practiced major-domo, he began to push Caleb out the door.

"Is that so?" Caleb snarled as he gathered the startled man's starched shirt front in one hand and lifted him off his feet, setting him down at the side of the door. "Now point out the governor's rooms and then go about your business. I come here representing the Dutch West India Company, and it will go hard on you if you don't do as you're told."

"I understand," the footman said, wiping his perspiring brow. "However, sir, the governor has . . . there is . . . the governor is a man of . . ."

"Lusty tastes and he has a whore in his bed," Caleb finished shortly. "Stand by so you can usher the lady out."

Caleb didn't bother to knock at the governor's bedroom door but thrust open the carved structure. The sight that met his eyes was so ludicrous he guffawed loudly. Twin gelatinous globes of alabaster flesh pumped furiously at something hidden from Caleb's eyes. The dual mountains quivered and then collapsed, accompanied by deep, guttural moans.

"I hope that is the end of it," Caleb laughed as he strode across the room and threw a cover over the fish-belly white flesh. He looked down at Willem Kiefft and hated him on sight. Bald, completely hairless, he reminded Caleb of an egg. The governor was without eyebrows or lashes, and his beady eyes glittered at the intrusion. His full, pouting mouth drew back, revealing tiny white teeth.

"Out!" The one word was a command aimed at the woman, who was already gathering her clothes together.

"Bellamy!" the governor shouted in outrage.

"If you're calling for your footman, save your breath. He has been informed who his employer is. Now, get your fat ass out of that bed before I do it for you. Put on some clothes and we'll talk. By the way, I am Captain van der Rhys, representing the Dutch West India Company."

Fear momentarily glassed the governor's eyes and then was replaced with arrogance. "Now, see here,

I'm the governor! Duly appointed! And that was my woman, and what right do you have to come barging in here?" His sensibilities returning, Kiefft assumed his usual bravado.

"By this right." Caleb tossed a scroll of parchment onto the bed. "You are correct about one thing, though. She was a woman. Somehow I would have thought a man of your position would be more discriminating than to employ the services of a common whore. And you are governor only as long as I wish. And I don't wish! So get the hell out of that bed. Now!" A dark crimson color stained Caleb's face, his mouth drew into a bitter, cruel line, and there was no denying the authority he exuded.

Kiefft reached for the parchment Caleb had tossed him and scanned the message. "I have not received a dismissal order from Holland. Until I do, I am the acting governor, and neither you nor any stiff, crackling paper is going to say otherwise."

"How much would you be willing to wager?" Caleb asked, reaching down and throwing back the coverlet. He moved slightly and pressed his knee into the man's groin. "That whore will never have to worry about being pounded to death again. Now, I want to know what's going on, and I want to know now."

The governor gasped for breath, his face tinged blue from the pain Caleb was inflicting.

"You're using up precious time and you're also turning blue. A fat man like you shouldn't take such chances with his health. Why is the warehouse empty? Where are the furs that were to be ready for me to take to England? If you try to lie, I'll kill you here and now."

"Take your knee . . . take it off and I'll tell you whatever you want to know," the governor croaked. Caleb eased the pressure somewhat but didn't remove his knee. The fat man gulped air and drew in a deep breath. "The goddamn warehouse is empty because the goddamn Indians stole the furs. Now, will you get the hell off me before you kill me?"

"Why did they steal the furs? The Pequots were a peaceful tribe when I was last here. Their chief is a man of honor and peace."

"The old chief is dead. Sassacus is the chief now. He's no old man. He's a savage bastard, is what he is. He'd sooner cut out your tongue than look at you. He stole the furs."

"You aren't telling me why he stole them. I met Sassacus and I smoked the pipe with him and broke bread. If Sassacus has turned savage, then you made him that way. Tell me about the levy you fixed on his tribe."

The governor rolled his head. "A small matter to bring them into line. All they had to do was spend a few more hours trapping and they could come up with the furs. They want everything handed to them on a silver platter. That's what happens when you teach them our language and try to make them civilized. They're like mad dogs and they turn on you every chance they get. They're savages. They're not fit to polish my boots."

"What you mean is, they're too good to polish your boots. Were they good enough to lay that long, circular driveway and tend your lawns and flowers? What else are they good enough for? How do they work that off, you fat bastard?" Caleb gritted through clenched teeth.

"Someone had to do it!" Kiefft protested sharply, his heavy jowls quivering with tension. "For the pride of the Company! It's expected. While the Indians worked, they were fed. If extraordinary measures were needed to bring about their cooperation, then so be it!"

Caleb's lip curled into an ugly line, his distaste and contempt for Kiefft evident. "And a promise of food and a whip could insure their cooperation! Is that it?" he boomed. "Get up and get dressed. We've a long night ahead of us to discuss these 'savages,' as you call them. When I return to Holland, I want to be able to tell the burghers what an excellent choice they made in selecting you governor of New Netherland."

Kiefft bounded out of bed and ran to the adjacent dressing room in search of his clothes. He was frightened of van der Rhys, frightened of his authority and his contempt. A report from him to the right person in Holland would mean the end of his own governorship here in New Netherland. Kiefft knew he would have to watch his markers; if reform was necessary in this Dutch West India Company territory, it would behoove his own political career to see that he was the one who brought it about, instead of an upstart fresh from Holland in pursuit of grandeur and glory here in America.

Caleb sat down and looked around the room. It was decorated like a French brothel, a successful one at that. Rich burgundy draperies adorned the long windows, and heavy tapestries hung on the walls. A thick, tapestried carpet made him frown. The bedcovers were satin and luxurious, and he knew they whispered all night long to the naked bodies that cavorted between them. Gold goblets and a decanter of wine stood on a carved table next to the bed. Kiefft certainly didn't deny himself.

Caleb reached for the decanter and drank from it, swallowing deeply. He stretched out on a plum brocade chaise and stared at his booted feet. Mentally, he calculated his forthcoming discussion with Kiefft, knowing he could never turn the man's prejudice around but hoping he could somehow control his greed and subsequent mistreatment of the red man with threats of impeachment. Kiefft and men like him had stirred the cookpot situation between the colonists and the Indians into a boiling cauldron of discontent and fear.

Tomorrow he would see the other side of that fear.

321

He would ride north, past Saybrook, to the Pequot village on the shores of Mystic.

Governor Kiefft had given in to Caleb's demands too easily. The man should have fought to his last breath to retain what he had cheated to obtain. Instead, he had listened and nodded his head in agreement, promising to revise his methods of filling the Company's storehouses and administering justice to whites and red men alike. Something was afoot, Caleb knew it, and whatever it was, it boded ill for the Indian.

With a sinking feeling, Caleb admitted to himself that nothing he could say or do would turn the tide and prevent a confrontation between the Pequots and the settlers. At best, he could avert that disaster by going to see Sassacus and telling him of the governor's promised reform. He doubted that the Indian chief would listen to him, but he had to try. The Pequots were a small tribe, beset by problems from more aggressive and larger tribes—most specifically the Narragansetts. War with the settlers now would mean the complete annihilation of their people.

His conference with Kiefft had taken most of the night, and he had gotten only three hours of sleep in the governor's guest room before setting out to see Sassacus.

The nag which had carried him from Saybrook to New Amsterdam could never have made the return trip, and Kiefft had accommodated him with a russet stallion, complete with saddlebags brimming with food and drink. For this Caleb had been grateful, as it meant he would not have to stop in Saybrook overnight but could camp in the woods and arrive at the Pequot village well before noon the next day.

After spending a restful night in the woods, he rose early and continued his trek along the dense shoreline, his eyes watchful as the horse pounded the sandy terrain. From time to time he heard a bird call and knew that Sassacus's braves were warning their chief of a lone rider approaching.

The moment Caleb came within sight of the Indian fort, he reined in the horse and waited. He sat tall and straight, his dark hair falling low on his forehead. An Indian approached, his face inscrutable in the bright sunshine. Neither man said a word. Caleb allowed the stallion to trot behind the Indian at a slow pace, holding himself erect and proud.

The squaws and the children paid him no heed as they went about their tasks. One old man looked up from his pipe and went back to his dozing. A canvas flap was thrown back across the doorway of a small lodge, and Caleb dismounted and entered the dim room. A man sat cross-legged before a smoldering pile of ashes. He was dark-skinned and had bright, intelligent-looking eyes. His long black hair was coiled into a single thick braid hanging down his back, and his folded arms revealed rippling muscles.

"Welcome," Sassacus said, rising with one fluid motion. "How are you, Captain van der Rhys?" He spoke an almost perfect English.

Caleb held out his hand and the Indian grasped it firmly. Caleb caught his breath but made no move to withdraw his hand. The Indian smiled and nodded. "You've gained strength since we did this last."

Caleb laughed. "I'm two years older. Each year we gain strength." The Indian looked skeptical but accepted the statement. Both men sat down, Caleb deferring first to the Pequot chief.

"My people have watched the waters for many days now. I knew of your arrival in Saybrook." Sassacus eyed Caleb warily, to see if the honest, forthright man he had met two years ago was still present.

"I heard of the passing of your father, Sassacus. He was a great chief. Now you sit in his place, another great chief, and you look the part." Caleb grinned.

"If only it were so simple. Looking the part of a

323

great leader is not the deed done." The Indian smiled, showing square white teeth. "Many things have happened to our people. Many per—" He hesitated.

"Persecutions," Caleb volunteered.

"Many times the words do not come to my lips. White men talk many words. White men talk too much."

Caleb threw back his head and laughed. "Why talk when a grunt will do just as well?"

Sassacus looked sheepish. "My people think I am a god now that I know so many white man's words. I am pleased to see you, Caleb van der Rhys. My greetings to your honorable father."

"I'm here, Sassacus, to speak of the Dutch West India Company's business. I have just come from the home of the governor and bring his greetings. Also, I bring you word of his reform."

"Bah! It is too late for reform. The deed is done— empty promises. First we will eat. Perhaps lies and deceptions will sit better on a full belly."

When they had partaken of the simple food, Caleb leaned back on his haunches and studied Sassacus carefully. The chief's eyes shone brightly in the dimness of the hut, and the oil from his swarthy skin made him look as though he were perspiring freely. He too, was waiting, waiting for Caleb to say something, to make some sign that he knew there was more to discuss than the little that had transpired in the past hour. Each played a waiting game, each wanting the other to speak first to show there was no distrust in his heart.

Caleb took the initiative. "This could go on all day, Sassacus. I'm as good at waiting as you are. I learned much from you and your father on my last visit. No games, Sassacus. I can't help you if you won't confide in me."

The Indian nodded, his lean, hard body relaxed and he crossed his legs in front of him. As always when he spoke, Caleb was stunned by his clear tone and his almost perfect command of the English language. Without the braid and the buckskins, he might have passed for a scholar. "A crooked trader named Captain John Smith came to the settlement and aligned himself with your governor. He arrived about six months ago and set up trading posts along the Connecticut River. Your own people feared him almost as much as the Indians. I understand from some of your settlers that he drew a knife on the governor of Plymouth and spoke lewdly and contemptuously to the officials in the Massachusetts Bay. Everywhere he had been, he was charged with drunkenness and adultery. It's not a pretty story, Caleb, and one I do not relish telling you. As I said, your own people wished him dead. One night his ship was riding anchor at the mouth of the river, and a band of Indians, not my tribe, but Pequots nevertheless, swarmed aboard and massacred all hands, including Captain Smith. He had cheated us and raped our women. His cutthroats had raped small children and then left them to die. In truth, if it had been your people, would you have done less?" Caleb said nothing, motioning Sassacus to continue. "You've come at a volatile time, my friend. The Massachusetts Bay authorities have demanded that we surrender the murderers to English justice. We cannot do that," Sassacus stated firmly.

"My people are already at war with the Narragansetts and have made our peace with your Dutch brothers," he went on. "I will attend a council meeting of my people. We plan to agree to a treaty if it meets with our approval. They"—he made the word sound obscene—"want us to hand over the murderers along with a heavy indemnity. I will tell them that our people retaliated only because of the rape of our women and children and for the murder of our chief. They kidnaped him, Caleb, and after we paid the ransom, they sent us back his dead body. If this is your English justice, we want no part of it. I know that we must

325

concede somewhere along the way, but we must have terms." Sassacus's voice was soft, almost humble, when he spoke again. "There are those who say the Dutch were responsible for the death of my father. In my heart," he said, placing a dark hand on his chest, "I know this is not true. Still, I cannot think for my people. I can only disagree and protest."

Caleb's own voice was soft when he spoke. "How soon will your people unite, and how soon will the war begin?"

Sassacus's smile was sad. "Ah, my friend, then you, too, see that war is inevitable. War solves nothing. Man must learn to talk and work out the problems. I was and am willing, but it is the white man who wants to pillage and plunder. The white man knows only war and greed." He leaned forward, his eyes imploring. "We were a peaceful people until the whites came here. We would have shared, but they took from us without asking. Would you allow what belongs to you to be taken by force without striking back? You can back a stray dog into a tree, but sooner or later he will find a way to free himself, and then he will become a wild renegade. I have hope for the meeting, but that's all it is—hope."

"What can I do? You haven't told me, Sassacus. I must know."

The Indian shrugged. He would say no more, and Caleb understood.

"Do you know what happened to all the furs?"

Again Sassacus shrugged. "Whose blood runs in your veins, Caleb van der Rhys?" the Indian asked harshly.

"You ask a foolish question for a wise chief. I agree with all that you've told me. Perhaps we can figure out a way to avert a war."

Sassacus laughed. "Now tell me who is being foolish. It is inevitable."

Caleb's face was troubled as he got to his feet. He

looked down at Sassacus, and his voice was stern when he spoke. "I see by your face and hear in your voice that you are hungry for war."

"Wise words spoken by a wise man," Sassacus said sarcastically. He rose in one fluid motion. "It is *your* people who will not listen! They will turn a deaf ear to you. For that I am sorry. There is something else you should know, Caleb van der Rhys. If it comes to war, and should we face each other in battle, I will fight to kill for what is mine. I want to be certain you understand what I am saying. If we meet in battle, one of us will die."

Caleb stared at the Indian for a long moment. "Understood, Sassacus."

The Pequot chief watched Caleb ride from the fort, his heart heavy in his chest. A pity all white men weren't like Caleb. He appreciated the relationship they had, one man to another, not white man and red man, but simply two men. Soon that would change, and it would be white man against red man, Caleb against Sassacus. Who would win? Sassacus's shoulders slumped. The white man always won. He squared his shoulders. Perhaps this time it would be different. Perhaps he could make it different.

He left the hut and walked to the clearing in the center of the fort. For a long time he stood there staring straight ahead of him. His bearing was proud as his eyes sought out one figure and then another. His jaw was grim, his high cheekbones lending a quality of arrogance to his face. Perhaps this time it would be different.

Chapter Twenty-one

While Malcolm Weatherly made his way downriver to confront Caleb and extort ransom for Wren, she was struggling to free herself from the ropes which bound her to a massive tree trunk. She cried in agony as the bands around her waist became tighter instead of loosening with her efforts. If she had to be grateful for one thing, it was the fact that Malcolm had secured her in a grassy nook close to the water's edge, shaded by goliath-like trees. If the sun were beating down on her, she wouldn't last the day. Already she was thirsty, and Malcolm hadn't left her any water. Her mouth was dry and her lips were cracked and sore, and the glimpses she caught of the fresh river water were maddening because it was unreachable.

She drifted between wakefulness and sleep, exhausted from her struggles. Suddenly, a crawling on the back of her leg awakened her. Images of horrible multi-eyed insects shot through her mind. Frantically she tried to reach the spot but could not bend forward. Revulsion constricted her chest and her spine stiffened as she became aware of a parade of red ants crawling up the front of her leg. She succeeded in brushing them off by rubbing her legs together, but they returned for the attack. A soundless scream leapt from her throat as the long, endless column of shiny red insects, their antennae quivering, inched farther up her leg, their grinding mandibles growing clearer and more horrible every moment.

While the inch-long red ants tormented Wren, Malcolm traveled downriver, his eye constantly searching out the terrain to the left and to the right. He sang loudly and lustily as his oars dipped and spurred the dinghy onward. He should be in sight of the settlement soon. An hour, perhaps less, for his business, and then back to the woods. He was pleased with himself that things were going according to plan.

He rowed contentedly. Soon he would be face to face with Aubrey Farrington and collecting his half of the jewels. He had decided long ago that he wouldn't wait for the gambler to sell them off in Martinique. He wanted them, and he wanted them now. He could sell them wherever and whenever he wanted. And with the ransom money from Caleb, he would have ready cash, which was the main thing for the time being. His world was slowly coming to rights.

There they were—the sails of the *Sea Siren*. Malcolm maneuvered the dinghy to the left and got as close to the shoreline as he could. He swiftly calculated the distance and decided it would be a small matter to cover it on foot. He worked slowly and efficiently to beach the dinghy and then broke off branches from the low-hanging trees to camouflage the small craft.

He reached the shore rapidly, his heart pounding in his chest. Only once did he falter even slightly, and that was when he saw a new grave with a stout wooden cross on it. He stepped over it lightly, paying it no heed, and continued his short journey.

Malcolm walked through the stockaded walls surrounding Saybrook, and after making certain no one had seen him, quickly skirted behind the buildings as he searched for the offices of the Dutch West India Company, where he knew he would find Caleb. He was well aware of his disfigurement and realized he could never go unnoticed for long among the people of the settlement. Hunkering down against the stable wall behind the Company's office, he waited, squinting his one good eye up at the sky. It was only an hour or so past noon. He was prepared to wait all day if necessary. He had already waited over two days in the woods, and one more day would be worth the end results.

His patience was well rewarded. Within the hour he spied Caleb handing his horse's reins to a small boy and heard him give the lad orders to curry and feed the animal.

Quickly, like a wraith, he stepped out into the open and called, "Van der Rhys!"

Caleb turned at the sound of his name and for a full moment didn't recognize Malcolm. The change in his appearance was so startling . . . so pitiful. "Weatherly!"

"Why do you look so surprised? After all, it was your ship that brought me here. Of course, Farrington helped, but if you want the truth, I was hiding in what you call your locker box. I'd appreciate it if you could tell me where I can find the old man."

Caleb was stunned. He shook his head to clear it. "You were on the *Siren* all the time, and none of us were aware of it?" He shook his head again as he recalled Aubrey's late-night comings and goings. He should have known better, or at least suspected. "Your friend, and mine, rests over there," Caleb said, pointing in the direction of the new grave.

"No lies, van der Rhys. Where's that old sinner? We have business to take care of."

"Ask anyone." Caleb waved his hand around the settlement. "Somebody on board ship clubbed him to death the night before we touched land. We buried him when we docked three nights ago."

It was Malcolm's turn to be stunned. "What about the jewels—where are they? That old fox wouldn't go to his death without leaving some clue to their whereabouts."

"So that was what he was trying to hide! You've just given me the answer to his death. I could find no reason why someone would kill a harmless old man. You'll have to look elsewhere for your jewels, Weatherly. Whoever killed Aubrey Farrington has them," Caleb lied smoothly.

Malcolm was beside himself with rage. "I don't believe a word you're saying. I think you have the jewels —in fact, I know you do. Well, I'll just show you how much good they're going to do you. Listen to me, van der Rhys, and listen carefully, for I have no intention of repeating myself. I want those jewels, all of them, plus fifty thousand pounds sterling for your sister, Wren."

Caleb's face went blank and his limbs froze. "Wren is dead," he choked. Then he remembered the misery Weatherly had caused her. "As dead as you're going to be!" He lunged at Malcolm, who deftly sidestepped the attack.

Malcolm laughed, a tinny cackle that nearly froze the blood in Caleb's veins. "She's not dead, but she might be soon. I have her safe and sound . . . for the time being. She was in the locker box with me. You look ill. Take some time, until noon tomorrow, to adjust yourself to the idea that your sister is alive and well . . . as I said, for the time being. You deliver the jewels and money to me tomorrow, and you can have her!"

"If you're lying to me, Weatherly, I'll carve you up in little pieces and feed you to the sharks!" Caleb's teeth were clenched as he advanced a step and then another. Malcolm held his ground, although his heart pumped rapidly.

"Keep your hands to yourself, van der Rhys. I said she's alive and well. I'll turn her over to you tomorrow on the noon hour, providing you meet my demands. Any tricks and she gets it." He made a rough motion of running his hand under his throat to show his intent.

Caleb understood the action all too well and also that the former dandy would do just as he threatened. For now, it would have to be his way, but tomorrow was another day and he would be off guard. Caleb remained still, knowing in his gut that if he made a move or said a word, he would kill the man standing before him. For now, he would have to wait. That Wren was alive was all he needed to know. There must be something to all that praying, after all.

Caleb squatted down on the dusty road, in full view of every one of the settlers. His legs were rubbery and his arms trembled. That damn mist was clouding his vision again. When he was in control of himself, he looked up. Malcolm Weatherly was gone, almost as if he had never appeared, had never said the words that made Caleb a whole man again. Tomorrow was another day.

Malcolm ran through the woods fronting the riverbank, hardly daring to breathe. So one small thing was not in his favor. Now, who could have killed the old man? The Dutchman was probably right—someone who wanted the jewels. Malcolm could almost see the jeweled collar in Caleb's hand tomorrow at noon. He had it—he wasn't fooling Malcolm. Somebody might have killed Farrington thinking he had it, only to realize after the bludgeoning that the jewels were in the Dutchman's safekeeping, probably hidden in the ship's safe. A child could have figured that out with one look at the sea captain's face. Tomorrow the jewels would be in his, Malcolm's, pocket.

Cautiously he made his way to the dinghy, stopping every few seconds to see if he was being followed. Satisfied that he wasn't, he removed the branches and carried them deeper into the woods, to be used again the following day.

As he rowed the boat swiftly upriver, he glanced at the sky. He was right on schedule. He would be back before sundown. He felt surprisingly good, good enough for a little play with Wren. Maybe this time she would welcome him. And if she didn't . . . If she knew what was good for her, she would, and he would make that clear before he untied her.

Wren was in agony; the clawing red ants were all over her, beneath her garments and in her hair, and one of them seemed to be caught in her thick eyelash. She let out a shrill scream and then fainted.

Two small girls playing in the woods stopped in their tracks as the high-pitched wail reached their ears. Hearing no further cries, they tiptoed on moccasined feet to where they thought the sound had come from. They held hands and giggled slightly at this small adventure. A wounded bird perhaps, and they would nurse it back to health. A small animal caught in a snare, and they would free it so it could return to its natural lair. The smaller of the two, who resembled a precocious squirrel with her bright, merry gaze, nudged the taller one and pushed her forward. At the sight that met their eyes they backed off quickly and held a whispered conversation with much pointing and stamping of feet. The smaller girl tilted her head to one side and advanced closer, taking in Wren's dark gown. She looked at her friend, and they both nodded. The taller girl ran down to the river and came back with her hands full of mud. Together they ripped off Wren's clothing and smeared her with mud from head to toe. They clucked their tongues in sympathy when they noticed the ants in her hair. Another brief conference and another trip to the river. Within minutes Wren resembled a grotesque river monster.

The two girls sat back on their haunches and surveyed their handiwork. They had a problem. Should they go back to the fort for help, or should they try to take the "creature" with them? Could they make a litter and carry her? How? Again they put their heads together and whispered. Within minutes they had removed every lace on their persons, from those on their moccasins to the ties that bound their hair. Fir branches were broken by the smaller child's standing on the taller one's shoulders and swinging from a branch till it collapsed. Then, they tied the branches together and dragged Wren's unprotesting body to the makeshift litter.

The mudpack seemed to be working; Wren had come to and was feeling better. She wanted to say something to the children but knew they wouldn't understand. She tried to thank them with her eyes and a gentle touch of her hand. She wanted to tell them to hurry, to get her out of here before Malcolm returned. Her gaze became pleading as she motioned to the rope they had removed.

It was the smaller child who understood first. Gesturing wildly and pointing to the rope, she danced around in agitation. Her companion nodded solemnly to show she, too, understood, and bent to help her friend with the litter. They made their way deep into the woods, certain it was the wisest route to follow. Every so often they stopped to smooth the pine needles and cover their tracks. Their eyes met from time to time and expressed their awareness that this was serious business, and it wasn't just the boys in the fort who knew how to do things. Chief Sassacus would be proud of them, proud because they had helped a white sister. If they were lucky, he might even give them a sweet to suck on. Already the little one's tongue was tasting the rock candy she adored.

By the time they reached their village, they were completely out of breath, their titian skin wet with perspiration. They dragged the litter the last few feet to a shady tree and stood back expectantly, each rubbing at the blisters on her hands from contact with the rough bark.

The women of the fort meandered over to the litter and stared down at Wren and then at the girls. Each began to babble, and much hand waving ensued. The girls looked at each other when one of the women said Sassacus was downriver. There would be no sweet. Disappointed at this news, they ran off to pick berries, their mouths watering.

The children had probably saved Wren's life, the women agreed. But who was she and where did she come from? Because there were no answers to their questions, they lifted Wren gently and took her into one of the lodges, where they worked industriously to wash off the dry mud and to apply fresh, wet compresses all over her body. Their eyes met when they saw the raw rope burns around her waist, but they said nothing. A white woman who had been tied up somewhere meant trouble. They placed Wren on a clean blanket and then sat down around her.

Wren relaxed within the protective circle of women. She knew they were Indians and that they meant her no harm. The children had managed to bring her here and now she was safe, away from Malcolm and his deranged ideas and threats. These women, with serene understanding in their eyes, would never harm her, she was convinced of that. Her eyes closed wearily and Caleb's face intruded into her dreams.

The women took turns sitting in the tight circle. They watched the girl with compassionate eyes as she slept fitfully, calling on someone named Caleb to help her. They rolled the strange name around on their

335

tongues so that they would have it right when they told it to Chief Sassacus on his return.

Malcolm felt elated as he stepped from the dinghy. By this time tomorrow he would have the ransom and the jewels and would be well on his way to a new life here in the colonies. He would set himself up in grand style and have servants wait on him hand and foot. He would be a generous employer and would lavish his servants with good food and fine lodgings. Money, he thought, could buy anything.

It was too quiet. There should be leaves rustling, small animals running through the underbrush. Even the birds were silent. Something was wrong. His jubilant mood of moments ago disappeared. What could have gone wrong? He had left Wren securely tied. He had the dinghy and he had seen Caleb, and he knew for certain that he hadn't been followed.

Malcolm's good eye nearly popped from its socket when he saw Wren's gown lying on the ground, covered with a lacy pattern of holes made by the red bugs. His mind refused to accept the visual evidence before him. What is holy hell happened to Wren's dress? he asked himself. Did she free herself? She couldn't have, he answered silently. Someone must have helped her escape. Who? He looked around and felt the first rumblings of fear in his gut. This was Indian territory, after all.

He reached down and picked up the tattered dress, trying to imagine what had happened. It was too much for him to comprehend, and he slumped against the tree. All his fine dreams of mere moments ago were shattered. There would be no fine house and no servants. Not only would the ransom be lost to him, but the jewels would be lost as well. He had nothing. He had never had anything except a pocketful of dreams, and now that was gone, just like his handsome face. His eyes burned with tears and the injustice of it all. What was he going to do now? Without Wren, van der Rhys would kill him. Unless . . . he wiped at his eye with the back of his hand . . . unless he could come up with a plan to outwit van der Rhys and get the gems and the money first. How? He couldn't think. All he knew was that he didn't want to die. He couldn't die; his whole life was ahead of him. But, he sobbed silently, I can't have any kind of life without money and someone to take care of me. I don't even have a weapon to defend myself against Caleb. I have to think—to come up with some sort of plan. He prayed that wherever Wren was, it was far away from Caleb. And, he thought maliciously, whoever has her, I hope it's the Indians and that she's strung up somewhere for all the grief she's caused me. Whatever is happening to her, she deserves it.

Malcolm made himself a small campsite and settled down to sleep. Normally, under the present circumstances, he would have slept with one eye open. Now, thanks to that bitch Wren, he couldn't even do that. However, because he was so tired and needed to sleep, he would simply have to take his chances.

Dawn crept up on him and woke him with tenacious fingers. He stirred, trying to orient himself to his surroundings. He itched; God, how he itched. In the early light he could barely make out the red bugs that were crawling all over him. He screamed shrilly and ran down to the river and dunked himself, hoping to wash the crawling insects from his person. At least now he knew what had happened to Wren's gown. He had dreamed of that tattered garment all night long, wondering, imagining, what had made those holes. Now, if he could just figure out how she had gotten loose, he would feel less anxious.

He shivered in the cool air as he made his way back to the campsite. He had no blanket to warm himself, and his flint was wet. He sat with his arms wrapped around his knees and cursed everything in sight. That didn't alter anything, but it made him feel better—until he started to think about how Caleb would react when he found Wren was gone. Malcolm had to find a way to wriggle out of taking Caleb to where Wren was supposed to be. He would just demand the ransom brazenly and give him directions; if the bastard didn't like it, that would be that. No ransom, no information. After all, one didn't divulge everything. Caleb was probably thinking the same thing—no Wren, no ransom. It would be a stalemate, and it would depend on how hungry Caleb was to see that bitch Wren. Malcolm would have to act convincingly; otherwise he would have to give up that scheme and start all over.

He settled himself as comfortably as he could and was soon asleep again, his dreams now invaded by a tall, dark-haired Dutchman who chased him from one end of the Saybrook settlement to the other, finally catching him and locking him in the locker box aboard the *Sea Siren*. He woke, drenched in his own sweat. There would be no more rest for him now. He rekindled the fire and sat shivering as he nibbled sparingly on the food he had brought with him from the ship.

Sometime during the morning hours his eye became glazed and his mouth curled down, making him look more grotesque than before. When he walked down to the water to wash himself, he stared at his reflection for a long time; for some reason the face that gazed back at him pleased him and at the same time frightened him.

His movements were slow, sure and precise as he readied the dinghy for his trip to Saybrook and Caleb. He stuffed the sack of provisions beneath the bench-like seat, placed the oar in its lock and then stood back to survey his campsite. The fire was nothing more than charred embers, with a few smoldering coals that hissed at him when he kicked out with his foot to scatter the ashes. He decided to leave Wren's gown as evidence that she had been here. Caleb would want proof, and the gown was as good as anything.

Malcolm sat down before the dying fire and stared morosely at the hole in the sole of his boot. Not only was there a hole in his boot, but there was also a hole in his stocking through which pink-gray skin glared up at him. A man shouldn't have holes in his boots, he thought. Caleb van der Rhys' boots flashed before him—soft black kid that cleaved to his legs and looked as though they had been made expressly for him. And what did *he* have? Boots and stockings with holes in them. All that would change as soon as possible. The first thing he would do with his money would be to find a bootmaker and order a dozen pairs just like Caleb's. And the second thing he would do would be to order seven pairs of stockings, one pair for each day of the week. If he had boots without holes and fresh stockings, no one would look at his face and see his disfigurement. He knew this was a flimsy rationalization, and he grimaced in despair. Why was he fooling himself? In his gut he realized that his life was over and van der Rhys had won. Even that bitch Wren had won by getting away from him. He was alone. All he had was a little food, the rags on his back and the dinghy. A man deserved to have more. A lone tear trickled down his cheek and he wiped at it angrily. His entire predicament was all Wren's fault. Women, he decided, were not even a necessary evil. Yet they made fools of men and caused wars, and a few besotted men had even lost empires because of them. A fierce, scorching hatred erupted in him and he spit vehemently. One way or another, they always won, always managed to come out on top and stand laughing at some man. Or was it just he? Women didn't laugh at Caleb van der Rhys; it was the other way around. The thought caused Malcolm such anguish that he rolled over on the ground and pounded his fists into the still-warm embers of the fire.

He had wasted enough precious time with his woolgathering. He had to begin his journey.

Chapter Twenty-two

When Caleb rowed away from the *Sea Siren* to meet Malcolm, his thoughts were only on Wren. God, he had thought he would never see her again or feel her in his arms. And now, within hours, he would have his dearest wish come true. There would be no more sleepless nights, no more recriminations. He would do, say, whatever she wanted as long as she loved him. He would lay down his life for her, if that was what she wanted. The thought stunned him and he grinned to himself. If that would make her happy, he would do it unflinchingly. God, how he had envied Regan with his love for Sirena! And now he had the same thing, the same wonderful thing that had made Regan a whole man. He would hold her in his arms and whisper all the right words in her ear. He would say them over and over until she begged him to stop. God, how he loved her! And how he hated Malcolm Weatherly! It had taken every ounce of his self-restraint not to have killed Malcolm on the spot when he told him about Wren. But Caleb hadn't, because if he had given in to his vicious impulses, he would never find Wren. If he had killed Malcolm, he would not be feeling what he was feeling now, this deep love for another person, the desire to give his life to Wren's happiness. After he had found her and held her in his arms, he would kill Weatherly and toss him to the sharks for fodder. He had never killed a man out of pure hate, but there was always a first time for everything.

Idly, his booted feet scuffing the dusty patch of ground he was now standing on, he watched Bascom Stoneham lead his flock to the outer perimeters of the settlement. His eyes narrowed slightly as he saw Bascom cup the elbow of a young girl in a possessive manner. His eyes narrowed again as he spotted a young man weaving his way through the ranks of the Puritans with a look of determination and purpose on his face, and not to attend a prayer meeting. Even from this distance Caleb knew the young man was interested only in the stiff-backed girl being escorted by the preacher. He recognized impending trouble when he saw it. But the Puritans were no longer his concern. His only concern now was for Wren. He turned his back on the parade of Puritans and watched both the shoreline and the woods for Malcolm to make his presence known. He was a patient man, and he would wait forever if in the end he could hold Wren in his arms. That terrible mist is covering my eyes again, he groaned inwardly. One of these days— He didn't finish the thought, because when his vision cleared, Malcolm was standing about ten feet away from him.

Caleb hadn't really expected Wren to be with him, but he had secretly hoped that maybe Malcolm would decide to turn her over at the point of exchange. He should have known better. The weasel wasn't going to give an inch, and from the looks of the stout club in his hand, Weatherly wasn't taking any chances on Caleb's emotions. Caleb wanted to kill him, to strangle him with his bare hands and hear him beg for the mercy that he would deny. At last he forced the words from between clenched teeth. "Where's Wren?"

Malcolm laughed, a shrill sound that sent the hackles on Caleb's neck to twanging. "First the ransom and the jewels. Now!" Malcolm demanded arrogantly as he waved the club in the air. "And no tricks, van der Rhys, or you'll never see her alive. Toss it here for me to see."

There was nothing for Caleb to do but toss to Malcolm the oilskin pouch he had hidden inside his shirt before leaving the ship. Malcolm laughed again as he stuffed the pouch inside his own shirt, satisfied that Caleb had kept his end of the bargain.

"All right, you bastard, you got what you wanted. Now, where's Wren? I'm warning you—if she's been harmed, I'll kill you." Caleb said this so softly, Malcolm had to strain to hear him.

"She's upriver. Ride the shoreline, and when you come to the bend with the cove and the sandbar, head to your right. That's where I made camp. Wren is tied to a tree, just waiting for you."

Caleb's heart turned over at the words. "Oh, no, we go together, and if you're lying, I'll kill you on the spot."

"I'd like to oblige you, van der Rhys, but I have other fish to fry. And this club I'm holding makes for the odds on my side. If you want your sister, you'll have to get her yourself, without any help from me. And if I were you, I'd get a move on, for the camp is infested with red ants that can eat a person alive." He added nonchalantly, "I wouldn't waste any time if I were you."

Dark sparks of fury shot from Caleb's eyes and Malcolm backed off, the club held out in front of him.

"It'll take more than that measly weapon to get

me," Caleb gritted as he reached out to grab it from Malcolm's shaking hand. They fought like animals, with Caleb having the advantage over the wiry Malcolm. Weatherly gouged and scratched, fighting like a woman, while Caleb struck out with his fist, letting it find its mark in Malcolm's good eye. He was momentarily taken off guard when Malcolm screamed shrilly in his ear. That moment was all Weatherly needed to race off into the woods and disappear from Caleb's sight.

Caleb leapt on his horse and dug his heels into the animal's flanks, enraged because he had to rely on Malcolm's word that Wren was alive and safe. But he had to believe that!

As Caleb's horse pounded the sandy riverbank, Malcolm raced wildly through the woods, going in circles in his blind panic. His vision was poor, and pain creased his head in spasms as he continued his erratic flight. Soon, he gasped to himself, I should be out of the woods and near the dinghy.

Exhausted, he fell to the ground and cried, the sounds like those of a whimpering child. He had to find a safe place where he could hide from Caleb. Caleb would kill him as soon as he found Wren gone. Pitiful mewing noises came from Malcolm's mouth as he wiped at his eye that was rapidly closing, almost obscuring what little vision he had left. Where was there a safe place in this Godforsaken land? He couldn't live in the woods like a wild animal. If he did that, he would never have his fine house and his servants. Wherever he went, Caleb would find him. He knew it, accepted it. Now he had to go on, to look for a place that would be free from Caleb's searching eyes. If Caleb did manage to find Wren and she was dead, the Dutchman would devote the rest of his life to hunting down Malcolm and then would kill him in slow, easy stages.

Malcolm curled himself into the fetal position and

rocked back and forth, his soft moans of anguish shattering the quiet of the forest. He didn't want to die; God, he didn't want to die. Safety, that was all he needed, and he needed it only until Caleb set sail. He sat upright, his spine straight, as a thought occurred to him. Once before he had been safely hidden from Caleb's eyes. True, Farrington had helped him then, but he could make his way back to the *Sea Siren* and hide in the locker box right under Caleb's unsuspecting nose. Van der Rhys would never think to look there. Malcolm would row out to the ship under cover of darkness and creep aboard. He sighed. This was the answer to all his problems, he was certain. Survival was all that mattered. His survival.

Caleb crouched low on the stallion's broad back, making it easier for the animal to race across the soggy terrain. He rode for what seemed like hours, every muscle, every nerve in his body strained to the breaking point. From time to time he shouted Wren's name to let her know he was coming. Each time his cry was more muffled and carried away on the brisk wind. Perspiration dripped down his back and drenched the horse.

His eye peeled for the sandbar, Caleb almost missed it with the wind stinging his face. He slid from the galloping steed and rolled over several times. Then he was on his feet, shouting Wren's name as he raced into the woods. In his heart he knew she wouldn't be there; it was his mind that refused to accept the thought. His broad shoulders heaved and then slumped as he bent down to pick up a black rag. He blinked at the lacy, cobwebby holes and at the dried blood that was caked to them. He ground his teeth together in a helpless fit of rage as he poked a finger through one of the holes. This couldn't be happening to him. No, it was impossible. To have come this far and then have the joy snatched away from him. It was like

344

drowning and coming up for air one last time, only to get pulled back down by the undertow.

The thought that he refused entry into his mind surfaced, and he looked at it squarely. What if this were a devious trick and Wren weren't alive after all? What if she had really gone over the rail, as Sara had said she had? What if she had been dead all along, and this was just some rotten, macabre joke of Malcolm's seedy little mind? "Oh, God," Caleb moaned. She couldn't be dead. His mind and heart could not accept that now. She was here, somewhere. There was blood on the gown, Wren's blood. He had to believe it was her blood and that somewhere, some place, she was free of Malcolm and alive. He had to find her. He had to clear his mind of all the cobwebs so he could think logically.

Caleb sat down, his long legs crossed in front of him. He forced his lean body to relax and let his mind take over. He would go with his original idea that Wren had been here tied to a tree as Malcolm had said. She had either escaped or been freed by someone. That person hadn't been Malcolm; therefore, it had to be someone who inhabited this section of the country. Only the Indians lived here. Caleb had ridden over two hours, at a hard and fast pace, to arrive at the sandbar. Another hour and a half and he would be at the mouth of the Mystic River and Sassacus's fort. Other Indian tribes inhabited this area, not just the Pequots. Any tribe could have found her and taken her for reasons of its own. Gory tales of Indians' vengeance made him shudder when he thought about them, and he forced them from his mind, refusing to believe Wren was anything but alive and well. A negative attitude would get him nowhere.

She could be anywhere, and if he didn't have a plan of action, he would go in circles for days or even months. The forest was all-encompassing, dark and forbidden to those who didn't belong. The thought frightened him. He would appeal to Sassacus, who knew the forest intimately. Sassacus would help him. Caleb would promise whatever was necessary to secure the chief's help and would work the rest of his life to repay his debt to him. He had no other choice, and he knew in his gut that the red man would help him.

The rough-hewn stockade gates of the Mystic fort opened and Caleb rode into the compound. He reined in his horse, visible to all, and waited. He knew that no message would be sent to the chief, informing him of his arrival. Sassacus had probably been aware an hour ago that Caleb was heading in this direction. When he was ready, and when he thought Caleb had waited long enough, the chief would come out and welcome him.

Caleb waited patiently, his eyes circling the huts and coming to rest on a small group of chattering women. An eerie feeling crawled up his spine, and his forehead became dotted with perspiration. He was used to seeing the Indians behave in a solemn-faced manner, their great dark eyes staring unwaveringly before them. Something must have happened for the women to be chattering the way they were. And they weren't paying any attention to him, which was equally strange. He shrugged, but the eerie feeling remained.

Sassacus pushed aside the canvas flap covering the doorway of his lodge and came out to greet his guest. His eye followed Caleb's to the babbling women, and he shrugged as if to say, "Women!"

"A small matter, probably something to do with one of the children. It's of no importance—a little harsh to the ear, but of no concern. I am pleased to see you again so soon, Captain."

"And I am pleased to see you, Sassacus," Caleb said, clasping the Indian's wrist in both his hands. "We must talk and then I must go back downriver.

But first I need your help." Once inside the chief's quarters, he explained about Wren and how he had found her gone from the woods.

Sassacus nodded. "We will help you. But only when it becomes light at dawn. One Indian tracking another Indian in the dark is a foolish waste of time. Each of us learned from our fathers how to hide tracks. The daylight hours will give us a small advantage. My men will set out at first light. I see this woman means much to you—here." He placed his hand over his heart.

"She is my heart," Caleb said simply, and smiled.

Sassacus returned the smile. "I understand. Now, tell me, what is the other thing that brings you here?"

"What have your chiefs decided? When will you start the war? You notice I said *when*, not if. I will go once more to the authorities and plead with them. More than that I cannot do. I sail back to England and Holland shortly."

Sassacus motioned for Caleb to follow him outside. He pointed toward the rising moon. "You understand, Caleb?"

Caleb felt a great sadness envelop him as he stared at the orange ball in the sky. "I understand. Before another full moon the war will have begun."

Sassacus nodded and his shoulders slumped. "By that time, my friend, you will be halfway to your homeland. We will not see each other again in this life. In the next one, perhaps we will stand side by side and hunt and fish like the brothers we are. I must do what is right for my people, just as you must do what is right for yours. We both understand this. You are my friend and I am yours. Nothing—war, man, Indian or white—can change that."

There were no words to say, and if there were, Caleb could not have uttered them for the knot that was choking him. Instead, he placed his arm around the Indian's shoulder and went back with him into the lodge.

Sassacus smiled. "We will eat and drink, and you will tell me of this woman who has captured your heart and I will lie to you and tell you all the women in the village want me as their man." At the concerned look on Caleb's face, Sassacus added, "You must not pity me. At some distant time, if you want, grieve for me and my people. If just one white man grieves for one red man, then we have made progress. It will be up to the others who follow me to continue where we have left off. Is that not so, Caleb van der Rhys?"

"That is so, Sassacus."

Wren woke, disoriented in the dimness of the hut. She didn't move, but her eyes took in the squaws and their watchful attitude. A feeling of incredible loss swept over her. What had she lost? Certainly not Malcolm. Tears sprang to her eyes as she remembered the name falling from her lips when she had surrendered to sleep. Caleb. Had something happened to Caleb? Why did she feel this way? She had to get up, move, do something.

Two of the Indian women, sensing her intention, gently pushed her back onto the blanket with a motion for her to lie still. Wren obeyed. She slept again, her arms folded across her chest. How empty they felt. Arms were meant to hold someone. "Caleb," she cried aloud heartbrokenly.

The women looked at one another and again repeated the strange name—Ca-leb. Soon Chief Sassacus would make his rounds of the fort, and then they would tell him of the strange name and how they came to have the white woman in their hut.

Sassacus walked around the compound as it began to come alive for the start of a new day. How he loved these quiet, gentle people who were entrusted to his care. He prayed that he would always have the wisdom to do the right thing where they were concerned. And if he couldn't do the right thing, he prayed that his people would forgive him.

As he neared the squaws' lodge, he waited expectantly for the women to bid him entrance. There was something they wanted him to see. A treat of some sort. His eyes widened when he saw a white woman lying on a blanket and gazing up at him with bright amber eyes. He had to clap his hands to quiet the women as they all babbled at once, pointing to Wren and then to the children and always ending with the word "Ca-leb."

Wren moistened dry lips and looked up at the tall chief. "I think they are trying to tell you that I have been calling that name in my sleep. I am Wren van der Rhys. I sailed with Captain van der Rhys from England and was kidnaped by someone who hoped for a ransom." A note of hysteria crept into her voice as she gazed at the Indian. "Where am I? What is this place?"

Sassacus dropped to his knees, stunned. "You are a van der Rhys woman?" he asked incredulously. "Caleb and I are old friends. I am Sassacus, the chief of my people. He was here last night and we talked for many hours. I did not know of your presence here." He shrugged. "My people do not always see fit to tell me all things immediately. I cannot chastise them, for I see that they have taken excellent care of you."

Wren smiled. "Yes, your people must have taken very good care of me, for I feel much better. I am glad you are Caleb's friend. Tell me, do you know where he is?"

Sassacus smiled. "I see much love in your eyes for him. I will have my men take you to him soon. You will be returned to your people. We wish you no harm, you must believe that."

"I do believe that, and I wish to thank you and especially the children who brought me here. Is there something I can do, some way I can repay you for your help?"

"Seeing you back with your people will be payment enough. Caleb is my friend, and you will be my friend. Now, you must allow the women to remove these compresses and clean you up. They will bring food and you will eat. When you have rested and are able to travel, you will be on your way to your people." He smiled again, a dazzling smile of happiness because he would be able to do something for his friend Caleb.

Chapter Twenty-three

Caleb rode into Saybrook and handed over the reins of the stallion to the young boy, Sammy. He was tired and discouraged. There was a deep ache within him, an emptiness that only Wren could fill. To have come so close to finding her and to lose her again! Damn that Weatherly! The first order of the day would be to find him and wring the truth out of him.

He looked around the bustling settlement and was impressed by the amount of activity at this early hour. Sounds of furious hammering pounded in his ears. Bascom's congregation was hard at work building its new homes with the aid of the present settlers. Before long, there would be a hundred new houses. Progress had already been accomplished on the construction of the new church. The skeleton was up and men were busy nailing planks to the timbers.

Caleb slouched against a stout oak tree and watched the proceedings as the men worked in companionable silence. Companionable, that is, until Bascom arrived on the scene, prayer book in hand. He shouted to be heard over the noise of the hammers and waited for the men to acknowledge him. The workers held their tools loosely in their hands, and at the exchange of words that passed between Bascom and them, Caleb almost guffawed aloud.

"It's time for a prayer meeting. Lay down your hammers and join me in asking the Lord for forgiveness for our sins and to help us see the light of His ways. My flock waits over there," Bascom said, pointing a bony hand.

"We can't rightly be attending your meeting," a red-faced, burly man protested. "We have a goal set for us each day, and until it's met, we have to keep on with the building. We could do with a few more hands. How about yourself, Preacher?" he sneered.

"Prayer and forgiveness are more important than work, even if that work is building a house of the Lord," Bascom declared virtuously.

"You won't be thinking like that if those redskins come riding in here, Preacher," the man shouted. "We work from sunup till the moon is directly overhead. We do our praying on Sundays." He motioned the workers to resume their tasks and lifted his own hammer to bang in a nail.

"One can never set aside just one day for the Lord. Every day is for the Lord. That's something I'll have to teach you, and teach you now. There must be no dissension among us now that I've arrived." Bascom drew himself up to his full height. "I am the Lord's messenger."

One of the settlers grinned at another and muttered, "Then deliver your message some place else." He banged a nail with undue emphasis to make his point.

Rather than lose face by continuing an already lost argument, Bascom turned angrily away from the area.

"The Lord wasn't using all His wits when He sent this preacher to us," the burly man said to a worker near him. They laughed heartily, the sound reaching Bascom's ears as he strode off. He knew they were laughing at him and mocking him. His thin lips tightened. He'd call down the wrath of God on the lot of them for ridiculing him! Things hadn't gone right ever since Lydia had walked out on him. Each day he could see a look of speculation on the faces of his flock. If a man couldn't control his own wife, how could he minister to and aid his own people? And dotty Sara certainly wasn't helping his image. Today he planned to ostracize her in front of his congregation. Unmarried women who found themselves with child had to be punished for their sins. He would see that she was punished severely.

The sun was already low in the west when Wren and her small entourage of Pequot braves followed the trail south through the dense Connecticut woods to the Old Saybrook settlement. The late June weather held a warm promise for the summer about to emerge upon the land. Songbirds were singing their last song before roosting at dusk, and a gentle breeze wafted up from the Sound. Wren's heart sang with happiness at the thought of being reunited with her people, and she was grateful for the superb care the Pequot women had given her. She still bore nasty welts from the rope Malcolm had used to bind her, but the minuscule ruddy insect bites had all but disappeared

352

because of the cooling mudpacks the Indians had administered.

Because of the hostilities between the colonists and the Indians, the braves indicated to Wren that it was time to leave her, here by a small stream that fed into the river. They would go on alone to find either Captain van der Rhys or his first mate, Peter, and alert them to her whereabouts. One brave, noting the concern on her face, motioned to the sky and pointed at the sun, dipping his arm slightly. She understood that this undertaking would be accomplished before dark.

Alone in the lengthening shadows, Wren rested alongside the stream, delighting in the reflection of the sun's reds and golds upon the water. The trek along the trail had been difficult, and she had sensed the Indians' eagerness to complete their task and immediately return to their camp. The woods offered no safety these days to a small band of red men who might encounter a hunting party of white men. Before Wren had left Sassacus's fort, one of the squaws had offered her a beautifully stitched buckskin dress, complete with intricate beadwork and fringes along the hemline. Her long dark hair had been bound with rawhide thongs atop her head to bare her neck to any cool breeze. But the day had been hot and the trail dusty, and Wren looked longingly at the cool water rushing past her.

Impulsively, she stood up and stripped off her dress and moccasins, stepped forward and tested the water with her toe. Wishing for a bar of perfumed soap, she waded into the stream and found that at its deepest level it was waist-high. As she submerged herself, she was uncertain if she trembled from the cool water or from the prospect of seeing Caleb again. Always Caleb. He had been uppermost in her mind throughout the trek back to Saybrook. She had no idea what his reaction to her might be. The last she had known about him before being trapped in the locker box with Malcolm was that Sara had claimed he was the father of her child. Knowing what an honorable man Caleb was, Wren was certain he had married Sara by now.

A sob caught in Wren's throat, but she was determined not to cry. She was a little girl no longer. She was a woman. Perhaps if she had behaved like a woman, had shown Caleb how much she loved him, instead of letting her fears override her passions . . . She willed her mind to come to a halt, to accept things the way they were, not the way she wished they could be. Yet she couldn't discipline her memories. Caleb's face swam before her time and time again . . . his night-dark eyes sweeping over her, warming her skin with an unseen flame, letting her know she was beautiful and desirable . . . his mouth taking possession of her, his strong, white teeth nibbling at her lower lip in tender, teasing touches . . . his arms, hard and powerful, capable of crushing her and yet so tender, so gentle and persuasive. She remembered the feel of his thick thatch of hair beneath her fingers, the way his lean, steel-hard thighs had pressed against her legs, making her weak-kneed and helpless. She heard the sound of his voice, confident and commanding when giving orders to his crew, soft and murmuring when he whispered love words into her ears. The crinkles of humor at the corners of his eyes, the almost invisible little scar near his upper lip . . . everything . . . everything . . . was Caleb.

Wren lifted her eyes and saw him standing there. At first she thought he was a figment of her imagination, so great was her desire to see him. He stood tall, feet planted apart, arms folded akimbo across his chest. He was still, as still as the giant oak behind him; only his eyes were alive . . . alive with the joy of seeing her. Slowly he stretched out an arm, extending it toward her, reaching out for her. All doubts left her; all answers were there to be seen in his eyes.

As though in a dream, she floated toward him. Oblivious of her nakedness, untouched by the breeze that chilled her wet skin and ruffled her hair, she emerged from the stream, arms extended, her heart in her eyes.

She was in his arms, holding him, being held, knowing her world had come right again, finding her answers in his eyes, on his lips.

Caleb was speechless with a happiness so deep and wondrous, it filled his soul and throbbed through his veins. She was real, she was here, in his arms, and he would never let her go.

Two long tresses trailed down from her tumbled hair, framing her lovely face. Her skin shone golden in the last rays of the sun, making her body appear as though it had been carved from copper. He held her close to him, pressing his hands possessively against her hips.

Lightheaded, delirious with joy, her legs trembling beneath her, she clung to him for support and felt herself being lowered to the shady bank, knowing he was beside her, wrapping her in his arms, cherishing the feel of her and the love he offered.

She offered her lips and possessed his in return. She offered her body and enslaved his passions. A hundred times his lips touched hers, seeking, finding, caressing. A thousand times his hands stroked her; still he could not satisfy his desire for her. She intoxicated him with her beauty: the elegant length of her legs, the clear curve of her thighs, the sleekness of her haunches, the provocative appeal of her breasts. It was toward these visual signs of her beauty that he directed the ardor of his caresses and kisses.

Wren thrilled beneath his touch and turned herself voluptuously in his arms, encouraging him to voyage again with his lips along her supple thighs, allowing him access to the threshold of her sensuality, maddening him with her responses, inspiring his caresses.

With closed eyes and his name upon her lips, he led her into the kingdom of love.

The night air was warm and soft. When Wren awakened, her first thought was of Caleb. For an instant she thought she had only dreamed he had come to her, loved her. She realized she was alone, her naked body covered by his shirt. Thinking they had been separated again, she gave a frightened start and sat up. The first stars of evening twinkled in the darkening sky.

A splash from the stream attracted her attention; a plume of white shot up as Caleb threw the water over his body. Wren was mesmerized by the sight of him. The water swirled about his hips, revealing to her view the hardness of his chest, his well-muscled arms, the strong column of his neck, the proud set of his head. Droplets glistened off his skin like jewels, his panther-dark hair tumbling over his brow.

She rose, casting aside his shirt, and waded into the stream, oblivious of the chill, knowing only that she had to be near him, to feel his arms encircle her once again.

Around them there was no movement save for the flow of the stream and the scud of distant clouds. A night bird issued a song that strummed through their veins and pounded at their pulses, reawakening their desires. She stood before him, an arm's reach away, and faced him proudly, shoulders back, head erect. "You understand. I have no regrets." Her voice was soft, a whisper in the night. "Not a single action do I regret. I surrendered myself to your embraces, responded to your caresses. I know no regret." Her eyes burned with unspoken questions.

"I sensed in you a hesitation, a withdrawal. No matter how slight, it was there." His voice was deep and husky with emotion. His mind whirled with arguments and approved of the consideration he had

356

given to her fears; his imagination summoned up visions of Wren's total surrender to him, to his love for her.

She lowered her eyes. "You know me well. You know me through and through. There's not an inch of my body whose response to your touch you do not know. But what do I know of you?" Her words were less than a whisper.

He reached for her hand, drawing her closer, guiding her hand to him and laying it upon his chest. She placed her head on his shoulder with a movement already familiar and one that he loved. Her hand, lightly touching his chest, trembled slightly on coming in contact with his skin. Then, in a slow and delicate progression, her fingers slid along his body, awakening in him a tidal wave of desire that rippled down to his aching loins.

He caught her up in his arms and carried her to the mossy bank, laying her gently upon their discarded clothing and coming to rest beside her. The moon was in his eyes, the stars in hers. With tender advances she learned the mysteries of his body and became the mistress of his soul.

Wren, his enchantress, summoned his passions and invoked his love. Each sensual caress that she learned from him, she turned about and practiced upon him, captivating him, enslaving him. A cry broke from his lips, a sound of passion and joy, and the cry became her name. *Wren.*

At daybreak Caleb waited impatiently for Sammy to saddle his horse. His thoughts were on the coming day, and when he spoke to Wren, Lydia and Peter, his tone was curt, almost abrasive. "Stay within the confines of the settlement. There's no telling when I'll come back. See about setting in ship's stores. If and when the situation between the Pequots and the colonists comes to a head, I want us to be well out to sea." His dark glance rested on Wren's upturned face, his meaning clear. He wanted no harm to come to her. Now that he had found her again, he wanted to keep her near him, always.

As Lydia and Wren walked off arm in arm, Caleb motioned Peter aside. "Weatherly is still lurking about. I know it as well as I know my name. He can't live in the woods forever without coming into Saybrook at some point. That can only mean trouble for all of us, especially for Wren. Keep a sharp eye out. I'm placing both women in your hands. Don't fail me, Peter."

"Aye, Captain. And we'll see about setting in ship's stores as well as rounding up the crew. If you see any of the louts hanging about New Amsterdam while you're there, be sure to tell them to high-tail it back to the ship before their scalps are on a redskin's belt."

Caleb took a last look in the direction that Wren and Lydia had taken. He ached to see her face again and hold her in his arms. Determinedly, he mounted, turned his steed in the direction of New Amsterdam and headed out of the settlement. What he hoped to accomplish by confronting Kiefft one last time was based more on elusive dream than on tangible reality. Sassacus had meant every word he had said, and war was inevitable. Were the colonists prepared? Would they be a match for the Indians with their knowledge of the woods and their deadly bows and arrows and stealthy attacks in the middle of the night? He shuddered to think of what an Indian rampage could do to the young town of Saybrook. For that reason alone, he wanted to take Wren and his crew as far away as possible. He had lost Farrington and had come so close to losing Wren that he couldn't chance it again.

While Caleb continued his journey, Wren and Lydia spoke with the women in the settlement and listened intently as one of them gave directions to a thriving berry field. Lydia's eyes sparkled as she made plans to bake pies for that evening's dinner and make preserves for the ship's galley.

"If we pick the berries, will you give us flour?" Wren asked the smiling woman. An agreement was made, and Wren herded Lydia in front of her.

As they walked down a dusty road, Lydia talked all the while about pie baking and said the secret lay in lemon and butter. She fretted that here there would be no lemon for her pies, and was busily improvising a replacement when Wren placed a hand on her arm and forced her to stop in the middle of the road. "Look," she whispered.

Lydia drew in her breath at the sight of her husband leading Sara into the center of a circle of people. Tears stung Wren's eyes on seeing Sara's unkempt look, her hair in wild disarray, her gown torn and tattered. Sara raised an arm to cover her face, either in shame or from fear.

"What's he going to do?" Wren hissed, fear for Sara alive in her face.

"Oh, no," Lydia moaned. "He's going to disown her as a sister, and then he'll make his parents come forward and do the same thing. He'll announce to all the people what she's done and how God is punishing her. Oh, Wren, we can't let him do that to Sara. She deserves better. I know," she said quickly, seeing the tight look on Wren's face, "what Sara did to you, but that's over and done with, and because of that you have Caleb. Always remember that because of Sara you have Caleb. And she no longer has the full mind she once had. You have only to look in her eyes and see the madness that rests there. My pity is for the child she carries."

"What will happen to her?" Wren asked as she glanced around to see if even one person would intervene in Sara's behalf. No one stepped forward.

"What would you do if a messenger of the Lord stood before you and said he had the answer to Sara's salvation? It's simple, really: Bascom will banish her. He'll take her by the hand and lead her from the circle, and from that moment on, she will belong to no one. She will have to forage for food like a wild animal, and she'll learn to live like one. According to Bascom, that is God's punishment. Sara will go completely mad and eventually die. He did this once before to a poor old soul who had told him she had no more coins to give the Lord. Bascom said she was giving her money to the devil and visiting a local tavern. She eventually threw herself into the river. Bascom prayed for her soul."

"My God!" Wren exploded. She looked at Lydia and grinned. "Do we wait for him to start his rantings and ravings, or do we snatch her out of that damnable circle here and now?"

"I'll agree to anything if it gets us out of Bascom's sight. Now!" Lydia declared firmly, her head high.

"Will he try to stop us? Perhaps we should arm ourselves with some sort of weapon. Here," Wren said, picking up two stout sticks. "If he makes one false move, club him."

"Of course he'll try to stop us. This is a big moment for Bascom. It isn't every day that a messenger of the Lord gets to ostracize his very own sister!" Lydia snatched one of the sticks from Wren, and before Wren could gather her wits, Lydia had marched ahead, waving the makeshift weapon in front of her. Wren had to run to catch up to her. Together they elbowed their way through the tight circle of praying men and women.

Bascom read their intent the moment he spotted the sticks clutched in their hands. "You're not welcome here," he said harshly, advancing to the center of the circle to stand next to Sara whose manner was docile, as though she were a child waiting to be punished for some trifling, mischievous act.

"As if I care what you think, Bascom Stoneham!"

Wren scoffed disdainfully, raising the stick over her head. "We're taking Sara with us. We'll take care of her!"

"Oh, no, you won't! Sinners, both of you! Do you think I would trust my sister to two sinners?" he screamed in outrage as Lydia raised her stick, too.

"The only sinner around here is you for what you're planning to do to your own flesh and blood. If you were truly a messenger of the Lord, you would forgive her, not turn her out to live like an animal in the forest. You're the sinner, Bascom!" Wren shouted to be heard over the mutterings of his flock. "Sara goes with us!"

"Sara stays!"

Wren and Lydia lashed out at the same moment, one cracking Bascom on the head, the other jabbing him in his midsection. He fell on the ground, dazed. Wren reached out to grasp Sara, as did Lydia, before the confused Puritans could take action.

"My God," Lydia wailed, "she won't move!"

"Then drag her, but get her out of here!" Wren groaned as she bent to pick up her stick to ward off any possible attack from Bascom's followers.

Bascom's followers, however, merely stood there, stunned, their mouths agape. Wren grabbed Sara by the arm, and she and Lydia managed to drag the girl from the circle of speechless onlookers.

"Damnation, Sara, if you don't pick up your feet, I'm going to leave you here!" Wren stopped a moment and tilted Sara's head upward. There was no sign of awareness in her eyes. "You were right, Lydia. She doesn't even know what's happening. Hurry, before that ranting, raving bastard decides to come after us. I can barely understand how you ever married that man and lived with him and still were able to keep all the brains God gave you," she scolded as they dragged a limp Sara down the dusty road and out of sight.

"We have to rest, Wren. Sara's a dead weight. He won't come after us. I'm sure. And if I'm not mistaken, this is something else that will give Bascom's flock pause about the merits of its spiritual leader."

Panting and struggling, they managed to prop Sara against a gnarled old oak tree. The moment they released their hold on her, she slid to the ground. Wren grimaced but made no move to lift her. "I'm trying to be charitable. Lydia, I really am, but I don't have the strength to get her back on her feet. What in the name of God are we going to do with her? Don't even suggest taking her back to Caleb's ship. He would kill both of us and ask questions later. He's had all he's going to take from Bascom and his relatives."

"Sit down, we have to think," Lydia mumbled. After several minutes of silence, she said, "Maybe the Indians will take her."

"If that's the best idea you can come up with, you better stop thinking," Wren grumbled.

"What *are* we going to do with her? If we can't take her back to the ship, then there's nothing we can do. This isn't England, Wren. There is no housing here unless you build it yourself. Somehow, I can't see either of us taking on *that* task. And Sara needs care and constant looking after. For now, we can both do that or take turns, but what will happen when it's time to sail?"

"Maybe your idea of the Indians wasn't so bad after all. A hut is a lot easier to build than a house. All we really need is some sort of shelter that will protect her from the elements. Surely there must be some kind soul who would take pity on her and let her live within the confines of this settlement," Wren said hopefully.

"Don't count on it. These people are a strange lot. They don't understand that Sara is mind-sick. They fear things like this and say it's devil's work. Whatever we do, we have to do it ourselves. I know in my heart it won't be long before Bascom disgraces himself." Lydia paused. "I know his appetites for young girls. Saybrook is too small to contain that kind of secret. As soon as he's out on his ear, I *know* Sara's parents will come to her rescue. If only we could find someone to care for her until then. Do you recall seeing that old Indian woman tending a fire when we started out earlier?"

Wren nodded. "She looked as if she was mixing something in a pot. Come to think of it, what's an Indian doing here if all these people are afraid of them? A deal!" she cried excitedly. "Maybe we could lure her away to care for Sara. We could give her all those gems that we won from Farrington. Indians love trinkets."

"But Caleb was going to return them anonymously to the King," Lydia fretted.

"The King doesn't need them. His neck is fat enough already," Wren sniffed. "Besides, I won those gems fair and square in a game of cards. Caleb has no right to make decisions about my property."

"But you gave them to me and I gave them to Caleb for safekeeping," Lydia said dejectedly.

"Then we'll just have to steal them back. Where did he put them?"

"In a strongbox in his cabin," Lydia answered.

"You stay here with Sara, and I'll go back to the ship and get the stones. If I find Peter along the way, I'll send him to you. Don't let Sara out of your sight. See if you can't get her down to the river and give her a good dunking; she smells."

"Does this mean we aren't going berry picking and won't have any pies for dessert?"

"Perhaps the children will pick them for us if we give them a stone or two. All children like pretties. Or I could give them one of the playing cards with the pictures on them." She jumped to her feet and scrambled off.

"Oh, God," Lydia groaned as she watched Wren disappear around the bend. She shrugged. Somehow or other, she knew they wouldn't have to pick the berries or bake the pies. Somewhere in the settlement there was a person who was just waiting for Wren to make him a target for her conniving ways. Lydia could taste the pie already, even though there wouldn't be any lemon juice to add the finishing touches.

On her walk through the small settlement Wren stopped from time to time, carrying on low-voiced conversations and waving her arms for emphasis. Lydia would have her pies.

Back on board the ship, she hurried to Caleb's quarters and searched out his strongbox. With a steady hand she dexterously worked a hairpin into the lock, and soon the pouch of gems was in her hand. Better hers and the old Indian woman's than the King of England's. He had enough jewels and would never miss these.

An hour later she was dragging an unwilling Indian woman by the arm to where Sara sat propped up. It looked as though Sara hadn't moved since Wren had left. Lydia verified this wearily.

"Now comes the hard part," Wren said. "We have to communicate to this woman that we need a shelter and want her to take care of Sara. How are we going to explain that Sara is . . . is . . . isn't right in the head?"

"She already knows," Lydia grimaced as the Indian squatted down and peered at Sara with bright shoe-button eyes. The woman tapped her head and then shook it vigorously. Lydia grimaced again. "I think that means she's not interested."

"I think you're right, Lydia. But we have to convince her that the most important thing in the world to her is taking care of Sara. Maybe if we tell her about the baby, she'll feel differently."

"She'll feel differently, all right," Lydia said sourly. "Try. You don't have anything to lose."

"Damnation, Lydia, I don't know how to converse with an Indian!"

"I trust you. You'll think of something; you usually do."

"Madame," Wren said imperiously, "we need your help." She gestured with her hands to indicate they wanted a hut. She pointed to the woman and then to Sara to show she wanted her to care for the not-too-bright girl.

The old woman shook her head and uttered one word. "Loco."

"A temporary state of affairs," Wren continued. Then she made a cradle with her arms and rocked back and forth, pointing to Sara.

The Indian woman still shook her head and held up two fingers. "Loco," she said.

"There's nothing to do but show her the gems and see what she does," Wren grumbled. She withdrew two emeralds and a shimmering ruby and held them out in the palm of her hand The old woman's eyes lit up and she cocked her head from side to side. First she looked at the stones and then at Sara, as if she were weighing the worth of both.

Lydia and Wren held their breath, waiting to see what she would decide. The gems won out and she reached for them. This time it was Wren who shook her head negatively and again made motions for a place of shelter. After much gesticulating the old woman scurried off and returned sometime later with several long branches and some sheets of bark. Deftly, she set about erecting them into a makeshift shelter. When she finished, she held out her hand for the gems. Again Wren shook her head and pointed to Sara. With no wasted motion the old woman had Sara up off the ground and in her arms. She dragged her under the shelter and both girls clenched their teeth and winced at the thump they heard. This time when she held out her hands Wren placed the gems in her dark palm.

Dramatically, Wren dusted her hands and laughed. "We did almost a day's work. Convincing that woman to take care of Sara was more work than cheating Farrington for the jewels. If anyone deserves berry pie for dessert, it's us."

"There seems to be some commotion going on," Lydia said as they neared the center of the settlement. "All the people have stopped what they were doing. Look—even Bascom is paying attention to the man who's speaking. It must be serious if Bascom would interrupt his prayer meeting!"

"Then let's see what it's all about," Wren said, pulling Lydia by the arm.

"Do you always have to be in the thick of things? Peter is there; he can tell us what's happening. Why don't we just wait here and let him come to us?"

"That won't do. I like to hear things firsthand. Walk faster, Lydia, before we miss something." Wren quickened her step.

"Whoever the man is who's doing the talking, he certainly is dressed for society and not this wilderness. Wren, he must be someone important." Her own curiosity aroused, Lydia matched her steps to Wren's long-legged stride.

The two women made their way to where Peter was standing and waited for the man to continue speaking. They were too late; he was turning and walking away, his face hateful and mean. Peter looked at the women, and his face, too, wore a strange expression.

"What's going on?" Wren demanded. "Who was that man, Peter? Why is he dressed in those elaborate clothes?"

Peter shrugged. "He said he was Willem Kiefft, the governor. He means trouble for Caleb and for us, too. He's calling us Indian sympathizers and traitors to our own kind. Do you see the looks we're getting? Walk with me, quickly now, and don't waste time. We're going back to the ship."

The women needed no second urging. They, too, heard the mutterings and saw the unrest that seemed to be gripping the people. "Why wasn't Caleb here?" Wren fretted as she forced her legs to keep up with Peter's loping walk.

"Does this mean we're not going to get the berry pies? I knew I should have picked the damn things myself and made them," Lydia grumbled.

"For shame, Lydia. Blasphemy coming out of your sweet mouth," Wren chided.

"I don't feel particularly sweet right now," Lydia said, glancing over her shoulder as they sped to the shoreline.

"Peter, tell us what happened. What was he saying? Why are those people looking at us that way?"

"Politics! Kiefft isn't happy about Caleb dictating to him and holding him under the knife of the Dutch West India Company. He said the captain was ready to toss him out on his ear. I know the captain, and it wasn't his ear he was about to be tossed out on." Peter hurried the two women along to the riverbank and the waiting jolly boat. "Kiefft wants the settlers to unite, to break away from the influence of 'interlopers,' as he referred to the captain. There was all kind of talk about being sacrificed to the Indians for the profits of the Company. Add to that the promises he has no intention of keeping, and it spells trouble for the captain and ourselves. Did you notice that when he walked away, he took three men with him, the most influential men in the settlement? They reminded me of puppets waiting to have their strings pulled."

"Will we be safe on board?" Lydia asked, a quiver in her voice.

"We're going to do our best," Peter said softly, his hand reaching for hers, causing Wren to wish with all her heart that Caleb were here to reassure her. "I doubt if they'll do anything tonight, but we have to prepare ourselves. There's no way of knowing if the captain will make it back from New Amsterdam tonight or even tomorrow. We're on our own, and each of us will have to depend on the other."

"But why?" Lydia protested. "We did nothing! The captain didn't do anything wrong!"

"Little matter when a man like Kiefft decides which way he's going to jump. I don't think his grievance is against us. Mostly it's against the captain and the ship. The last thing he wants is to have the *Siren* pull into port without the cargo he guaranteed to the Dutch West India Company. I've seen seeds of unrest planted in the past, and I've also seen the results. They aren't too pretty."

"I'll be damned before I let them touch Caleb's ship!" Wren snapped.

"That goes for me, too!" Lydia avowed, hands on her hips, red hair tossing, blue eyes full of fire. "That's not just a ship to me, it's a symbol of my independence!"

Peter's stomach churned. Two women and him. What kind of showing could they make against a band of angry settlers who were looking for a good fight and some sort of retribution, just or not? Not much, he told himself. And why had the captain given the crew shore liberty? The men were scattered all over Hell and creation, probably drunk as lords and no good to anyone even if he could track them down.

"We have a good number of daylight hours left," Wren said. "If you feel that something might happen tonight after dark, then we should think about taking some precautions the moment we're back on board.

368

I don't know exactly *what* we can do, but one of us is bound to get an idea. I'll die before I let them harm the *Sea Siren!*" A chill washed over her when she remembered that the *Sea Siren* was really Sirena's maiden ship, the *Rana*. If she let anything happen to this ship, the van der Rhyses would never forgive her.

Bright afternoon sunshine faded into soft twilight as the trio battened down the *Sea Siren*. Secure in the knowledge that they had done all they could, for the time being, they dragged tack boxes to advantageous lookouts and proceeded to keep watch.

Chapter Twenty-four

The same twilight that wrapped the *Sea Siren* in its arms slowly descended on the Pequot fort. Sassacus liked this time of day when the children were tired and played quietly as their mothers cleaned up after the evening meal. Soon it would be time for the chiefs to take their places at the council meeting. For hours the young men worked, laying the twigs and gathering the dried out logs that would make the bonfire stretch to the heavens.

Sassacus looked around the compound at the newly erected lodges that housed the representatives of the other Indian chiefs. They would remain inside, eating the sweetmeats the women had prepared as they waited to be called to the meeting. Each would come out adorned in his richest attire and then sit cross-legged, face impassive, eyes blank.

He should be in his own lodge, dressing, but he hated the thought of being cooped up. He wanted the soft night around him with the brilliant stars overhead and the rich smell of the earth wafting up to his nostrils. His eyes traveled to the stockade fence and he cringed. He hated the sight of it. Man, red or white, did not belong behind a barricade. Children and women should be able to walk about freely without fear. This was a white man's fence, this ugly log structure that glared back at him in the lavender light. The white man built stockade fences to ward off the Indian, and the Indian built stockade fences to ward off the white man. It made no sense. His eyes were sad and troubled as he reached out a hand to touch the rough bark. He and his people were prisoners of the white man, even though there were no guards outside the heavy gates. He knew in his heart that he and his people had seen the last of their peaceful days. He had to do what was best for them. If that meant going to war, then he would go to war with the other chiefs. They would unite and hope against impossible odds that they could regain that elusive thing called peace.

As Sassacus pondered and weighed his problem, Bascom Stoneham strolled from the makeshift quarters that had been allotted to his flock, his eyes on a dark form directly ahead. He neither saw nor appreciated the quiet star-filled night or the soft evening sounds that meant people were living and breathing and loving in this tiny village. His thoughts were full of lust and what he was going to do when he came upon the young girl walking along the river.

His voice was sharp, hostile, when he grasped the

370

frightened girl's thin shoulder. He turned her to face him his grip painful and strong. Her name was Anna and she was frightened, as any child of thirteen would be. She swallowed hard, tears gathering in her eyes at the pain the preacher was inflicting on her. She wanted to cry out, but the eyes boring into her forbade it. She swallowed again and tried to speak.

"You must not speak in my presence. I feel a visitation coming on," Bascom said, forcing the girl to her knees. "Clasp your hands and pray with me. Pray to the Lord and beg Him to forgive you for straying from your parents. I saw the way you've been looking at the Emery boy and the way he's been looking at you. Pray to the Lord that He drives your lustful wants from your body. Pray," he commanded.

Fear coursed through Anna as she again tried to speak. Saliva gathered in her mouth and dribbled down her chin. "Truly, Preacher Stoneham, I was not lusting after William Emery. Our eyes met once and I lowered mine immediately. It was an accident."

"A sorry story, indeed, and one I cannot believe," Bascom intoned piously. "I know what I say. You have the body of a woman, and all women lust after men. You throw your wanton bodies before men and flaunt your wares like a hawker. Disgusting!" he all but spit. "Now, pray, and don't stop till I tell you, or I'll have a long talk with your parents about your wicked ways."

Anna dropped her eyes and bowed her head, muttering and half moaning prayers she didn't know she knew, saying words that had no meaning to her. Saying anything to keep the preacher from telling her parents of what he called her wicked ways.

While Anna prayed, Bascom positioned her more carefully in front of him and forced her head upright. "Close your eyes when you pray to the Lord!" he cried in an excited voice. His hands worked feverishly with the belt buckle of his trousers as the girl's prayers invaded his ears. Quickly, before she knew what was happening, Bascom forced his manhood to her mouth, his bony hands gripping her head. His body moved in a frenzy as the girl choked and sobbed.

"Wanton slut," Bascom shouted hoarsely as he thrust her from him and snapped his buckle together. "I'm going to take pity on you and not tell your parents of your sinful ways. I'll stay here all night and pray for your soul. The devil's blood runs in your veins," he muttered as he opened his prayer book and then dropped to his knees.

Anna rubbed her hands across her mouth and ran, her eyes blinded with tears. She wasn't a wanton slut, she wasn't! She ran till she collapsed, exhausted and numb. She had to tell someone. Who? Billy Emery? She cradled her head in the crook of her arm and sobbed, great racking sobs that tore at her very being. "I'm not what he said I am. I'm not!" she cried over and over. Eventually she slept, and it was Billy Emery who found her hours later and carried her back to her worried parents.

At seventeen, he felt very manly as he approached Anna's parents and smiled to reassure them the girl was safe, only sleeping. No one noticed the dried tears on her cheeks except Billy, and he promised himself he would find out why Anna had been sobbing. Morning would be time enough. He was also the only one who noticed that the preacher wasn't anywhere to be seen. And that, he told himself, is unlike Bascom Stoneham, who likes to be in the thick of things with his prayer book. The young man's eyes narrowed to slits as Anna's father took her from his arms and carried her off to her bed.

Caleb had never been so angry in his entire life. Sassacus was right—the white man was stupid, even ignorant. The men sitting before him with their glasses of wine, their jovial attitudes and their elegant clothes made him want to kill. They heard him out and then laughed. Ridiculous! Sassacus? There was no fight in Sassacus. Sassacus liked the white man. Unite? The Pequots were so scattered they couldn't unite as one and make war. They knew the white man was superior and would take what he wanted. Who really cared if those savages had been here first? You had to be strong and eager to conquer new worlds. The white man was strong; he had already proved this. Even if the Pequots did band together, they would be no match for the English and the Dutch. There might be a skirmish or two, but those bastard savages would be put in their place.

Caleb watched the men raise their wineglasses and drink to the demise of the Indians.

A portly gentleman, attired in a crimson waistcoat with a ruffled shirt, slapped Caleb resoundingly on the back. He was already drunk, and his facial muscles hung slackly as he tried to bring Caleb's angry face into focus. "You, van der Rhys, think you have control of the Dutch West India Company. You don't," he blustered. "We do what we think is best. You come sailing into port and think you have all the answers. You don't—as Governor Kiefft will soon show you!"

Caleb seethed and fumed but realized he couldn't argue with a group of drunken men. And from the looks of things, that was a state more common to them than sobriety. He was on his own. The letter giving him full authority from the Dutch West India Company meant nothing to these sodden fools.

Sassacus took his place before the council fire, his spokesman calling the names of the visiting chiefs. Although they were not in the Pequot fort in person, their representatives answered to their chiefs' names. When all were assembled, they sat side by side,

373

forming a straight line. Sassacus, on the far side of the fire, faced them. Through the flames he could see the visages of his enemies.

There sat the spokesman for Miantonomo, chief of the Narragansetts, who had no love for the Pequots. When Sassacus had approached Miantonomo nearly a year before with terms for an alliance, he had been cruelly rejected.

Beside the Narragansett, rested the representative for the Mohegans, speaking in the name of Chief Uncas. There was no friendship to be found in this face, either. Little more than two months earlier, sixty Mohegans, who were related to the Pequot tribe, had set out from Hartford town with ninety militiamen. When their loyalty had been doubted, Chief Uncas himself had soon reassured the English by attacking a nearby hunting party of Pequots and returning to the militia with four heads and one prisoner. This prisoner, nephew to Sassacus, had shown great courage; he had lost his life by suffering an atrocious torture: one leg had been tied to a post, the other to a frisky horse.

Even the spokesman for Ninigret, chief of the Eastern Niantic warriors, was no friend to the Pequot. Sassacus had learned that afternoon that Ninigret was joining with nearly six hundred Narragansetts and, with the English, was preparing to attack the Mystic fort.

It was into these hostile eyes that he peered, stating his pleas. "All red men are brothers. We are all of the Algonquian family and language. We are brother to the Narragansett, the Niantic, the Mohegan and the Mohican of the Hudson Valley. We who are the children of the earth must live for the earth. Now it is the Pequot time to face his enemy. But soon, very soon, each of you will suffer the fate of the Pequot. Our bones will rot and make the earth richer, more fertile.

We will become fodder for the white man's crops as he fishes our streams and hunts in our woods."

Sassacus spoke slowly and precisely, to be certain they understood and would deliver his message to their chiefs. "We are the people. We will die. All of us. Women. Children. There will be no heritage. The leaves will fall and cover our graves, and within the lifetime of the eagle, there will be none to say that a red brother lived on the land."

It was difficult for Sassacus to keep his shoulders straight, his head high and proud, as he left the ceremonial fire and walked to his lodge, where he would await their answer. Would they stand beside their brothers, the Pequots? Even as Sassacus crossed his legs and lowered himself to the floor, he knew his people would face their destiny alone.

The shadows of twilight had deepened before Malcolm withdrew from his hiding place in the woods and pressed forward, tripping and falling over vines and rocks. The swelling over his eye had eased since his battle with Caleb, and he had enough vision to see where he was going.

He trekked for hours until he saw lantern lights winking in the settlement of Saybrook. He was familiar with the territory. During the past two nights, he had skulked into the compound to forage for food and had succeeded in garnering eggs, early radishes and peas from kitchen gardens, and, wonder of wonders, a stray chicken. Belly full, confidence high, he stood still, orienting himself in the darkness and determining the best way to get to the riverbank without being seen.

He crept through the trees as silently as he could, stopping every so often to see if he was being observed. His thoughts rumbled with curses, damning Wren and Caleb van der Rhys. He knew that Caleb's influence in the region was far from minimal because of his position with the Dutch West India Company. Owing to the fiasco Malcolm had brought about with his attempt to ransom Wren, van der Rhys had no doubt placed a bounty on his head. There was no welcome for Malcolm Weatherly anywhere in this new world. His only chance for safety lay among the masses in England. There, among the riffraff of the slums, his disfigurement would be accepted, almost unnoticed.

Excitement coursed through him. He was so close to precious safety—the ship! He was almost to the shore and even from this distance he could see the *Sea Siren*'s sails and masts stabbing the dark sky. She was close, close enough for him to swim out to her. She had been his haven once before, taking him away from England, and she would be his haven again. He looked around, held his breath and was just about to weave his way to the sandy, gritty strip of land that would lead him to the Sound when he heard a voice, soft at first, then raised in anger. Malcolm drew back fearfully and waited. The voice was familiar, one he had heard before. He strained to distinguish the words, but with the rustling of the branches overhead and the soft lap of the water, he could only make out sounds. He crept back through the trees, careful to be quiet.

It was the preacher! And two other people. No, one other person. The third person seemed to be hiding, peering around a tree. A woman was with the preacher. Malcolm leered. This was something he understood. The preacher was out dallying with another man's wife, and the husband was waiting to catch him in a compromising position. Malcom shook his head. Whatever happened to Bascom, he deserved it. Malcolm certainly wasn't going to intervene. He had enough problems of his own without adding more to the list. He would just wait and see what happened.

He watched in shock as Bascom forced the girl to her knees and then prevented her from getting away. She was clumsy, not like that sure-footed she-cat, Wren. Bascom had her in his clutches before she could get one foot solidly planted in the sand. She was crying, sobbing at what the preacher was making her do. So it wasn't a mutual feeling of lust. This Malcolm understood also. His eye went to the figure standing behind the tree, and he wanted to urge him on, to shout at him to take the preacher by the neck and throttle him for what he was making the girl do. From the looks of things, the preacher wouldn't have to wait for God to punish him. The man behind the tree would do it for Him.

Malcolm saw the glint of a knife in the moonlight and the direction in which it was traveling. He winced. There were other ways to die, better ways, less painful ways.

The man, whoever he was, had things well in hand. He was leading the girl away, his arm protecting her from the grisly sight at their feet. Malcolm saw the knife fall to the ground and fought the desire to rush to it and pick it up. Instead, he crawled silently on his hands and knees to the water and struck out for the ship.

Ahead of him, Malcolm could see the dark hull of the *Sea Siren* against the starlit sky. He swam, kicking with his feet, straining one arm in front of the other, willing himself to reach his goal.

Minute after agonizing minute passed; from time to time, exhausted, he rolled over on his back and floated. Still the ship seemed no nearer. His arms ached and trembled. His legs were cold and becoming stiff. Each breath he took seemed to fill his lungs and expand his chest and was squeezed out of him as though he were trapped in a vise. His clothing and the pouch of jewels, still stuffed inside his shirt, weighed him down; a cramp jolted through his calf muscles.

The *Siren* continued to elude him. Glancing back, he saw that he hadn't even swum half the distance. In the darkness the shoreline was nearly impossible to discern. The inky, black waves became his enemy. Overpowering him, filling his mouth and nose, shutting out his air. Valiantly, he struggled onward, one goal in mind—the darkness of the locker box, where no one would find him. Safety. Security. Almost a homecoming. His exhausted muscles refused to work in coordination. It was increasingly fatiguing to keep his head above water, to gasp the next breath.

Tears mixed with the swells of the Sound. Tears of self-pity and rage against the injustice of his fate. He had come so close to having it all, everything, and now he had nothing. And it was all because of Wren. She had actually killed him back in the flat in London when she had robbed him of his one marketable asset —his good looks. Even Sara hadn't wanted him after she had seen his ruined face. Wren had destroyed him as calculatingly as if she had put a knife to his heart and pierced it.

The black waters closed over his head. Once. Twice. He felt himself going under for the third time, and instead of uttering a prayer of contrition, he heard himself cry out wretchedly, "Wren!"

Chapter Twenty-five

Caleb rode his mount hard and fast, stopping once for a few quick hours of much needed rest. When he awoke, darkness had settled around him. He had wasted too much time rounding up the stragglers of his crew. Traveling alone was much quicker, and he had instructed the men to wait for him to make port in New Amsterdam, where they would take on additional stores for the return trip to England.

The horse's hooves tore up chunks of turf as he raced toward Saybrook. Ahead of him, Caleb could see lanterns and torches lining the riverbank. On perceiving so much activity near the water, he rightly assumed it had something to do with the *Sea Siren*. Dismounting, he cautiously approached the thronging colonists from the trees and soon realized they were discussing the fate of his ship.

It was several moments before he began to understand that Kiefft had paid a visit to Saybrook and convinced the settlers that Caleb and his crew were Indian partisans, supplying the Pequots with weapons and spying on their behalf. It was a ridiculous statement, yet Caleb knew there was nothing he could say to refute it. Tempers were high and hostilities were fed by fear. The Pequots offered a very real threat, and he *had* been with Sassacus on several occasions.

Peering through the trees toward the ship, he felt his stomach tighten. She was a good mile out into the Sound. Without a chance of retrieving his jolly, it would be a long swim.

Suddenly a cry went up. "The preacher! The preacher, Stoneham!" the voice shrilled. "He's dead! Murdered!"

Caleb's ears pricked as he listened. One man, whose modish clothing revealed he was not one of the settlers but was probably one of Kiefft's men, linked Caleb's name with Bascom's murder. Outraged, the throng drew closer to the water, looking toward the *Siren* and waving clenched fists.

Knowing it would be only a matter of time until they ventured out in their boats to attack the ship, Caleb also knew it was time to take his chances.

He ran as though his life depended on it, and it did. Gasping, his long arms giving him momentum, he skidded to a stop at the river's edge. One quick look over his shoulder at the advancing colonists, and he leapt into the murky waters of the Sound. When he surfaced some distance from the shoreline, he kicked off his boots, the shouts of "Murderer!" and "Indian lover!" ringing in his ears.

His feet free of the weighty boots, he struck out just as his own jolly was launched from the shore, full of shouting, cursing men, intent only on his capture. Another quick look over his shoulder told him four members of his crew who had returned to Saybrook were behind him. Their intent was the same as his.

As Caleb's arms slashed through the water, he realized how the past days had taken their toll of him. Farrington's death, Sara's duplicity, Wren's supposed death and then her miraculous reappearance, along with his hatred for Malcolm Weatherly, had left him drained of emotion. Too many sleepless nights worrying what might or might not have been with Wren were now in the past, and he had to force his body to keep moving in the churning black water. He had to reach the ship and Wren. He was tired. The crewmen were almost abreast of him, and they had hit the water after he had. He had to make it; he couldn't fail now, not after all that had happened. Deep, even strokes would bring him to the *Siren*.

Lifting his head as his arms knifed through the water, he saw the four crew members, two each abreast of him. They were good men, his men, and they knew that his strokes were less than even and measured and that his breathing was ragged, much more so than theirs. If he faltered, they were there. Determination and anger raced through him. He couldn't let the crew bring in its captain. He'd die first. Even if he slowed, as long as his strokes were measured, he would make it.

Wren stood on the quarterdeck of the *Sea Siren*, her face softly lit by the gimbaled lantern. Her anxious gaze was fixed on the commotion ashore, when suddenly she realized what she was seeing. "Peter! Look! It's Caleb!" Excitement rang in her voice and mingled with her anxiety.

"Aye! And it seems as though four of our men have finally found their way back to the ship!" His eyes were pressed tightly against the ship's glass as he looked toward shore. "And look what's behind them and gaining distance!"

Wren peered out, her hand shielding her eyes from the lantern's light. In the distance, behind Caleb and the crewmen, was the *Siren*'s jolly boat, manned by Kiefft's men, their muskets raised and ready to fire.

Peter ran to the foredeck, hoisting the winch which would lower the second jolly. "I'll row out and pick them up. You and Lydia go below and lock the cabin doors."

"I'm going with you," Wren stated, lifting her skirts in preparation of climbing down the Jacob's ladder.

"No, you're not! Stay below—that's an order!"

"I'll be damned if I'll go below and hide like a criminal. My running and hiding days are over, Peter. I'm going with you!"

"And leave Lydia alone? You must stay here. Now, do as you're told. Now!" Peter thundered.

Wren gulped and seized Lydia by the arm. "We'll do as you say. Hurry, Peter."

With the boat lowered into the dark water, Peter cast a last, longing look at his Lydia and slid down into the jolly. Every muscle in his back bunched into knots as he dipped the oars and then swung back, only to dip and swing again. There they were, he could see them struggling in the churning tides. He prayed he would reach them in time. The governor's men were fast closing the distance. Soon they would be within shooting range.

On deck, Lydia was trembling with the force of her fear. "Wren, I'm frightened," she whispered. "Why is this happening? Why would Governor Kiefft do this?"

"You heard what Peter said before. What better way to insure that Caleb never makes his report to the burghers in Holland? This way, we will all be victims of mass hysteria, not of coldblooded murder."

"Wren, we have to do something. If they come aboard . . . I've heard what men can do to women . . ."

"They're not pirates, Lydia, they won't rape us. That's not what they have in mind. Right now they just wouldn't want any witnesses to say what really did happen." Wren's voice conveyed a confidence she did not feel. "Be brave, Lydia. When Caleb comes aboard, he'll know what to do." She hugged Lydia close.

Several shots rang out through the darkness. Kiefft's men were firing on the swimmers and Peter.

"Dear God! They're firing on our men!" Lydia squealed.

Wren's heart constricted in panic, her amber eyes flashing with rage. "Lydia! Come with me. We have a gun, too! The ship's cannon."

"The cannon! You must be crazy! We can't fire that!"

"Why not? Caleb said it's always loaded. All we need to do is add powder. Do you know where it's kept?"

Lydia glanced at the cumbersome, lethal cannon whose muzzle pointed through a bay abaft the starboard beam. She froze with terror.

Wren seized her shoulders and shook her. "Do you know where the powder is kept? It's in the stern, in the magazine!" Lydia shook her head in the affirmative, like a puppet whose string had been pulled. "Get it!" Wren ordered, pushing Lydia toward the stern. "If you can't carry it, roll it down!"

Wren ran down the starboard side, stopping at each gun sight, peering over the gunwale to assess the best aim. At sea, the crew would bring a ship about for the best firing vantage. Trapped on a sandbar the way they were, there was no chance of doing that. The best she could do was choose the cannon facing the target; then hope and pray that when she fired it, it would at least alarm Caleb's pursuers and give him time to get aboard safely. Cannon 2 on the starboard beam seemed to fit her specifications.

Lydia came forward, hunched over, carrying the twenty-pound powder cask on her back, supporting it with a rope drawn forward over her shoulders like Wren had seen peasants do in Java. The cask thudded to the deck and spilled open, saving Wren the trouble of breaking into it. "How much powder do we use?" Lydia gasped.

"I don't know. But I've seen it done before, when Regan was testing the guns on his ships in the Batavia harbor. Help me, Lydia. There's little time left!"

The women worked quickly, uncertain of what they were doing. At the last moment Wren remembered to use the long plunger to tamp down the powder. Exerting all their strength, they rolled the gun into place. Wren grabbed the lantern and lifted the chimney, holding the naked flame to the fuse. Squeezing her eyes shut, she fired the cannon. It reeled backward on its mounts from the force of the explosion.

An oily, inky cloud exuded from the gun, and when the smoke cleared, Wren hardly dared to look, fearing that somehow she had miscalculated and that Caleb and Peter had also taken the brunt of the shot.

"Look! Look!" Lydia squealed. "I see the jolly and our men! Throw down the ladder so they can board!"

Caleb had one foot on the ladder, a dumbfounded expression on his face. "Did they fire on us or on Kiefft's men?" he muttered. "That was too close for comfort."

Wren was loading the cannon again when she felt a hand on her shoulder and swung around, a silent scream in her throat. "Caleb! I didn't know what to do. We thought Peter wouldn't get to you in time, and those men were firing at you!" She collapsed into his arms.

"Hush, now! You did everything just right. You saved our lives and gave us the time we needed." He hugged her to him and then released her, shouting orders to the crew.

"Peter, there's little chance we can keep them from boarding the ship," Caleb said. "The cannons were meant for long-range firing. Once they're on board, we've lost firing range. We'd better prepare to fight." He drew Peter aside. "Listen to me carefully. If they manage to board and the fight is all to their favor, set

384

fire to the *Siren* and go over the side. We'll take our chances in the water."

"Aye, Captain. And I'm sorry about the sandbar. I panicked with the responsibility of the women. If only the tide had been right, we could have turned the ship around and headed for sea. It's my fault, Captain, and if anything happens to you and the others, I'm to blame."

"There's no blame being placed on your shoulders, Peter. You did the best you could, and that's all I ask of any man. Tomorrow the tide will be right and we'll sail away from here. I hope," he muttered under his breath.

At the first sound of the grappling hooks, Wren's eyes took on a feverish glaze and her body began to tremble. Kiefft's men wanted Caleb, and the only way they would get him would be to kill her first.

She flinched at the sound of a pistol being cocked, and then another and another. The four crew members were stationed broadside, while Peter stood a little to the left of Caleb to give him backup support should his volley miss. Where was Lydia? "Lydia, where are you?" she hissed.

"Shhh, over here. See, I have a rapier, too."

"Good. Use it, don't just hold it," Wren whispered back.

"It's the same principle as jabbing a hairpin, isn't that so?"

"Oh, Christ," Caleb moaned to Peter, who rolled his eyes at Lydia's words.

"Yes," Wren told her, "but be sure that you use force."

There was no time to give Lydia an exercise on the finer points of fencing. Wren was only glad that as a little girl she had pretended to be the infamous Sea Siren and that Regan had seen to her lessons himself.

Over the port rail climbed Kiefft's men, aided by

colonists from Old Saybrook. The decks became alive with sharp cries and mayhem. Lydia jabbed out with her weapon, delaying an attacker until Peter could see to him himself.

Wren waited in the darkness, undecided where she was needed most. How could eight people survive this attack? she wondered fearfully. She refused to speculate whether or not she could actually use a rapier to kill a man. Her fencing lessons had been child's play, meant more for form than for actual defense. Her mouth became a thin line of concentration as she emerged onto the deck, the sword clutched in her hand.

She stepped over two fallen bodies and advanced warily on an unsuspecting man bent upon cutting Peter down from behind. The point of her blade plunged deep into the back of his neck, and he dropped before her. She pulled her weapon free of his resisting flesh and grimaced, but the expression on Peter's face was all she needed to keep going.

Again and again she lashed out, mentally counting the odds against them as three to one. She jabbed and feinted, cracking one man over the head with the rapier's handle, only to stun him. Lydia saved her in the nick of time by running her own rapier through the man's arm. Peter finished him off.

Wren was seized with a panic which choked off all reason. Averting her eyes from the gore, she backed against the foremast, weapon held loosely in her hand. One of Kiefft's men advanced on her, his eyes raking her and taking in the sword she held. She was an easy target, stunned by panic, immobile with fear. Even as he approached her, she was defenseless against him. He wielded a cutlass, held at a menacing angle, ready to slash out at her if she made a move.

Her mouth was dry, her gaze fixed; she was helpless. None of the polite and genteel lessons she had learned from Regan had prepared her for this. Just as the man's hand reached out for her, she turned to run. He grabbed for her viciously, pulling at the fabric of her skirts, tearing the stitches at the waistline. The material trapped her legs and caused her to sprawl onto the deck.

A soundless plea rose to her lips as he ripped the fabric away from her legs and feasted his eyes on the elegant length of her legs stripped bare to his view. Frozen by terror and what she read in his face, Wren was paralyzed. Amid the frenzied happenings around her, she knew there would be no help from anyone: only herself. Slowly, unseen by her attacker, she groped the deck near her side, searching for the hilt of her rapier. Just as her fingers found their target, he lunged for her, naked lust casting dark shadows over his eyes. The tip of her weapon found his breast, and with a deliberate, unhurried action, she plunged it deep into his flesh. Rolling onto her side, she avoided his dead weight falling on top of her. "That was for you and all the Malcolms of this world!" she screamed, beyond the edge of panic now and into the grip of deadly willfulness. "No one will ever do that to me again!"

She had killed before and she had done it again; *would* kill still again, if necessary, but never would she allow herself to be at the mercy of a man's lust.

Silently she crept from her seclusion near the foremast and took stock of the situation. Her eyes widened as she watched Caleb square off against a burly attacker who wielded a wicked cutlass. Another of Kiefft's men was creeping up behind him, his intent only too clear.

With a wild whoop Wren was on the man's back, smacking him over the head with the hilt of her weapon. Startled, Caleb turned and took a blow on his shoulder. He grinned as Wren slid from the dead man's back, her eyes gleaming in the dim light. It couldn't be possible! Her dark hair was flying about her shoulders and her skirt was gone, revealing her long, curvaceous legs. With her tattered clothes and wild hair, she looked just like the Sea Siren.

"I couldn't let him kill you. Not after I've only just found you again." She smiled. "Are we winning or losing?"

Caleb threw back his head and laughed. "You might look like the Sea Siren, but she'd never ask a question like that. Look around—we've repelled them for the time being. But they'll be back." His expression changed, his voice became deeper, his eyes lingered on her face. "Sweetheart," he said, gathering her into his arms, "I, for one, am proud to fight beside you."

"Then you believe they'll come back?" she asked, her eyes darkening with an unspoken fear.

"Aye, sweetheart, we can almost bet on it. Are you frightened?"

Wren clutched at him, her lips close against his chest. "Yes," she whispered, her voice barely audible. "I'm frightened that something will happen to one of us." She lifted her head and looked directly at him, her eyes filled with meaning. "I want you, Caleb. I love you and I want you to make love to me. If something should happen . . . I don't want to die without knowing you completely, totally."

Caleb's eyes grew darker with pent-up desire. Wren, his beautiful Wren, had at last become a woman. A woman who loved and wanted to be loved. Wordlessly, he lifted her into his arms and carried her across the deck, taking her to the captain's cabin. And as he did, he whispered against her ear, telling her of the first time Regan had made love to his Siren, there in the same cabin, behind the shroud of an isolating fog.

Wren touched her fingers delicately to his lips. "Shh. Ours is the first love, the only love. Never have two people loved the way we do. Ever since I was a little girl I've wanted to be like the Sea Siren. For the longest time I hadn't even dreamed that Sirena was that woman and that Regan was her handsome captain. But I'm grown up now, Caleb. And the only woman I want to be is your woman."

With his foot he swung the cabin door shut, his mouth closed over hers, his heart filling with an overpowering love for her. He worked the laces of her bodice, stripping her of the confining cloth. Her clothing came away piece by piece, and always his mouth kissed and tasted the freshly exposed skin. She was naked in his arms, turning her body beneath his caresses, offering herself, tempting him again and again with her sighs of pleasure and low moans of passion.

Finally, having little patience for the restrictions his own clothing imposed, he broke away from her, tearing and ripping at the material, eager to be naked in the arms of the woman he loved.

Wren's senses soared and whirled, making her dizzy with yearning and a deep hunger for him. Gone were the fears she had known. She was a woman, Caleb's woman, and she wanted him, needed him, demanded he possess her. She answered his caresses with a sizzling response that bordered on an animal lust. Wantonly, she explored his body with her lips, brazened the most sensuous caresses and invited him to partake of her passions with an exquisite joy.

Caleb delighted in his bewitching partner, withholding the moment of completion to savor her charms further. He rejoiced to find his desires met by hers. In the darkness he perceived her through his fingers, through his lips, and was intoxicated with their love for each other.

Straining toward him, throbbing with unfulfilled desire, her body rose and fell in rhythmic obedience to an instinctive yearning. And then a cry came from her: "Take me! Have me! Make me your own!" She

389

pulled him to her, gathering him into her, making his flesh a part of her own.

Hours later, sitting on the quiet deck, Wren snuggled deep into Caleb's arms. "Did you really think I looked like the Sea Siren?"

"For a moment I really did. But there's only one Sea Siren and only one Wren. Do you understand?"

"Yes," she breathed contentedly. "You love me because I'm who I am."

Caleb frowned and then laughed. "That's exactly what I'm saying, but somehow when you say it, it sounds different."

"That's because men use too many words when action is needed." Her silken arms embraced him, her lips covered his.

"Caleb, tell me about the boys back in Java. I can't wait to see them again. I was in England three years, and Wynde was just a baby when I left."

Caleb's voice took on a faraway tone as he recalled the last time he had seen his half brothers. "I imagine they've grown at least a head taller since I've seen them. At times they're so much alike I can hardly separate them in my mind. Let's see if I have it right. Thor is the oldest. Strong and domineering and quite aware of the responsibility of his younger brothers. Then comes Storm, serious and inquisitive, always asking 'Why?' Rein is third in line." Caleb laughed, remembering. "Rein is always complaining that he gets left out of everything, but he's the most headstrong of them all. Sometimes I think he gets himself into trouble just to gain attention. And Wynde is the baby. He's still hanging on to Sirena's skirts, but that will soon change. You see, I know a secret."

At the mention of a secret, Wren's head popped up from his shoulder. "Tell me. I love secrets."

"Sirena is expecting another child. By now she and Regan should be in Java awaiting the birth. I pray it will be a girl. Regan will need a daughter now that I'm taking you away from him."

"I wonder what Sirena will name the baby if it is a girl. All the boys managed to be born during some of the worst storms in Java's history."

"Knowing Sirena and Regan, could you expect anything else?" Caleb asked, laughing. "Regardless of the weather when this child is born, Regan said if he had a daughter he would call her Fury."

"Fury," Wren whispered, trying the name on her lips.

Caleb smiled again. "Regan will have his daughter, and she'll be born during a storm, and she'll carry the name Fury van der Rhys. Sirena will see to it."

All through the rest of the night the crew of the *Sea Siren* was on watch, scanning the water and the shoreline.

"What do you think, Captain?" Peter asked in a whisper, careful not to wake Wren, who was sleeping contentedly in the crook of Caleb's arm.

"I don't think they'll be back anymore tonight, but tomorrow will tell another story. The only thing that saved us is the fact that they're not fighters but farmers, men of the earth. There was no heart in most of them for what they were doing. As their friends fell at their feet, some of them went over the side. God alone knows how many will return in the morning. How one man can and did make such a mess of things, I'll never understand." Caleb shook his head. "I find it hard to believe that Kiefft would kill innocent people just to prevent me from going back to Holland to make my report. We're playing a waiting game for now. If it weren't for the sandbar . . ."

". . . we'd be out to sea by now," Peter said softly. "Captain, I . . ."

"I told you I place no blame on you for our circumstances, nor do the women or the crew. Full tide will get us out of here."

"Only if full tide arrives before Kiefft and his men."

"We can't think of that now," Caleb said as he shifted slightly to ease Wren into a more comfortable position. Then he dozed off.

When the first pearly gray streak of light heralded the coming dawn, Caleb blinked and was instantly awake. Joining Peter at the rail, he watched as dawn fought the darkness for supremacy. His eyes, like Peter's, were on the shoreline. Even from this distance they could make out hurrying figures and frenzied activity.

"Two more hours till full tide," Peter said morosely.

Caleb's gut rumbled and his face became a mask of hatred for what his eyes were seeing. They would all be killed. He would never make it back to England and Holland and would never live to enjoy his new life with Wren. There were at least fifty men assembling on the shore. As each minute raced on, more arrived carrying guns.

"Captain, look! Upriver! Do you see what I see?" Peter cried excitedly.

"By God, I do, and I don't believe it!" Caleb exclaimed, tossing his seaman's cap in the air. "It's Sassacus!"

"How many canoes do you count, Captain?"

"At least two dozen."

"They're coming to help. Never have I been so glad to see an Indian in my life!" Peter shouted hoarsely.

"Peter, they're not coming to fight. Sassacus will not intervene between the white men, just as I wouldn't intervene between the red men. He's bringing those canoes to pull us off the sandbar. Lord, if I live to be a thousand, I'll never forget this sight. Order the crew on deck to help secure the lines. Make fast work of it. Sassacus timed it just right. As soon as we're free of the sandbar, the tide will carry us out. The settlers will have no stomach for a fight on water with all those Indians. They would be hopelessly outnumbered and it would be a slaughter."

Caleb drew in his breath as he watched the Indians strain with their paddles to cross the Sound. Their bodies gleaming with sweat, they surrounded the *Siren* and worked to free her from the spit that held her down. A mighty lurch, and the lady crashed into the water.

There were no happy shouts from the Indians at the success of their efforts. Their expressions were staid, placid. They didn't understand why they had done what they had, only that their chief and the captain, who was a white man, were friends.

No words were spoken, and Caleb raised his hand to his head in a jaunty salute to Sassacus, who returned it in kind. This time Caleb put a name to the damnable mist that clouded his vision. He was shedding tears for a friend he would never see again. How could he ever repay his debt to the courageous Indian?

A single tear formed in the corner of Sassacus's eye and he wiped at it unashamedly; at the same time Caleb ran the back of his hand over both his eyes.

"Another time, another place, Caleb van der Rhys, and we will again be brothers," Sassacus said softly.

Only Wren was close enough to Caleb to hear him say, "Look for me in that other world one day, Sassacus, and we will hunt and fish together, good friend."

Bestsellers from BALLANTINE